Robert Michael Ballantyne

Dusty Diamonds Cut and Polished

A Tale of City-arab Life and Adventure

Robert Michael Ballantyne

Dusty Diamonds Cut and Polished
A Tale of City-arab Life and Adventure

ISBN/EAN: 9783744751810

Printed in Europe, USA, Canada, Australia, Japan

Cover: Foto ©Andreas Hilbeck / pixelio.de

More available books at **www.hansebooks.com**

Robert Michael Ballantyne

Dusty Diamonds Cut and Polished
A Tale of City-arab Life and Adventure

ISBN/EAN: 9783744751810

Printed in Europe, USA, Canada, Australia, Japan

Cover: Foto ©Andreas Hilbeck / pixelio.de

More available books at **www.hansebooks.com**

DUSTY DIAMONDS

CUT AND POLISHED

A TALE OF CITY-ARAB LIFE AND ADVENTURE.

BY R. M. BALLANTYNE,

AUTHOR OF "THE BATTERY AND THE BOILER;" "THE GIANT OF THE NORTH;" "THE
LONELY ISLAND;" "POST HASTE; A TALE OF HER MAJESTY'S MAILS;" "IN THE TRACK
OF THE TROOPS;" "THE SETTLER AND THE SAVAGE;" "UNDER THE WAVES;"
"RIVERS OF ICE;" "BLACK IVORY;" "THE PIRATE CITY;" "THE NORSEMEN
IN THE WEST;" "THE IRON HORSE;" "THE FLOATING LIGHT OF THE
GOODWIN SANDS;" "ERLING THE BOLD;" "FIGHTING THE FLAMES;"
"SHIFTING WINDS;" "DEEP DOWN;" "THE LIGHTHOUSE;"
"GASCOYNE;" "THE LIFE BOAT;" "THE GOLDEN
DREAM," ETC. ETC.

With Illustrations.

LONDON:

JAMES NISBET & CO., 21 BERNERS STREET.

1884.

PREFACE.

THIS tale is founded on well-authenticated facts. I commend the subject of which it treats to the reader's earnest consideration.

R. M. B.

HARROW-ON-THE-HILL,
1883.

CONTENTS.

CONTENTS.

LIST OF ILLUSTRATIONS.

DUSTY DIAMONDS.

CHAPTER I.

AN ACCIDENT AND SOME OF ITS CURIOUS RESULTS.

EVERY one has heard of those ponies—those shaggy, chubby, innocent-looking little creatures— for which the world is indebted, we suppose, to Shetland.

Well, once on a time, one of the most innocent-looking, chubbiest, and shaggiest of Shetland ponies —a dark brown one—stood at the door of a mansion in the west end of London.

It was attached to a wickerwork vehicle which resembled a large clothes-basket on small wheels. We do not mean, of course, that the pony was affectionately attached to it. No; the attachment was involuntary and unavoidable, by reason of a brand-new yellow leather harness with brass buckles. It objected to the attachment, obviously, for it sidled this way, and straddled that way, and whisked its enormous little tail, and tossed its

A

rotund little head, and stamped its ridiculously small feet, and champed its miniature bit, as if it had been a war-horse of the largest size, fit to carry a Wallace, a Bruce, or a Richard of the Lion-heart into the midst of raging battle.

And no wonder; for many months had not elapsed since that brown creature had kicked up its little heels, and twirled its tail, and shaken its shaggy mane in all the wild exuberance of early youth and unfettered freedom on the heather hills of its native island.

In the four-wheeled basket sat a little girl whom it is useless to describe as beautiful. She was far beyond that! Her delicate colour, her little straight nose, her sparkling teeth, her rosebud of a mouth, her enormous blue eyes, and floods of yellow hair—pooh! these are not worth mentioning in the same sentence with her expression. It was that which carried all before it, and swept up the adoration of man-and-woman-kind as with the besom of fascination.

She was the only child of Sir Richard Brandon. Sir Richard was a knight and a widower. He was knighted, not because of personal merit, but because he had been mayor of some place, sometime or other, when some one connected with royalty had something important to do with it! Little Diana was all that this knight and widower had on earth to care for, except, of course, his horses and dogs, and guns, and club, and food. He was very particular as to his food. Not that he was an epicure, or a gourmand, or luxurious, or a hard drinker, or anything of that sort—by no means. He could rough it (so he said) as well as any man, and put up with whatever chanced to be going, but, when there was no occasion for roughing it, he did like to see things well cooked and nicely served; and wine, you know, was not worth drinking—positively nauseous—if it was not of the best.

Sir Richard was a poor man—a very poor man. He had only five thousand a year—a mere pittance; and he managed this sum in such a peculiar way that he never had anything wherewith to help a struggling friend, or to give to the poor, or to assist the various religious and charitable institutions by which he was surrounded; while at certain intervals in the year he experienced exasperating difficulty in meeting the demands of those torments to society the tradespeople—people who ought to be ashamed of themselves for not being willing to supply the nobility and gentry with food and clothing gratuitously! Moreover, Sir Richard never by any chance laid anything by.

Standing by the pony's head, and making tender efforts to restrain his waywardness, stood a boy— a street boy—a city Arab. To a Londoner any description of this boy would be superfluous, but it may be well to state, for the benefit of the world at large, that the class to which he belonged embodies within its pale the quintessence of rollicking mischief, and the sublimate of consummate insolence.

This remarkable boy was afflicted with a species of dance—not that of St. Vitus, but a sort of double shuffle, with a stamp of the right foot at the end—which he was prone to indulge, consciously and unconsciously, at all times, and the tendency to which he sometimes found it difficult to resist. He was beginning to hum the sharply-defined air to which he was in the habit of performing this dance, when little Diana said, in a silvery voice quite in keeping with her beauty—

"Let go his head, boy; I'm quite sure that he cannot bear restraint."

It may be remarked here that little Di was probably a good judge on that point, being herself nearly incapable of bearing restraint.

"I'd better not, miss," replied the boy with profound respect in tone and manner, for he had yet to be paid for the job; "he seems raither frisky, an' might take à fancy to bolt, you know."

"Let his head go, I say!" returned Miss Diana with a flashing of the blue eyes, and a pursing of the rosebud mouth that proved her to be one of Adam's race after all.

DI RUN AWAY WITH.—Page 5

"Vell, now, don't you think," rejoined the boy, in an expostulating tone, "that it would be as vell to vait for the guv'nor before givin' 'im 'is 'ead ?"

"Do as I bid you, sir!" said Di, drawing herself up like an empress.

Still the street boy held the pony's head, and it is probable that he would have come off the victor in this controversy, had not Diana's dignified action given to the reins which she held a jerk. The brown pony, deeming this full permission to go on, went off with a bound that overturned the boy, and caused the fore-wheel to strike him on the leg as it passed.

Springing up with the intention of giving chase to the runaway, the little fellow again fell, with a sharp cry of pain, for his leg was broken.

At the same moment Sir Richard Brandon issued from the door of his mansion leisurely, and with an air of calm serenity, pulling on his gloves. It was one of the knight's maxims that, under all circumstances, a gentleman should maintain an appearance of imperturbable serenity. When, however, he suddenly beheld the street boy falling, and his daughter standing up in her wickerwork chariot, holding on to the brown pony like an Amazon warrior of ancient times, his maxim somehow evaporated. His serenity vanished. So did his hat as he bounded from beneath it, and left it far behind in his mad and hopeless career after the runaway.

A policeman, coming up just as Sir Richard disappeared, went to the assistance of the street boy.

"Not much hurt, youngster," he said kindly, as he observed that the boy was very pale, and seemed to be struggling hard to repress his feelings.

"Vell, p'raps I is an' p'raps I ain't, Bobby," replied the boy with an unsuccessful attempt at a smile, for he felt safe to chaff or insult his foe in the circumstances, "but vether hurt or not it vont much matter to you, vill it?"

He fainted as he spoke, and the look of half humorous impudence, as well as that of pain, gave place to an expression of infantine repose.

The policeman was so struck by the unusual sight of a street boy looking innocent and unconscious, that he stooped and raised him quite tenderly in his arms.

"You'd better carry him in here," said Sir Richard Brandon's butler, who had come out. "I saw it 'appen, and suspect he must be a good deal damaged."

Sir Richard's footman backing the invitation, the boy was carried into the house accordingly, laid on the housemaid's bed, and attended to by the cook, while the policeman went out to look after the runaways.

"Oh! what ever shall we do?" exclaimed the

cook, as the boy showed symptoms of returning consciousness.

" Send for the doctor," suggested the housemaid.

" No," said the butler, " send for a cab, and 'ave the boy sent home. I fear that master will blame me for givin' way to my feelin's, and won't thank me for bringin' 'im in here. You know he is rather averse to the lower orders. Besides, the poor boy will be better attended to at 'ome, no doubt. I dare say you 'd like to go 'ome, wouldn't you ?" he said, observing that the boy was looking at him with a rather curious expression.

" I dessay I should, if I could," he answered, with a mingled glance of mischief and pain, " but if you 'll undertake to carry me, old cock, I 'll be 'appy to go."

" I 'll send you in a cab, my poor boy," returned the butler, " and git a cabman as I 'm acquainted with to take care of you."

" All right ! go a'ead, ye cripples," returned the boy, as the cook approached him with a cup of warm soup.

" Oh ! ain't it prime !" he said, opening his eyes very wide indeed, and smacking his lips. " I think I 'd go in for a smashed pin every day o' my life for a drop o' that stuff. Surely it must be wot they drinks in 'eaven ! Have 'ee got much more o' the same on 'and ?"

" Never mind, but you drink away while you 've

got the chance," replied the amiable cook; "there's the cab coming, so you've no time to lose."

"Vell, I *am* sorry I ain't able to 'old more, an' my pockets wont 'old it neither, bein' the wuss for wear.   Thankee, missus."

He managed, by a strong effort, to dispose of a little more soup before the cab drew up.

"Where do you live?" asked the butler, as he placed the boy carefully in the bottom of the cab with his unkempt head resting on a hassock, which he gave him to understand was a parting gift from the housemaid.

"Vere do I live?" he repeated.   "Vy, mostly in the streets; my last 'ome was a sugar barrel, the one before was a donkey cart, but I do sometimes condescend to wisit my parents in their mansion 'ouse in Vitechapel."

"And what is your name? Sir Richard may wish to inquire for you—perhaps."

"May he?   Oh! I'm sorry I ain't got my card to leave, but you just tell him, John—is it, or Thomas? —Ah! Thomas.   I knowed it couldn't 'elp to be one or t'other;—you just tell your master that my name is Robert, better known as Bobby, Frog.   But I've lots of aliases, if that name don't please 'im. Good-bye, Thomas.   Farewell, and if for ever, then —you know the rest o' the quotation, if your eddication's not bin neglected, w'ich is probable it

was. Oh! by the way. This 'assik is the gift of
the 'ousemaid? You observe the answer, cabby, in
case you and I may differ about it 'ereafter."

"Yes," said the amused butler, "a gift from
Jessie."

" Ah!—jus' so. An' she's tender-'earted an' on'y
fifteen. Wots 'er tother name? Summers, eh?
Vell, it's prettier than Vinters. Tell 'er I'll not
forget 'er. Now, cabman—'ome!"

A few minutes more, and Bobby Frog was on
his way to the mansion in Whitechapel, highly
delighted with his recent feast, but suffering extremely from his broken limb.

Meanwhile, the brown pony—having passed a bold
costermonger, who stood shouting defiance at it,
and waving both arms till it was close on him, when
he stepped quickly out of its way—eluded a drayman, and entered on a fine sweep of street, where
there seemed to be no obstruction worth mentioning.
By that time it had left the agonised father far
behind.

The day was fine; the air bracing. The utmost
strength of poor little Diana, and she applied it
well, made no impression whatever on the pony's
tough mouth. Influences of every kind were
favourable. On the illogical principle, probably,
that being " in for a penny " justified being " in for a
pound," the pony laid himself out for a glorious run.

He warmed to his work, caused the dust to fly, and the clothes-basket to advance with irregular bounds and swayings as he scampered along, driving many little dogs wild with delight, and two or three cats mad with fear. Gradually he drew towards the more populous streets, and here, of course, the efforts on the part of the public to arrest him became more frequent, also more decided, though not more successful. At last an inanimate object effected what man and boy had failed to accomplish.

In a wild effort to elude a demonstrative cabman near the corner of one of the main thoroughfares, the brown pony brought the wheels of the vehicle into collision with a lamp-post. That lamp-post went down before the shock like a tall head of grain before the sickle. The front wheels doubled up into a sudden embrace, broke loose, and went across the road, one into a greengrocer's shop, the other into a chemist's window. Thus diversely end many careers that begin on a footing of equality! The hind wheels went careering along the road like a new species of bicycle, until brought up by a donkey cart, while the basket chariot rolled itself violently round the lamp-post, like a shattered remnant, as if resolved, before perishing, to strangle the author of all the mischief. As to the pony, it stopped, and seemed surprised at first by the unexpected finale, but the look quickly changed—or appeared to change—to one of calm contentment as it surveyed the ruin.

But what of the fair little charioteer? Truly, in regard to her, a miracle, or something little short of one, had occurred. The doctrine that extremes meet contains much truth in it—truth which is illustrated and exemplified more frequently, we think, than is generally supposed. A tremendous accident is often much less damaging to the person who experiences it than a slight one. In little Diana's case, the extremes had met, and the result was absolute safety. She was shot out of her basket carriage after the manner of a sky-rocket, but the impulse was so effective that, instead of causing her to fall on her head and break her pretty little neck, it made her perform a complete somersault, and alight upon her feet. Moreover, the spot on which she alighted was opportune, as well as admirably suited to the circumstances.

At the moment, ignorant of what was about to happen, police-constable No. 666—we are not quite sure of what division—in all the plenitude of power, and blue, and six-feet-two, approached the end of a street entering at right angles to the one down which our little heroine had flown. He was a superb specimen of humanity, this constable, with a chest and shoulders like Hercules, and the figure of Apollo. He turned the corner just as the child had

completed her somersault and received her two
little feet fairly in the centre of his broad breast,
driving him flat on his back more effectively than
could have been done by the best prize-fighter in
England! ·

No. 666 proved a most effectual buffer, for Di,
after planting her blow on his chest, sat plump
down on his stomach, off which she sprang in an
agony of consternation, exclaiming—

"Oh! I have killed him! I 've killed him!" and
burst into tears.

"No, my little lady," said No. 666, as he rose
with one or two coughs and replaced his helmet,
"you 've not quite done for me, though you've come
nearer the mark than any *man* has ever yet accomplished.   Come, now, what can I do for you?
You 're not hurt, I hope?"

This sally was received with a laugh, almost
amounting to a cheer, by the half-horrified crowd
which had quickly assembled to witness, as it
expected, a fatal accident.

"Hurt? oh! no, I 'm not hurt," exclaimed Di, while
tears still converted her eyes into blue lakelets as
she looked anxiously up in the face of No. 666;
"but I'm quite sure you must be hurt—awfully.
I'm *so* sorry!   Indeed I am, for I didn't mean to
knock you down."

This also was received by the crowd with a hearty

laugh, while No. 666 sought to comfort the child by earnestly assuring her that he was not hurt in the least—only a little stunned at first, but that was quite gone.

"Wot does she mean by knockin' of 'im down?" asked a small butcher's boy, who had come on the scene just too late, of a small baker's boy who had, happily, been there from the beginning.

"She means wot she says," replied the small baker's boy with the dignified reticence of superior knowledge, "she knocked the constable down."

"Wot! a leetle gurl knock a six-foot bobby down?—walk-*er*!"

"Very good; you've no call to b'lieve it unless you like," replied the baker's boy, with a look of pity at the unbelieving butcher, "but she did it, though—an' that's six month with 'ard labour, if it ain't five year."

At this point the crowd opened up to let a maniac enter. He was breathless, hatless, moist, and frantic.

"My child! my darling! my dear Di!" he gasped.

"Papa!" responded Diana, with a little scream, and, leaping into his arms, grasped him in a genuine hug.

"Oh! I say," whispered the small butcher, "it's a melly-drammy—all for nuffin!"

"My!" responded the small baker, with a solemn

look, "won't the Lord left-tenant be down on 'em for play-actin' without a licence, just!"

"Is the pony killed?" inquired Sir Richard, recovering himself.

"Not in the least, sir. 'Ere 'e is, sir; all alive an' kickin'," answered the small butcher, delighted to have the chance of making himself offensively useful, "but the hinsurance offices wouldn't 'ave the clo'se-baskit at no price. Shall I order up the remains of your carriage, sir?"

"Oh! I'm so glad he's not dead," said Diana, looking hastily up, "but this policeman was nearly killed, and *I* did it! He saved my life, papa."

A chorus of voices here explained to Sir Richard how No. 666 had come up in the nick of time to receive the flying child upon his bosom.

"I am deeply grateful to you," said the knight, turning to the constable, and extending his hand, which the latter shook modestly while disclaiming any merit for having merely performed his duty— he might say, involuntarily.

"Will you come to my house?" said Sir Richard. "Here is my card. I should like to see you again, and pray, see that some one looks after my pony and—"

"And the remains," suggested the small butcher, seeing that Sir Richard hesitated.

"Be so good as to call a cab," said Sir Richard in a general way to any one who chose to obey.

"Here you are, sir!" cried a peculiarly sharp cabby, who, correctly judging from the state of affairs that his services would be required, had drawn near to bide his time.

Sir Richard and his little daughter got in and were driven home, leaving No. 666 to look after the pony and the remains.

Thus curiously were introduced to each other some of the characters in our tale.

CHAPTER II.

THE IRRESISTIBLE POWER OF LOVE.

NEED we remark that there was a great deal of embracing on the part of Di and her nurse when the former returned home? The child was an affectionate creature as well as passionate. The nurse, Mrs. Screwbury, was also affectionate without being passionate. Poor Diana had never known a mother's love or care; but good, steady, stout Mrs. Screwbury did what in her lay to fill the place of mother.

Sir Richard filled the place of father pretty much as a lamp-post might have done had it owned a child. He illuminated her to some extent—explained things in general, stiffly, and shed a feeble ray around himself; but his light did not extend far. He was proud of her, however, and very fond of her—when good. When not good, he was—or rather had been—in the habit of dismissing her to the nursery.

Nevertheless, the child exercised very considerable and ever-increasing influence over her father;

for, although stiff, the knight was by no means
destitute of natural affection, and sometimes observed, with moist eyes, strong traces of resemblance
to his lost wife in the beautiful child. Indeed, as
years advanced, he became a more and more
obedient father, and was obviously on the high
road to abject slavery.

"Papa," said Di, while they were at luncheon
that day, not long after the accident, " I *am* so sorry
for that poor policeman. It seems such a dreadful
thing to have actually jumped upon him! and oh!
you should have heard his poor head hit the pavement, and seen his pretty helmet go spinning along
like a boy's top, ever so far. I wonder it didn't
kill him. I'm *so* sorry."

Di emphasised her sorrow by laughing, for she
had a keen sense of the ludicrous, and the memory of
the spinning helmet was strong upon her just then.

"It must indeed have been an unpleasant blow,"
replied Sir Richard, gravely, "but then, dear, you
couldn't help it, you know—and I dare say he is
none the worse for it now. Men like him are not
easily injured. I fear we cannot say as much for
the boy who was holding the pony."

"Oh! I quite forgot about him," exclaimed Di;
"the naughty boy! he wouldn't let go the pony's
reins when I bid him, but I saw he tumbled down
when we set off."

"Yes, he has been somewhat severely punished, I fear, for his disobedience. His leg has been broken. Is it not so, Balls?"

"Yes, sir," replied the butler, "'e 'as 'ad 'is"——

Balls got no farther, for Diana, who had been struck dumb for the moment by the news, recovered herself.

"His leg broken!" she exclaimed with a look of consternation; "Oh! the poor, poor boy!—the dear boy! and it was me did that too, as well as knocking down the poor policeman!"

There is no saying to what lengths the remorseful child would have gone in the way of self-condemnation if her father had not turned her thoughts from herself by asking what had been done for the boy.

"We sent 'im 'ome, sir. in a cab."

"I'm afraid that was a little too prompt," returned the knight thoughtfully. "A broken leg requires careful treatment, I suppose. You should have had him into the house and sent for a doctor."

Balls coughed. He was slightly chagrined to find that the violation of his own humane feelings had been needless, and that his attempt to do as he thought his master would have wished was in vain.

"I thought, Sir Richard, that you didn't like the lower orders to go about the 'ouse more"——

Again little Di interrupted the butler by asking excitedly where the boy's home was.

"In the neighbour'ood of W'itechapel, Miss Di."

"Then, papa, we will go straight off to see him," said the child, in the tone of one whose mind is fully made up. "You and I shall go together—won't we? good papa!"

"That will do, Balls, you may go. No, my dear Di, I think we had better not. I will write to one of the city missionaries whom I know, and ask him to "——

"No, but, papa—*dear* papa, we *must* go. The city missionary could never say how very, *very* sorry I am that he should have broken his leg while helping me. And then I should *so* like to sit by him and tell him stories, and give him his soup and gruel, and read to him. Poor, *poor* boy, we *must* go, papa, won't you?"

"Not to-day, dear. It is impossible to go to-day. There, now, don't begin to cry. Perhaps—*perhaps* to-morrow—but think, my love; you have no idea how dirty—how *very* nasty—the places are in which our lower orders live."

"Oh! yes I have," said Di eagerly. "Haven't I seen our nursery on cleaning days?"

A faint flicker of a smile passed over the knight's countenance.

"True, darling, but the places are far, far dirtier

than that. Then the smells. Oh! they are very dreadful"——

"What—worse than *we* have when there's cabbage for dinner?"

"Yes, much worse than that."

"I don't care, papa. We *must* go to see the boy —the poor, *poor* boy, in spite of dirt and smells. And then, you know—let me up on your knee and I'll tell you all about it. There! Well, then, you know, I'd tidy the room up, and even wash it a little. Oh, you can't think how nicely I washed up my doll's room—her corner, you know,—that day when I spilt all her soup in trying to feed her, and then, while trying to wipe it up, I accidentally burst her, and all her inside came out—the sawdust, I mean. It was the worst mess I ever made, but I cleaned it up as well as Jessie herself could have done—so nurse said."

"But the messes down in Whitechapel are much worse than you have described, dear," expostulated the parent, who felt that his powers of resistance were going.

"So much the better, papa," replied Di, kissing her sire's lethargic visage. "I should like *so* much to try if I could clean up something worse than my doll's room. And you've promised, you know."

"No—only said 'perhaps,'" returned Sir Richard quickly.

" Well, that's the same thing; and now that it's all nicely settled, I'll go and see nurse. Good-bye, papa."

"Good-bye, dear," returned the knight, resigning himself to his fate and the newspaper.

CHAPTER III.

POVERTY MANAGES TO BOARD OUT HER INFANT FOR NOTHING.

ON the night of the day about which we have been writing, a woman, dressed in "unwomanly rags" crept out of the shadow of the houses near London Bridge. She was a thin, middle-aged woman, with a countenance from which sorrow, suffering, and sin had not been able to obliterate entirely the traces of beauty. She carried a bundle in her arms which was easily recognisable as a baby, from the careful and affectionate manner in which the woman's thin, out-spread fingers grasped it.

Hurrying on to the bridge till she reached the middle of one of the arches, she paused and looked over. The Thames was black and gurgling, for it was intensely dark, and the tide half ebb at the time. The turbid waters chafed noisily on the stone piers as if the sins and sorrows of the great city had been somehow communicated to them.

But the distance from the parapet to the surface of the stream was great. It seemed awful in the woman's eyes. She shuddered and drew back.

"Oh! for courage—only for one minute!" she murmured, clasping the bundle closer to her breast.

The action drew off a corner of the scanty rag which she called a shawl, and revealed a small and round, yet exceedingly thin face, the black eyes of which seemed to gaze in solemn wonder at the scene of darkness visible which was revealed. The woman stood between two lamps in the darkest place she could find, but enough of light reached her to glitter in the baby's solemn eyes as they met her gaze, and it made a pitiful attempt to smile as it recognised its mother.

"God help me! I can't," muttered the woman with a shiver, as if an ice-block had touched her heart.

She drew the rag hastily over the baby's head again, pressed it closer to her breast, retraced her steps, and dived into the shadows from which she had emerged.

This was one of the "lower orders" to whom Sir Richard Brandon had such an objection, whom he found it, he said, so difficult to deal with (no wonder, for he never tried to deal with them at all, in any sense worthy of the name) and whom it was, he said, useless to assist, because all *he* could do in such a vast accumulation of poverty would be a mere drop in the bucket. Hence Sir Richard thought it best to keep the drop in his pocket where it could be felt and do good—at least to him-

self, rather than dissipate it in an almost empty
bucket. The bucket, however, was not quite empty
—thanks to a few thousands of people who differed
from the knight upon that point.

The thin woman hastened through the streets as
regardless of passers-by as they were of her, until
she reached the neighbourhood of Commercial Street,
Spitalfields.

Here she paused and looked anxiously round her.
She had left the main thoroughfare, and the spot on
which she stood was dimly lighted. Whatever she
looked or waited for, did not, however, soon appear,
for she stood under a lamp-post, muttering to herself,
"I *must* git rid of it. Better to do so than see it
starved to death before my eyes."

Presently a foot-fall was heard, and a man drew
near. The woman gazed intently into his face. It
was not a pleasant face. There was a scowl on it.
She drew back and let him pass. Then several
women passed, but she took no notice of them.
Then another man appeared. His face seemed a
jolly one. The woman stepped forward at once and
confronted him.

"Please, sir," she began, but the man was too
sharp for her.

"Come now—you've brought out that baby on
purpose to humbug people with it. Don't fancy
you'll throw dust in *my* eyes. I'm too old a cock

for that. Don't you know that you're breaking the law by begging ?"

"I'm *not* begging," retorted the woman, almost fiercely.

"Oh! indeed. Why do you stop me, then ?"

"I merely wished to ask if your name is Thompson."

"Ah! hem!" ejaculated the man with a broad grin, "well no, madam, my name is *not* Thompson."

"Well, then," rejoined the woman, still indignantly, "you may move on."

She had used an expression all too familiar to herself, and the man, obeying the order with a bow and a mocking laugh, disappeared like those who had gone before him.

For some time no one else appeared save a policeman. When he approached, the woman went past him down the street, as if bent on some business, but when he was out of sight she returned to the old spot, which was near the entrance to an alley.

At last the woman's patience was rewarded by the sight of a burly little elderly man, whose face of benignity was unmistakably genuine. Remembering the previous man's reference to the baby, she covered it up carefully, and held it more like a bundle.

Stepping up to the newcomer at once, she put the same question as to name, and also asked if he lived in Russell Square.

"No, my good woman," replied the burly little man, with a look of mingled surprise and pity, my name is *not* Thompson. It is Twitter—Samuel Twitter, of Twitter, Slime and—— but," he added, checking himself, under a sudden and rare impulse of prudence, "why do you ask my name and address?"

The woman gave an almost hysterical laugh at having been so successful in her somewhat clumsy scheme, and, without uttering another word, darted down the alley. She passed rapidly round by a back way to another point of the same street she had left —well ahead of the spot where she had stood so long and so patiently that night. Here she suddenly uncovered the baby's face and kissed it passionately for a few moments. Then, wrapping it in the ragged shawl, with its little head out, she laid it on the middle of the footpath full in the light of a lamp, and retired to await the result.

When the woman rushed away, as above related, Mr. Samuel Twitter stood for some minutes rooted to the spot, lost in amazement. He was found in that condition by the returning policeman.

"Constable," said he, cocking his hat to one side the better to scratch his bald head, "there are strange people in this region."

"Indeed there are, sir."

"Yes, but I mean *very* strange people."

" Well, sir, if you insist on it, I won't deny that some of them are *very* strange."

" Yes, well—good-night, constable," said Mr. Twitter, moving slowly forward in a mystified state of mind, while the guardian of the night continued his rounds, thinking to himself that he had just parted from one of the very strangest of the people.

Suddenly Samuel Twitter came to a full stop, for there lay the small baby gazing at him with its solemn eyes, apparently quite indifferent to the hardness and coldness of its bed of stone.

" Abandoned!" gasped the burly little man.

Whether Mr. Twitter referred to the infant's moral character, or to its being shamefully forsaken, we cannot now prove, but he instantly caught the bundle in his arms and gazed at it. Possibly his gaze may have been too intense, for the mild little creature opened a small mouth that bore no propor- tion whatever to the eyes, and attempted to cry, but the attempt was a failure. It had not strength to cry.

The burly little man's soul was touched to the centre by the sight. He kissed the baby's forehead, pressed it to his ample breast, and hurried away. If he had taken time to think he might have gone to a police-office, or a night refuge, or some such haven of rest for the weary, but when Twitter's feelings were touched he became a man of impulse.

He did not take time to think—except to the
extent that, on reaching the main thoroughfare, he
hailed a cab and was driven home.

The poor mother had followed him with the intention of seeing him home.   Of course the cab put
an end to that.   She felt comparatively easy, however, knowing, as she did, that her child was in the
keeping of "Twitter, Slime and ——."   That was
quite enough to enable her to trace Mr. Twitter
out.   Comforting herself as well as she could with
this reflection, she sat down in a dark corner on a
cold door-step, and, covering her face with both
hands, wept as though her heart would break.

Gradually her sobs subsided, and, rising, she
hurried away, shivering with cold, for her thin
cotton dress was a poor protection against the night
chills, and her ragged shawl was gone—with the
baby.

In a few minutes she reached a part of the
Whitechapel district where some of the deepest
poverty and wretchedness in London is to be found.
Turning into a labyrinth of small streets and alleys,
she paused in the neighbourhood of the court in
which was her home—if such it could be called.

"Is it worth while going back to him?" she
muttered.   "He nearly killed baby, and it wouldn't
take much to make him kill me.   And oh! he was
so different—once!"

While she stood irresolute, the man of whom she spoke chanced to turn the corner, and ran against her, somewhat roughly.

"Hallo! is that you?" he demanded, in tones that told too clearly where he had been spending the night.

"Yes, Ned, it's me. I was just thinking about going home."

"Home, indeed—'stime to b' goin' home. Where'v you bin? The babby 'll 'v bin squallin' pretty stiff by this time."

"No fear of baby now," returned the wife almost defiantly; "it's gone."

"Gone!" almost shouted the husband. "You haven't murdered it, have you?"

"No, but I've put it in safe keeping, where *you* can't get at it, and, now I know *that*, I don't care what you do to *me*."

"Ha! we'll see about that. Come along."

He seized the woman by the arm and hurried her towards their dwelling.

.It was little better than a cellar, the door being reached by a descent of five or six much-worn steps. To the surprise of the couple the door, which was usually shut at that hour, stood partly open, and a bright light shone within.

"Wastin' coal and candle," growled the man with an angry oath, as he approached.

"Hetty didn't use to be so extravagant," remarked the woman, in some surprise.

As she spoke the door was flung wide open, and an overgrown but very handsome girl peered out.

"Oh! father, I thought it was your voice," she said. "Mother, is that you? Come in, quick. Here's Bobby brought home in a cab with a broken leg."

On hearing this the man's voice softened, and, entering the room, he went up to a heap of straw in one corner whereon our little friend Bobby Frog —the street Arab—lay.

"Hallo! Bobby, wot's wrong with'ee? You ain't used to come to grief," said the father, laying his hand on the boy's shoulder, and giving him a rough shake.

Things oftentimes "are not what they seem." The shake was the man's mode of expressing sympathy, for he was fond of his son, regarding him, with some reason, as a most hopeful pupil in the ways of wickedness.

"It's o' no use, father," said the boy, drawing his breath quickly and knitting his brows, "you can't stir me up with a long pole now. I'm past that."

"What! have 'ee bin runned over?"

"No—on'y run down, or knocked down."

"Who did it? On'y give me his name an' address, an' as sure as my name's Ned I'll—"

He finished the sentence with a sufficiently expressive scowl and clenching of a huge fist, which
had many a time done great execution in the prize
ring.

"It wasn't a he, father, it was a she."

"Well, no matter, if I on'y had my fingers on her
windpipe I'd squeeze it summat."

"If you did I'd bang your nose! She didn't go
for to do it a-purpose, you old grampus," retorted
Bobby, intending the remark to be taken as a gentle
yet affectionate reproof. "A doctor's bin an' set
my leg," continued the boy, "an' made it as stiff as
a poker wi' what 'e calls splints. He says I won't be
able to go about for ever so many weeks."

"An' who's to feed you, I wonder, doorin' them
weeks? An' who sent for the doctor? Was it
him as supplied the fire an' candle to-night?"

"No, father, it was me," answered Hetty, who
was engaged in stirring something in a small saucepan, the loose handle of which was attached to its
battered body by only one rivet; the other rivet had
given way on an occasion when Ned Frog sent it
flying through the doorway after his retreating wife.
"You see I was paid my wages to-night, so I could
afford it, as well as to buy some coal and a candle,
for the doctor said Bobby must be kept warm."

"Afford it!" exclaimed Ned, in rising wrath, "how
can 'ee say you can afford it w'en I 'aven't had

enough grog to *half* screw me, an' not a brown left. Did the doctor ask a fee ?"

"No, father, I offered him one, but he wouldn't take it."

" Ah—very good on 'im ! I wonder them fellows has the cheek to ask fees for on'y givin' advice. W'y, I'd give advice myself all day long at a penny an hour, an' think myself well off too if I got that— better off than them as got the advice anyhow What are you sittin' starin' at an' sulkin' there for ?"

This last remark was addressed gruffly to Mrs. Frog, who, during the previous conversation, had seated herself on a low three-legged stool, and, clasping her hands over her knees, gazed at the dirty blank walls in blanker despair.

The poor woman realised the situation better than her drunken husband did. As a bird-fancier he contributed little, almost nothing, to the general fund on which this family subsisted. He was a huge, powerful fellow, and had various methods of obtaining money—some obvious and others mysterious— but nearly all his earnings went to the gin-palace, for Ned was a man of might, and could stand an enormous quantity of drink. Hetty, who worked, perhaps we should say slaved, for a firm which paid her one shilling a week, could not manage to find food for them all. Mrs. Frog herself, with her infant to care for, had found it hard work at any time to earn a few pence, and now Bobby's active little limbs were reduced to inaction, converting him into a consumer instead of a producer. In short, the glaring fact that the family expenses would be increased while the family income was diminished, stared Mrs. Frog as blankly in the face as she stared at the dirty blank wall.

And her case was worse, even, than people in better circumstances might imagine, for the family lived so literally from hand to mouth that there was no time even to think when a difficulty arose or disaster befell. They rented their room from a man who styled it a furnished apartment, in virtue of a rickety table, a broken chair, a worn-out sheet or two, a dilapidated counterpane, four ragged blankets, and the infirm saucepan before mentioned, besides a few articles of cracked or broken crockery. For this accommodation the landlord charged ninepence per day, which sum had to be paid *every night* before the family was allowed to retire to rest! In the event of failure to pay they would have been turned out into the street at once, and the door padlocked. Thus the necessity for a constant, though small, supply of cash became urgent, and the consequent instability of " home " very depressing.

To preserve his goods from the pawnbroker, and prevent a moonlight flitting, this landlord had

printed on his sheets the words "stolen from ——"
and on the blankets and counterpane were stamped
the words "stop thief!"

Mrs. Frog made no reply to her husband's gruff
question, which induced the man to seize an empty
bottle as being the best way of rousing her attention.

"Come, you let mother alone, dad," suggested
Bobby, "she ain't a-aggrawatin' of you just now."

"Why, mother," exclaimed Hetty, who was so
busy with Bobby's supper, and, withal, so accustomed to the woman's looks of hopeless misery that
she had failed to observe anything unusual until
her attention was thus called to her, "what ever
have you done with the baby?"

"Ah—you may well ask that," growled Ned.

Even the boy seemed to forget his pain for a
moment as he now observed, anxiously, that his
mother had not the usual bundle on her breast.

"The baby's gone!" she said, bitterly, still keeping her eyes on the blank wall.

"Gone!—how?—lost? killed? speak, mother,"
burst from Hetty and the boy.

"No, only gone to where it will be better cared
for than here."

"Come, explain, old woman," said Ned, again
laying his hand on the bottle.

As Hetty went and took her hand gently, Mrs.

Frog condescended to explain, but absolutely refused to tell to whose care the baby had been consigned.

"Well—it ain't a bad riddance, after all," said the man, as he rose, and, staggering into a corner where another bundle of straw was spread on the floor, flung himself down. Appropriately drawing two of the "stop thief" blankets over him, he went to sleep.

Then Mrs. Frog, feeling comparatively sure of quiet for the remainder of the night, drew her stool close to the side of her son, and held such intercourse with him as she seldom had the chance of holding while Bobby was in a state of full health and bodily vigour. Hetty, meanwhile, ministered to them both, for she was one of those dusty diamonds of what may be styled the East-end diggings of London—not so rare, perhaps, as many people may suppose—whose lustre is dimmed and intrinsic value somewhat concealed by the neglect and the moral as well as physical filth by which they are surrounded.

"Of course you 've paid the ninepence, Hetty ?"

"Yes, mother."

"You might 'ave guessed that," said Bobby, "for, if she 'adn't we shouldn't 'ave bin here."

"That and the firing and candle, with what the doctor ordered, has used up all I had earned, even though I did some extra work and was paid for it," said Hetty with a sigh. "But I don't grudge it, Bobby—I'm only sorry because there's nothing more coming to me till next week."

"Meanwhile there is nothing for *this* week," said Mrs. Frog with a return of the despair, as she looked at her prostrate son, "for all I can manage to earn will barely make up the rent—if it does even that—and father, you know, drinks nearly all he makes. God help us!"

"God *will* help us," said Hetty, sitting down on the floor and gently stroking the back of her mother's hand, "for He sent the trouble, and will hear us when we cry to Him."

"Pray to Him, then, Hetty, for it's no use askin' me to join you. I can't pray. An' don't let your father hear, else he'll be wild."

The poor girl bent her head on her knees as she sat, and prayed silently. Her mother and brother, neither of whom had any faith in prayer, remained silent, while her father, breathing stertorously in the corner, slept the sleep of the drunkard.

CHAPTER IV.

SAMUEL TWITTER ASTONISHES MRS. TWITTER AND HER FRIENDS.

IN a former chapter we described, to some extent, the person and belongings of a very poor man with five thousand a year. Let us now make the acquaintance of a very rich one with an income of five hundred.

He has already introduced himself to the reader under the name of Samuel Twitter.

On the night of which we write Mrs. Twitter happened to have a "few friends" to tea. And let no one suppose that Mrs. Twitter's few friends were to be put off with afternoon tea—that miserable invention of modern times—nor with a sham meal of sweet warm water and thin bread and butter. By no means. We have said that Samuel Twitter was rich, and Mrs. Twitter, conscious of her husband's riches, as well as grateful for them, went in for the substantial and luxurious to an amazing extent.

Unlimited pork sausages and inexhaustible buttered toast, balanced with muffins or crumpets, was

her idea of "tea." The liquid was a secondary
point—in one sense—but it was always strong. It
was the only strong liquid in fact allowed in the
house, for Mr. Twitter, Mrs. Twitter, and all the
little Twitters were members of the Blue Ribbon
Army; more or less enthusiastic according to their
light and capacity.

The young Twitters descended in a graduated
scale from Sammy, the eldest (about sixteen), down
through Molly, and Willie, and Fred, and Lucy, to
Alice the so-called "baby"—though she was at
that time a remarkably robust baby of four years.

Mrs. Twitter's few friends were aware of her
tendencies, and appreciated her hospitality, insomuch that the "few" bade fair to develop by
degrees into many.

Well, Mrs. Twitter had her few friends to tea,
and conviviality was at its height. The subject of
conversation was poverty. Mrs. Loper, a weak-
minded but amiable lady, asserted that a large
family with £500 a year was a poor family. Mrs.
Loper did not know that Mrs. Twitter's income was
five hundred, but she suspected it. Mrs. T. herself
carefully avoided giving the slightest hint on the
subject.

"Of course," continued Mrs. Loper, "I don't
mean to say that people with five hundred are *very*
poor, you know; indeed it all depends on the

family. With six children like you, now, to feed and clothe and educate, and with everything so dear as it is now, I should say that five hundred was poverty."

"Well, I don't quite agree with you, Mrs. Loper, on that point. To my mind it does not so much depend on the family, as on the notions, and the capacity to manage, in the head of the family. I remember one family just now, whose head was cut off suddenly, I may say in the prime of life.' A hundred and fifty a year or thereabouts was the income the widow had to count on, and she was left with five little ones to rear. She trained them well, gave them good educations, made most of their garments with her own hands when they were little, and sent one of her boys to college, yet was noted for the amount of time she spent in visiting the poor, the sick, and the afflicted, for whom she had always a little to spare out of her limited income. Now, if wealth is to be measured by results, I think we may say that that poor lady was rich. She was deeply mourned by a large circle of poor people when she was taken home to the better land. Her small means, having been judiciously invested by a brother, increased a little towards the close of life, but she never was what the world esteems rich."

Mrs. Twitter looked at a very tall man with a

dark unhandsome countenance, as if to invite his opinion.

"I quite agree with you," he said, helping himself to a crumpet, "there are some people with small incomes who seem to be always in funds, just as there are other people with large incomes who are always hard-up. The former are really rich, the latter really poor."

Having delivered himself of these sentiments somewhat sententiously, Mr. Crackaby,—that was his name,—proceeded to consume the crumpet.

There was a general tendency on the part of the other guests to agree with their hostess, but one black sheep in the flock objected. He quite agreed, of course, with the general principle that liberality with small means was beautiful to behold as well as desirable to possess—the liberality, not the small means—and that, on the other hand, riches with a narrow niggardly spirit was abominable, but then— and the black sheep came, usually, to the strongest part of his argument when he said "but then"— it was an uncommonly difficult thing, when everything was up to famine prices, and gold was depreciated in value owing to the gold-fields, and silver was nowhere, and coppers were changed into bronze,—exceedingly difficult to practise liberality and at the same time to make the two ends meet.

As no one clearly saw the exact bearing of the

black sheep's argument, they all replied with that half idiotic simper with which Ignorance seeks to conceal herself, and which Politeness substitutes for the more emphatic " pooh," or the inelegant " bosh." Then, applying themselves with renewed zest to the muffins, they put about ship, nautically speaking, and went off on a new tack.

" Mr. Twitter is rather late to-night, I think?" said Mr. Crackaby, consulting his watch, which was antique and turnipy in character.

" He is, indeed," replied the hostess, " business must have detained him, for he is the very soul of punctuality. That is one of his many good qualities, and it is *such* a comfort, for I can always depend on him to the minute,—breakfast, dinner, tea; he never keeps us waiting, as too many men do, except, of course, when he is unavoidably detained by business."

" Ah, yes, business has much to answer for," remarked Mrs. Loper, in a tone which suggested that she held business to be an incorrigibly bad fellow; " whatever mischief happens with one's husband it's sure to be business that did it."

" Pardon me, madam," objected the black sheep, whose name, by the way, was Stickler, " business does bring about much of the disaster that often appertains to wedded life, but mischief is sometimes done by other means, such, for instance, as accidents, robberies, murders "—

"Oh! Mr. Stickler," suddenly interrupted a stout, smiling lady, named Larrabel, who usually did the audience part of Mrs. Twitter's little tea parties, "how *can* you suggest such ideas, especially when Mr. Twitter is unusually late?"

Mr. Stickler protested that he had no intention of alarming the company by disagreeable suggestions, that he had spoken of accident, robbery, and murder in the abstract.

"There, you've said it all over again," interrupted Mrs. Larrabel, with an unwonted frown.

"But then," continued Stickler, regardless of the interruption, "a broken leg, or a rifled pocket and stunned person, or a cut windpipe, may be applicable to the argument in hand without being applied to Mr. Twitter."

"Surely," said Mrs. Loper, who deemed the reply unanswerable.

In this edifying strain the conversation flowed on until the evening grew late and the party began to grow alarmed.

"I do hope nothing has happened to him," said Mrs. Loper, with a solemnised face.

"I think not. I have seen him come home much later than this—though not often," said the hostess, the only one of the party who seemed quite at ease, and who led the conversation back again into shallower channels.

As the night advanced, however, the alarm became deeper, and it was even suggested by Mrs. Loper that Crackaby should proceed to Twitter's office —a distance of three miles—to inquire whether and when he had left; while the smiling Mrs. Larrabel proposed to send information to the headquarters of the police in Scotland Yard, because the police knew everything, and could find out anything.

"You have no idea, my dear," she said, "how clever they are at Scotland Yard. Would you believe it, I left my umbrellar the other day in a cab, and I didn't know the number of the cab, for numbers won't remain in my head, nor the look of the cabman, for I never look at cabmen, they are so rude sometimes. I didn't even remember the place where I got into the cab, for I can't remember places when I've to go to so many, so I gave up my umbrellar for lost and was going away, when a policeman stepped up to me and asked in a very civil tone if I had lost anything. He was so polite and pleasant that I told him of my loss, though I knew it would do me no good, as he had not seen the cab or the cabman.

"'I think, madam,' he said, 'that if you go down to Scotland Yard to-morrow morning, you may probably find it there.'

"'Young man,' said I, 'do you take me for a fool!'

"'No, madam, I don't,' he replied.

"'Or do you take my umbrellar for a fool,' said I, 'that it should walk down to Scotland Yard of its own accord and wait there till I called for it?'

"'Certainly not, madam,' he answered with such a pleasant smile that I half forgave him.

"'Nevertheless if you happen to be in the neighbourhood of Scotland Yard to-morrow,' he added, 'it might be as well to call in and inquire.'

"'Thank you,' said I, with a stiff bow as I left him. On the way home, however, I thought there might be something in it, so I did go down to Scotland Yard next day, where I was received with as much civility as if I had been a lady of quality, and was taken to a room as full of umbrellas as an egg's full of meat—almost.

"'You'd know the umbrellar if you saw it, madam,' said the polite constable who escorted me.

"'Know it, sir!' said I, 'yes, I should think I would. Seven and sixpence it cost me—new, and I've only had it a week—brown silk with a plain handle—why, there it is!' And there it was sure enough, and he gave it to me at once, only requiring me to write my name in a book, which I did with great difficulty because of my gloves, and being so nervous. Now, how did the young policeman that spoke to me the day before know that my umbrellar would go there, and how did it get there? They say the days of miracles are over, but I don't

think so, for that was a miracle if ever there was
one."

"The days of miracles are indeed over, ma'am,"
said the black sheep, "but then that is no reason
why things which are in themselves commonplace
should not appear miraculous to the uninstructed
mind. When I inform you that our laws compel
cabmen under heavy penalties to convey left
umbrellas and parcels to the police office, the
miracle may not seem quite so surprising."

Most people dislike to have their miracles un-
masked. Mrs. Larrabel turned from the black
sheep to her hostess without replying, and repeated
her suggestion about making inquiries at Scotland
Yard—thus delicately showing that although, possibly, convinced, she was by no means converted.

They were interrupted at this point by a hurried
knock at the street door.

"There he is at last," exclaimed every one.

"It is his knock, certainly," said Mrs. Twitter,
with a perplexed look, "but rather peculiar—not so
firm as usual—there it is again! Impatient! I
never knew my Sam impatient before in all our
wedded life. You'd better open the door, dear,"
she said, turning to the eldest Twitter, he being the
only one of the six who was privileged to sit up late,
"Mary seems to have fallen asleep."

Before the eldest Twitter could obey, the maligned

Mary was heard to open the door and utter an ex-
clamation of surprise, and her master's step was
heard to ascend the stair rather unsteadily.

The guests looked at each other anxiously. It
might be that to some minds—certainly to that of
the black sheep—visions of violated blue-ribbonism
occurred. As certainly these visions did *not* occur to
Mrs. Twitter. She would sooner have doubted her
clergyman than her husband. Trustfulness formed
a prominent part of her character, and her confidence
in her Sam was unbounded.

Even when her husband came against the drawing-
room door with an awkward bang—the passage being
dark—opened it with a fling, and stood before the
guests with a flushed countenance, blazing eyes, a
peculiar deprecatory smile, and a dirty ragged
bundle in his arms, she did not doubt him.

"Forgive me, my dear," he said, gazing at his wife
in a manner that might well have justified the black
sheep's thought, "screwed," "I—I—business kept
me in the office very late, and then"— He cast
an imbecile glance at the bundle.

"What *ever* have you got there, Sam?" asked his
wondering wife.

"Goodness me! it moves!" exclaimed Mrs. Loper.

"Live poultry!" thought the black sheep, and
visions of police cells and penal servitude floated
before his depraved mental vision.

"Yes, Mrs. Loper, it moves. It is alive—though not very much alive, I fear. My dear, I've found—found a baby—picked it up in the street. Not a soul there but me. Would have perished or been trodden on if I had not taken it up. See here!"

He untied the dirty bundle as he spoke, and uncovered the round little pinched face with the great solemn eyes, which gazed, still wonderingly, at the assembled company.

It is due to the assembled company to add that it returned the gaze with compound interest.

CHAPTER V.

TREATS STILL FURTHER OF RICHES, POVERTY, BABIES, AND POLICE.

WHEN Mr. and Mrs. Twitter had dismissed the few friends that night, they sat down at their own fireside, with no one near them but the little foundling, which lay in the youngest Twitter's disused cradle, gazing at them with its usual solemnity, for it did not seem to require sleep. They opened up their minds to each other thus :—

"Now, Samuel," said Mrs. Twitter, "the question is, what are you going to do with it?"

"Well, Mariar," returned her spouse, with an assumption of profound gravity, "I suppose we must send it to the workhouse."

"You know quite well, Sam, that you don't mean that," said Mrs. Twitter, "the dear little forsaken mite! Just look at its solemn eyes. It has been clearly cast upon us, Sam, and it seems to me that we are bound to look after it."

"What! with six of our own, Mariar?"

"Yes, Sam. Isn't there a song which says something about luck in odd numbers?"

"And with only £500 a year?" objected Mr. Twitter.

"'Only' five hundred. How can you speak so? We are *rich* with five hundred. Can we not educate our little ones?"

"Yes, my dear."

"And entertain our friends?"

"Yes, my love,—with crumpets and tea."

"Don't forget muffins and bloater paste, and German sausage and occasional legs of mutton, you ungrateful man!"

"I don't forget 'em, Mariar. My recollection of 'em is powerful; I may even say vivid."

"Well," continued the lady, "haven't you been able to lend small sums on several occasions to friends"—

"Yes, my dear,—and they are *still* loans," murmured the husband.

"And don't we give a little—I sometimes think too little—regularly to the poor, and to the church, and haven't we got a nest-egg laid by in the Post-office savings-bank?"

"All true, Mariar, and all *your* doing. But for your thrifty ways, and economical tendencies, and rare financial abilities, I should have been bankrupt long ere now."

Mr. Twitter was nothing more than just in this statement of his wife's character. She was one of those happily constituted women who make the

D

best and the most of everything, and who, while by
no means turning her eyes away from the dark
sides of things, nevertheless gave people the impression that she saw only their bright sides. Her
economy would have degenerated into nearness if
it had not been commensurate with her liberality,
for while, on the one hand, she was ever anxious,
almost eager, to give to the needy and suffering
every penny that she could spare, she was, on the
other hand, strictly economical in trifles. Indeed
Mrs. Twitter's vocabulary did not contain the word
trifle. One of her favourite texts of Scripture, which
was always in her mind, and which she had illuminated in gold and hung on her bed-room walls
with many other words of God, was, "Gather up
the fragments, that nothing be lost." Acting on
this principle with all her heart, she gathered up
the fragments of time, so that she had always a
good deal of that commodity to spare, and was
never in a hurry. She gathered up bits of twine
and made neat little rings of them, which · she
deposited in a basket—a pretty large basket—
which in time became such a repository of wealth
in that respect that the six Twitters never failed
to find the exact size and quality of cordage wanted
by them—and, indeed, even after the eldest,
Sammy, came to the years of discretion, if he had
suddenly required a cable suited to restrain a

first-rate iron-clad, his mind would, in the first
blush of the thing, have reverted to mother's basket!
If friends wrote short notes to Mrs. Twitter—
which they often did, for the sympathetic find plenty
of correspondents—the blank leaves were always
torn off and consigned to a scrap-paper box, and the
pile grew big enough at last to have set up a small
stationer in business. And so with everything that
came under her influence at home or abroad. She
emphatically did what she could to prevent waste,
and became a living fulfilment of the well-known
proverb, for as she wasted not she wanted not.

But to return from this digression—

"Well, then," said Mrs. Twitter, "don't go and
find fault, Samuel (she used the name in full when
anxious to be impressive) with what Providence has
given us, by putting the word 'only' to it, for we
are *rich* with five hundred a year."

Mr. Twitter freely admitted that he was wrong,
and said he would be more careful in future of the
use to which he put the word "only."

"But," said he, "we haven't a hole or corner in
the house to put the poor thing in. To be sure,
there's the coal-cellar and the scuttle might be
rigged up as a cradle, but—"

He paused, and looked at his wife. The deceiver
did not mean all this to be taken as a real objection.
He was himself anxious to retain the infant, and

only made this show of opposition to enlist Maria more certainly on his side.

"Not a corner!" she exclaimed, "why, is there not the whole parlour? Do you suppose that a baby requires a four-post bed, and a wash-hand-stand, and a five-foot mirror? Couldn't we lift the poor darling in and out in half a minute? Besides, there is our own room. I feel as if there was an uncomfortable want of some sort ever since *our* baby was transplanted to the nursery. So we will establish the old bassinet and put the mite there."

"And what shall we call it, Maria?"

"Call it—why, call it—call it—Mite—no name could be more appropriate."

"But, my love, Mite, if a name at all, is a man's —that is, it sounds like a masculine name."

"Call it Mita, then."

And so it was named, and thus that poor little waif came to be adopted by that "rich" family.

It seems to be our mission, at this time, to introduce our readers to various homes—the homes of England, so to speak! But let not our readers become impatient, while we lead the way to one more home, and open the door with our secret latch-key.

This home is in some respects peculiar. It is not a poor one, for it is comfortable and clean. Neither is it a rich one, for there are few ornaments, and no luxuries about it. Over the fire stoops a comely young woman, as well as one can judge, at least, from the rather faint light that enters through a small window facing a brick wall. The wall is only five feet from the window, and some previous occupant of the rooms had painted on it a rough landscape, with three very green trees and a very blue lake, and a swan in the middle thereof, sitting on an inverted swan which was meant to be his reflection, but somehow seemed rather more real than himself. The picture is better, perhaps, than the bricks were, yet it is not enlivening. The only other objects in the room worth mentioning are, a particularly small book-shelf in a corner; a cuckoo-clock on the mantel-shelf, an engraved portrait of Queen Victoria on the wall opposite in a gilt frame, and a portrait of Sir Robert Peel in a frame of rosewood beside it.

On a little table in the centre of the room are the remains of a repast. Under the table is a very small child, probably four years of age. Near the window is another small, but older child—a boy of about six or seven. He is engaged in fitting on his little head a great black cloth helmet with a bronze badge, and a peak behind as well as before.

Having nearly extinguished himself with the helmet, the small boy seizes a very large truncheon, and makes a desperate effort to flourish it.

Close to the comely woman stands a very tall, very handsome, and very powerful man, who is putting in the uppermost buttons of a police constable's uniform.

Behold, reader, the *tableau vivant* to which we would call your attention!

"Where d'you go on duty to-day, Giles," asked the comely young woman, raising her face to that of her husband.

"Oxford Circus," replied the policeman. "It is the first time I've been put on fixed-point duty. That's the reason I'm able to breakfast with you and the children, Molly, instead of being off at half-past five in the morning as usual. I shall be on for a month."

"I'm glad of it, Giles, for it gives the children a chance of seeing something of you. I wish you'd let me look at that cut on your shoulder. Do!"

"No, no, Molly," returned the man, as he pushed his wife playfully away from him. "Hands off! You know the punishment for assaulting the police is heavy! Now then, Monty (to the boy), give up my helmet and truncheon. I must be off."

"Not yet, daddy," cried Monty, "I's a pleeceman of the A Division, No. 2, 'ats me, an' I'm goin' to catch a t'ief. I 'mell 'im."

"You smell him, do you? Where is he, d'you think?"

"Oh! I know," replied the small policeman—here he came close up to his father, and, getting on tiptoe, said in a very audible whisper, "he's under de table, but don' tell 'im I know. His name's Joe!"

"All right, I'll keep quiet, Monty, but look alive and nab him quick, for I must be off."

Thus urged the small policeman went on tiptoe to the table, made a sudden dive under it, and collared his little brother.

The arrest, however, being far more prompt than had been expected, the "t'ief" refused to be captured. A struggle ensued, in the course of which the helmet rolled off, a corner of the table-cloth was pulled down, and the earthenware teapot fell with a crash to the floor.

"It's my duty, I fear," said Giles, "to take you both into custody and lock you up in a cell for breaking the teapot as well as the peace, but I'll be merciful and let you off this time, Monty, if you lend your mother a hand to pick up the pieces."

Monty agreed to accept this compromise. The helmet and truncheon were put to their proper uses, and the merciful police constable went out "on duty."

CHAPTER VI.

WEALTH PAYS A VISIT TO POVERTY.

It was an interesting sight to watch police constable No. 666 as he went through the performance
of his arduous duties that day at the Regent Circus
in Oxford Street.

To those who are unacquainted with London, it
may be necessary to remark that this circus is one
of those great centres of traffic where two main
arteries cross and tend to cause so much obstruction,
that complete stoppages would become frequent
were it not for the admirable management of the
several members of the police force who are stationed
there to keep order. The "Oxford Circus," as it is
sometimes called, is by no means the largest or most
crowded of such crossings, nevertheless the tide of
traffic is sufficiently strong and continuous there to
require several police-constables on constant duty.
When men are detailed for such "Fixed-Point" duty
they go on it for a month at a time, and have
different hours from the other men, namely, from
nine in the morning till five in the afternoon.

We have said it was interesting to watch our big

hero, No. 666, in the performance of his arduous duties. He occupied the crossing on the city side of the circus.

It was a magnificent afternoon, and all the metropolitan butterflies were out. Busses flowed on in a a continuous stream, looking like big bullies who incline to use their weight and strength to crush through all obstruction. The drivers of these were for the most part wise men, and restrained themselves and their steeds. In one or two instances, where the drivers were unwise, a glance from the bright eye of Giles Scott was quite sufficient to keep all right.

And Giles could only afford to bestow a fragmentary glance at any time on the refractory, for, almost at one and the same moment he had to check the impetuous, hold up a warning hand to the unruly, rescue a runaway child from innumerable horse-legs, pilot a stout but timid lady from what we may call refuge-island, in the middle of the roadway, to the pavement, answer an imbecile's question as to the whereabouts of the Tower or St. Paul's, order a loitering cabby to move on, and look out for his own toes, as well as give moderate attention to the carriage-poles which perpetually threatened the small of his own back.

We should imagine that the premium of insurance on the life of No. 666 was fabulous in amount, but cannot tell.

Besides his great height, Giles possessed a drooping moustache, which added much to his dignified
appearance. He was also imperturbably grave,
except when offering aid to a lady or a little child,
on which occasions the faintest symptoms of a smile
floated for a moment on his visage like an April
sunbeam. At all other times his expression was
that of incorruptible justice and awful immobility.
No amount of chaff, no quantity of abuse, no kind
of flattery, no sort of threat could move him any
more than the seething billows of the Mediterranean
can move Gibraltar. Costermongers growled at him
hopelessly. Irate cabmen saw that their wisdom
lay in submission. Criminals felt that once in his
grasp their case was hopeless, just as, conversely,
old ladies felt that once under his protection they
were in absolute security. Even street boys felt
that references to " bobbies," " coppers," and " slops;"
questions as to how 'is 'ead felt up there ; who rolled
'im hout so long; whether his mother knew 'e was
hout; whether 'e 'd sell 'em a bit of 'is legs; with
advice to come down off the ladder, or to go 'ome to
bed—that all these were utterly thrown away and
lost upon Giles Scott.

The garb of the London policeman is not, as every
one knows, founded on the principles of æsthetics.
Neither has it been devised on utilitarian principles.
Indeed we doubt whether the originator of it (and

we are happy to profess ignorance of his name) proceeded on any principle whatever, except the gratification of a wild and degraded fancy. The colour, of course, is not objectionable, and the helmet might be worse, but the tunic is such that the idea of grace or elegance may not consist with it.

We mention these facts because Giles Scott was so well made that he forced his tunic to look well, and thus added one more to the already numerous "exceptions" which are said to "prove the rule."

"Allow me, madam," said Giles, offering his right hand to an elderly female, who, having screwed up her courage to make a rush, got into sudden danger and became mentally hysterical in the midst of a conglomerate of hoofs, poles, horse-heads, and wheels.

The female allowed him, and the result was sudden safety, a gasp of relief, and departure of hysteria.

"Not yet, please," said Giles, holding up a warning right hand to the crowd on refuge-island, while with his left waving gently to and fro he gave permission to the mighty stream to flow. "Now," he added, holding up the left hand suddenly. The stream was stopped as abruptly as were the waters of Jordan in days of old, and the storm-staid crew on refuge-island made a rush for the mainland. It was a trifling matter to most of them that rush, but of serious moment to the few whose limbs had lost their elasticity, or whose minds could not shake off the memory of the fact that between 200 and 300 lives are lost in London streets by accidents every year, and that between 3000 and 4000 are more or less severely injured annually.

Before the human stream had got quite across, an impatient hansom made a push. The eagle eye of No. 666 had observed the intention, and in a moment his gigantic figure stood calmly in front of the horse, whose head was raised high above his helmet as the driver tightened the reins violently.

Just then a small slipshod girl made an anxious dash from refuge-island, lost courage, and turned to run back, changed her mind, got bewildered, stopped suddenly and yelled.

Giles caught her by the arm, bore her to the pavement, and turned, just in time to see the hansom dash on in the hope of being overlooked. Vain hope! No. 666 saw the number of the hansom, booked it in his memory while he assisted in raising up an old gentleman who had been overturned, though not injured, in endeavouring to avoid it.

During the lull—for there are lulls in the rush of London traffic, as in the storms of nature,— Giles transferred the number of that hansom to his note-book, thereby laying up a little treat for its driver in the shape of a little trial the next day, terminating, probably, with a fine.

Towards five in the afternoon the strain of all this began to tell even on the powerful frame of Giles Scott, but no symptom did he show of fatigue, and so much reserve force did he possess that it is probable he would have exhibited as calm and unwearied a front if he had remained on duty for eighteen hours instead of eight.

About that hour, also, there came an unusual glut to the traffic, in the form of a troop of the horse-guards. These magnificent creatures, resplendent in glittering steel, white plumes, and black boots, were passing westward. Giles stood in front of the arrested stream. A number of people stood, as it were, under his shadow. Refuge-island was over-flowing. Comments, chiefly eulogistic, were being freely made and some impatience was being mani-fested by drivers, when a little shriek was heard, and a child's voice exclaimed :—

"Oh! papa, papa—there's *my* policeman—the one I so nearly killed. He's *not* dead after all!"

Giles forgot his dignity for one moment, and, look-ing round, met the eager gaze of little Di Brandon.

Another moment and duty required his undivided attention, so that he lost sight of her, but Di took good care not to lose sight of him.

"We will wait here, darling," said her father, referring to refuge-island on which he stood, "and when he is disengaged we can speak to him."

"Oh! I'm *so* glad he's not dead," said little Di, "and p'raps he'll be able to show us the way to my boy's home."

Di had a method of adopting, in a motherly way, all who, in the remotest manner, came into her life. Thus she not only spoke of our butcher and our baker, which was natural, but referred to "my policeman" and "my boy" ever since the day of the accident.

When Giles had set his portion of the traffic in harmonious motion he returned to his island, and was not sorry to receive the dignified greeting of Sir Richard Brandon, while he was delighted as well as amused by the enthusiastic grasp with which Di seized his huge hand in both of her little ones, and the earnest manner in which she inquired after his health, and if she had hurt him much.

"Did they put you to bed and give you hot gruel?" she asked, with touching pathos.

"No, miss, they didn't think I was hurt quite enough to require it," answered Giles, his drooping moustache curling slightly as he spoke.

"I had hoped to see you at my house," said Sir Richard, "you did not call."

"Thank you, sir, I did not think the little service I rendered your daughter worth making so much of. I called, however, the same evening, to inquire for her, but did not wish to intrude on you."

"It would have been no intrusion, friend," returned Sir Richard, with grand condescension. "One who has saved my child's life has a claim upon my consideration."

"A dook 'e must be," said a small street boy in a loud stage whisper to a drayman—for small street boys are sown broadcast in London, and turn up at all places on every occasion, "or p'raps," he added on reflection, "'e 's on'y a markiss."

"Now then," said Giles to the drayman with a motion of the hand that caused him to move on, while he cast a look on the boy which induced him to move off.

"By the way, constable," said Sir Richard, "I am on my way to visit a poor boy whose leg was broken on the day my pony ran away. He was holding the pony at the time. He lives in Whitechapel somewhere. I have the address here in my note-book."

"Excuse me, sir, one moment," said No. 666, going towards a crowd which had gathered round a fallen horse. "I happen to be going to that district myself," he continued on returning, "what is the boy's name?"

"Robert—perhaps I should rather say Bobby Frog," answered Sir Richard.

"The name is familiar," returned the policeman, "but in London there are so many—what's his

address, sir,—Roy's Court, near Commercial Street?
Oh! I know it well—one of the worst parts of
London. I know the boy too. He is somewhat
noted in that neighbourhood for giving the police
trouble. Not a bad-hearted fellow, I believe, but
full of mischief, and has been brought up among
thieves from his birth. His father is, or was, a bird-
fancier and seller of penny articles on the streets,
besides being a professional pugilist. You will be
the better for protection there, sir. I would advise
you not to go alone. If you can wait for five or ten
minutes," added Giles, "I shall be off duty and
will be happy to accompany you."

Sir Richard agreed to wait. Within the time
mentioned Giles was relieved, and, entering a cab
with his friends, drove towards Whitechapel. They
had to pass near our policeman's lodgings on the
way.

"Would you object, sir, stopping at my house for
five minutes?" he asked.

"Certainly not," returned the knight, "I am in no
hurry."

No. 666 stopped the cab, leaped out and disappeared through a narrow passage. In less than
five minutes a very tall gentlemanly man issued
from the same passage and approached them.
Little Di opened her blue eyes to their very uttermost. It was *her* policeman in plain clothes!

She did not like the change at all at first, but before the end of the drive got used to him in his new aspect—all the more readily that he seemed to have cast off much of his stiffness and reserve with his blue skin.

Near the metropolitan railway station in White-chapel the cab was dismissed, and Giles led the father and child along the crowded thoroughfare until they reached Commercial Street, along which they proceeded a short distance.

"We are now near some of the worst parts of London, sir," said Giles, "where great numbers of the criminal and most abandoned characters dwell."

"Indeed," said Sir Richard, who did not seem to be much gratified by the information.

As for Di, she was nearly crying. The news that *her* boy was a thief and was born in the midst of such naughty people had fallen with chilling influence on her heart, for she had never thought of anything but the story-book "poor but honest parents!"

"What large building is that?" inquired the knight, who began to wish that he had not given way to his daughter's importunities, "the one opposite, I mean, with placards under the windows."

"That is the well-known Home of Industry, instituted and managed by Miss Macpherson and a staff of volunteer workers. They do a deal of good, sir, in this neighbourhood."

"Ah! indeed," said Sir Richard, who had never before heard of the Home of Industry. "And, pray, what particular industry does this Miss Mac— what did you call her?"

"Macpherson. The lady, you know, who sends out so many rescued waifs and strays to Canada, and spends all her time in caring for the poorest of the poor in the East End and in preaching the gospel to them. You've often seen accounts of her work, no doubt, in the *Christian?*"

"Well—n—no. I read the *Times*, but, now you mention it, I have some faint remembrance of see-ing reference to such matters. Very self-denying, no doubt, and praiseworthy, though I must say that I doubt the use of preaching the gospel to such persons. From what I have seen of these lowest people I should think they were too deeply sunk in depravity to be capable of appreciating the lofty and sublime sentiments of Christianity."

No. 666 felt a touch of surprise at these words, though he was too well-bred a policeman to express his feelings by word or look. In fact, although not pre-eminently noted for piety, he had been led by training, and afterwards by personal experience, to view this matter from a very different standpoint from that of Sir Richard. He made no reply, how-ever, but, turning round the corner of the Home of Industry, entered a narrow street which bore palpable evidence of being the abode of deepest poverty. From the faces and garments of the inhabitants it was also evidently associated with the deepest depravity.

As little Di saw some of the residents sitting on their doorsteps with scratched faces, swelled lips and cheeks, and dishevelled hair, and beheld the children in half-naked condition rolling in the kennel and extremely filthy, she clung closer to her father's side and began to suspect there were some phases of life she had never seen—had not even dreamt of!

What the knight's thoughts were we cannot tell, for he said nothing, but disgust was more prominent than pity on his fine countenance. Those who sat on the doorsteps, or lolled with a dissipated air against the doorposts, seemed to appreciate him at his proper value, for they scowled at him as he passed. They recognised No. 666, however (perhaps by his bearing), and gave him only a passing glance of indifference.

"You said it would be dangerous for me to come here by myself," said Sir Richard, turning to Giles, as he entered another and even worse street. "Are they then so violent?"

"Many of them are among the worst criminals in London, sir. Here is the court of which you are in search : Roy's Court."

As he spoke, Ned Frog staggered out of his own doorway, clenched his fists, and looked with a vindictive scowl at the strangers. A second glance induced him to unclench his fists and reel round the corner on his way to a neighbouring grog-shop. Whatever other shops may decay in that region, the grog-shops, like noxious weeds, always flourish.

The court was apparently much deserted at that hour, for the men had not yet returned from their work—whatever that might be—and most of the women were within doors.

"This is the house," continued Giles, descending the few steps, and tapping at the door; "I have been here before. They know me."

The door was opened by Hetty, and for the first time since entering those regions of poverty and crime, little Di felt a slight rise in her spirits, for through Hetty's face shone the bright spirit within; albeit the shining was through some dirt and dishevelment, good principle not being able altogether to overcome the depressing influences of extreme poverty and suffering.

"Is your mother at home, Hetty?"

"Oh! yes, sir. Mother, here's Mr. Scott. Come in, sir. We are so glad to see you, and—"

She stopped, and gazed inquiringly at the visitors who followed.

"I've brought some friends of Bobby to inquire for him. Sir Richard Brandon—Mrs. Frog."

No. 666 stood aside, and, with something like a smile on his face, ceremoniously presented Wealth to Poverty.

Wealth made a slightly confused bow to Poverty, and Poverty, looking askance at Wealth, dropt a mild courtesy.

"Vell now, I'm a Dutchman if it ain't the hangel!" exclaimed a voice in the corner of the small room, before either Wealth or Poverty could utter a word.

"Oh! it's *my* boy," exclaimed Di with delight, forgetting or ignoring the poverty, dirt, and extremely bad air, as she ran forward and took hold of Bobby's hand.

It was a pre-eminently dirty hand, and formed a remarkable contrast to the little hands that grasped it!

The small street boy was, for the first time in his life, bereft of speech! When that faculty returned, he remarked in language which was obscure to Di:—

"Vell, if this ain't a go!"

"What is a go?" asked Di with innocent surprise.

Instead of answering, Bobby Frog burst into a fit of laughter, but stopped rather suddenly with an expression of pain.

"Oh! 'old on! I say. This won't do. Doctor 'e said I musn't larf, 'cause it shakes the leg too much. But, you know, wot's a cove to do ven a hangel comes to him and axes sitch rum questions?"

Again he laughed, and again stopped short in pain.

"I'm *so* sorry! Does it feel *very* painful? You can't think how constantly I 've been thinking of you since the accident; for it was all my fault. If I hadn't jumped up in such a passion, the pony wouldn't have run away, and you wouldn't have been hurt. I'm so *very, very* sorry, and I got dear papa to bring me here to tell you so, and to see if we could do anything to make you well."

Again Bobby was rendered speechless, but his mind was active.

"Wot! I ain't dreamin', am I? 'As a hangel *really* come to my bed-side all the vay from the Vest-end, an' brought 'er dear pa'—vich means the guv'nor, I fancy—all for to tell me—a kid whose life is spent in 'movin' on'—that she 's wery, wery, sorry I 've got my leg broke, an' that she 's bin an' done it, an' she would like to know if she can do hanythink as 'll make me vell! But it ain't true. It 's a big lie! I 'm dreamin', that 's all. I 've been took to hospital, an' got d'lirious—that 's wot it is. I 'll try to sleep!"

With this end in view he shut his eyes, and remained quite still for a few seconds, and when Di looked at his pinched and pale face in this placid condition, the tears *would* overflow their natural boundary, and sobs *would* rise up in her pretty throat, but she choked them back for fear of disturbing her boy.

Presently the boy opened his eyes.

"Wot, are you there yet?" he asked.

"Oh yes. Did you think I was going away?" she replied, with a look of innocent surprise. "I won't leave you now. I'll stay here and nurse you, if papa will let me. I have slept once on a shake-down, when I was forced by a storm to stay all night at a juv'nile party. So if you've a corner here, it will do nicely—"

"My dear child," interrupted her amazed father, "you are talking nonsense. And—do keep a little further from the bed. There may be—you know—infection—"

"Oh! you needn't fear infection here, sir," said Mrs. Frog, somewhat sharply. "We are poor enough, God knows, though I *have* seen better times, but we keep ourselves pretty clean, though we can't afford to spend much on soap when food is so dear, and money so scarce—so *very* scarce!"

"Forgive me, my good woman," said Sir Richard, hastily, "I did not mean to offend, but circumstances would seem to favour the idea—of—of—"

And here Wealth—although a bank director and chairman of several boards, and capable of making a neat, if weakly, speech on economic laws and the currency when occasion required—was dumb before Poverty. Indeed, though he had often theorised about that stricken creature, he had never before fairly hunted her down, run her into her den, and fairly looked her in the face.

"The fact is, Mrs. Frog," said Giles Scott, coming to the rescue, "Sir Richard is anxious to know something about your affairs—your family, you know, and your means of—by the way, where is baby?" he said, looking round the room.

"She's gone lost," said Mrs. Frog.

"Lost?" repeated Giles, with a significant look.

"Ay, lost," repeated Mrs. Frog, with a look of equal significance.

"Bless me, how did you lose your child?" asked Sir Richard, in some surprise.

"Oh! sir, that often happens to us poor folk. We're used to it," said Mrs. Frog, in a half bantering half bitter tone.

Sir Richard suddenly called to mind the fact—which had not before impressed him, though he had read and commented on it—that 11,835 children under ten years of age had been lost that year (and it was no exceptional year, as police reports will show) in the streets of London, and that 23 of these children were *never found*.

He now beheld, as he imagined, one of the losers of the lost ones, and felt stricken.

"Well now," said Giles to Mrs. Frog, "let's hear how you get along. What does your husband do?"

"He mostly does nothin' but drink. Sometimes he sells little birds; sometimes he sells penny watches or boot-laces in Cheapside, an' turns in a little that way, but it all goes to the grog-shop; none of it comes here. Then he has a mill now an' again—"

"A mill?" said Sir Richard,—"is it a snuff or flour—"

"He's a professional pugilist," explained Giles.

"An' he's employed at a music-hall," continued Mrs. Frog, "to call out the songs an' keep order. An' Bobby always used to pick a few coppers by runnin' messages, sellin' matches, and odd jobs. But he's knocked over now."

"And yourself. How do you add to the general fund?" asked Sir Richard, becoming interested in the household management of Poverty.

"Well, I char a bit an' wash a bit, sir, when I'm well enough—which ain't often. An' sometimes I lights the Jews' fires for 'em, an' clean up their 'earths on Saturdays—w'ich is their Sundays, sir. But Hetty works like a horse. It's she as keeps us from the work'us, sir. She's got employment at a slop shop, and by workin' 'ard all day manages to make about one shillin' a week."

"I beg your pardon—how much?"

"One shillin', sir."

"Ah, you mean one shilling a day, I suppose."

"No, sir, I mean one shillin' a *week*. Mr. Scott there knows that I'm tellin' what's true."

Giles nodded, and Sir Richard said, "ha—a-hem" having nothing more lucid to remark on such an amazing financial problem as was here set before him. "But," continued Mrs. Frog, "poor Hetty has had a sad disappointment this week—"

"Oh! mother," interrupted Hetty, "don't trouble the gentleman with that. Perhaps he wouldn't understand it, for of course he hasn't heard about all the outs and ins of slop work."

"Pardon me, my good girl," said Sir Richard, "I have not, as you truly remark, studied the details of slop-work minutely, but my mind is not unaccustomed to financial matters. Pray let me hear about this—"

A savage growling, something between a mastiff and a man, outside the door, here interrupted the visitor, and a hand was heard fumbling about the latch. As the hand seemed to lack skill to open the door the foot considerately took the duty in hand and burst it open, whereupon the huge frame of Ned Frog stumbled into the room and fell prostrate at the feet of Sir Richard, who rose hastily and stepped back.

The pugilist sprang up, doubled his ever ready

fists, and, glaring at the knight, asked savagely :—
" Who the—"

He was checked in the utterance of a ferocious
oath, for at that moment he encountered the grave
eye of No. 666.

Relaxing his fists he thrust them into his coat
pockets, and, with a subdued air, staggered out of
the house.

" My 'usband, sir," said Mrs. Frog, in answer to her
visitor's inquiring glance.

" Oh ! is that his usual mode of returning home ? "

" No, sir," answered Bobby from his corner, for
he was beginning to be amused by the succession
of surprises which Wealth was receiving, " 'e don't
always come in so. Sometimes 'e sends 'is 'ead first
an' the feet come afterwards. In any case the furniture's apt to suffer, not to mention the in'abi-
tants, but you 've saved us to-night, sir, or, raither,
Mr. Scott 'as saved both us an' you."

Poor little Di, who had been terribly frightened,
clung closer to her father's arm on hearing this.

" Perhaps," said Sir Richard, " it would be as
well that we should go, in case Mr. Frog should
return."

He was about to say good-bye when Di checked
him, and, despite her fears, urged a short delay.

" We haven't heard, you know, about the slops yet.
Do stop just one minute, dear papa. I wonder if

it's like the beef-tea nurse makes for me when I'm ill."

"It's not that kind of slops, darling, but ready-made clothing to which reference is made. But you are right. Let us hear about it, Miss Hetty."

The idea of "Miss" being applied to Hetty and slops compared to beef-tea proved almost too much for the broken-legged boy in the corner, but he put strong constraint on himself and listened.

"Indeed, sir, I do not complain," said Hetty, quite distressed at being thus forcibly dragged into notice. "I am thankful for what has been sent—indeed I am—only it *was* a great disappointment, particularly at this time, when we so much needed all we could make amongst us."

She stopped and had difficulty in restraining tears.

"Go on, Hetty," said her mother, "and don't be afraid. Bless you, he's not goin' to report what you say."

"I know that, mother. Well, sir, this was the way on it. They sometimes—"

"Excuse me—who are 'they'?"

"I beg pardon, sir, I—I'd rather not tell."

"Very well. I respect your feelings, my girl. Some slop-making firm, I suppose. Go on."

"Yes, sir. Well—they sometimes gives me extra work to do at home. It do come pretty hard on me after goin' through the regular day's work, from early mornin' till night, but then, you see, it brings in a little more money—and, I'm strong, thank God."

Sir Richard looked at Hetty's thin and colourless though pretty face, and thought it possible that she might be stronger with advantage.

"Of late," continued the girl, "I've bin havin' extra work in this way, and last week I got twelve children's ulsters to make up. This job when finished would bring me six and sixpence."

"How much?"

"Six and sixpence, sir."

"For the whole twelve?" asked Sir Richard.

"Yes, sir—that was sixpence halfpenny for makin' up each ulster. It's not much, sir."

"No," murmured Wealth in an absent manner, "sixpence halfpenny is *not* much."

"But when I took them back," continued Hetty— and here the tears became again obstreperous and difficult to restrain—"the master said he'd forgot to tell me that this order was for the colonies, that he had taken it at a very low price, and that he could only give me three shillin's for the job. Of— of course three shillin's is better than nothin', but after workin' hard for such a long long time an' expectin' six, it was—"

Here the tears refused to be pent up any longer, and the poor girl quietly bending forward hid her face in her hand.

" Come, I think we will go now," said Sir Richard, rising hastily. " Good-night, Mrs. Frog, I shall probably see you again—at least—you shall hear from me. Now, Di—say good-night to your boy."

In a few minutes Sir Richard stood outside, taking in deep draughts of the comparatively fresher air of the court.

" The old screw," growled Bobby, when the door was shut. " 'E didn't leave us so much as a single bob—not even a brown, though 'e pretends that six of 'em ain't much."

" Don't be hard on him, Bobby," said Hetty, drying her eyes; " he spoke very kind, you know, an' p'raps he means to help us afterwards."

" Spoke kind," retorted the indignant boy; " I tell 'ee wot, Hetty, you're far too soft an' forgivin'. I s'pose that's wot they teaches you in Sunday-school at George Yard—eh? Vill speakin' kind feed us, vill it clothe us, vill it pay for our lodgin's?"

The door opened at that moment, and No. 666 re-entered.

" The gentleman sent me back to give you this, Mrs. Frog (laying a sovereign on the rickety table). He said he didn't like to offer it to you himself for fear of hurting your feelings, but I told him he needn't be afraid on that score! Was I right, Missis? Look well after it, now, an' see that Ned don't get his fingers on it."

Giles left the room, and Mrs. Frog, taking up the piece of gold, fondled it for some time in her thin fingers, as though she wished to make quite sure of its reality. Then wrapping it carefully in a piece of old newspaper, she thrust it into her bosom.

Bobby gazed at her in silence up to this point, and then turned his face to the wall. He did not speak, but we cannot say that he did not pray, for, mentally he said, " I beg your parding, old gen'l'm'n, an' I on'y pray that a lot of fellers like you may come 'ere sometimes to 'urt our feelin's in that vay !"

At that moment Hetty bent over the bed, and, softly kissing her brother's dirty face, whispered, " Yes, Bobby, that's what they teach me in Sunday-school at George Yard."

Thereafter Wealth drove home in a cab, and Poverty went to bed in her rags.

CHAPTER VII.

BICYCLING AND ITS OCCASIONAL RESULTS.

It is pleasant to turn from the smoke and turmoil of the city to the fresh air and quiet of the country.

To the man who spends most of his time in the heart of London, going into the country—even for a short distance—is like passing into the fields of Elysium. This was, at all events, the opinion of Stephen Welland; and Stephen must have been a good judge, for he tried the change frequently, being exceedingly fond of bicycling, and occasionally taking what he termed long spins on that remarkable instrument.

One morning, early in the summer-time, young Welland (he was only eighteen) mounted his iron horse in the neighbourhood of Kensington, and glided away at a leisurely pace through the crowded streets. Arrived in the suburbs of London he got up steam, to use his own phrase, and went at a rapid pace until he met a "chum," by appointment. This chum was also mounted on a bicycle, and was none other than our friend Samuel Twitter, Junior—known at home as Sammy, and by his companions as Sam.

"Isn't it a glorious day, Sam?" said Welland as he rode up and sprang off his steed.

"Magnificent!" answered his friend, also dismounting and shaking hands. "Why, Stephen, what an enormous machine you ride!"

"Yes, it's pretty high—48 inches. My legs are long, you see. Well, where are we to run to-day?"

"Wherever you like," said Sam, "only let it be a short run, not more than forty miles, for I've got an appointment this afternoon with my old dad which I can't get off."

"That 'll do very well," said Welland, "so we can go round by—"

Here he described a route by country road and village, which we pretend not to remember. It is sufficient to know that it represented the required "short" run of forty miles—such is the estimate of distance by the youth of the present day!

"Now then, off we go," said Welland, giving his wheel—he quite ignored the existence of the little thing at the back—a shove, putting his left foot on the treddle, and flinging his right leg gracefully over.

Young Twitter followed suit, but Sammy was neither expert nor graceful. True, he could ride easily, and travel long distances, but he could only

F

mount by means of the somewhat clumsy process of hopping behind for several yards.

Once up, however, he went swiftly enough alongside his tall companion, and the two friends thereafter kept abreast.

"Oh ! isn't it a charming sensation to have the cool air fanning one's cheeks, and feel the soft tremor of the wheel, and see the trees and houses flow past at such a pace ? It is the likest thing to flying I ever felt," said Welland, as they descended a slight incline at, probably, fifteen miles an hour.

"It is delightful," replied Sam, " but, I say, we'd better put on the brakes here a bit. It gets much steeper further down."

Instead of applying the brake, however, young Welland, in the exuberance of his joy, threw his long legs over the handles, and went down the slope at railway speed, ready, as he remarked, for a jump if anything should go wrong.

Twitter was by no means as bold as his friend, but, being ashamed to show the white feather, he quietly threw his shorter legs over the handles, and thus the two, perched—from a fore-and-aft point of view—upon nothing, went in triumph to the bottom of the hill.

A long stretch of smooth level road now lay before them. It required the merest touch on the treddles to send them skimming along like skaters on smooth ice, or swallows flying low. Like gentle ghosts they fleeted along with little more than a muffled sound, for their axles turned in ball-sockets and their warning bells were silent save when touched.

Onward they went with untiring energy, mile after mile, passing everything on the way—pedestrians, equestrians, carts and gigs; driving over the level ground with easy force, taking the hills with a rush to keep up the pace, and descending on the other sides at what Welland styled a "lightning run."

Now they were skimming along a road which skirted the margin of a canal, the one with hands in his coat pockets, the other with his arms crossed, and both steering with their feet; now passing under a railway-arch, and giving a wild shout, partly to rouse the slumbering echoes that lodged there, and partly to rouse the spirit of a small dog which chanced to be passing under it—in both cases successfully! Anon they were gliding over a piece of exposed ground on which the sun beat with intense light, causing their shadows to race along with them. Again they were down in a hollow, gliding under a row of trees, where they shut off a little of the steam and removed their caps, the better to enjoy the grateful shade. Soon they were out in the sunshine again, the spokes of their wheels invisible, as they topped a small eminence from the summit of which they took in one comprehensive view of undulating lands, with villages scattered all round, farm-houses here and there, green fields and flowering meadows, traversed by rivulet or canal, with cattle, sheep, and horses gazing at them in silent or startled wonder, and birds twittering welcome from the trees and hedge-rows everywhere.

Now they were crossing a bridge and nearing a small town where they had to put hands to the handles again and steer with precaution, for little dogs had a tendency to bolt out at them from unexpected corners, and poultry is prone to lose its heads and rush into the very jaws of danger, in a cackling effort to avoid it. Stray kittens and pigs, too, exhibited obstinate tendencies, and only gave in when it was nearly too late for repentance. Little children, also, became sources of danger, standing in the middle of roads until, perceiving a possible catastrophe, they dashed wildly aside—always to the very side on which the riders had resolved to pass, —and escaped by absolute miracle !

Presently they came to a steep hill. It was not steep enough to necessitate dismounting, but it rendered a rush inadvisable. They therefore worked up slowly, and, on gaining the top, got off to breathe and rest a while.

"That *was* a glorious run, wasn't it, Sam ?" said Welland, flicking the dust from his knees with his handkerchief. "What d'ye say to a glass of beer?"

"Can't do it, Stephen, I'm Blue Ribbon."

"Oh! nonsense. Why not do as I do—drink in moderation?"

"Well, I didn't think much about it when I put it on," said Sam, who was a very sensitive, and not very strong-minded youth; "the rest of us did it, you know, by father's advice, and I joined because they did."

Welland laughed rather sarcastically at this, but made no rejoinder, and Sam, who could not stand being laughed at, said—

"Well, come, I'll go in for one glass. I'll be my own doctor, and prescribe it medicinally! Besides, it's an exceptional occasion this, for it is awfully hot."

"It's about the best run I ever had in the same space of time," said Welland on quitting the beer shop.

"First-rate," returned Sam, "I wish my old dad could ride with us. He *would* enjoy it so."

"Couldn't we bring him out on a horse? He could ride that, I suppose?"

"Never saw him on a horse but once," said Sam, "and that time he fell off. But it's worth suggesting to him."

"Better if he got a tricycle," said Welland.

"I don't think that would do, for he's too old for long rides, and too short-winded. Now, Stephen, I'm not going to run down this hill. We *must* take it easy, for it's far too steep."

"Nonsense, man, it's nothing to speak of; see, I'll go first and show you the way."

He gave the treadle a thrust that sent him off like an arrow from a bow.

"Stay! there's a caravan or something at the bottom—wild beasts' show, I think! Stop! hold on!"

But Sam Twitter shouted in vain. Welland's was a joyous spirit, apt to run away with him. He placed his legs over the handles for security, and allowed the machine to run. It gathered speed as it went, for the hill became steeper, insomuch that the rider once or twice felt the hind-wheel rise, and had to lean well back to keep it on the ground. The pace began to exceed even Welland's idea of pleasure, but now it was too late to use the brake, for well did he know that on such a slope and going at such a pace the slightest check on the front wheel would send him over. He did not feel alarmed however, for he was now near the bottom of the hill, and half a minute more would send him in safety on the level road at the foot.

But just at the foot there was a sharpish turn in the road, and Welland looked at it earnestly. At an ordinary pace such a turn could have been easily taken, but at such a rate as he had by that time attained, he felt it would require a tremendous lean over to accomplish it. Still he lost no confidence, for he was an athlete by practice if not by profession, and he gathered up his energies for the moment of action.

The people of the caravan—whoever they were—had seen him coming, and, beginning to realise his danger to some extent, had hastily cleared the road to let him pass.

Welland considered the rate of speed; felt, rather than calculated, the angle of inclination; leaned over boldly until the tire almost slipped sideways on the road, and came rushing round with a magnificent sweep, when, horrible sight! a slight ridge of what is called road-metal crossed the entire road from side to side! A drain or water pipe had recently been repaired, and the new ridge had not yet been worn down by traffic. There was no time for thought or change of action. Another moment and the wheel was upon it, the crash came, and the rider went off with such force that he was shot well in advance of the machine, as it went with tremendous violence into the ditch. If Welland's feet had been on the treadles he must have turned a complete somersault. As it was he alighted on his feet, but came to the ground with such force that he failed to save himself. One frantic effort he made

and then went down headlong and rolled over on
his back in a state of insensibility.

When Sam Twitter came to the bottom of the
hill with the brake well applied he was able to
check himself in time to escape the danger, and ran
to where his friend lay.

For a few minutes the unfortunate youth lay as if
he had been dead.   Then his blood resumed its
flow, and when the eyes opened he found Sam kneeling on one side of him with a smelling bottle which
some lady had lent him, and a kindly-faced elderly
man with an iron-grey beard kneeling on the other
side and holding a cup of water to his lips.

"That's right, Stephen, look up," said Sam, who
was terribly frightened, "you're not much hurt, are
you?"

"Hurt, old fellow, eh?" sighed Stephen, "why
should I be hurt?   Where am I?   What has happened?"

"Take a sip, my young friend, it will revive you,"
said the man with the kindly face.   "You have had
a narrow escape, but God has mercifully spared you.
Try to move now; gently—we must see that no
bones have been broken before allowing you to
rise."

By this time Welland had completely recovered,
and was anxious to rise; all the more that a crowd
of children surrounded him, among whom he ob-

served several ladies and gentlemen, but he lay still until the kindly stranger had felt him all over and come to the conclusion that no serious damage had been done.

"Oh! I'm all right, thank you," said the youth on rising, and affecting to move as though nothing had happened, but he was constrained to catch hold of the stranger rather suddenly, and sat down on the grass by the road-side.

"I do believe I've got a shake after all," he said with a perplexed smile and sigh. "But," he added, looking round with an attempt at gaiety, "I suspect my poor bicycle has got a worse shake. Do look after it, Sam, and see how it is."

Twitter soon returned with a crestfallen expression. "It's done for, Stephen. I'm sorry to say the whole concern seems to be mashed up into a kind of wire-fencing!"

"Is it past mending, Sam?"

"Past mending by any ordinary blacksmith, certainly. No one but the maker can doctor it, and I should think it would take him a fortnight at least."

"What is to be done?" said Stephen, with some of his companion's regret of tone. "What a fool I was to take such a hill—spoilt such a glorious day too—for you as well as myself, Sam. I'm *very* sorry, but that won't mend matters."

"Are you far from home, gentlemen?" asked the man with the iron-grey beard, who had listened to the conversation with a look of sympathy.

"Ay, much too far to walk," said Welland. "D'you happen to know how far off the nearest railway station is?"

"Three miles," answered the stranger, "and in your condition you are quite unfit to walk that distance."

"I'm not so sure of that," replied the youth, with a pitiful look. "I think I'm game for three miles, if I had nothing to carry but myself, but I can't leave my bicycle in the ditch, you know!"

"Of course you can't," rejoined the stranger in a cheery tone, "and I think we can help you in this difficulty. I am a London City Missionary. My name is John Seaward. We have, as you see, brought out a · number of our Sunday-school children, to give them a sight of God's beautiful earth; poor things, they've been used to bricks, mortar, and stone all their lives hitherto. Now, if you choose to spend the remainder of the day with us, we will be happy to give you and the injured bicycle a place in our vans till we reach a cabstand or a railway station. What say you? It will give much pleasure to me and the teachers."

Welland glanced at his friend. "You see, Sam, there's no help for it, old boy. You'll have to return alone."

"Unless your friend will also join us," said the missionary.

"You are very kind," said Sam, "but I cannot stay, as I have an engagement which must be kept. Never mind, Stephen. I'll just complete the trip alone, and comfort myself with the assurance that I leave you in good hands. So, good-bye, old boy."

"Good-bye, Twitter," said Stephen, grasping his friend's hand.

"Twitter," repeated the missionary, "I heard your friend call you Sam just now. Excuse my asking—are you related to Samuel Twitter of Twitter, Slime, and Co., in the city ?"

"I'm his eldest son," said Sam.

"Then I have much pleasure in making your acquaintance," returned the other, extending his hand, "for although I have never met your father, I know your mother well. She is one of the best and most regular teachers in our Sunday-schools. Is she not, Hetty?" he said, turning to a sweet-faced girl who stood near him.

"Indeed she is, I was her pupil for some years, and now I teach one of her old classes," replied the girl.

"I work in the neighbourhood of Whitechapel, sir," continued the missionary, "and most of the children here attend the Institution in George Yard."

"Well, I shall tell my mother of this unexpected meeting," said Sam, as he remounted his bicycle. "Good-bye, Stephen. Don't romp too much with the children!"

"Adieu, Sam, and don't break your neck on the bicycle."

In a few minutes Sam Twitter and his bicycle were out of sight.

CHAPTER VIII.

A GREAT AND MEMORABLE DAY.

WHEN young Stephen Welland was conducted by
John Seaward the missionary into a large field
dotted with trees, close to where his accident had
happened, he found that the children and their
guardians were busily engaged in making arrangements for the spending of an enjoyable day.

And then he also found that this was not a mere
monster excursion of ordinary Sunday-schools, but
one of exceedingly poor children, whose garments,
faces, and general condition, told too surely that
they belonged to the lowest grade in the social scale.

"Yes," said the missionary, in reply to some
question from Welland, "the agency at George
Yard, to which I have referred, has a wide-embrac-
ing influence—though but a small lump of leaven
when compared with the mass of corruption around
it. This is a flock of the ragged and utterly forlorn,
to many of whom green fields and fresh air are
absolutely new, but we have other flocks besides
these."

"Indeed! Well, now I look at them more carefully, I see that their garments do speak of squalid poverty. I have never before seen such a ragged crew, though I have sometimes encountered individuals of the class on the streets."

"Hm!" coughed the missionary with a peculiar smile. "They are not so ragged as they were. Neither are they as ragged as they will be in an hour or two."

"What do you mean?"

"I mean that these very rough little ones have to receive peculiar treatment before we can give them such an outing as they are having to-day. As you see, swings and see-saws have been put up here, toys are now being distributed, and a plentiful feast will ere long be forthcoming, through the kindness of a Christian gentleman whose heart the Lord has inclined to 'consider the poor;' but before we could venture to move the little band, much of their ragged clothing had to be stitched up to prevent it falling off on the journey, and we had to make them move carefully on their way to the train—for vans have brought us only part of the way. Now that they are here, our minds are somewhat relieved, but I suspect that the effect of games and romping will undo much of our handiwork. Come, let us watch them."

The youth and the missionary advanced towards

a group of the children, whose souls, for the time being, were steeped in a see-saw. This instrument of delight consisted of a strong plank balanced on the trunk of a noble tree which had been recently felled, with many others, to thin the woods of the philanthropist's park. It was an enormous see-saw! such as the ragged creatures had never before seen —perhaps never conceived of, their experiences in such joys having been hitherto confined to small bits of broken plank placed over empty beer barrels, or back-yard fences. No fewer than eight children were able to find accommodation on it at one and the same time, besides one of the bigger boys to straddle in the centre; and it required the utmost vigilance on the part of a young man teacher at one end of the machine, and Hetty Frog at the other end, to prevent the little ragamuffins at either extremity from being forced off.

Already the missionary's anticipation in regard to the undoing of their labour had begun to be verified. There were at least four of the eight whose nether garments had succumbed to the effort made in mounting the plank, and various patches of flesh-colour revealed the fact that the poor little wearers were innocent of flannels. But it was summer-time, and the fact had little effect either on wearers or spectators. The missionary, however, was not so absorbed in the present but that he felt impelled to remark to Welland: "That is their winter as well as summer clothing."

The bicyclist said nothing in reply, but the remark was not lost upon him.

"Now, Dick Swiller," said the young man teacher, "I see what you're up to. You mustn't do it!"

Richard Swiller, who was a particularly rugged as well as ragged boy of about thirteen, not being in the habit of taking advice, did do it. That is, he sent his end of the plank up with such violence that the other end came to the ground with a shock which caused those who sat there to gasp, while it all but unseated most of those who were on the higher end. Indeed one very small and pinched but intelligent little boy, named by his companions Blobby, who looked as if Time, through the influence of privation and suffering, had been dwindling instead of developing him,—actually did come off with a cry of alarm, which, however, changed into a laugh of glee when he found himself in his teacher's arms, instead of lying "busted on the ground," as he afterwards expressed it when relating the incident to an admiring audience of fellow ragamuffins in the slums of Spitalfields.

Blobby was immediately restored to his lost position, and Swiller was degraded, besides being made to stand behind a large tree for a quarter of an hour in forced inaction, so that he might have time to meditate on the evil consequences of disobedience.

"Take care, Robin," said Hetty, to a very small but astonishingly energetic fellow, at her end of the see-saw, who was impressed with the notion that he was doing good service by wriggling his own body up and down, "if you go on so, you'll push Lilly Snow off."

Robin, unlike Dick, was obedient. He ceased his efforts, and thereby saved the last button which held his much too small waistcoat across his bare bosom.

"What a sweet face the child she calls Lilly Snow has—if it were only clean," observed Welland. "A little soap and water with a hair brush would make her quite beautiful."

"Yes, she is very pretty," said the missionary, and the kindly smile with which he had been watching the fun vanished, as he added in a sorrowful voice, "her case is a very sad one, dear child. Her mother is a poor but deserving woman who earns a little now and then by tailoring, but she has been crushed for years by a wicked and drunken husband who has at last deserted her. We know not where he is, perhaps dead. Five times has her home been broken up by him, and many a time has she with her little one been obliged to sit on door-steps all night, when homeless. Little Lilly attends

G

our Sunday-school regularly, and Hetty is her
teacher. It is not long since Hetty herself was a
scholar, and I know that she is very anxious to lead
Lilly to the Lord. The sufferings and sorrows to
which this poor child has been exposed have told
upon her severely, and I fear that her health will
give way. A day in the country like this may do
her good perhaps."

As the missionary spoke little Lilly threw up her
arms and uttered a cry of alarm. Robin, although
obedient, was short of memory, and his energetic
spirit being too strong for his excitable little frame,
he had recommenced his wriggling, with the effect
of bursting the last button off his waistcoat and
thrusting Lilly off the plank. She was received,
however, on Hetty's breast, who fell with her to the
ground.

"Not hurt, Hetty!" exclaimed the missionary,
running forward to help the girl up.

"Oh! no, sir," replied Hetty with a short laugh,
as she rose and placed Lilly on a safer part of the
see-saw.

"Come here, Hetty," said John Seaward, "and
rest a while. You have done enough just now; let
some one else take your place."

After repairing the buttonless waistcoat with a
pin and giving its owner a caution, Hetty went and
sat down on the grass beside the missionary.

"How is Bobby?" asked the latter, "I have not found a moment to speak to you till now."

"Thank you, sir, he's better; much better. I fear he will be well too soon."

"How so? That's a strange remark, my girl."

"It may seem strange, sir, but—you know—father's very fond of Bobby."

"Well, Hetty, that's not a bad sign of your father."

"Oh but, sir, father sits at his bed-side when he's sober, an' has such long talks with him about robberies and burglaries, and presses him very hard to agree to go out with him when he's well. I can't bear to hear it, for dear Bobby seems to listen to what he says, though sometimes he refuses, and defies him to do his worst, especially when he—"

"Stay, dear girl. It is very very sad, but don't tell me anything more about your father. Tell it all to Jesus, Hetty. He not only sympathises with, but is able to save—even to the uttermost."

"Yes, thank God for that 'uttermost,'" said the poor girl, clasping her hands quickly together. "Oh, I understood that when He saved me, and I will trust to it now."

"And the gentleman who called on you,—has he been again?" asked the missionary.

"No, sir, he has only come once, but he has sent his butler three or four times with some money for us,

and always with the message that it is from Miss
Diana, to be divided between Bobby and me.
Unfortunately father chanced to be at home the
first time he came and got it all, so we got none of
it. But he was out the other times. The butler is
an oldish man, and a very strange one. He went
about our court crying."

"Crying! Hetty, that's a curious condition for
an oldish butler to be in."

"Oh, of course I don't mean cryin' out like a baby,"
said Hetty, looking down with a modest smile, "but
I saw tears in his eyes, and sometimes they got on
his cheeks. I can't think what's the matter with
him."

Whatever Mr. Seaward thought on this point he
said nothing, but asked if Bobby was able to go out.

Oh yes, he was quite able to walk about now
with a little help, Hetty said, and she had taken
several walks with him and tried to get him to
speak about his soul, but he only laughed at that,
and said he had too much trouble with his body to
think about his soul—there was time enough for
that!

They were interrupted at this point by a merry
shout of glee, and, looking up, found that young
Welland had mounted the see-saw, taken Lilly Snow
in front of him, had Dick Swiller reinstated to
counterbalance his extra weight, and was enjoying

himself in a most hilarious manner among the fluttering rags. Assuredly, the fluttering rags did not enjoy themselves a whit less hilariously than he.

In this condition he was found by the owner of the grounds, George Brisbane, Esq., of Lively Hall, who, accompanied by his wife, and a tall, dignified friend with a little girl, approached the see-saw.

" I am glad you enjoy yourself so much, my young friend," he said to Welland; " to which of the ragged schools may you belong ?"

In much confusion—for he was rather shy—Welland made several abortive efforts to check the see-saw, which efforts Dick Swiller resisted to the uttermost, to the intense amusement of a little girl who held Mrs. Brisbane's hand. At last he succeeded in arresting it and leaped off.

" I beg pardon," he said, taking off his cap to the lady as he advanced, " for intruding uninvited on— "

" Pray don't speak of intrusion," interrupted Mr. Brisbane, extending his hand; " if you are here as Mr. Seaward's friend you are a welcome guest. Your only intrusion was among the little ones, but as they seem not to resent it neither do I."

Welland grasped the proffered hand. " Thank you very much," he returned, " but I can scarcely lay claim to Mr. Seaward's friendship. The fact is,

I am here in consequence of an accident to my bicyle."

"Oh! then you *are* one of the poor unfortunates after all," said the host. "Come, you are doubly welcome. Not hurt much, I hope. No? That's all right. But don't let me keep you from your amusements. Remember, we shall expect you at the feast on the lawn. You see, Sir Richard," he added, turning to his dignified friend, "when we go in for this sort of thing we don't do it by halves. To have any lasting effect, it must make a deep impression. So we have got up all sorts of amusements, as you observe, and shall have no fewer than two good feeds. Come, let us visit some other— Why, what are you gazing at so intently?"

He might well ask the question, for Sir Richard Brandon had just observed Hetty Frog, and she, unaccustomed to such marked attention, was gazing in perplexed confusion on the ground. At the same time little Di, having caught sight of her, quitted Mrs. Brisbane, ran towards her with a delighted scream, and clasping her hand in both of hers, proclaimed her the sister of "my boy"!

Hetty's was not the nature to refuse such affection. Though among the poorest of the poor, and clothed in the shabbiest and most patchy of garments (which in her case, however, were neat, clean and well mended), she was rich in a loving disposition;

so that, forgetting herself and the presence of others, she stooped and folded the little girl in her arms. And, when the soft brown hair and pale pretty face of Poverty were thus seen as it were co-mingling with the golden locks and rosy cheeks of Wealth, even Sir Richard was forced to admit to himself that it was not after all a very outrageous piece of impropriety!

"Oh! I 'm *so* glad to hear that he 's much better, and been out too! I would have come to see him again long long ago, but p—"

She checked herself, for Mrs. Screwbury had carefully explained to her that no good girl ever said anything against her parents; and little Di had swallowed the lesson, for, when not led by passion, she was extremely teachable.

"And oh!" she continued, opening her great blue lakelets to their widest state of solemnity, "you haven't the smallest bit of notion how I have dreamt about my boy—and my policeman too! I never can get over the feeling that they might both have been killed, and if they had, you know, it would have been me that did it; only think! I would have—been—a murderer! P'raps they'd have hanged me!"

"But they weren't killed, dear," said Hetty, unable to restrain a smile at the awful solemnity of the child, and the terrible fate referred to.

"No—I'm *so* glad, but I can't get over it," continued Di, while those near to her stood quietly by unable to avoid overhearing, even if they had wished to do so. "And they do such strange things in my dreams," continued Di, "you can't think. Only last night I was in our basket-cart—the dream-one, you know, not the real one—and the dream-pony ran away again, and gave my boy such a dreadful knock that he fell flat down on his back, tumbled over two or three times, and rose up—a policeman! Not *my* policeman, you know, but quite another one that I had never seen before! But the very oddest thing of all was that it made me so angry that I jumped with all my might on to his breast, and when I got there it wasn't the policeman but the pony! and it was dead—quite dead, for I had killed it, and I wasn't sorry at all—not a bit!"

This was too much for Hetty, who burst into a laugh, and Sir Richard thought it time to go and see the games that were going on in other parts of the field, accompanied by Welland and the missionary, while Hetty returned to her special pet Lilly Snow.

And, truly, if "one touch of nature makes the whole world kin," there were touches of nature enough seen that day among these outcasts of society to have warranted their claiming kin with the whole world.

Leap-frog was greatly in favour, because the practitioners could abandon themselves to a squirrel-and-cat sort of bound on the soft grass, which they had never dared to indulge in on the London pavements. It was a trying game, however, to the rags, which not only betrayed their character to the eye by the exhibition of flesh tints through numerous holes, but addressed themselves also to the ears by means of frequent and explosive rendings. Pins, however, were applied to the worst of these with admirable though temporary effect, and the fun became faster and more furious,—especially so when the points of some of the pins touched up the flesh-tints unexpectedly.

On these occasions the touches of nature became strongly pronounced—expressing themselves generally in a yell. Another evidence of worldly kinship was, that the touched-up ones, instead of attributing the misfortune to accident, were prone to turn round with fierce scowl and doubled fists under the impression that a guilty comrade was in rear!

The proceedings were totally arrested for one hour at mid-day, when unlimited food was issued, and many of the forlorn ones began to feel the rare sensation of being stuffed quite full and rendered incapable of wishing for more! But this was a mere interlude. Like little giants refreshed they rose up again to play—to swing, to leap, to wrestle, to ramble, to gather flowers, to roll on the grass, to bask in the gladdening sunshine, and, in some cases, to thank God for all His mercies, in spite of the latent feeling of regret that there was so little of all that enjoyment in the slums, and dark courts, and filthy back-streets of the monster city.

Of course all the pins were extracted in this second act of the play, and innumerable new and gaping wounds were introduced into the clothing, insomuch that all ordinary civilised people, except philanthropists, would have been shocked with the appearance of the little ones.

But it was during the third and closing act of the play that the affair culminated. The scene was laid on the lawn in front of Mr. Brisbane's mansion.

Enter, at one end of the lawn, a band of small and dirty but flushed and happy boys and girls, in rags which might appropriately be styled ribbons. At the other end of the lawn a train of domestics bearing trays with tea, cakes, buns, pies, fruits, and other delectable things, to which the ragged army sits down.

Enter host and hostess, with Sir Richard, friends and attendants.

(*Host.*)—after asking a blessing—"My little friends, this afternoon we meet to eat, and only one request have I to make—that you shall do your duty well. (Small boy in ribbons.—Von't I, just!) No platter shall return to my house till it be empty.

No little one shall quit these premises till he be full ;
what cannot be eaten must be carried away."

(The ragged army cheers.)

(*Host.*)—Enough.   Fall-to.

[They fall-to.]

(*Little boy* in tatters, pausing.)—"*I* shan't fall two,
I 'll fall three or four."

(*Another little boy*, in worse tatters.)—"So shall
I."

(*First little boy.*)—" I say, Jim, wot would mother
say if she was here ? "

(*Jim.*)—" She 'd say nothin'. 'Er mouth 'ud be too
full to speak."

(Prolonged silence.   Only mastication heard,
mingled with a few cases of choking, which are
promptly dealt with.)

(*Blobby*, with a sigh.)—" I say, Robin, I 'm gettin'
tight."

(*Robin*, with a gasp.)—"So am I; I 'm about
bustin'."

(*Blobby*, coming to another pause.)—" I say, Robin,
I 'm as full as I can 'old.   So 's all my pockits, an'
there 's some left over !"

(*Robin*—sharply.)—" Stick it in your 'at, then."

(Blobby takes off his billycock, thrusts the
remnant of food therein, and puts it on.)

Enter the brass band of the neighbouring village
(the bandsmen being boys), which plays a selection

of airs, and sends a few of the smaller ragamuffins to sleep.

(*Sir Richard Brandon*, confidentially to his friend.) —" It is an amazing sight."

(*Host.*)—" Would that it were a more common sight ! "

Enter more domestics with more tea, buns, and fruit; but the army is glutted, and the pockets are brought into requisition: much pinning being a necessary consequence.

(*Lilly Snow*, softly.)—" It 's like 'eaven ! "

(*Hetty*, remonstratingly.)—" Oh ! Lilly, 'eaven is quite different."

(*Dick Swiller.*)—" I 'm sorry for it. Couldn't be much 'appier to my mind."

(*Host.*)—" Now, dear boys and girls, before we close the proceedings of this happy day, my excellent friend, your missionary, Mr. Seaward, will say a few words."

(John Seaward steps to the front, and says a few words—says them so well, too, so simply, so kindly, yet so heartily, that the army is roused to a pitch of great enthusiasm; but we leave this speech to the reader's imagination: after which—

Exeunt Omnes.

And, as the curtain of night falls on these ragged ones, scattered now, many of them, to varied homes of vice, and filth, and misery, the heavy eyelids close to open again, perchance, in ecstatic dreams of food, and fun and green fields, fresh air and sunshine, which impress them more or less with the idea embodied in the aphorism, that "God made the country, but man made the town."

CHAPTER IX.

HOW THE POOR ARE SUCCOURED.

"I AM obliged to you, Mr. Seaward, for coming out of your way to see me," said Sir Richard Brandon, while little Di brought their visitor a chair. "I know that your time is fully occupied, and would not have asked you to call had not my friend Mr. Brisbane assured me that you had to pass my house daily on your way to—to business."

"No apology, Sir Richard, pray. I am at all times ready to answer a call whether of the poor or the rich, if by any means I may help my Lord's cause."

The knight thought for a moment that he might claim to be classed among the poor, seeing that his miserable pittance of five thousand barely enabled him to make the two ends meet, but he only said: "Ever since we had the pleasure of meeting at that gathering of ragged children, my little girl here has been asking so many questions about poor people—the lower orders, I mean—which I could not answer, that I have asked you to call, that we may get some information about them. You see, Diana is an eccentric little puss " (Di opened her eyes very wide at this, wondering what " eccentric " could mean), " and she has got into a most unaccountable habit of thinking and planning about poor people."

" A good habit, Sir Richard," said the missionary. "' Blessed are they that consider the poor.' "

Sir Richard acknowledged this remark with a little bow. " Now, we should like to ask, if you have no objection, what is your chief object in the mission at—what did you say its name—ah! George Yard ?"

" To save souls," said Mr. Seaward.

" Oh—ah—precisely," said the knight, taken somewhat aback by the nature and brevity of the answer, " that of course; but I meant, how do you proceed ? What is the method, and what the machinery that you put in motion ?"

" Perhaps," said the missionary, drawing a small pamphlet from his pocket, " this will furnish you with all the information you desire. You can read it over to Miss Diana at your leisure—and don't return it; I have plenty more. Meanwhile I may briefly state that the mission premises are in George Yard, High Street, Whitechapel, one of the worst parts of the east of London, where the fire of sin and crime rages most fiercely ; where the soldiers of the Cross are comparatively few, and would be overwhelmed by mere numbers, were it not that they

are invincible, carrying on the war as they do in
the strength of Him who said, 'Lo, I am with you
alway."

"In the old coaching days," continued Mr. Seaward, "this was a great centre, a starting-point for
mail-coaches.   For nigh thirty years the mission has
been there.   The 'Black Horse' was a public-house
in George Yard, once known to the magistrates as
one of the worst gin-shops and resort of thieves and
nurseries of crime in London.   That public-house is
now a shelter for friendless girls, and a place where
sick children of the poor are gratuitously fed."

From this point the missionary went off into a
graphic account of incidents illustrative of the great
work done by the mission, and succeeded in deeply
interesting both Diana and her father, though the
latter held himself well in hand, knowing, as he was
fond of remarking, that there were two sides to every
question.

Checking his visitor at one point, he said, "You
have mentioned ragged schools and the good that is
done by them, but why should not the school-boards
look after such children?"

"Because, Sir Richard, the school-boards cannot
reach them.   There are upwards of 150,000 people
in London who have never lived more than three
months in one place.   No law reaches this class,
because they do not stay long enough in any

neighbourhood for the school-board authorities to put the law into operation. Now, nearly three hundred of the children of these wanderers meet in our Free Ragged Day Schools twice a day for instruction. Here we teach them as efficiently as we can in secular matters, and of course they are taught the Word of God, and told of Jesus the Saviour of sinners; but our difficulties are great, for children as well as parents are often in extremest poverty, the former suffering from hunger even when sent to school—and they never stay with us long. Let me give you an instance:—

"One morning a mother came and begged to have her children admitted. She had just left the workhouse. Three children in rags, that did not suffice to cover much less to protect them, stood by her side. She did not know where they were to sleep that night, but hoped to obtain a little charing and earn enough to obtain a lodging somewhere. She could not take the children with her while seeking work—Would we take them in? for, if not, they would have to be left in the streets, and as they were very young they might lose themselves or be run over. We took them in, fed, sympathised with, and taught them. In the afternoon the mother returned weary, hungry, dejected. She had failed to obtain employment, and took the children away to apply for admission to a casual ward."

H

"What is a casual ward, Mr. Missionary?" asked Di.

"Seaward, my love,—his name is not Missionary," said Sir Richard.

"A casual ward," answered the visitor, "is an exceedingly plain room with rows of very poor beds; mere wooden frames with canvas stretched on them, in which any miserable beggars who choose to submit to the rules may sleep for a night after eating a bit of bread and a basin of gruel—for all which they pay nothing. It is a very poor and comfortless place—at least you would think it so—and is meant to save poor people from sleeping, perhaps dying, in the streets."

"Do some people sleep in the streets?" asked Di in great surprise.

"Yes, dear, I'm sorry to say that many do."

"D'you mean on the stones, in their night-dresses?" asked the child with increasing surprise.

"Yes, love," said her father, "but in their ordinary clothes, not in their night-dresses—they have no night-dresses."

Little Di had now reached a pitch of surprise which rendered her dumb, so the missionary continued:—

"Here is another case. A poor widow called once, and said she would be so grateful if we would admit her little girl and boy into the schools. She looked, clean and tidy, and the children had not been neglected. She could not afford to pay for them, as she had not a penny in the world, and applied to us because we made no charge. The children were admitted and supplied with a plain but nourishing meal, while their mother went away to seek for work. We did not hear how she sped, but she had probably taken her case to God, and found Him faithful, for she had said, before going away, 'I know that God is the Father of the fatherless, and the husband of the widow.'"

"Again, another poor woman came. Her husband had fallen sick. Till within a few days her children had been at a school and paid for, but now the bread-winner was ill—might never recover—and had gone to the hospital. These children were at once admitted, and in each case investigation was made to test the veracity of the applicants.

"Of course," continued the missionary, "I have spoken chiefly about the agencies with which I happen to have come personally in contact, but it must not be supposed that therefore I ignore or am indifferent to the other grand centres of influence which are elsewhere at work in London; such as, for instance, the various agencies set agoing and superintended by Dr. Barnardo, whose *Home for Working and Destitute Boys*, in Stepney Causeway, is a shelter from which thousands of rescued little ones go forth to labour as honest and useful members of society, instead of dying miserably in the slums of London, or growing up to recruit the ranks of our criminal classes. These agencies, besides rescuing destitute and neglected children, include *Homes for destitute girls* and for *little boys* in Ilford and Jersey, an *Infirmary for sick children of the destitute classes* in Stepney, *Orphan Homes, Ragged and Day schools, Free dinner-table to destitute children, Mission Halls, Coffee Palaces*, and, in short, a grand net-work of beneficent agencies—Evangelistic, Temperance, and Medical—for the conduct of which is required not far short of One Hundred Pounds a day!"

Even Sir Richard Brandon, with all his supposed financial capacities, seemed struck with the magnitude of this sum.

"And where does Dr. Barnardo obtain so large an amount?" he asked.

"From the voluntary gifts of those who sympathise with and consider the poor," replied Seaward.

"Then," he added, "there is that noble work carried on by Miss Rye of the *Emigration Home for Destitute Little Girls*, at the Avenue House, Peckham, from which a stream of destitute little ones continually flows to Canada, where they are much wanted, and who, if allowed to remain here, would almost certainly be *lost*. Strong testimony to the value of this work has been given by the Bishops of Toronto and Niagara, and other competent judges.

Let me mention a case of one of Miss Rye's little ones, which speaks for itself.

"A little girl of six was deserted by both father and mother."

"Oh! *poor* little thing!" exclaimed the sympathetic Di, with an amazing series of pitiful curves about her eyebrows.

"Yes, poor indeed!" responded Seaward. "The mother forsook her first; then her father took her on the tramp, but the little feet could not travel fast enough, so he got tired of her and offered her to a workhouse. They refused her, so the tramping was continued, and at last baby was sold for three shillings to a stranger man. On taking his purchase home, however, the man found that his wife was unwilling to receive her; he therefore sent poor little baby adrift in the streets of London!"

"*What* a shame!" cried Di, with flashing orbs.

"Was it not? But, when father and mother cast this little one off, the Lord cared for it. An inspector of police, who found it, took it to his wife, and she carried it to Miss Rye's Home, where it was at once received and cared for, and, doubtless, this little foundling girl is now dwelling happily and usefully with a Canadian family."

"How nice!" exclaimed Di, her eyes, lips, and teeth bearing eloquent witness to her satisfaction.

"But no doubt you have heard of Miss Rye's work,

as well as that of Miss Annie Macpherson at the Home of Industry, and, perhaps, contributed to—"

"No," interrupted Sir Richard, quickly, "I do not contribute; but pray, Mr. Seaward, are there other institutions of this sort in London?"

"Oh! yes, there are several. It would take me too long to go into the details of the various agencies we have for. succouring the poor. There is, among others, The Church of England '*Central Home for, Waifs and Strays,*' with a 'Receiving House' for boys in Upper Clapton, and one for girls in East Dulwich, with the Archbishop of Canterbury for its President. Possibly you may have heard of the '*Strangers' Rest,*' in St. George Street, Ratcliff Highway, where, as far as man can judge, great and permanent good is being constantly done to the souls of sailors. A sailor once entered this 'Rest' considerably the worse for drink. He was spoken to by Christian friends, and asked to sign the pledge. He did so, and has now been steadfast for years. Returning from a long voyage lately, he went to revisit the *Rest*, and there, at the Bible-class, prayed. Part of his prayer was—'God bless the Strangers' Rest. O Lord, we thank Thee for this place, and we shall thank Thee to all eternity.' This is a sample of the feeling with which the place is regarded by those who have received blessing there. In the same street, only a few doors from this Rest, is the '*Sailor's Welcome Home*.' This is more of a home than the other, for it furnishes lodging and unintoxicating refreshment, while its devoted soul-loving manager, Miss Child, and her assistant workers, go fearlessly into the very dens of iniquity, and do all they can to bring sailors to Jesus, and induce them to take the pledge against strong drink, in which work they are, through God's blessing, wonderfully successful. These two missions work, as it were, into each other's hands. In the 'Rest' are held prayer-meetings and Bible-classes, and when these are dismissed, the sailors find the open door of the 'Welcome Home' ready to receive them, and the inmates there seek to deepen the good influence that has been brought to bear at the meetings—and this in the midst of one of the very worst parts of London, where temptation to every species of evil is rampant, on the right hand and on the left, before and behind.

"But, Sir Richard, although I say that a grand and extensive work of salvation to soul, body, and spirit is being done to thousands of men, and women, and children, by the agencies which I have mentioned, and by many similar agencies which I have not now time to mention, as well as by the band of City Missionaries to which I have the honour to belong, I would earnestly point out that these all put together only scratch the surface of

the vast mass of corruption which has to be dealt
with in this seething world of London, the population
of which is, as you are aware, equal to that of all
Scotland; and very specially would I remark that
the work is almost exclusively carried on by the
voluntary contributions of those who 'consider the
poor'!

"The little tract which I have given you will explain much of the details of this great work, as
carried on in the George Yard Mission. When you
have read that, if you desire it, I will call on you
again. Meanwhile engagements compel me to take
my leave."

After luncheon, that day, Sir Richard drew his
chair to the window, but instead of taking up the
newspaper and recommending his little one to visit
the nursery, he said :—

"Come here, Di. You and I will examine this
pamphlet—this little book—and I'll try to explain
it, for reports are usually very dry."

Di looked innocently puzzled. "Should reports
always be wet, papa ?"

Sir Richard came nearer to the confines of a laugh
than he had reached for a long time past.

"No, love—not exactly wet, but—hm—you shall
hear. Draw the stool close to my knee and lay your
head on it."

With his large hand on the golden tresses, Sir

Richard Brandon began to examine the record of work done in the George Yard Mission.

"What is this?" he said. *Toy Classes,*—why, this must be something quite in your way, Di."

"Oh yes, I'm sure of that, for I adore toys. Tell me about it."

"These toy classes are for the cheerless and neglected," said the knight, frowning in a business-like way at the pamphlet. "Sometimes so many as eighty neglected little ones attend these classes. On one occasion, only one of these had boots on, which were very old, much too large, and both lefts. When they were seated, toys and scrap-books were lent to them. There were puzzles, and toy-bricks, and many other things which kept them quite happy for an hour. Of course the opportunity was seized to tell them about Jesus and His love. A blessed lesson which they would not have had a chance of learning at home—if they had homes; but many of them had none. When it was time to go they said —'Can't we stay longer?'

"The beginning of this class was interesting," said Sir Richard, continuing to read. "The thought arose—'gather in the most forlorn and wretched children; those who are seldom seen to smile, or heard to laugh; there are many such who require Christian sympathy.' The thought was immediately acted on. A little barefooted ragged boy was sent into the streets to bring in the children. Soon there was a crowd round the school door. The most miserable among the little ones were admitted. The proceedings commenced with prayer—then the toys were distributed, the dirty little hands became active, and the dirty little faces began to look happy. When the toys were gathered up, some could not be found, so, at the next meeting, some of the bigger children were set to watch the smaller ones. Presently one little detective said: 'Please, teacher, Teddy's got a horse in his pocket;' and another said that Sally had an elephant in her pinafore! Occasion was thus found to show the evil of stealing, and teach the blessedness of honesty. They soon gave up pilfering, and they now play with the toys without desiring to take them away."

"How nice!" said Di. "Go on, papa."

"What can this be?" continued Sir Richard, quoting—" *Wild Flowers of the Forest Day Nursery.* Oh! I see—very good idea. I'll not read it, Di. I'll tell you about it. There are many poor widows, you must know, and women whose husbands are bad, who have no money to buy food and shelter for themseves and little ones except what they can earn each day. But some of these poor women have babies, and they can't work, you know, with babies in their arms, neither can they leave the babies at home with no one to look after them, except, perhaps, little sisters or brothers not much older than themselves, so they take their babies to this Cradle-Home, and each pays only twopence, for which small sum her baby is taken in, washed, clothed, warmed, fed, and amused by kind nurses, who keep it till the mother returns from her work to get it back again. Isn't that good ?"

"Oh! yes," assented Di, with all her heart.

"And I read here," continued her father, "that thousands of the infants of the poor die every year because they have not enough food, or enough clothing to keep them warm."

"Oh *what* a pity!" exclaimed Di, the tears of ready sympathy rushing hot into her upturned eyes.

"So you see," continued Sir Richard, who had unconsciously, as it were, become a pleader for the poor, "if there were a great many nurseries of this kind all over London, a great many little lives would be saved."

"And why are there not a great many nurseries of that kind, papa?"

"Well, I suppose, it is because there are no funds."

"No what? papa."

"Not enough of money, dear."

"Oh! *what* a pity! I wish I had lots and lots of money, and then wouldn't I have Cradle-Homes everywhere?"

Sir Richard, knowing that he had "lots and lots" of money, but had not hitherto contributed one farthing to the object under consideration, thought it best to change the subject by going on with the George Yard Record.

But we will not conduct the reader through it all—interesting though the subject certainly is. Suffice it to say that he found the account classed under several heads. Under "*Feeding the Hungry*," for instance, he learned that many poor children are entirely without food, sometimes, for a whole day, so that only two courses are open to them—to steal food and become criminals, or drift into sickness and die. From which fate many hundreds are annually rescued by timely aid at George Yard, the supplies for which are sent by liberal-minded Christians in all ranks of life—from Mr. Crackaby with his £150 a year, up through Mr. Brisbane and his class to the present Earl of Shaftesbury—who, by the way, has taken a deep interest and lent able support to this particular Mission for more than a quarter of a century. But the name of Sir Richard Brandon did not appear on the roll of contributors. He had not studied the "lower orders" much, except from a politico-economical-argumentative-after-dinner-port-winy point of view.

Under the head of "*Clothing necessitous Children*," he found that some of the little ones presented themselves at the school-door in such a net-work of rags, probably infected, as to be unfit even for a Ragged School. They were therefore taken in, had their garments destroyed, and were supplied with new clothes. Also, that about 1000 children between the ages of three and fourteen years were connected with the Institution—scattered among the various works of usefulness conducted for the young.

Under " *Work among Lads,*" he found that those big boys whom one sees idling about corners of streets, fancying themselves men, smoking with obvious dislike and pretended pleasure, and on the highroad to the jail and the gallows—that those boys were enticed into classes opened for carpentry, turning, fretwork, and other attractive industrial pursuits—including even printing, at a press supplied by Lord Shaftesbury. This, in connection with evening classes for reading, writing, and arithmetic—the whole leading up to the grand object and aim of all—the salvation of souls.

Under other heads he found that outcast boys were received, sheltered, sent to Industrial Homes, or returned to friends and parents ; that temperance meetings were held, and drunkards, male and female, sought out, prayed for, lovingly reasoned with, and reclaimed from this perhaps the greatest curse of the land ; that Juvenile Bands of Hope were formed, on the ground of prevention being better than cure; that lodging-houses, where the poorest of the poor, and the lowest of the low do congregate, were visited, and the gospel proclaimed to ears that were deaf to nearly every good influence; that mothers' meetings were held—one of them at that old head-quarters of sin, the "Black Horse," where counsel and sympathy were mingled with a Clothing Club and a Bible-woman; that there were a Working Men's Benefit Society, Bible Classes, Sunday Schools, a Sewing Class, a Mutual Labour Loan Society, a Shelter for Homeless Girls, a library, an Invalid Children's Dinner, a bath-room and lavatory, a Flower Mission, and—hear it, ye who fancy that a penny stands very low in the scale of financial little-ness—a Farthing Bank! All this free—conducted by an unpaid band of considerably over a hundred Christian workers, male and female—and leaven-ing the foundations of society, without which, and similar missions, there would be very few leavening influences at all, and the superstructure of society would stand a pretty fair chance of being burst up or blown to atoms—though the superstructure is not very willing to believe the fact!

In addition to all this, Sir Richard learned, to his great amazement, that the Jews won't light their fires on the Sabbath-day—that is, on our Saturday—that they won't even poke it, and that this abstinence is the immediate cause of a source of revenue to the un-Jewish poor, whom the Jews hire to light and poke their fires for them.

And, lastly, Sir Richard Brandon learned that Mr. George Holland, who had managed that mission for more than quarter of a century, was resolved, in the strength of the Lord, to seek out the lost and rescue the perishing, even though he, Sir Richard, and all who resembled him, should refuse to aid by tongue or hand in the glorious work of rescuing the poor from sin and its consequences.

CHAPTER X.

BALLS, BOBBY, SIR RICHARD, AND GILES APPEAR ON THE STAGE.

As from the sublime to the ridiculous there is but a step, so, from the dining-room to the kitchen there is but a stair. Let us descend the stair and learn that while Sir Richard was expounding the subject of "the poor" to little Di, Mr. Balls, the butler, was engaged on the same subject in the servants' hall.

"I cannot tell you," said Balls, "what a impression the sight o' these poor people made on me."

"La! Mr. Balls," said the cook, who was not unacquainted with low life in London, having herself been born within sound of Bow-Bells, "you've got no occasion to worrit yourself about it. It 'as never bin different."

"That makes it all the worse, cook," returned Balls, standing with his back to the fireplace and his legs wide apart; "if it was only a temporary depression in trade, or the repeal of the corn laws that did it, one could stand it, but to think that such a state of things *always* goes on is something fearful. You know I'm a country-bred man myself, and ain't used to the town, or to such awful sights of squalor. It almost made me weep, I do assure you. One room that I looked into had a mother and two children in it, and I declare to you that the little boy was going about stark naked, and his sister was only just a slight degree better."

"P'raps they was goin' to bed," suggested Mrs. Screwbury.

"No, nurse, they wasn't; they was playing about evidently in their usual costume—for that evenin' at least. I would not have believed it if I had not seen it. And the mother was so tattered and draggled and dirty—which, also, was the room."

"Was that in the court where the Frogs live?" asked Jessie Summers.

"It was, and a dreadful court too—shocking!"

"By the way, Mr. Balls," asked the cook, "is there any chance o' that brat of a boy Bobby, as they call him, coming here? I can't think why master has offered to take such a creeter into his service."

"No, cook, there is no chance. I forgot to tell you about that little matter. The boy was here yesterday and he refused—absolutely declined a splendid offer."

"I'm glad to hear it," returned the cook.

"Tell us about it, Mr. Balls," said Jessie Summers with a reproachful look at the other. "I'm quite

I

fond of that boy—he's such a smart fellow, and wouldn't be bad-looking if he'd only wash his face and comb his hair."

"He's smart enough, no doubt, but impudence is his strong point," rejoined the butler with a laugh. The way he spoke to the master beats everything.

"'I've sent for you, my boy,' said Sir Richard, in his usual dignified, kindly way, 'to offer you the situation of under-gardener in my establishment.'

"'Oh! that's wot you wants with me, is it?' said the boy, as bold as brass; indeed I may say as bold as gun-metal, for his eyes an' teeth glittered as he spoke, and he said it with the air of a dook. Master didn't quite seem to like it, but I saw he laid restraint on himself and said: 'You have to thank my daughter for this offer—'

"'Thank you, Miss,' said the boy, turnin' to Miss Di with a low bow, imitatin' Sir Richard's manner, I thought, as much as he could."

"'Of course,' continued the master, rather sharply, 'I offer you this situation out of mere charity—'

"'Oh! you do, do you?' said the extraordinary boy in the coolest manner, 'but wot if I objec' to receive charity? Ven I 'olds a 'orse I expecs to be paid for so doin', same as you expecs to be paid w'en you attends a board-meetin' to grin an' do nuffin.'

"'Come, come, boy,' said Sir Richard, gettin'

redder in the face than I ever before saw him, 'I am not accustomed to low pleasantry, and—'

"'An' I ain't accustomed,' broke in the boy, 'to 'igh hinsults. Do you think that every gent what vears a coat an' pants with 'oles in 'em is a beggar?'

"For some moments master seemed to be struck speechless, an' I feared that in spite of his well-known gentleness of character he 'd throw the ink-stand at the boy's head, but he didn't; he merely said in a low voice, 'I would dismiss you at once, boy, were it not that I have promised my daughter to offer you employment, and you can see by her looks how much your unnatural conduct grieves her.'

"An' this was true, for poor Miss Di sat there with her hands clasped, her eyes full of tears, her eyebrows disappearin' among her hair with astonishment, and her whole appearance the very pictur' of distress. 'However,' continued Sir Richard, 'I still make you the offer, though I doubt much whether you will be able to retain the situation. Your wages will—'

"'Please sir,' pleaded the boy, 'don't mention the wages. I couldn't stand that. Indeed I couldn't. It would really be too much for me.'

"'Why, what do you mean?' says master.

"'I mean,' says Impudence, 'that I agree with you. I don't think I *could* retain the sitivation, cos w'y?

In the fust place, I a'int got no talent at gardenin'. The on'y time I tried it was w'en I planted a toolip in a flower-pot, an' w'en I dug it up to see 'ow it was a-gittin on a cove told me I 'd planted it upside down. Howsever, I wasn't goin' to be beat by that cove, so I say to 'im, Jack, I says, I planted it so a-purpus, an' w'en it sprouts I 'm agoin' to 'ang it up to see if it won't grow through the 'ole in the bottom. In the second place, I couldn't retain the sitivation 'cause I don't intend to take it, though you was to offer me six thousand no shillin's an' no pence no farthin's a year as salary.'

"I r'ally did think master would ha' dropt out of his chair at that. As for Miss Di, she was so tickled that she gave a sort of hysterical laugh.

"'Balls,' said master, 'show him out, and—' he pulled up short, but I knew he meant to say have an eye on the great-coats and umbrellas, so I showed the boy out, an' he went down-stairs quite quiet, but the last thing I saw of him was performin' a sort of minstrel dance at the end of the street just before he turned the corner and disappeared."

"Imp'rence!" exclaimed the cook.

"Naughty, ungrateful boy!" said Mrs. Screwbury

"But it was plucky of him," said Jessie Summers.

"I would call it cheeky," said Balls, "I can't think what put it into his head to go on so."

If Mr. Balls had followed Bobby Frog in spirit, watched his subsequent movements, and listened to his remarks, perhaps he might have understood the meaning of his conduct a little better.

After he had turned the corner of the street, as above mentioned, Bobby trotted on for a short space, and then, coming to a full stop, executed a few steps of the minstrel dance, at the end of which he brought his foot down with tremendous emphasis on the pavement, and said—" Yes, I've bin an' done it. I know'd I was game for a good deal, but I did *not* think I was up to that. One never knows wot 'e's fit for till 'e tries. Wot'll Hetty think, I wonder?"

What Hetty thought he soon found out, for he overtook her on the Thames embankment on her way home. Bobby was fond of that route, though a little out of his way, because he loved the running water, though it *was* muddy, and the sight of steamers and barges.

" Well, Bobby," she said, laying her hand on his shoulder, " where have you been?"

" To see old Swallow'd-the-poker, Hetty."

" What took you there?" asked the girl in surprise.

" My legs. You don't suppose I've set up my carriage yet, do you?"

" Come, you know what I mean."

"Vell, then, I went because I was sent for, an' wot d'ye think? the old gen'l'man hoffered me the sitivation of under-gardener!"

"You don't say so! Oh! Bobby, what a lucky boy—an' what a kind gentleman! Tell me all about it now," said Hetty, pressing her hand more tenderly on her brother's shoulder. "What wages is he to give you?"

"No wages wotsomever."

Hetty looked into her brother's face with an expression of concerned surprise. She knew some tradespeople who made her work hard for so very little, that it was not difficult to believe in a gentleman asking her brother to work for nothing! Still she had thought better of Sir Richard, and expected to hear something more creditable to him.

"Ah, you may look, but I do assure you he is to give me no wages, an' I'm to do no work."

Here Bobby executed a few steps of his favourite dance, but evidently from mere habit, and unconsciously, for he left off in the middle, and seemed to forget the salient point of emphasis with his foot.

"What *do* you mean, Bobby?—be earnest, like a dear boy, for once."

"Earnest!" exclaimed the urchin with vehemence. "I never was more in earnest in my life. You should 'ave seen Swallow'd-the-poker w'en I refused to 'ave it."

" Refused it ?"

" Ay—re-fused it. Come Hetty, I 'll explain."

The boy dropped his facetious tone and manner while he rapidly ran over the chief points of his interview with Sir Richard.

" But why did you refuse so good an offer ?" asked Hetty, still unable to repress her surprise.

" Because of daddy."

" Daddy ?"

" Ay, daddy. You know he 's fond o' me, is daddy, and, d'ye know, though p'r'aps you mayn't believe it, I 'm raither fond o' *him;* but 'e 's a bad-un is daddy. He 's bent on mischief, you see, an' 'e 's set his 'art on my 'elpin' of 'im. But I *wont* 'elp 'im —that 's flat. Now, what d'ye think, Hetty " (here he dropped his voice to almost a whisper and looked solemn), " dad wants to make use o' me to commit a burglary on Swallow'd-the-poker's 'ouse."

" You don't mean it, Bobby !",

" But I do, Hetty. Dad found out from that rediklous butler that goes veepin' around our court like a leeky pump, that the old gen'l'man was goin' to hoffer me this sitivation, an 'e 's bin wery 'ard on me to accept it, so that I may find out the ways o' the 'ouse where the plate an' waluables lay, let 'im in some fine dark night an' 'elp 'im to carry off the swag."

A distressed expression marked poor Hetty's re- ception of this news, but she said never a word.

" Now you won't tell, Hetty ?" said the boy with
a look of real anxiety on his face. " It's not so
much his killin' me I cares about, but I wouldn't
bring daddy to grief for any money. I'd raither 'elp
'im than that. You 'll not say a word to nobody ?"

" No, Bobby, I won't say a word."

" Vell, you see," continued the boy, " ven I'd
made myself so disagreeable that the old gen'l'man
would 'ave nothin' to do with me, I came straight
away, an' 'ere I am ; but it *was* a trial, let me tell
you, specially ven 'e come to mention wages—an'
sitch a 'eavenly smell o' roasted wittles come up
from the kitchen too at the moment, but I 'ad only
to look at Miss Di, to make me as stubborn as a
hox or a hass. ' Wot!' thinks I to myself, ' betray
that hangel—no, never !' yet if I was to go into that
'ouse I know I'd do it, for daddy's got sitch a
wheedlin' way with 'im w'en 'e likes, that I couldn't
'old hout long—so I giv' old Swallowed-the-poker
sitch a lot o' cheek that I thought 'e'd kick me
right through the winder. He was considerable
astonished as well as riled, I can tell you, an' Miss
Di's face was a pictur', but the old butler was the
sight. He'd got 'is face screwed up into sitch a
state o' surprise that it looked like a eight-day clock
with a gumboil. Now, Hetty, I'm goin' to tell 'ee
what 'll take your breath away. I've made up my
mind to go to Canada !"

Hetty did, on hearing this, look as if her breath had been taken away. When it returned sufficiently she said :—

"Bobby, what put that into your head?"

"The 'Ome of Hindustry," said Bobby with a mysterious look.

"The Home of Industry," repeated the girl in surprise, for she knew that Institution well, having frequently assisted its workers in their labour of love.

"Yes, that's the name—'Ome of Hindustry, what sends off so many ragged boys to Canada under Miss Macpherson."

"Ay, Bobby, it does a great deal more than that," returned the girl. "Sending off poor boys and girls to Canada is only one branch of its work. If you'd bin to its tea-meetin's for the destitute, as I have, an' its clothin' meetin's and its mothers' meetin's an' —"

"'Ow d'ye know I 'aven't bin at 'em all?" asked the boy with an impudent look.

"Well, you know, you couldn't have been at the mothers' meetings, Bobby."

"Oh! for the matter o' that, no more could you."

"True, but I've heard of them all many and many a time; but come, tell me all about it. How did you come to go near the Home of Industry at all after refusing so often to go with me?"

"Vell, I didn't go because of bein' axed to go, you may be sure o' that, but my little dosser, Tim Lumpy, you remember 'im? The cove wi' the nose like a button, an' no body to speak of—all legs an' arms, like a 'uman win'-mill; vell, you must know they've nabbed 'im, an' given 'im a rig-out o' noo slops, an' they're goin' to send 'im to Canada. So I 'appened to be down near the 'Ome one day three weeks past, an' I see Lumpy a-goin' in. ''Allo!' says I. ''Allo!' says 'e; an' then 'e told me all about it. 'Does they feed you well?' I axed. 'Oh! don't they, just!' said 'e. 'There's to be a blow hout this wery night,' said 'e. 'I wonder,' says I, 'if they'd let me in, for I'm uncommon 'ungry, I tell you; 'ad nuffin to heat since last night.' Just as I said that, a lot o' fellers like me came tumblin' up to the door—so I sneaked in wi' the rest—for I thought they'd kick me hout if they knowed I'd come without inwitation."

"Well, and what then?" asked Hetty.

Here our little street Arab began to tell, in his own peculiar language and style, how that he went in, and found a number of ladies in an upper room with forms set, and hot tea and bread to be had—as much as they could stuff—for nothing; that the boys were very wild and unruly at first, but that after the chief lady had prayed they became better, and that when half-a-dozen nice little girls were brought in and had sung a hymn or two they were quite quiet and ready to listen. Like many other people, this city Arab did not like to speak out freely, even to his sister, on matters that touched his feelings deeply, but he said enough to let the eager and thankful Hetty know that not only had Jesus and His love been preached to the boys, but she perceived that what had been said and sung had made an unusual impression, though the little ragged waif sought to conceal it under the veil of cool pleasantry, and she now recognised the fact that the prayers which she had been putting up for many a day in her brother's behalf had been answered.

"Oh! I'm so happy," she said; and, unable to restrain herself, flung her arms round Bobby's neck and kissed him.

It was evident that the little fellow rather liked this, though he pretended that he did not.

"Come, old gal," he said brusquely, "none o' that sort o' thing. I can't stand it. Don't you see, the popilation is lookin' at us in surprise; besides, you've bin an' crushed all my shirt front!"

"But," continued Hetty, as they walked on again, "I'm not happy to hear that you are goin' to Canada. What ever will I do without you, Bobby?"

Poor girl, she could well afford to do without him in one sense, for he had hitherto been chiefly an object of anxiety and expense to her, though also an object of love.

"I 'm sorry to think of goin' too, Hetty, for your sake an' mother's, but for daddy's sake and my own I *must* go. You see, I can't 'old hout agin 'im. W'en 'e makes up 'is mind to a thing you know 'e sticks to it, for 'e 's a tough un; an' 'e 's got sitch a wheedlin' sort o' way with 'im that I can't 'elp givin' in a'most. So, you see, it 'll be better for both of us that I should go away. But I 'll come back, you know, Hetty, with a fortin—see if I don't—an' then, oh! won't I keep a carridge an' a ridin' 'oss for daddy, an' feed mother an' you on plum-duff an' pork sassengers to breakfast, dinner, an' supper, with ice cream for a relish!"

Poor Hetty did not even smile at this prospect of temporal felicity. She felt that in the main the boy was right, and that the only chance he had of escaping the toils in which her father was wrapping him by the strange union of affection and villainy, was to leave the country. She knew, also, that, thanks to the Home of Industry and its promoters, the sending of a ragged, friendless, penniless London waif, clothed and in his right mind, to a new land of bright and hopeful prospects, was an event brought within the bounds of possibility.

That night Bob Frog stood with his dosser (*i.e.* his friend) Tim Lumpy, discussing their future prospects in the partial privacy of a railway arch. They talked long, and, for waifs, earnestly—both as to the land they were about to quit and that to which they were going; and the surprising fact might have been noted by a listener—had there been any such present, save a homeless cat—that neither of the boys perpetrated a joke for the space of at least ten minutes.

"Vy," observed little Frog at length, "you seem to 'ave got all the fun drove out o' you, Lumpy."

"Not a bit on it," returned the other, with a hurt look, as though he had been charged with some serious misdemeanour, " but it do seem sitch a shabby thing to go an' forsake my blind old mother."

"But yer blind old mother wants you to go," said Bobby, "an' says she 'll be well looked arter by the ladies of the 'Ome, and that she wouldn't stand in the way o' your prospec's. Besides, she ain't yer mother !"

This was true. Tim Lumpy had neither father nor mother, nor relative on earth, and the old woman who, out of sheer pity, had taken him in and allowed him to call her " mother," was a widow at the lowest possible round of that social ladder, at the top of which—figuratively speaking—sits Her Gracious Majesty the Queen. Mrs. Lumpy had found him on her door-step, weeping and in rags, at the early age of five years. She had taken him in,

and fed him on part of a penny loaf which formed
the sole edible substance for her own breakfast. She
had mended his rags to the extent of her ability, but
she had not washed his face, having no soap of her
own, and not caring to borrow from neighbours who
were in the same destitute condition. Besides, she
had too hard a battle to fight with an ever-present
and pressing foe, to care much about dirt, and
no doubt deemed a wash of tears now and then
sufficient. Lumpy himself seemed to agree with
her as to this, for he washed himself in that fashion
frequently.

Having sought for his parents in vain, with the
aid of the police, Mrs. Lumpy quietly kept the boy
on; gave him her surname, prefixed that of Timothy,
answered to the call of mother, and then left him to
do very much as he pleased.

In these circumstances, it was not surprising that
little Tim soon grew to be one of the pests of his
alley. Tim was a weak-eyed boy, and remarkably
thin, being, as his friend had said, composed chiefly
of legs and arms. There must have been a good deal
of brain also, for he was keen-witted, as people soon
began to find out to their cost. Tim was observant
also. He observed, on nearing the age of ten years,
that in the great river of life which daily flowed past
him, there were certain faces which indicated tender
and kindly hearts, coupled with defective brain-

action, and a good deal of self-will. He became painfully shrewd in reading such faces, and, on wet days, would present himself to them with his bare little red feet and half-naked body, rain water (doing duty for tears), running from his weak bloodshot eyes, and falsehoods of the most pitiable, complex, and impudent character pouring from his thin blue lips, whilst awful solemnity seemed to shine on his visage. The certain result was—coppers!

These kindly ones have, unwittingly of course, changed a text of Scripture, and, for the words "*consider* the poor," read "throw coppers to the poor!" You see, it is much easier to relieve one's feelings by giving away a few pence, than to take the trouble of visiting, inquiring about, and otherwise *considering*, the poor! At all events it would seem so, for Tim began to grow comparatively rich, and corrupted, still more deeply, associates who were already buried sufficiently in the depths of corruption.

At last little Tim was met by a lady who had befriended him more than once, and who asked him why he preferred begging in the streets to going to the ragged school, where he would get not only food for the body, but for the soul. He replied that he was hungry, and his mother had no victuals to give him, so he had gone out to beg. The lady went straight to Mrs. Lumpy, found the story to be true, and that the poor half-blind old woman was quite unable to support the boy and herself. The lady prevailed on the old woman to attend the meetings for poor, aged, and infirm women in Miss Macpherson's "Bee-hive," and little Tim was taken into the "Home for Destitute Little Boys under ten years of age."

It was not all smooth sailing in that Home after Tim Lumpy entered it! Being utterly untamed, Tim had many a sore struggle ere the temper was brought under control. One day he was so bad that the governess was obliged to punish him by leaving him behind, while the other boys went out for a walk. When left alone, the lady-superintendent tried to converse with him about obedience, but he became frightfully violent, and demanded his rags that he might return again to the streets. Finally he escaped, rushed to his old home in a paroxysm of rage, and then, getting on the roof, declared to the assembled neighbours that he would throw himself down and dash out his brains. In this state a Bible-woman found him. After offering the mental prayer, "Lord, help me," she entreated him to come down and join her in a cup of tea with his old mother. The invitation perhaps struck the little rebel as having a touch of humour in it. At all events he accepted it and forthwith descended.

Over the tea, the Bible-woman prayed aloud

for him, and the poor boy broke down, burst into tears, and begged forgiveness. Soon afterwards he was heard tapping at the door of the Home— gentle and subdued.

Thus was this waif rescued, and he now discussed with his former comrade the prospect of transferring themselves and their powers, mental and physical, to Canada. Diverging from this subject to Bobby's father, and his dark designs, Tim asked if Ned Frog had absolutely decided to break into Sir Richard Brandon's house, and Bobby replied that he had; that his father had wormed out of the butler, who was a soft stupid sort of cove, where the plate and valuables were kept, and that he and another man had arranged to do it.

" Is the partikler night fixed ?" asked Tim.

" Yes; it's to be the last night o' this month."

" Why not give notice ?" asked Tim.

" 'Cause I won't peach on daddy," said Bob Frog stoutly.

Little Tim received this with a "quite right, old dosser," and then proposed that the meeting should adjourn, as he was expected back at the Home by that time.

Two weeks or so after that, Police Constable No. 666 was walking quietly along one of the streets of his particular beat in the West-end, with that state-

liness of step which seems to be inseparable from
place, power, and six feet two.

It was a quiet street, such as Wealth loves to
inhabit. There were few carriages passing along it,
and fewer passengers. No. 666 had nothing particular to do—the inhabitants being painfully well-
behaved, and the sun high. His mind, therefore,
roamed about aimlessly, sometimes bringing playfully before him a small abode, not very far distant,
where a pretty woman was busy with household
operations, and a ferocious policeman, about three
feet high, was taking into custody an incorrigible
criminal of still smaller size.

A little boy, with very long arms and legs, might
have been seen following our friend Giles Scott,
until the latter entered upon one of those narrow
paths made by builders on the pavements of streets
when houses are undergoing repairs. Watching
until Giles was half way along it, the boy ran
nimbly up and accosted him with a familiar—

"Well, old man, 'ow are you?"

"Pretty bobbish, thank you," returned the constable, for he was a good-natured man, and rather
liked a little quiet chaff with street-boys when not
too much engaged with duty.

"Well, now, are you aweer that there's agoin' to
be a burglairy committed in this 'ere quarter?" asked
the boy, thrusting both hands deep into his pockets,

and bending his body a little back, so as to look more easily up at his tall friend.

"Ah! indeed, well no, I didn't know it, for I forgot to examine the books at Scotland Yard this morning, but I've no doubt it's entered there by your friend who's goin' to commit it."

"No, it ain't entered there," said the boy, with a manner and tone that rather surprised No. 666; "and I'd advise you to git out your note-book, an' clap down wot I'm agoin' to tell ye. You know the 'ouse of Sir Richard Brandon?"

"Yes, I know it."

"Well, that 'ouse is to be cracked on the 31st night o' this month."

"How d'you know that, lad?" asked Giles, moving towards the end of the barricade, so as to get nearer to his informant.

"No use, bobby," said Tim, "big as you are, you can't nab me. Believe me or not as you like, but I advise you to look arter that there 'ouse on the 31st if you valley your repitation."

Tim went off like a congreve rocket, dashed down a side street, sloped into an alley, and melted into a wilderness of bricks and mortar.

Of course Giles did not attempt to follow, but some mysterious communications passed between him and his superintendent that night before he went to bed.

CHAPTER XI.

SIR RICHARD AND MR. BRISBANE DISCUSS, AND DI LISTENS.

"My dear sir," said Sir Richard Brandon, over a glass of sherry one evening after dinner, to George Brisbane, Esq. of Lively Hall, "the management of the poor is a difficult, a very difficult subject to deal with."

"It is, unquestionably," assented Brisbane, "so difficult, that I am afraid some of our legislators are unwilling to face it; but it ought to be faced, for there is much to be done in the way of improving the poor-laws, which at present tend to foster pauperism in the young, and bear heavily on the aged. Meanwhile, philanthropists find it necessary to take up the case of the poor as a private enterprise."

"Pardon me, Brisbane, there I think you are in error. Everything requisite to afford relief to the poor is provided by the state. If the poor will not take advantage of the provision, or the machinery is not well oiled and worked by the officials, the remedy lies in greater wisdom on the part of the poor, and supervision of officials—not in further legislation. But what do you mean by our poor-laws bearing heavily on the aged?"

"I mean that the old people should be better cared for, simply because of their age. Great age is a sufficient argument of itself, I think, for throwing a veil of oblivion over the past, and extending charity with a liberal, pitying hand, because of present distress, and irremediable infirmities. Whatever may be the truth with regard to paupers and workhouses in general, there ought to be a distinct refuge for the aged, which should be attractive—not repulsive, as at present—and age, without reference to character or antecedents, should constitute the title to enter it. 'God pity the aged poor,' is often my prayer, 'and enable us to feel more for them in the dreary, pitiful termination of their career.'"

"But, my dear sir," returned Sir Richard, "you would have old paupers crowding into such workhouses, or refuges as you call them, by the thousand."

"Well, better that they should do so than that they should die miserably by thousands in filthy and empty rooms—sometimes without fire, or food, or physic, or a single word of kindness to ease their sad descent into the grave."

"But, then, Brisbane, as I said, it is their own fault—they have the workhouse to go to."

"But, then, as *I* said, Sir Richard, the workhouse

is rendered so repulsive to them that they keep out of it as long as they can, and too often keep out so long that it is too late, and their end is as I have described. However, until things are better arranged, we must do what we can for them in a private way. Indeed Scripture teaches distinctly the necessity for private charity, by such words as—'the poor ye have always with you,' and, 'blessed are they who consider the poor.' Don't you agree with me, Mr. Welland?"

Stephen Welland—who, since the day of his accident, had become intimate with Mr. Brisbane and Sir Richard—replied that although deeply interested in the discussion going on, his knowledge of the subject was too slight to justify his holding any decided opinion.

"Take another glass of sherry," said Sir Richard, pushing the decanter towards the young man; "it will stir your brain and enable you to see your way more clearly through this knotty point."

"No more, thank you, Sir Richard."

"Come, come—fill your glass," said the knight; "you and I must set an example of moderate drinking to Brisbane, as a counter-blast to his Blue Ribbonism."

Welland smiled and re-filled his glass.

"Nay, I never thrust my opinions on that point on people," said Brisbane, with a laugh, "but if you *will* draw the sword and challenge me, I won't refuse the combat!"

"No, no, Brisbane. Please spare us! I re-sheath the sword, and need not that you should go all over it again. I quite understand that you are no bigot, that you think the Bible clearly permits and encourages total abstinence in certain circumstances, though it does not teach it; that, although a total abstainer yourself, you do not refuse to give drink to your friends if they desire it—and all that sort of thing; but pray let it pass, and I won't offend again."

"Ah! Sir Richard, you are an unfair foe. You draw your sword to give me a wound through our young friend, and then sheath it before I can return on you. However, you have stated my position so well that I forgive you and shake hands. But, to return to the matter of private charity, are you aware how little suffices to support the poor—how very far the mere crumbs that fall from a rich man's table will go to sustain them? Now, just take the glass of wine which Welland has swallowed—against his expressed wish, observe, and merely to oblige you, Sir Richard. Its value is, say, sixpence. Excuse me, I do not of course refer to its real value, but to its recognised restaurant-value! Well, I happened the other day to be at a meeting of old women at the 'Beehive' in Spitalfields; there were some eighty or a hundred of them. With dim eyes and trembling fingers they were sewing garments for the boys who are to be sent out to Canada. Such feeble workers could not find employment elsewhere, but by liberal hearts a plan has been devised whereby many an aged one, past work, can earn a few pence. Twopence an hour is the pay. They are in the habit of meeting once a week for three hours, and thus earn sixpence. Many of these women, I may remark, are true Christians. I wondered how far such a sum would go, and how the poor old things spent it. One woman sixty-three years of age enlightened me. She was a feeble old creature, suffering from chronic rheumatism and a dislocated hip. When I questioned her she said—

"'I have difficulties indeed, but I tell my Father all. Sometimes, when I'm very hungry and have nothing to eat, I tell Him, and I know He hears me, for He takes the feeling away, and it only leaves me a little faint.'"

"'But how do you spend the sixpence that you earn here?' I asked."

"'Well, sir,' she said, 'sometimes, when very hard up, I spend part of it this way:—I buy a hap'orth o' tea, a hap'orth o' sugar, a hap'orth o' drippin', a hap'orth o' wood and a penn'orth o' bread. Sometimes when better off than usual I get a heap of coals at a time, perhaps quarter of a cwt., because I save a farthing by getting the whole quarter, an' that lasts me a long time, and wi' the farthing I mayhap treat myself to a drop o' milk. Sometimes, too, I buy my penn'orth o' wood from the coopers and chop it myself, for I can make it go further that way.'

"So, you see, Welland," continued Brisbane, "your glass of sherry would have gone a long way in the domestic calculations of a poor old woman, who very likely once had sons who were as fond of her and as proud of her, as you now are of your own mother."

"It is very sad that any class of human beings should be reduced to so low an ebb," returned the young man seriously.

"Yes, and it is very difficult," said Sir Richard, "to reduce one's mental action so as to fully understand the exact bearing of such minute monetary arrangements, especially for one who is accustomed to regard the subject of finance from a different standpoint."

"But the saddest thing of all to me, and the most difficult to understand," resumed Brisbane, "is the state of mind and feeling of those professing Christians, who, with ample means, give exceedingly little towards the alleviation of such distress, take little or no interest in the condition of the poor, and allow as much waste in their establishments as would, if turned to account, become streamlets of absolute wealth to many of the destitute."

This latter remark was a thrust which told pretty severely on the host—all the more so, perhaps, that he knew Brisbane did not intend it as a thrust at all, for he was utterly ignorant of the fact that his friend seldom gave anything away in charity, and even found it difficult to pay his way and make the two ends meet with his poor little five thousand a year —for, you see, if a man has to keep up a fairly large establishment,. with a town and country house, and have his yacht, and a good stable, and indulge in betting, and give frequent dinners, and take shootings in Scotland, and amuse himself with jewellery, etc., why, he must pay for it, you know!

"The greatest trouble of these poor women, I found," continued Brisbane, "is their rent, which varies from 2s. to 3s. a week for their little rooms, and it is a constant struggle with them to keep out of ' the House," so greatly dreaded by the respectable poor. One of them told me she had lately saved up a shilling with which she bought a pair of ' specs,' and was greatly comforted thereby, for they helped her fading eyesight. I thought at the time what a deal of good might be done and comfort given if people whose sight is changing would send their disused spectacles to the Home of Industry in Commercial Street, Spitalfields, for the poor. By the way, your sight must have changed more than once, Sir Richard! Have you not a pair or two of disused spectacles to spare ?"

"Well, yes, I have a pair or two, but they have gold rims, which would be rather incongruous on the noses of poor people, don't you think ?"

"Oh! by no means. We could manage to convert the rims into blue steel, and leave something over for sugar and tea."

"Well, I'll send them," said Sir Richard with a laugh. "By the way, you mentioned a plan whereby those poor women were enabled to do useful work, although too old for much. What plan might that be ?"

"It is a very simple plan," answered Brisbane, "and consists chiefly in the work being apportioned according to ability. Worn garments and odds and ends of stuff are sent to the Beehive from all parts of the country by sympathising friends. These are heaped together in one corner of the room where the poor old things work. Down before this mass of stuff are set certain of the company who have large constructive powers. These skilfully contrive, cut out, alter, and piece together all kinds of clothing, including the house slippers and Glengarry caps worn by the little rescued boys. Even handkerchiefs and babies' long frocks are conjured out of a petticoat or muslin lining! The work, thus selected and arranged, is put into the hands of those who, though not skilful in originating, have the plodding patience to carry out the designs of the more ingenious, and so garments are produced to cover the shivering limbs of any destitute child that may enter the Refuge as well as to complete the outfits of the little emigrants."

"Well, Brisbane, I freely confess," said Sir Richard, " that you have roused a degree of interest in poor old women which I never felt before, and it does seem to me that we might do a good deal more for them with our mere superfluities and cast-off clothing. Do the old women receive any food on these working nights besides the pence they earn ?"

" No, I am sorry to say they do not—at least not usually. You see it takes a hundred or more six-pences every Monday merely to keep that sewing-class going, and more than once there has been a talk of closing it for want of funds, but the poor creatures have pleaded so pitifully that they might still be allowed to attend, even though they should work at *half-price*, that it has been hitherto continued. You see it is a matter of no small moment for those women merely to spend three hours in a room with a good fire, besides which they delight in the hymns and prayers and the loving counsel and comfort they receive. It enables them to go out into the cold, even though hungry, with more heart

and trust in God as they limp slowly back again to
their fireless grates and bare cupboards.

"The day on which I visited the place I could
not bear the thought of this, so I gave a sovereign
to let them have a good meal. This sufficed. Large
kettles are always kept in readiness for such occasions. These were put on immediately by the
matron. The elder girls in training on the floor
above set to work to cut thick slices of bread and
butter, the tea urns were soon brought down, and in
twenty minutes I had the satisfaction of seeing the
whole hundred eating heartily and enjoying a hot
meal. My own soul was fed, too—for the words
came to me, 'I was an hungered and ye gave me
meat,' and one old woman, sitting near me, said, 'I
have a long walk home, and have been casting over
in my mind all the afternoon whether I could spare
a penny for a cup of tea on the way. How good the
Lord is to send this!'"

With large, round, glittering eyes and parted lips,
and heightened colour and varying expression, sat
little Di Brandon at her father's elbow, almost
motionless, her little hands clasped tight, and uttering never a word, but gazing intently at the speakers
and drinking it all in, while sorrow, surprise, sympathy, indignation, and intense pity stirred her little
heart to its very centre.

In the nursery she retailed it all over, with an

eager face and rapid commentary, to the sympathetic
Mrs. Screwbury, and finally, in bed, presided over
millions of old women who made up mountains of
old garments, devoured fields of buttered bread, and
drank oceans of steaming tea !

CHAPTER XII.

SAMMY TWITTER'S FALL.

WE must turn now to Samuel Twitter, senior. That genial old man was busy one morning in the nursery, amusing little Mita, who had by that time attained to what we may style the dawn-of-intelligence period of life, and was what Mrs. Loper, Mr. Crackaby, and Mr. Stickler called "engaging."

"Mariar!" shouted Mr. Twitter to his amiable spouse, who was finishing her toilet in the adjoining room. "She's makin' faces at me—yes, she's actually attempting to laugh!"

"The darling!" came from the next room, in emphatic tones.

"Mariar!"

"Well, dear."

"Is Sammy down in the parlour?"

"I don't know. Why?"

"Because he's not in his room—tumti-iddidy-too-too—you charming thing!"

It must be understood that the latter part of this

sentence had reference to the baby, not to Mrs. Twitter.

Having expended his affections and all his spare time on Mita,—who, to do her justice, made faces enough at him to repay his attentions in full,— Mr. Twitter descended to the breakfast parlour and asked the domestic if she had seen Sammy yet.

"No, sir, I hain't."

"Are you sure he's not in his room?"

"Well, no, sir, but I knocked twice and got no answer."

"Very odd; Sammy didn't use to be late, nor to' sleep so soundly," said Mr. Twitter, ascending to the attic of his eldest son.

Obtaining no reply to his knock, he opened the door and found that the room was empty. More than that, he discovered, to his surprise and alarm, that Sammy's bed was unruffled, so that Sammy himself must have slept elsewhere!

In silent consternation the father descended to his bedroom and said, "Mariar, Sammy's gone!"

"Dead!" exclaimed Mrs. Twitter with a look of horror.

"No, no; not dead, but gone—gone out of the house. Did not sleep in it last night, apparently."

Poor Mrs. Twitter sank into a chair and gazed at her husband with a stricken face.

Up to that date the family had prospered steadily,

and, may we not add, deservedly; their children having been trained in the knowledge of God, their duties having been conscientiously discharged, their sympathies with suffering humanity encouraged, and their general principles carried into practical effect. The consequence was that they were a well-ordered and loving family. There are many such in our land—families which are guided by the Spirit and the Word of God. The sudden disappearance, therefore, of the eldest son of the Twitter family was not an event to be taken lightly, for he had never slept out of his own particular bed without the distinct knowledge of his father and mother since he was born, and his appearance at the breakfast-table had been hitherto as certain as the rising of the sun or the winding of the eight-day clock by his father every Saturday night.

In addition to all this, Sammy was of an amiable disposition, and had been trustworthy, so that when he came to the years of discretion—which his father had fixed at fifteen—he was allowed a latch-key, as he had frequently to work at his employer's books till a latish hour,—sometimes eleven o'clock—after the family, including the domestic, had gone to rest.

"Now, Samuel," said Mrs. Twitter, with a slight return of her wonted energy, "there can be only two explanations of this. Either the dear boy has met with an accident, or—"

L

"Well, Mariar, why do you pause?"

"Because it seems so absurd to think of, much more to talk of, his going wrong or running away! The first thing I've got to do, Samuel, is to go to the police-office, report the case, and hear what they have to advise."

"The very thing I was thinking of, Mariar; but don't it strike you it might be better that *I* should go to the station?"

"No, Samuel, the station is near. I can do that, while you take a cab, go straight away to his office and find out at what hour he left. Now, go; we have not a moment to lose. Mary" (this was the next in order to Sammy) "will look after the children's breakfast. Make haste!"

Mr. Twitter made haste—made it so fast that he made too much of it, over-shot the mark, and went down-stairs head foremost, saluting the front door with a rap that threw that of the postman entirely into the shade. But Twitter was a springy as well as an athletic man. He arose undamaged, made no remark to his more than astonished children, and went his way.

Mrs. Twitter immediately followed her husband's example in a less violent and eccentric manner. The superintendent of police received her with that affable display of grave good-will which is a characteristic of the force. He listened with patient attention to the rather incoherent tale which she told with much agitation—unbosoming herself to this officer to a quite unnecessary extent as to private feelings and opinions, and, somehow, feeling as if he were a trusted and confidential friend though he was an absolute stranger—such is the wonderful influence of Power in self-possessed repose, over Weakness in distressful uncertainty!

Having heard all that the good lady had to say, with scarcely a word of interruption; having put a few pertinent and relevant questions and noted the replies, the superintendent advised Mrs. Twitter to calm herself, for that it would soon be " all right;" to return home, and abide the issue of his exertions; to make herself as easy in the circumstances as possible, and, finally, sent her away with the first ray of comfort that had entered her heart since the news of Sammy's disappearance had burst upon her like a thunderclap.

" What a thing it is," she muttered to herself on her way home, " to put things into the hands of a *man !*—one you can feel sure will do everything sensibly and well, and without fuss." The good lady meant no disparagement to her sex by this— far from it; she referred to a manly man as compared with an unmanly one, and she thought, for one moment, rather disparagingly about the salute which her Samuel's bald pate had given to the door that morning.   Probably she failed to think of the fussy manner in which she herself had assaulted the superintendent of police, for it is said that people seldom see themselves !

But Mrs. Twitter was by no means bitter in her thoughts, and her conscience twitted her a little for having perhaps done Samuel a slight injustice.

Indeed she *had* done him injustice, for that estimable little man went about his inquiries after the lost Sammy with a lump as big as a walnut on the top of his head, and with a degree of persistent energy that might have made the superintendent himself envious.

"Not been at the office for two days, sir !" exclaimed Mr. Twitter, repeating—in surprised indignation, for he could not believe it—the words of Sammy's employer, who was a merchant in the hardware line.

"No, sir," said the hardware man, whose face seemed as hard as his ware.

"Do—you—mean—to—tell—me," said Twitter, with deliberate solemnity, "that my son Samuel has not been in this office for *two days?*"

"That is precisely what I mean to tell you," returned the hardware man, "and I mean to tell you, moreover, that your son has been very irregular of late in his attendance, and that on more than one occasion he has come here drunk."

"Drunk!" repeated Twitter, almost in a shout.

"Yes, sir, drunk—intoxicated."

The hardware man seemed at that moment to Mr. Twitter the hardest-ware man that ever confronted him. He stood for some moments aghast and speechless.

"Are you aware, sir," he said at last, in impressive tones, "that my son Samuel wears the blue ribbon?"

The hardware man inquired, with an expression of affected surprise, what that had to do with the question; and further, gave it as his opinion that a bit of blue ribbon was no better than a bit of red or green ribbon if it had not something better behind it.

This latter remark, although by no means meant to soothe, had the effect of reducing Mr. Twitter to a condition of sudden humility.

"There, sir," said he, "I entirely agree with you, but I had believed—indeed it seems to me almost ·impossible to believe otherwise—that my poor boy had religious principle behind his blue ribbon."

This was said in such a meek tone, and with such a wo-begone look—as the conviction began to dawn that Sammy was not immaculate—that the hardware man began visibly to soften, and at last a confidential talk was established, in which was revealed such a series of irregularities on the part of the erring son, that the poor father's heart was crushed, for the time, and, as it were, trodden in the dust. In his extremity, he looked up to God and found relief in rolling his care upon Him.

As he slowly recovered from the shock, Twitter's brain resumed its wonted activity.

"You have a number of clerks, I believe?" he suddenly asked the hardware man.

"Yes, I have—four of them."

"Would you object to taking me through your warehouse, as if to show it to me, and allow me to look at your clerks?"

"Certainly not. Come along."

On entering, they found one tying up a parcel, one writing busily, one reading a book, and one balancing a ruler on his nose. The latter, on being thus caught in the act, gave a short laugh, returned the ruler to its place, and quietly went on with his work. The reader of the book started, endeavoured to conceal the volume, in which effort he was unsuccessful, and became very red in the face as he resumed his pen.

The employer took no notice, and Mr. Twitter looked very hard at the hardware in the distant end of the warehouse, just over the desk at which the clerks sat. He made a few undertoned remarks to the master, and then, crossing over to the desk, said:—

"Mr. Dobbs, may I have the pleasure of a few minutes' conversation with you outside?"

"C—certainly, sir," replied Dobbs, rising with a redder face than ever, and putting on his hat.

"Will you be so good as to tell me, Mr. Dobbs," said Twitter, in a quiet but very decided way when outside, "where my son Samuel Twitter spent last night?"

Twitter looked steadily in the clerk's eyes as he put this question. He was making a bold stroke for success as an amateur detective, and, as is frequently the result of bold strokes, he succeeded.

"Eh! you—your—y—son S—Samuel," stammered Dobbs, looking at Twitter's breast-pin, and then at the ground, while varying expressions of guilty shame and defiance flitted across his face.

He had a heavy, somewhat sulky face, with indecision of character stamped on it. Mr. Twitter saw that and took advantage of the latter quality.

"My poor boy," he said, "don't attempt to deceive me. You are guilty, and you know it. Stay, don't speak yet. I have no wish to injure you. On the contrary, I pray God to bless and save you; but what I want with you at this moment is to learn where my dear boy is. If you tell me, no further notice shall be taken of this matter, I assure you."

"Does—does—*he* know anything about this?' asked Dobbs, glancing in the direction of the warehouse of the hardware man.

"No, nothing of your having led Sammy astray,

if that's what you mean,—at least, not from me, and you may depend on it he shall hear nothing, if you only confide in me. Of course he may have his suspicions."

"Well, sir," said Dobbs, with a sigh of relief, "he's in my lodgings."

Having ascertained the address of the lodgings, the poor father called a cab and soon stood by the side of a bed on which his son Sammy lay sprawling in the helpless attitude in which he had fallen down the night before, after a season of drunken riot. He was in a heavy sleep, with his still inno- cent-looking features tinged with the first blight of dissipation.

"Sammy," said the father, in a husky voice, as he shook him gently by the arm; but the poor boy made no answer—even a roughish shake failed to draw from him more than the grumbled desire, "let me alone."

"Oh! God spare and save him!" murmured the father, in a still husky voice, as he fell on his knees by the bedside and prayed—prayed as though his heart were breaking, while the object of his prayer lay apparently unconscious through it all.

He rose, and was standing by the bedside, uncer- tain how to act, when a heavy tread was heard on the landing, the door was thrown open, and the landlady, announcing "a gentleman, sir," ushered in the superintendent of police, who looked at Mr. Twitter with a slight expression of surprise.

" You are here before me, I see, sir," he said.

" Yes, but how did you come to find out that he was here ? "

" Well, I had not much difficulty. You see it is part of our duty to keep our eyes open," replied the superintendent, with a peculiar smile, " and I have on several occasions observed your son entering this house with a companion in a condition which did not quite harmonise with his blue ribbon, so, after your good lady explained the matter to me this morning I came straight here."

" Thank you—thank you. It is *very* kind. I— you—it could not have been better managed."

Mr. Twitter stopped and looked helplessly at the figure on the bed.

" Perhaps," said the superintendent, with much delicacy of feeling, " you would prefer to be alone with your boy when he awakes. If I can be of any further use to you, you know where to find me. Good-day, sir."

Without waiting for a reply the considerate superintendent left the room.

" Oh ! Sammy, Sammy, speak to me, my dear boy—speak to your old father ! " he cried, turning again to the bed and kneeling beside it ; but the drunken sleeper did not move.

Rising hastily he went to the door and called the landlady.

"I'll go home, missis," he said, "and send the poor lad's mother to him."

"Very well, sir, I'll look well after 'im till she comes."

Twitter was gone in a moment, and the old landlady returned to her lodger's room. There, to her surprise, she found Sammy up and hastily pulling on his boots.

In truth he had been only shamming sleep, and, although still very drunk, was quite capable of looking after himself. He had indeed been asleep when his father's entrance awoke him, but a feeling of intense shame had induced him to remain quite still, and then, having commenced with this unspoken lie, he felt constrained to carry it out. But the thought of facing his mother he could not bear, for the boy had a sensitive spirit and was keenly alive to the terrible fall he had made. At the same time he was too cowardly to face the consequences. Dressing himself as well as he could, he rushed from the house in spite of the earnest entreaties of the old landlady, so that when the distracted mother came to embrace and forgive her erring child she found that he had fled.

Plunging into the crowded thoroughfares of the great city, and walking swiftly along without aim or

desire, eaten up with shame, and rendered desperate by remorse, the now reckless youth sought
refuge in a low grog-shop, and called for a glass
of beer.

" Well, I say, you're com—comin' it raither
strong, ain't you, young feller?" said a voice at his
elbow.

He looked up hastily, and saw a blear-eyed youth
in a state of drivelling intoxication, staring at him
with the expression of an idiot.

" That's no business of yours," replied Sam Twitter, sharply.

" Well, thash true, 'tain't no b—busnish o' mine.
I—I 'm pretty far gone m'self, I allow ; but I ain't
quite got the l—length o' drinkin' in a p—pub,
k 'ouse wi' th' bl—blue ribb'n on."

The fallen lad glanced at his breast. There it
was,—forgotten, desecrated ! He tore it fiercely
from his button-hole, amid the laughter of the by-
standers—most of whom were women of the lowest
grade—and dashed it on the floor.

" Thash right—you 're a berrer feller than I took
you for," said the sot at his elbow.

To avoid further attention Sammy took his beer
into a dark corner and was quickly forgotten.

He had not been seated more than a few minutes
when the door opened, and a man with a mild, gentle,
yet manly face entered.

" Have a glass, ol' feller ?" said the sot, the instant he caught sight of him.

"Thank you, no—not to-day," replied John Sea· ward, for it was our city missionary on what he sometimes called a fishing excursion—fishing for men! "I have come to give *you* a glass to-day, friends."

"Well, that's friendly," said a gruff voice in a secluded box, out of which next minute staggered Ned Frog. "Come, what is 't to be, old man ?"

" A looking-glass," replied the missionary, picking out a tract from the bundle he held in his hand and offering it to the ex-prize-fighter. "But the tract is not the glass I speak of, friend: here it is, in the Word of that God who made us all—made the throats that swallow the drink, and the brains that reel under it."

Here he read from a small Bible, "' But they also have erred through wine, and through strong drink are out of the way.'"

"Bah!" said Ned, flinging the tract on the floor, and exclaiming as he left the place with a swing; "I don't drink wine, old man; can't afford anything better than beer, though sometimes, when I'm in luck, I have a drop of Old Tom."

There was a great burst of ribald laughter at this, and numerous were the witticisms perpetrated at the expense of the missionary, but he took no notice of these for a time, occupying himself merely in turning over the leaves of his Bible. When there was a lull he said :—

"Now, dear sisters" (turning to the women who, with a more or less drunken aspect and slatternly air, were staring at him), "for sisters of mine you are, having been made by the same Heavenly Father; I won't offer you another glass,—not even a look-ing-glass,—for the one I have already held up to you will do, if God's Holy Spirit opens your eyes to see yourselves in it; but I'll give you a better object to look at. It is a Saviour—one who is able to save you from the drink, and from sin in every form. You know His name well, most of you; it is Jesus, and that name means Saviour, for He came to save His people from their sins."

At this point he was interrupted by one of the women, who seemed bent on keeping up the spirit of banter with which they had begun. She asked him with a leer if he had got a wife.

"No," he said, "but I have got a great respect and love for women, because I've got a mother, and if ever there was a woman on the face of this earth that deserves the love of a son, that woman is my mother. Sister," he added, turning to one of those who sat on a bench near him with a thin, puny, curly-haired boy wrapped up in her ragged shawl, "the best prayer that I could offer up for you—and

I *do* offer it—is, that the little chap in your arms may grow up to bless his mother as heartily as I bless mine, but that can never be so long as you love the strong drink and refuse the Saviour."

At that moment a loud cry was heard outside. They all rose and ran to the door, where a woman, in the lowest depths of depravity, with her eyes bloodshot, her hair tumbling about her half-naked shoulders, and her ragged garments draggled and wet, had fallen in her efforts to enter the public-house to obtain more of the poison which had already almost destroyed her. She had cut her forehead, and the blood flowed freely over her face as the missionary lifted her. He was a powerful man, and could take her up tenderly and with ease. She was not much hurt, however. After Seaward had bandaged the cut with his own handkerchief she professed to be much better.

This little incident completed the good influence which the missionary's words and manner had previously commenced. Most of the women began to weep as they listened to the words of love, encouragement, and hope addressed to them. A few of course remained obdurate, though not unimpressed.

All this time young Sam Twitter remained in his dark corner, with his head resting on his arms to prevent his being recognised. Well did he know John Seaward, and well did Seaward know him, for the missionary had long been a fellow-worker with Mrs. Twitter in George Yard and at the Home of Industry. The boy was very anxious to escape Seaward's observation. This was not a difficult matter. When the missionary left, after distributing his tracts, Sammy rose up and sought to hide himself--from himself, had that been possible—in the lowest slums of London.

CHAPTER XIII.

TELLS OF SOME CURIOUS AND VIGOROUS PECULIARITIES OF THE LOWER ORDERS.

Now it must not be supposed that Mrs. Frog, having provided for her baby and got rid of it, remained thereafter quite indifferent to it. On the contrary, she felt the blank more than she had expected, and her motherly heart began to yearn for it powerfully.

To gratify this yearning to some extent, she got into the habit of paying frequent visits, sometimes by night and sometimes by day, to the street in which Samuel Twitter lived, and tried to see her baby through the stone walls of the house! Her eyes being weak, as well as her imagination, she failed in this effort, but the mere sight of the house where little Matty was, sufficed to calm her maternal yearnings in some slight degree.

By the way, that name reminds us of our having omitted to mention that baby Frog's real name was Matilda, and her pet name Matty, so that the name

of Mita, fixed on by the Twitters, was not so wide
of the mark as it might have been.

One night Mrs. Frog, feeling the yearning strong
upon her, put on her bonnet and shawl—that is to
say, the bundle of dirty silk, pasteboard, and flowers
which represented the one, and the soiled tartan rag
that did duty for the other.

" Where are ye off to, old woman ?" asked Ned,
who, having been recently successful in some little
"job, " was in high good humour.

" I 'm goin' round to see Mrs. Tibbs, Ned. D' you
want me ?"

" No, on'y I 'm goin' that way too, so we 'll walk
together."

Mrs. Frog, we regret to say, was not particular as
to the matter of truth. She had no intention of
going near Mrs. Tibbs, but, having committed herself, made a virtue of necessity, and resolved to pay
that lady a visit.

The conversation by the way was not sufficiently
interesting to be worthy of record. Arrived at
Twitter's street an idea struck Mrs. Frog.

" Ned," said she, " I 'm tired."

" Well, old girl, you 'd better cut home."

" I think I will, Ned, but first I 'll sit down on
this step to rest a bit."

" All right, old girl," said Ned, who would have
said the same words if she had proposed to stand

on her head on the step—so easy was he in his
mind as to how his wife spent her time; "if you sit
for half-an-hour or so I'll be back to see you 'ome
again. I'm on'y goin' to Bundle's shop for a bit
o' baccy. Ain't I purlite now? Don't it mind you
of the courtin' days?"

"Ah! Ned," exclaimed the wife, while a sudden
gush of memory brought back the days when he
was handsome and kind,—but Ned was gone, and
the slightly thawed spring froze up again.

She sat down on the cold step of a door which
happened to be somewhat in the shade, and gazed at
the opposite windows. There was a light in one of
them. She knew it well. She had often watched
the shadows that crossed the blind after the gas
was lighted, and once she had seen some one carrying something which looked like a baby! It might
have been a bundle of soiled linen, or undarned
socks, but it *might* have been Matty, and the thought
sent a thrill to the forlorn creature's heart.

On the present occasion she was highly favoured,
for, soon after Ned had left, the shadows came again
on the blind, and came so near it as to be distinctly
visible. Yes, there could be no doubt now, it *was*
a baby, and as there was only one baby in that
house it followed that the baby was *her* baby—little
Matty! Here was something to carry home with her,
and think over and dream about. But there was

more in store for her. The baby, to judge from the shadowy action of its fat limbs on the blind, became what she called obstropolous. More than that, it yelled, and its mother heard the yell—faintly, it is true, but sufficiently to send a thrill of joy to her longing heart.

Then a sudden fear came over her. What if it was ill, and they were trying to soothe it to rest! How much better *she* could do that if she only had the baby!

"Oh! fool that I was to part with her!" she murmured, "but no. It was best. She would surely have bin dead by this time."

The sound of the little voice, however, had roused such a tempest of longing in Mrs. Frog's heart, that, under an irresistible impulse, she ran across the road and rang the bell. The door was promptly opened by Mrs. Twitter's domestic.

"Is—is the baby well?" stammered Mrs. Frog, scarce knowing what she said.

" *You 've* nothink to do wi' the baby that I knows on," returned Mrs. Twitter's domestic, who was not quite so polite as her mistress.

" No, honey," said Mrs. Frog in a wheedling tone, rendered almost desperate by the sudden necessity for instant invention, " but the doctor said I was to ask if baby had got over it, or if 'e was to send round the—the—I forget its name—at once."

"What doctor sent you?" asked Mrs. Twitter, who had come out of the parlour on hearing the voices through the doorway, and with her came a clear and distinct yell which Mrs. Frog treasured up in her thinly clad but warm bosom, as though it had been a strain from Paradise. "There must surely be some mistake, my good woman, for my baby is quite well."

"Oh! thank you, thank you—yes, there must have been some mistake," said Mrs. Frog, scarce able to restrain a laugh of joy at the success of her scheme, as she retired precipitately from the door and hurried away.

She did not go far, however, but, on hearing the door shut, turned back and took up her position again on the doorstep.

Poor Mrs. Frog had been hardened and saddened by sorrow, and suffering, and poverty, and bad treatment; nevertheless she was probably one of the happiest women in London just then.

"'*My* baby,'" she said, quoting part of Mrs. Twitter's remarks with a sarcastic laugh, "no, madam, she's not *your* baby *yet!*"

As she sat reflecting on this agreeable fact, a heavy step was heard approaching. It was too slow for that of Ned. She knew it well—a policeman!

There are hard-hearted policemen in the force—

not many, indeed, but nothing is perfect in this world, and there are a *few* hard-hearted policemen. He who approached was one of these.

"Move on," he said in a stern voice.

"Please, sir, I'm tired. On'y restin' a bit while I wait for my 'usband," pleaded Mrs. Frog.

"Come, move on," repeated the unyielding constable in a tone that there was no disputing. Indeed it was so strong that it reached the ears of Ned Frog himself, who chanced to come round the corner at the moment and saw the policeman, as he imagined, maltreating his wife.

Ned was a man who, while he claimed and exercised the right to treat his own wife as he pleased, was exceedingly jealous of the interference of others with his privileges. He advanced, therefore, at once, and planted his practised knuckles on the policeman's forehead with such power that the unfortunate limb of the law rolled over in one direction and his helmet in another.

As every one knows, the police sometimes suffer severely at the hands of roughs, and on this occasion that truth was verified, but the policeman who had been knocked down by this prize-fighter was by no means a feeble member of the force. Recovering from his astonishment in a moment, he sprang up and grappled with Ned Frog in such a manner as to convince that worthy he had "his work cut out for him." The tussle that ensued was tremendous, and Mrs. Frog retired into a doorway to enjoy it in safety. But it was brief. Before either wrestler could claim the victory, a brother constable came up, and Ned was secured and borne away to a not unfamiliar cell before he could enjoy even one pipe of the " baccy " which he had purchased.

Thus it came to pass, that when a certain comrade expected to find Ned Frog at a certain mansion in the West-end, prepared with a set of peculiar tools for a certain purpose, Ned was in the enjoyment of board and lodging at Her Majesty's expense.

The comrade, however, not being aware of Ned's incarceration, and believing, no doubt, that there was honour among thieves, was true to his day and hour. He had been engaged down somewhere in the country on business, and came up by express train for this particular job; hence his ignorance as to his partner's fate.

But this burglar was not a man to be easily balked in his purpose.

"Ned must be ill, or got a haccident o' some sort," he said to a very little but sharp boy who was to assist in the job. "Howsever, you an' me'll go at it alone, Sniveller."

"Wery good, Bunky," replied Sniveller, "'ow is it to be? By the winder, through the door, down the chimbly, up the spout—or wot?"

"The larder windy, my boy."

"Sorry for that," said Sniveller.

"Why?"

"'Cause it *is* so 'ard to go past the nice things an' smell 'em all without darin' to touch 'em till I lets you in. Couldn't you let me 'ave a feed first?"

"Unpossible," said the burglar.

"Wery good," returned the boy, with a sigh of resignation.

Now, while these two were whispering to each other in a box of an adjoining tavern, three police constables were making themselves at home in the premises of Sir Richard Brandon. One of these was No. 666.

It is not quite certain, even to this day, how and where these men were stationed, for their proceedings —though not deeds of evil—were done in the dark, at least in darkness which was rendered visible only now and then by bull's-eye lanterns. The only thing that was absolutely clear to the butler, Mr. Thomas Balls, was, that the mansion was given over entirely to the triumvirate to be dealt with as they thought fit.

Of course they did not know when the burglars would come, nor the particular point of the mansion where the assault would be delivered; therefore No. 666 laid his plans like a wise general, posted his troops where there was most likelihood of their being required, and kept himself in reserve for contingencies.

About that "wee short hour" of which the poet Burns writes, a small boy was lifted by a large man to the sill of the small window which lighted Sir Richard Brandon's pantry. To the surprise of the small boy, he found the window unfastened.

"They've bin an' forgot it!" he whispered.

"Git in," was the curt reply.

Sniveller got in, dropped to his extreme length from the sill, let go his hold, and came down lightly on the floor—not so lightly, however, but that a wooden stool placed there was overturned, and, falling against a blue plate, broke it with a crash.

Sniveller became as one petrified, and remained so for a considerable time, till he imagined all danger from sleepers having been awakened was over. He also thought of thieving cats, and thanked them mentally. He likewise became aware of the near presence of pastry. The smell was delicious, but a sense of duty restrained him.

No. 666 smiled to himself to think how well his trap had acted, but the smile was lost in darkness.

Meanwhile, the chief operator, Bunky, went round to the back door. Sniveller, who had been taught the geography of the mansion from a well-executed plan, proceeded to the same door inside. Giles could have patted his little head as he carefully drew back the bolts and turned the key. Another moment, and Bunky, on his stocking soles, stood within the mansion.

Yet another moment, and Bunky was enjoying an embrace that squeezed most of the wind out of his body, strong though he was, for No. 666 was apt to forget his excessive power when duty constrained him to act with promptitude.

"Now, then, show a light," said Giles, quietly.

Two bull's-eyes flashed out their rich beams at the word, and lit up a tableau of three, in attitudes faintly resembling those of the Laocoon, without the serpents.

"Fetch the bracelets," said Giles.

At these words the bull's-eyes converged, and Sniveller, bolting through the open door, vanished— he was never heard of more !

Then followed two sharp *clicks*, succeeded by a sigh of relief as No. 666 relaxed his arms.

"You needn't rouse the household unless you feel inclined, my man," said Giles to Bunky in a low voice.

Bunky did *not* feel inclined. He thought it better, on the whole, to let the sleeping dogs lie, and wisely submitted to inevitable fate. He was marched off to jail, while one of the constables remained behind to see the house made safe, and acquaint Sir Richard of his deliverance from the threatened danger.

Referring to this matter on the following day in the servants' hall, Thomas Balls filled a foaming tankard of ginger-beer—for, strange to say, he was an abstainer, though a butler—and proposed, in a highly eulogistic speech, the health and prosperity of that admirable body of men, the Metropolitan Police, with which toast he begged to couple the name of No. 666 !

CHAPTER XIV.

NO. 666 OFF DUTY.

SOME time after the attempt made upon Sir
Richard Brandon's house, Giles Scott was seated at
his own fireside, helmet and truncheon laid aside,
uniform taken off, and a free and easy suit of plain
clothes put on.

His pretty wife sat beside him darning a pair of
very large socks. The juvenile policeman, and the
incorrigible criminal were sound asleep in their re-
spective cribs, the one under the print of the Queen,
the other under that of Sir Robert Peel. Giles was
studying a small book of instructions as to the
duties of police constables, and pretty Molly was
commenting on the same, for she possessed that
charming quality of mind and heart which induces
the possessor to take a sympathetic and lively
interest in whatever may happen to be going on.

"They expect pretty hard work of you, Giles,"
remarked Molly with a sigh, as she thought of the
prolonged hours of absence from home, and the
frequent night duty.

"Why, Moll, you wouldn't have me wish for easy work at my time of life, would you?" replied the policeman, looking up from his little book with an amused smile. "Somebody must always be taking a heavy lift of the hard work of this world, and if a big hulking fellow like me in the prime o' life don't do it, who will?"

"True, Giles, but surely you won't deny me the small privilege of wishing that you had a *little* less to do, and a *little* more time with your family. You men, —especially you Scotchmen—are such an argumentative set, that a poor woman can't open her lips to say a word, but you pounce upon it and make an argument of it."

"Now Molly, there you go again, assuming my duties! Why do you take me up so sharp? Isn't taking-up the special privilege of the police?"

"Am I not entitled," said Molly, ignoring her husband's question, "to express regret that your work should include coming home now and then with scratched cheeks, and swelled noses, and black eyes?"

"Come now," returned Giles, "you must admit that I have fewer of these discomforts than most men of the force, owing, no doubt, to little men being unable to reach so high—and, d' you know, it is the little men who do most damage in life; they 're such a pugnacious and perverse generation! As to swelled noses, these are the fortune of war, at least of civil war like ours—and black eyes, why, my eyes are black by nature. If they were of a heavenly blue like yours, Molly, you might have some ground for complaint when they are blackened."

"And then there is such dreadful tear and wear of clothes," continued Molly; "just look at that, now!" She held up to view a sock with a hole in its heel large enough to let an orange through.

"Why, Molly, do you expect that I can walk the streets of London from early morning till late at night, protect life and property, and preserve public tranquillity, as this little book puts it, besides engaging in numerous scuffles and street rows without making a hole or two in my socks?"

"Ah! Giles, if you had only brain enough to take in a simple idea! it's not the making of holes that I complain of. It is the making of such awfully big ones before changing your socks! There now, don't let us get on domestic matters. You have no head for these, but tell me something about your little book. I am specially interested in it, you see, because the small policeman in the crib over there puts endless questions about his duties which I am quite unable to answer, and, you know, it is a good thing for a child to grow up with the idea that father and mother know everything."

"Just so, Molly. I hope you'll tell your little

recruit that the first and foremost duty of a good policeman is to obey orders. Let me see, then, if I can enlighten you a bit."

"But tell me first, Giles—for I really want to know—how many are there of you altogether, and when was the force established on its present footing, and who began it, and—in short, all about it. It's *so* nice to have you for once in a way for a quiet chat like this."

"You have laid down enough of heads, Molly, to serve for the foundation of a small volume. However, I'll give it you hot, since you wish it, and I'll begin at the end instead of the beginning. What would you say, now, to an army of eleven thousand men?"

"I would say it was a very large one, though I don't pretend to much knowledge about the size of armies," said Molly, commencing to another hole about the size of a turnip.

" Well, that, in round numbers, is the strength of the Metropolitan Police force at the present time— and not a man too much, let me tell you, for what with occasional illnesses and accidents, men employed on special duty, and men off duty—as I am just now—the actual available strength of the force at any moment is considerably below that number. Yes, it is a goodly army of picked and stalwart men (no self-praise intended), but, then, consider what we have to do."

"We have to guard and keep in order the population of the biggest city in the world ; a population greater than that of the whole of Scotland."

"Oh ! of course, you are sure to go to Scotland for your illustrations, as if there was no such place as England in the world," quietly remarked Molly, with a curl of her pretty lip.

"Ah ! Molly, dear, you are unjust. It is true I go to Scotland for an illustration, but didn't I come to England for a wife ? Now, don't go frowning at that hole as if it couldn't be bridged over."

"It is the worst hole you ever made," said the despairing wife, holding it up to view.

"You make a worsted hole of it then, Moll, and it 'll be all right. Besides, you don't speak truth, for I once made a worse hole in your heart."

"You never did, sir. Go on with your stupid illustrations," said Molly.

"Well, then, let me see—where was I ? "

"In Scotland, of course !"

"Ah, yes. The population of all Scotland is under four millions, and that of London—that is, of the area embraced in the Metropolitan Police District, is estimated at above four million seven hundred thousand—in round numbers. Of course I give it you all in round numbers."

"I don't mind how round the numbers are, Giles,

so long as they're all square," remarked the little wife with much simplicity.

"Well, just think of that number for our army to watch over; and that population—not all of it, you know, but part of it—succeeds in spite of us in committing, during one year, no fewer than 25,000 'Principal' offences such as murders, burglaries, robberies, thefts, and such-like. What they would accomplish if we were not ever on the watch I leave you to guess.

"Last year, for instance, 470 burglaries, as we style house-breaking by night, were committed in London. The wonder is that there are not more, when you consider the fact that the number of doors and windows found open by us at night during the twelve months was nearly 26,000. The total loss of property by theft during the year is estimated at about £100,000. Besides endeavouring to check crime of such magnitude, we had to search after above 15,000 persons who were reported lost and missing during the year, about 12,000 of whom were children."

"Oh! the *poor* darlings," said Molly, twisting her sympathetic eyebrows.

"Ay, and we found 7523 of these darlings," continued the practical Giles, and 720 of the adults. Of the rest some returned home or were found by their friends, but 154 adults and 23 children have been lost altogether. Then, we found within the twelve months 54 dead bodies which we had to take care of and have photographed for identification. During the same period (and remember that the record of every twelve months is much the same) we⁻ seized over 17,000 stray dogs and returned them to their owners or sent them to the Dogs' Home. We arrested over 18,000 persons for being drunk and disorderly. We inspected all the public vehicles and horses in London. We attended to 3527 accidents which occurred in the streets, 127 of which were fatal. We looked after more than 17,000 articles varying in value from 6d. to £1500, which were lost by a heedless public during the year, about 10,000 of which articles were restored to the owners. We had to regulate the street traffic; inspect common lodging-houses; attend the police and other courts to give evidence, and many other things which it would take me much too long to enumerate, and puzzle your pretty little head to take in."

"No, it wouldn't," said Molly, looking up with a bright expression; "I have a wonderful head for figures—especially for handsome manly figures! Go on, Giles."

"Then, look at what is expected of us," continued No. 666, not noticing the last remark. "We are told to exercise the greatest civility and affability towards every one—high and low, rich and poor. We are expected to show the utmost forbearance

N

under all circumstances; to take as much abuse and
as many blows as we can stand without inflicting
any in return; to be capable of answering almost
every question that an ignorant—not to say
arrogant—public may choose to put to us; to be
ready, single-handed and armed only with our
truncheons and the majesty of the law, to encoun-
ter burglars furnished with knives and revolvers;
to plunge into the midst of drunken maddened
crowds and make arrests in the teeth of tremendous
odds; to keep an eye upon strangers whose presence
may seem to be less desirable than their absence;
to stand any amount of unjust and ungenerous
criticism without a word of reply; to submit quietly
to the abhorrence and chaff of boys, labourers, cabmen, omnibus drivers, tramps, and fast young men;
to have a fair knowledge of the 'three R's' and a
smattering of law, so as to conduct ourselves with
propriety at fires, fairs, fights, and races, besides acting wisely as to mad dogs, German bands (which
are apt to produce mad *men*), organ-grinders, furious
drivers, and all other nuisances. In addition to all
which we must be men of good character, good
standing—as to inches—good proportions, physically,
and good sense. In short, we are expected to be—
and blamed if we are not—as near to a state of per-
fection as it is possible for mortal man to attain on
this side the grave, and all for the modest sum which

you are but too well aware is the extent of our income."

"Is one of the things expected of you," asked Molly, "to have an exceedingly high estimate of yourselves ?"

"Nay, Molly, don't you join the ranks of those who are against us. · It will be more than criminal if you do. You are aware that I am giving the opinion expressed by men of position who ought to know everything about the force. That we fulfil the conditions required of us not so badly is proved by the fact that last year, out of the whole 12,000 there were 215 officers and 1225 men who obtained rewards for zeal and activity, while only one man was discharged, and four men were fined or imprisoned. I speak not of number one—or, I should say No. 666. For myself I am ready to admit that I am the most insignificant of the force."

"O Giles! what a barefaced display of mock modesty !"

"Nay, Molly, I can prove it. Everything in this world goes by contrast, doesn't it ? Well, then, is there a man in the whole force except myself, I ask, whose wife is so bright and beautiful and good and sweet that she reduces him to mere insignificance by contrast ?"

"There's something in that, Giles," replied Molly with gravity, " but go on with your lecture."

"I've nothing more to say about the force," returned Giles; "if I have not said enough to convince you of our importance, and of the debt of gratitude that you and the public of London owe to us, you are past conviction, and—"

"You are wrong, Giles, as usual; I am never past conviction; you have only to take me before the police court in the morning, and any magistrate will at once convict me of stupidity for having married a Scotchman and a policeman!"

"I think it must be time to go on my beat, for you beat me hollow," said No. 666, consulting his watch.

"No, no, Giles, please sit still. It is not every day that I have such a chance of a chat with you."

"Such a chance of pitching into me, you mean," returned Giles. "However, before I go I would like to tell you just one or two facts regarding this great London itself, which needs so much guarding and such an army of guardians. You know that the Metropolitan District comprises all the parishes any portion of which are within 15 miles of Charing Cross—this area being 688 square miles. The rateable value of it is over twenty-six million eight hundred thousand pounds sterling. See, as you say you've a good head for *figures*, there's the sum on a bit of paper for you—£26,800,000.

During last year 26,170 new houses were built, forming 556 new streets and four new squares—the whole covering a length of 86 miles. The total number of new houses built during the last *ten* years within this area has been 162,525, extending over 500 miles of streets and squares!

"Stay, I can't stand it!" cried Molly, dropping her sock and putting her fingers in her ears.

" Why not, old girl ? "

" Because it is too much for me; why, even *your* figure is a mere nothing to such sums ! "

" Then," returned Giles, " you 've only got to stick me on to the end of them to make my information ten times more valuable."

"But are you quite sure that what you tell me is true, Giles ? "

" Quite sure, my girl—at least as sure as I am of the veracity of Colonel Henderson, who wrote the last Police Report."

At this point the chat was interrupted by the juvenile policeman in the crib under Sir Robert Peel. Whether it was the astounding information uttered in his sleepy presence, or the arduous nature of the duty required of him in dreams, we cannot tell, but certain it is that when No. 666 uttered the word "Report" there came a crash like the report of a great gun, and No. 2 of the A Division, having fallen overboard, was seen on the floor pommelling some imaginary criminal who stoutly refused to be captured.

Giles ran forward to the assistance of No. 2, as was his duty, and took him up in his arms. But No. 2 had awakened to the fact that he had hurt himself, and, notwithstanding the blandishments of his father, who swayed him about and put him on his broad shoulders, and raised his curly head to the ceiling, he refused for a long time to be comforted. At last he was subdued, and returned to the crib and the land of dreams.

"Now, Molly, I must really go," said Giles, putting on his uniform. "I hope No. 2 won't disturb you again. Good-bye, lass, for a few hours," he added, buckling his belt. "Here, look, do you see that little spot on the ceiling?"

"Yes,—well?" said Molly, looking up.

Giles took unfair advantage of her, stooped, and kissed the pretty little face, received a sounding slap on the back, and went out, to attend to his professional duties, with the profound gravity of an incapable magistrate.

There was a bright intelligent little street Arab on the opposite side of the way, who observed Giles with mingled feelings of admiration, envy, and hatred, as he strode sedately along the street like an imperturbable pillar. He knew No. 666 personally; had seen him under many and varied circumstances, and

had imagined him under many others—not unfre-
quently as hanging by the neck from a lamp post—
but never, even in the most daring flights of his
juvenile fancy, had he seen him as he has been
seen by the reader in the bosom of his poor but
happy home.

CHAPTER XV.

MRS FROG SINKS DEEPER AND DEEPER

"NOBODY cares," said poor Mrs. Frog, one raw afternoon in November, as she entered her miserable dwelling, where the main pieces of furniture were a rickety table, a broken chair, and a heap of straw, while the minor pieces were so insignificant as to be unworthy of mention. There was no fire in the grate, no bread in the cupboard, little fresh air in the room and less light, though there was a broken unlighted candle stuck in the mouth of a quart bottle which gave promise of light in the future— light enough at least to penetrate the November fog which had filled the room as if *it* had been en- dued with a pitying desire to throw a veil over such degradation and misery.

We say degradation, for Mrs. Frog had of late taken to "the bottle" as a last solace in her ex- treme misery, and the expression of her face, as she cowered on a low stool beside the empty grate and drew the shred of tartan shawl round her shivering form, showed all too clearly that she was at that time under its influence. She had been down to the river again, more than once, and had gazed into its dark waters until she had very nearly made up her mind to take the desperate leap, but God in mercy had hitherto interposed. At one time a policeman had passed with his weary "move on" —though sometimes he had not the heart to enforce his order. More frequently a little baby-face had looked up from the river with a smile, and sent her away to the well-known street where she would sit on the familiar door-step watching the shadows on the window-blind until cold and sorrow drove her to the gin-palace to seek for the miserable comfort to be found there.

Whatever that comfort might amount to, it did not last long, for, on the night of which we write, she had been to the palace, had got all the comfort that was to be had out of it, and returned to her desolate home more wretched than ever, to sit down, as we have seen, and murmur, almost fiercely, "Nobody cares!"

For a time she sat silent and motionless, while the deepening shadows gathered round her, as if they had united with all the rest to intensify the poor creature's woe.

Presently she began to mutter to herself aloud—

"What's the use o' your religion when it comes to this? What sort of religion is in the hearts of these (she pursed her lips, and paused for an expressive word, but found none), these rich folk in their silks and satins and broadcloth, with more than they can use, an' feedin' their pampered cats and dogs on what would be wealth to the likes o' me! Religion! bah!"

She stopped, for a Voice within her said as plainly as if it had spoken out: "Who gave you the sixpence the other day, and looked after you with a tender, pitying glance as you hurried away to the gin-shop without so much as stopping to say 'Thank you'? She wore silks, didn't she?"

"Ah, but there's not many like that," replied the poor woman, mentally, for the powers of good and evil were fighting fiercely within her just then.

"How do you know there are not many like that?" demanded the Voice.

"Well, but *all* the rich are not like that," said Mrs. Frog.

The Voice made no reply to that!

Again she sat silent for some time, save that a low moan escaped her occasionally, for she was very cold and very hungry, having spent the last few pence, which might have given her a meal, in drink, and the re-action of the poison helped to depress her. The evil spirit seemed to gain the mastery at this point, to judge from her muttered words.

"Nothing to eat, nothing to drink, no work to be

got, Hetty laid up in hospital, Ned in prison, Bobby gone to he bad again instead of goin' to Canada, and—nobody cares!"

"What about baby?" asked the Voice.

This time it was Mrs. Frog's turn to make no reply!

In a few minutes she seemed to become desperate, for, rising hastily, she went out, shut the door with a bang, locked it, and set out on the familiar journey to the gin-shop.

She had not far to go. It was at the corner. If it had not been at that corner, there was one to be found at the next—and the next—and the next again, and so on all round; so that, rushing *past*— as people sometimes do when endeavouring to avoid a danger—would have been of little or no avail in this case. But there was a very potent influence of a negative kind in her favour. She had no money! Recollecting this when she had nearly reached the door, she turned aside, and ran swiftly to the old door-step, where she sat down and hid her face in her hands.

A heavy footstep sounded at her side the next moment. She looked quickly up. It was a policeman. He did not apply the expected words, "move on." He was a man under whose blue uniform beat a tender and sympathetic heart. In fact, he was No. 666—changed from some cause that we cannot explain, and do not understand—from the Metropolitan to the City Police Force. His number also had been changed, but we refuse to be trammelled by police regulations. No. 666 he was and shall remain in this tale to the end of the chapter!

Instead of ordering the poor woman to go away, Giles was searching his pockets for a penny, when to his intense surprise he received a blow on the chest, and then a slap on the face!

Poor Mrs. Frog, misjudging his intentions, and roused to a fit of temporary insanity by her wrongs and sorrows, sprang at her supposed foe like a wild-cat. She was naturally a strong woman, and violent passion lent her unusual strength.

Oh! it was pitiful to witness the struggle that ensued!—to see a woman, forgetful of sex and everything else, striving with all her might to bite, scratch, and kick, while her hair tumbled down, and her bonnet and shawl falling off made more apparent the insufficiency of the rags with which she was covered.

Strong as he was, Giles received several ugly scratches and bites before he could effectually restrain her. Fortunately, there were no passers-by in the quiet street, and, therefore, no crowd assembled.

"My poor woman," said Giles, when he had her fast, "do keep quiet. I'm going to do you no harm. God help you, I was goin' to give you a copper when you flew at me so. Come, you'd better go with me to the station, for you're not fit to take care of yourself."

Whether it was the tender tone of Giles's voice, or the words that he uttered, or the strength of his grasp that subdued Mrs. Frog, we cannot tell, but she gave in suddenly, hung down her head, and allowed her captor to do as he pleased. Seeing this, he carefully replaced her bonnet on her head, drew the old shawl quite tenderly over her shoulders, and led her gently away.

Before they had got the length of the main thoroughfare, however, a female of a quiet, re-spectable appearance met them.

"Mrs. Frog!" she exclaimed, in amazement, stopping suddenly before them.

"If you know her, ma'am, perhaps you may direct me to her home."

"I know her well," said the female, who was none other than the Bible-nurse who visited the sick of that district; "if you have not arrested her for—for—"

"Oh no, madam," interrupted Giles, "I have not arrested her at all, but she seems to be unwell, and I was merely assisting her."

"Oh! then give her over to me, please. I know where she lives, and will take care of her."

Giles politely handed his charge over, and went on his way, sincerely hoping that the next to demand his care would be a man.

The Bible-woman drew the arm of poor Mrs. Frog through her own, and in a few minutes stood beside her in the desolate home.

"Nobody cares," muttered the wretched woman as she sank in apathy on her stool and leaned her head against the wall.

"You are wrong, dear Mrs. Frog. *I* care, for one, else I should not be here. Many other Christian people would care, too, if they knew of your sufferings; but, above all, God cares. Have you carried your troubles to Him?"

"Why should I? He has long ago forsaken me."

"Is it not, dear friend, that you have forsaken Him? Jesus says, as plain as words can put it; 'Come unto me, all ye that labour and are heavy laden, and I will give you rest.' You tell me it is of no use to go to Him, and you don't go, and then you complain that He has forsaken you! Where is my friend Hetty?"

"In hospital."

"Indeed! I have been here several times lately to inquire, but have always found your door locked. Your husband—"

"He's in prison, and Bobby's gone to the bad," said Mrs. Frog, still in a tone of sulky defiance.

"I see no sign of food," said the Bible-nurse, glancing quickly round; "are you hungry?"

"Hungry!" exclaimed the woman fiercely, "I've tasted nothin' at all since yesterday."

"Poor thing!" said the Bible-nurse in a low tone; "come—come with me. Don't say more. You cannot speak while you are famishing. Stay, first one word—"

She paused and looked up. She did not kneel; she did not clasp her hands or shut her eyes, but, with one hand on the door-latch, and the other grasping the poor woman's wrist, she prayed—"God bless and comfort poor Mrs. Frog, for Jesus' sake."

Then she hurried, without uttering a word, to the Institution in George Yard. The door happened to be open, and the figure of a man with white hair and a kind face was seen within.

Entering, the Bible-nurse whispered to this man. Another moment and Mrs. Frog was seated at a long deal table with a comfortable fire at her back, a basin of warm soup, and a lump of loaf bread before her. The Bible-nurse sat by and looked on.

"Somebody cares a little, don't you think?" she whispered, when the starving woman made a brief pause for breath.

"Yes, thank God," answered Mrs. Frog, returning to the meal as though she feared that some one might still snatch it from her thin lips before she got it all down.

When it was finished the Bible-nurse led Mrs. Frog into another room.

"You feel better—stronger?" she asked.

"Yes, much better—thank you, and quite able to go home."

"There is no occasion for you to go home to-night; you may sleep there (pointing to a corner), but I would like to pray with you now, and read a verse or two."

Mrs. Frog submitted, while her friend read to her words of comfort; pleaded that pardon and deliverance might be extended, and gave her loving words of counsel. Then the poor creature lay down in her corner, drew a warm blanket over her, and slept with a degree of comfort that she had not enjoyed for many a day.

When it was said by Mrs. Frog that her son Bobby had gone to the bad, it must not be supposed that any very serious change had come over him. As that little waif had once said of himself, when in a penitent mood, he was about as bad as he could be, so couldn't grow much badder. But when his sister lost her situation in the firm that paid her such splendid wages, and fell ill, and went into hospital in consequence, he lost heart, and had a relapse of wickedness. He grew savage with regard to life in general, and committed a petty theft, which, although not discovered, necessitated his absence from home for a time. It was while he was away that the scene which we have just described took place.

On the very next day he returned, and it so happened that on the same day Hetty was discharged from hospital "cured." That is to say, she left the place a thin, tottering, pallid shadow, but with no particular form of organic disease about her.

She and her mother had received some food from one who cared for them, through the Bible-nurse.

"Mother, you've been drinkin' again," said Hetty, looking earnestly at her parent's eyes.

"Well, dear," pleaded Mrs. Frog, "what could I do? You had all forsaken me, and I had nothin' else to comfort me."

"Oh! mother, darling mother," cried Hetty, "do promise me that you will give it up. I won't get ill or leave you again—God helping me; but it will kill me if you go on. *Do* promise."

"It's of no use, Hetty. Of course I can easily promise, but I can't keep my promise. I *know* I can't."

Hetty knew this to be too true. Without the grace of God in the heart, she was well aware that human efforts *must* fail, sooner or later. She was thinking what to reply, and praying in her heart for guidance, when the door opened and her brother Bobby swaggered in with an air that did not quite

o

accord with his filthy fluttering rags, unwashed face
and hands, bare feet and unkempt hair.

"Vell, mother, 'ow are ye? Hallo! Hetty! w'y,
wot a shadder you've become! Oh! I say, them
nusses at the hospital must 'ave stole all your flesh
an' blood from you, for they've left nothin' but the
bones and skin."

He went up to his sister, put an arm round her
neck, and kissed her. This was a very unusual display of affection. It was the first time Bobby had
volunteered an embrace, though he had often submitted to one with dignified complacency, and
Hetty, being weak, burst into tears.

"Hallo! I say, stop that now, yong gal," he said,
with a look of alarm, "I'm always took bad ven I
see that sort o' thing, I can't stand it."

By way of mending matters the poor girl, endeavouring to be agreeable, gave a hysterical laugh.

"Come, that's better, though it ain't much to
boast of"—and he kissed her again.

Finding that, although for the present they were
supplied with a small amount of food, Hetty had no
employment and his mother no money, our city
Arab said that he would undertake to sustain the
family.

"But oh! Bobby, dear, don't steal again."

"No, Hetty, I von't, I'll vork. I didn't go for to
do it a-purpose, but I was overtook some'ow—I

seed the umbrellar standin' handy, you know, and —etceterer. But I'm sorry I did it, an' I von't do it again."

Swelling with great intentions, Robert Frog thrust his dirty little hands into his trouser pockets —at least into the holes that once contained them —and went out whistling.

Soon he came to a large warehouse, where a portly gentleman stood at the door. Planting himself in front of this man, and ceasing to whistle in order that he might speak, he said :—

"Was you in want of a 'and, sir?"

"No, I wasn't," replied the man, with a glance of contempt.

"Sorry for that," returned Bobby, "'cause I'm in want of a sitivation."

"What can you do?" asked the man.

"Oh! hanythink."

"Ah, I thought so; I don't want hands who can do anything, I prefer those who can do something."

Bobby Frog resumed his whistling, at the exact bar where he had left off, and went on his way. He was used to rebuffs, and didn't mind them. But when he had spent all the forenoon in receiving rebuffs, had made no progress whatever in his efforts, and began to feel hungry, he ceased the whistling and became grave.

"This looks serious," he said, pausing in front of a pastry-cook's shop window. "But for that there plate glass *wot* a blow hout I might 'ave! Beggin' might be tried with advantage. It's agin the law, no doubt, but it ain't a *sin*. Yes, I'll try beggin'."

But our Arab was not a natural beggar, if we may say so. He scorned to whine, and did not even like to ask. His spirit was much more like that of a highwayman than a beggar.

Proceeding to a quiet neighbourhood which seemed to have been forgotten by the police, he turned down a narrow lane and looked out for a subject, as a privateer might search among "narrows" for a prize. He did not search long. An old lady soon hove in sight. She seemed a suitable old lady, well dressed, little, gentle, white-haired, a tottering gait, and a benign aspect.

Bobby went straight up and planted himself in front of her.

"Please, ma'am, will you oblige me with a copper?"

The poor old lady grew pale. Without a word she tremblingly, yet quickly, pulled out her purse, took therefrom a shilling, and offered it to the boy.

"Oh! marm," said Bobby, who was alarmed and conscience-smitten at the result of his scheme, "I didn't mean for to frighten you. Indeed I didn't, an' I von't 'ave your money at no price."

Saying which he turned abruptly round and walked away.

"Boy, boy, *boy!*" called the old lady in a voice so entreating, though tremulous, that Bobby felt constrained to return.

"You're a most remarkable boy," she said, putting the shilling back into her purse.

"I'm sorry to say, marm, that you're not the on'y indiwidooal as 'olds that opinion."

"What do you mean by your conduct, boy?"

"I mean, marm, that I'm wery 'ard up. *Uncommon* 'ard up; that I've tried to git vork an' can't git it, so that I'm redooced to beggary. But, I ain't a 'ighway robber, marm, by no means, an' don't want to frighten you hout o' your money if you ain't willin' to give it."

The little tremulous old lady was so pleased with this reply that she took half-a-crown out of her purse and put it into the boy's hand. He looked at her in silent surprise.

"It ain't a *copper*, marm!"

"I know that. It is half-a-crown, and I willingly give it you because you are an honest boy."

"But, marm," said Bobby, still holding out the piece of silver on his palm, "I *ain't* a honest boy. I'm a thief!"

"Tut, tut, don't talk nonsense; I don't believe you."

"Vel now, this beats all that I ever did come across. 'Ere's a old 'ooman as I tells as plain as mud that I'm a thief, an' nobody's better able to give a opinion on that pint than myself, yet she *von't* believe it!"

"No, I won't," said the old lady with a little nod and a smile, "so, put the money in your pocket, for you're an honest boy."

"Vell, it's pleasant to 'ear that, any'ow," returned Bobby, placing the silver coin in a vest pocket which was always kept in repair for coins of smaller value.

"Where do you live, boy? I should like to come and see you."

"My residence, marm, ain't a mansion in the vest-end. No, nor yet a willa in the subarbs. I'm afear'd, marm, that I live in a district that ain't quite suitable for the likes of you to wisit. But—".

Here Bobby paused, for at the moment his little friend Tim Lumpy recurred to his memory, and a bright thought struck him.

"Well, boy, why do you pause?"

"I was on'y thinkin', marm, that if you wants to befriend us poor boys—they calls us waifs an' strays an' all sorts of unpurlite names—you've on'y got to send a sov. or two to Miss Annie Macpherson, 'Ome of Hindustry, Commercial Street, Spitalfields, an' you'll be the means o' doin' a world o' good—

as I 'eard a old gen'l'm with a white choker on say the wery last time I was down there 'avin' a blow out o' bread an' soup."

"I know the lady and the Institution well, my boy," said the old lady, "and will act on your advice, but—"

Ere she finished the sentence Bobby Frog had turned and fled at the very top of his speed.

"Stop! stop! stop!" exclaimed the old lady in a weakly shout.

But the "remarkable boy" would neither stop nor stay. He had suddenly caught sight of a policeman turning into the lane, and forthwith took to his heels, under a vague and not unnatural impression that if that limb of the law found him in possession of a half-crown he would refuse to believe his innocence with as much obstinacy as the little old lady had refused to believe his guilt.

On reaching home he found his mother alone in a state of amused agitation which suggested to his mind the idea of Old Tom.

"Wot, bin at it again, mother?"

"No, no, Bobby, but somethin''s happened which amuses me much, an' I can't keep it to myself no longer, so I'll tell it to you, Bobby."

"Fire avay, then, mother, an' remember that the law don't compel no one to criminate hisself."

"You know, Bob, that a good while ago our

Matty disappeared. I saw that the dear child was dyin' for want o' food an' warmth an' fresh air, so I thinks to myself, 'why shouldn't I put 'er out to board wi' rich people for nothink?'"

"A wery correct notion, an' cleverer than I gave you credit for. I'm glad to 'ear it too, for I feared sometimes that you'd bin an' done it."

"Oh! Bobby, how could you ever think that! Well, I put the baby out to board with a family of the name of Twitter. Now it seems, all unbeknown to me, Mrs. Twitter is a great helper at the George Yard Ragged Schools, where our Hetty has often seen her; but as we've bin used never to speak about the work there, as your father didn't like it, of course I know'd nothin' about Mrs. Twitter bein' given to goin' there. Well, it seems she's very free with her money and gives a good deal away to poor people." (She's not the only one, thought the boy.) "So what does the Bible-nurse do when she hears about poor Hetty's illness but goes off and asks Mrs. Twitter to try an' git her a situation."

"'Oh! I know Hetty,' says Mrs. Twitter at once, 'That nice girl that teaches one o' the Sunday school classes. Send her to me. I want a nurse for our baby,' that's for Matty, Bob—"

"What! *our* baby!" exclaimed the boy with a sudden blaze of excitement.

"Yes—*our* baby. She calls it *hers!*"

"Well, now," said Bobby, after recovering from the fit of laughter and thigh-slapping into which this news had thrown him, "if this don't beat cockfightin' all to nuffin'! why, mother, Hetty'll know baby the moment she claps eyes on it."

"Of course she will," said Mrs. Frog; "it is really very awkward, an' I can't think what to do. I'm half afraid to tell Hetty."

"Oh! don't tell her—*don't* tell her," cried the boy, whose eyes sparkled with mischievous glee. "It'll be sich fun! If I 'ad on'y the chance to stand be'ind a door an' see the meetin' I wouldn't exchange it— no not for a feed of pork sassengers an' suet pud'n. I must go an' tell this to Tim Lumpy. It'll bust 'im—that's my on'y fear, but I must tell 'im wotever be the consikences."

With this stern resolve, to act regardless of results, Bob Frog went off in search of his little friend, whose departure for Canada had been delayed, from some unknown cause, much to Bob's satisfaction. He found Tim on his way to the Beehive, and was induced not only to go with him, but to decide, finally, to enter the Institution as a candidate for Canada. Being well known, both as to person and circumstances, he was accepted at once; taken in, washed, cropped, and transformed as if by magic.

CHAPTER XVI.

SIR RICHARD VISITS THE BEEHIVE, AND SEES MANY SURPRISING THINGS.

"My dear Mrs. Loper," said Mrs. Twitter over a cup of tea, "it is very kind of you to say so, and I really do think you are right, we have done full justice to our dear wee Mita. Who would ever have thought, remembering the thin starved sickly child she was the night that Sam brought her in, that she would come to be such a plump, rosy, lovely child? I declare to you that I feel as if she were one of my own."

"She is indeed a very lovely infant," returned Mrs. Loper. "Don't you think so, Mrs. Larrabel?"

The smiling lady expanded her mouth, and said, "very."

"But," continued Mrs. Twitter, "I really find that the entire care of her is too much for me, for, although dear Mary assists me, her studies require to be attended to, and, do you know, babies interfere with studies dreadfully. Not that I have time to do much in that way at present. I think the Bible is the only book I really study now, so, you see, I've been thinking of adding to our establishment by getting a new servant;—a sort of nursery governess, you know,—a cheap one, of course. Sam quite agrees with me, and, as it happens, I know a very nice little girl just now—a very very poor girl—who helps us so nicely on Sundays in George Yard, and has been recommended to me as a most deserving creature. I expect her to call to-night."

"Be cautious, Mrs. Twitter," said Mrs. Loper. "These *very* poor girls from the slums of White-chapel are sometimes dangerous, and, excuse me, rather dirty. Of course, if you know her, that is some security, but I would advise you to be very cautious."

"Thank you, my dear," said Mrs. Twitter, "I usually am very cautious, and will try to be so on this occasion. I mean her to be rather a sort of nursery governess than a servant.—That is probably the girl."

She referred to a rather timid knock at the front door. In another second the domestic announced Hetty Frog, who entered with a somewhat shy air, and seemed fluttered at meeting with unexpected company.

"Come in, Hetty, my dear; I'm glad to see you. My friends here know that you are a helper in our

Sunday-schools. Sit down, and have a cup of tea. You know why I have sent for you?"

"Yes, Mrs. Twitter. It—it is very kind. Our Bible-nurse told me, and I shall be so happy to come, because—but I fear I have interrupted you. I—I can easily come back—"

"No interruption at all, my dear. Here, take this cup of tea—"

"And a crumpet," added Mrs. Larrabel, who sympathised with the spirit of hospitality.

"Yes, take a crumpet, and let me hear about your last place."

Poor Hetty, who was still very weak from her recent illness, and would gladly have been excused sitting down with two strangers, felt constrained to comply, and was soon put at her ease by the kindly tone and manner of the hostess. She ran quickly over the chief points of her late engagements, and roused, without meaning to do so, the indignation of the ladies by the bare mention of the wages she had received for the amount of work done.

"Well, my dear," said the homely Mrs. Twitter, "we won't be so hard on you here. I want you to assist me with my sewing and darning—of which I have a very great deal—and help to take care of baby."

"Very well, ma'am," said Hetty, "when do you wish me to begin my duties?"

"Oh! to-morrow—after breakfast will do. It is too late to-night. But before you go, I may as well let you see the little one you are to have charge of. I hear she is awake."

There could be no doubt upon that point, for the very rafters of the house were ringing at the moment with the yells which issued from an adjoining room.

"Come this way, Hetty."

Mrs. Loper and Mrs. Larrabel, having formed a good opinion of the girl, looked on with approving smiles. The smiles changed to glances of surprise, however, when Hetty, having looked on the baby, uttered a most startling scream, while her eyes glared as though she saw a ghostly apparition.

Seizing the baby with unceremonious familiarity, Hetty struck Mrs. Twitter dumb by turning it on its face, pulling open its dress, glancing at a bright red spot on its back, and uttering a shriek of delight as she turned it round again, and hugged it with violent affection, exclaiming, "Oh! my blessed Matty!"

"The child's name is not Matty; it is Mita," said Mrs. Twitter, on recovering her breath. "What *do* you mean, girl?"

"Her name is *not* Mita, it is Matty," returned Hetty, with a flatness of contradiction that seemed impossible in one so naturally gentle.

Mrs. Twitter stood aghast—bereft of the power

of speech or motion.   Mrs. Loper and Mrs. Larrabel
were similarly affected.   They soon recovered, however, and exclaimed in chorus, "What *can* she
mean ?"

"Forgive me, ma'am," said Hetty, still holding on
to baby, who seemed to have an idea that she was
creating a sensation of some sort, without requiring
to yell, "forgive my rudeness, ma'am, but I really
couldn't help it, for this is my long-lost sister
Matilda."

"Sister Matilda!" echoed Mrs. Loper.

"Long-lost sister Matilda!" repeated Mrs. Larrabel.   "This—is—your—long—lost sister Matilda,"
rehearsed Mrs. Twitter, like one in a dream.

The situation was rendered still more complex
by the sudden entrance of Mr. Twitter and his
friend Crackaby.

"What—what—what's to do *now*, Mariar ?"

"Sister Matilda!" shouted all three with a gasp.

"Lunatics, every one of 'em," murmured Crackaby.

It is, perhaps, scarcely necessary to add that a full
explanation ensued 'when the party became calmer;
that Mrs. Twitter could not doubt the veracity of
Hetty Frog, but suspected her sanity; that Mrs.
Frog was sent for, and was recognised at once by Mr.
Twitter as the poor woman who had asked him such
wild and unmeaning questions the night on which
he had found the baby; and that Mr. and Mrs.

Twitter, Mrs. Loper, Mrs. Larrabel, and Crackaby
came to the unanimous conclusion that they had
never heard of such a thing before in the whole
course of their united lives—which lives, when
united, as some statisticians would take a pride in
recording, formed two hundred and forty-three years!
Poor Mrs. Twitter was as inconsolable at the loss of
her baby as Mrs. Frog was overjoyed at the recovery
of hers. She therefore besought the latter to leave
little Mita, *alias* Matty, with her just for one night
longer—only one night—and then she might come
for her in the morning, for, you know, it would have
been cruel to remove the child from her warm crib
at that hour to a cold and comfortless lodging.

Of course Mrs. Frog readily consented. If Mrs.
Frog had known the events that lay in the womb of
the next few hours, she would sooner have consented to have had her right hand cut off than have
agreed to that most reasonable request.

But we must not anticipate. A few of our
dramatis personæ took both an active and an
inactive part in the events of these hours. It is
therefore imperative that we should indicate how
some of them came to be in that region.

About five of the clock in the afternoon of the
day in question, Sir Richard Brandon, his daughter
and idol Diana, and his young friend Stephen
Welland, sat in the dining-room of the West-end

mansion concluding an early and rather hasty dinner. That something was pending was indicated by the fact that little Di sat accoutred in her hat and cloak.

"We shall have to make haste," said Sir Richard, rising, "for I should not like to be late, and it is a long drive to Whitechapel."

"When do they begin?" asked Welland.

"They have tea at six, I believe, and then the meeting commences at seven, but I wish to be early that I may have a short conversation with one of the ladies of the Home."

"Oh! it will be so nice, and such fun to see the dear little boys. How many are going to start for Canada, to-night, papa?"

"About fifty or sixty, I believe, but I'm not sure. They are sent off in batches of varying size from time to time."

"Is the demand for them so great?" asked Welland, "I should have thought that Canadian farmers and others would be afraid to receive into their dwellings what is often described as the scum of the London streets."

"They were afraid at first, I am told, but soon discovered that the little fellows who came from Miss Macpherson's Home had been subjected to such good training and influences before leaving that they almost invariably turned out valuable and trustworthy workmen. No doubt there are exceptions in this as in every other case, but the demand is, it seems, greater than the supply. It is, however, a false idea that little waifs and strays, however dirty or neglected, are in any sense the scum of London. Youth, in all circumstances, is cream, and only turns into scum when allowed to stagnate or run to waste. Come, now, let us be off. Mr. Seaward, the city missionary, is to meet us after the meeting, and show you and me something of those who have fallen very low in the social scale. Brisbane, who is also to be at the meeting, will bring Di home. By the way, have you heard anything yet about that poor comrade and fellow-clerk of yours—Twitter, I think, was his name—who disappeared so suddenly?"

"Nothing whatever. I have made inquiries in all directions—for I had a great liking for the poor fellow. I went also to see his parents, but they seemed too much cut up to talk on the subject at all, and knew nothing of his whereabouts."

"Ah! it is a very sad case—very," said Sir Richard, as they all descended to the street. "We might, perhaps, call at their house to-night in passing." Entering a cab, they drove away.

From the foregoing conversation the reader will have gathered that the party were about to visit the Beehive, or Home of Industry, and that Sir

Richard, through the instrumentality of little Di and the city missionary, had actually begun to think about the poor!

It was a special night at the Beehive. A number of diamonds with some of their dust rubbed off— namely, a band of little boys, rescued from the streets and from a probable life of crime, were to be assembled there to say farewell to such friends as took an interest in them.

The Hive had been a huge warehouse. It was now converted, with but slight structural alteration, into a great centre of Light in that morally dark region, from which emanated gospel truth and Christian influence, and in which was a refuge for the poor, the destitute, the sin-smitten, and the sorrowful. Not only poverty, but sin-in-rags, was sure of help in the Beehive. It had been set agoing to bring, not the righteous, but sinners, to repentance.

When Sir Richard arrived he found a large though low-roofed room crowded with people, many of whom, to judge from their appearance, were, like himself, diamond-seekers from the "west-end," while others were obviously from the "east-end," and had the appearance of men and women who had been but recently unearthed. There were also city missionaries and other workers for God in that humble-looking hall. Among them sat Mr. John Seaward and George Brisbane, Esquire.

Placing Di and Welland near the latter, Sir Richard retired to a corner where one of the ladies of the establishment was distributing tea to all comers.

"Where are your boys, may I ask?" said the knight, accepting a cup of tea.

"Over in the left corner," answered the lady. "You can hardly see them for the crowd, but they will stand presently."

At that moment, as if to justify her words, a large body of boys rose up, at a sign from the superintending genius of the place, and began to sing a beautiful hymn in soft, tuneful voices. It was a goodly array of dusty diamonds, and a few of them had already begun to shine.

"Surely," said Sir Richard, in a low voice, "these cannot be the ragged, dirty little fellows you pick up in the streets?"

"Indeed they are," returned the lady.

"But—but they seem to me quite respectable and cleanly fellows, not at all like—why, how has the change been accomplished?"

"By the united action, sir, of soap and water, needles and thread, scissors, cast-off garments, and Love."

Sir Richard smiled. Perchance the reader may also smile; nevertheless, this statement embodied probably the whole truth.

When an unkempt, dirty, ragged little savage

presents himself, or is presented, at the Refuge, or is "picked up" in the streets, his case is promptly and carefully inquired into. If he seems a suitable character—that is, one who is *utterly* friendless and parentless, or whose parents are worse than dead to him—he is received into the Home, and the work of transformation—both of body and soul—commences. First he is taken to the lavatory and scrubbed outwardly clean. His elfin locks are cropped close and cleansed. His rags are burned, and a new suit, made by the old women workers, is put upon him, after which, perhaps, he is fed. Then he is sent to a doctor to see that he is internally sound in wind and limb. If passed by the doctor, he receives a brief but important training in the rudiments of knowledge. In all of these various processes Love is the guiding principle of the operator—love to God and love to the boy. He is made to understand, and to *feel*, that it is in the name of Jesus, for the love of Jesus, and in the spirit of Jesus —not of mere philanthropy—that all this is done, and that his body is cared for *chiefly* in order that the soul may be won.

Little wonder, then, that a boy or girl, whose past experience has been the tender mercies of the world —and that the roughest part of the world—should become somewhat "respectable," as Sir Richard put it, under such new and blessed influences.

Suddenly a tiny shriek was heard in the midst of the crowd, and a sweet little voice exclaimed, as if its owner were in great surprise—

" Oh ! oh ! there is *my* boy !"

A hearty laugh from the audience greeted this outburst, and poor Di, shrinking down, tried to hide her pretty face on Welland's ready arm. Her remark was quickly forgotten in the proceedings that followed—but it was true.

There stood, in the midst of the group of boys, little Bobby Frog, with his face washed, his hair cropped and shining, his garments untattered, and himself looking as meek and " respectable " as the best of them. Beside him stood his fast friend Tim Lumpy. Bobby was not, however, one of the emigrant band. Having joined only that very evening, and been cropped, washed, and clothed for the first time, he was there merely as a privileged guest. Tim, also, was only a guest, not having quite attained to the dignity of a full-fledged emigrant at that time.

At the sound of the sweet little voice, Bobby Frog's meek look was replaced by one of bright intelligence, not unmingled with anxiety, as he tried unavailingly to see the child who had spoken.

We do not propose to give the proceedings of this meeting in detail, interesting though they were. Other matters of importance claim our attention. It will be sufficient to say that mingled with the semi-conversational, pleasantly free-and-easy, inter-course that ensued, there were most interesting short addresses from the lady-superintendents of "The Sailors' Welcome Home" and of the "Strangers' Rest," both of Ratcliff Highway, also from the chief of the Ragged schools in George Yard, and several city missionaries, as well as from city merchants who found time and inclination to traffic in the good things of the life to come as well as in those of the life that now is.

Before the proceedings had drawn to a close a voice whispered:—

"It is time to go, Sir Richard." It was the voice of John Seaward.

Following him, Sir Richard and Welland went out. It had grown dark by that time, and as there were no brilliantly lighted shops near, the place seemed gloomy, but the gloom was nothing to that of the filthy labyrinths into which Seaward quickly conducted his followers.

"You have no occasion to fear, sir," said the missionary, observing that Sir Richard hesitated at the mouth of one very dark alley. "It would, indeed, hardly be safe were you to come down here alone, but most of 'em know me. I remember being told by one of the greatest roughs I ever knew that at the very corner where we now stand he had many and many a time knocked down and robbed people. That man is now an earnest Christian, and, like Paul, goes about preaching the Name which he once despised."

At the moment a dark shadow seemed to pass them, and a gruff voice said, " Good-night, sir."

"Was that the man you were speaking of?" asked Sir Richard, quickly.

" Oh no, sir," replied Seaward with a laugh; " that's what he was once like, indeed, but not what he is like now. His voice is no longer gruff. Take care of the step, gentlemen, as you pass here; so, now we will go into this lodging. It is one of the common lodging-houses of London, which are regulated by law and under the supervision of the police. Each man pays fourpence a night here, for which he is entitled to a bed and the use of the kitchen and its fire to warm himself and cook his food. If he goes to the same lodging every night for a week he becomes entitled to a free night on Sundays."

The room into which they now entered was a long low chamber, which evidently traversed the whole width of the building, for it turned at a right angle at the inner end, and extended along the back to some extent. It was divided along one side into boxes or squares, after the fashion of some eating-houses, with a small table in the centre of each box, but, the partitions being little higher than those of a church-pew, the view of the whole room was

unobstructed. At the inner angle of the room blazed
a coal-fire so large that a sheep might have been
easily roasted whole at it. Gas jets, fixed along the
walls at intervals, gave a sufficient light to the place.

This was the kitchen of the lodging-house, and
formed the sitting-room of the place; and here was
assembled perhaps the most degraded and miserable
set of men that the world can produce. They were
not all of one class, by any means; nor were they
all criminal, though certainly many of them were.
The place was the last refuge of the destitute; the
social sink into which all that is improvident, foolish,
reckless, thriftless, or criminal finally descends.

Sir Richard and Welland had put on their oldest
greatcoats and shabbiest wideawakes; they had also
put off their gloves and rings and breast-pins in order
to attract as little attention as possible, but nothing
that they could have done could have reduced
their habiliments to anything like the garments of
the poor creatures with whom they now mingled.
If they had worn the same garments for months
or years without washing them, and had often slept
in them out of doors in dirty places, they might
perhaps have brought them to the same level, but
not otherwise.

Some of the people, however, were noisy enough.
Many of them were smoking, and the coarser sort
swore and talked loud. Those who had once

been in better circumstances sat and moped, or spoke in lower tones, or cooked their victuals with indifference to all else around, or ate them in abstracted silence; while not a few laid their heads and arms on the tables, and apparently slept. For sleeping in earnest there were rooms overhead containing many narrow beds with scant and coarse covering, which, however, the law compelled to be clean. One of the rooms contained seventy such beds.

Little notice was taken of the west-end visitors as they passed up the room, though some dark scowls of hatred were cast after them, and a few glanced at them with indifference. It was otherwise in regard to Seaward. He received many a "good-night, sir," as he passed, and a kindly nod greeted him here and there from men who at first looked as if kindness had been utterly eradicated from their systems.

One of those whom we have described as resting their heads and arms on the tables, looked hastily up, on hearing the visitors' voices, with an expression of mingled surprise and alarm. It was Sammy Twitter, with hands and visage filthy, hair dishevelled, eyes blood-shot, cheeks hollow, and garments beyond description disreputable. He seemed the very embodiment of woe and degradation. On seeing his old friend Welland he quickly laid his head down again and remained motionless.

Welland had not observed him.

"You would scarcely believe it, sir," said the missionary, in a low tone; "nearly all classes of society are occasionally represented here. You will sometimes find merchants, lawyers, doctors, military men, and even clergymen, who have fallen step by step, chiefly in consequence of that subtle demon drink, until the common lodging-house is their only home."

"Heaven help me!" said Sir Richard; "my friend Brisbane has often told me of this, but I have never quite believed it—certainly never realised it—until to-night. And even now I can hardly believe it. I see no one here who seems as if he ever had belonged to the classes you name."

"Do you see the old man in the last box in the room, on the left-hand side, sitting alone?" asked Seaward, turning his back to the spot indicated.

"Yes."

"Well, that is a clergyman. I know him well. You would never guess it from his wretched clothing, but you might readily believe it if you were to speak to him."

"That I will not do," returned the other firmly.

"You are right, sir," said Seaward, "I would not advise that you should—at least not here, or now. I have been in the habit of reading a verse or two of the Word and giving them a short address sometimes about this hour. Have you any objection to my doing so now? It won't detain us long."

"None in the world; pray, my good sir, don't let me disarrange your plans."

"Perhaps," added the missionary, "you would say a few words to—"

"No, no," interrupted the other, quickly; "no, they are preaching to *me* just now, Mr. Seaward, a very powerful sermon, I assure you."

During the foregoing conversation young Welland's thoughts had been very busy; ay, and his conscience had not been idle, for when mention was made of that great curse strong-drink, he vividly recalled the day when he had laughed at Sam Twitter's blue ribbon, and felt uneasy as to how far his conduct on that occasion had helped Sam in his downward career.

"My friends," said the missionary aloud, "we will sing a hymn."

Some of those whom he addressed turned towards the speaker; others paid no attention whatever, but went on with their cooking and smoking. They were used to it, as ordinary church-goers are to the "service." The missionary understood that well, but was not discouraged, because he knew that his "labour in the Lord" should not be in vain. He pulled out two small hymn-books and handed one to Sir Richard, the other to Welland.

Sir Richard suddenly found himself in what was to him a strange and uncomfortable position, called on to take a somewhat prominent part in a religious service in a low lodging-house!

The worst of it was that the poor knight could not sing a note. However, his deficiency in this respect was more than compensated by John Seaward, who possessed a telling tuneful voice, with a grateful heart to work it. Young Welland also could sing well, and joined heartily in that beautiful hymn which tells of " The wonderful words of life."

After a brief prayer the missionary preached the comforting gospel, and tried, with all the fervour of a sympathetic heart, to impress on his hearers that there really was Hope for the hopeless, and Rest for the weary in Jesus Christ.

When he had finished, Stephen Welland surprised him, as well as his friend Sir Richard and the audience generally, by suddenly exclaiming, in a subdued but impressive voice, which drew general attention :—

" Friends, I had no intention of saying a word when I came here, but, God forgive me, I have committed a sin, which seems to force me to speak and warn you against giving way to strong drink. I had —nay, I *have*—a dear friend who once put on the Blue Ribbon."

Here he related the episode at the road-side

tavern, and his friend's terrible fall, and wound up
with the warning :—

" Fellow-men, fellow-sinners, beware of being
laughed out of good resolves—beware of strong drink.
I know not where my comrade is now. He may be
dead, but I think not, for he has a mother and father
who pray for him without ceasing. Still better, as
you have just been told, he has an Advocate with
God, who is able and willing to save him to the
uttermost. Forgive me, Mr. Seaward, for speaking
without being asked. I could not help it."   ·

" No need to ask forgiveness of me, Mr. Welland.
You have spoken on the Lord's side, and I have
reason to thank you heartily."   ·

While this was being said, those who sat near the
door observed that a young man rose softly, and
slunk away like a criminal, with a face ashy pale
and his head bowed down. On reaching the door,
he rushed out like one who expected to be pursued.
It was young Sam Twitter. Few of the inmates
of the place observed him, none cared a straw
for him, and the incident was, no doubt, quickly
forgotten.

" We must hasten now, if we are to visit another
lodging-house," said Seaward, as they emerged into
the comparatively fresh air of the street, " for it grows
late, and riotous drunken characters are apt to be
met with as they stagger home."

" No ; I have had enough for one night," said Sir
Richard. "I shall not be able to digest it all in a
hurry. I 'll go home by the Metropolitan, if you
will conduct me to the nearest station."

" Come along, then. This way."

They had not gone far, and were passing through
a quiet side street, when they observed a poor
woman sitting on a door-step. It was Mrs. Frog,
who had returned to sit on the old familiar spot, and
watch the shadows on the blind, either from the
mere force of habit, or because this would probably
be the last occasion on which she could expect to
enjoy that treat.

A feeling of pity entered Sir Richard's soul as he
looked on the poorly clothed forlorn creature. He
little knew what rejoicing there was in her heart just
then—so deceptive are appearances at times! He
went towards her with an intention of some sort,
when a very tall policeman turned the corner, and
approached.

" Why, Giles Scott !" exclaimed the knight,
holding out his hand, which Giles shook respectfully, "you seem to be very far away from your
beat to-night."

" No, sir, not very far, for this is my beat, now.
I have exchanged into the city, for reasons that
I need not mention."

At this point a belated and half tipsy man passed

with his donkey-cart full of unsold vegetables and rubbish.

"Hallo! you big blue-coat-boy," he cried politely to Giles, "wot d'ye call *that?*"

Giles had caught sight of "*that*" at the same moment, and darted across the street.

"Why, it's fire!" he shouted. "Run, young fellow, you know the fire-station!"

"*I* know it," shouted the donkey-man, sobered in an instant, as he jumped off his cart, left it standing, dashed round the corner, and disappeared, while No. 666 beat a thundering tattoo on Samuel Twitter's front door.

CHAPTER XVII.

THINGS BECOME TOO HOT FOR THE TWITTER FAMILY.

BEFORE the thunder of Giles Scott's first rap had ceased, a pane of glass in one of the lower windows burst, and out came dense volumes of smoke, with a red tongue or two piercing them here and there, showing that the fire had been smouldering long, and had got well alight.

It was followed by an appalling shriek from Mrs. Frog, who rushed forward shouting, "Oh! baby! baby!"

"Hold her, sir," said Giles to young Welland, who sprang forward at the same moment.

Welland was aware of the immense value of prompt obedience, and saw that Giles was well fitted to command. He seized Mrs. Frog and held her fast, while Giles, knowing that there was no time to stand on ceremony, stepped a few paces back, ran at the door with all his might, and applied his foot with his great weight and momentum to it. As the oak is shattered by the thunderbolt, so was Samuel

Twitter's door by the foot of No. 666.   But the bold
constable was met by a volume of black smoke which
was too much even for him.   It drove him back half
suffocated, while, at the same time, it drove the
domestic out of the house into his arms.   She had
rushed from the lower regions just in time to escape
death.

A single minute had not yet elapsed, and only
half-a-dozen persons had assembled, with two or
three policemen, who instantly sought to obtain an
entrance by a back door.

" Hold her, Sir Richard," said Welland, handing
the struggling Mrs. Frog over.   The knight accepted
the charge, while Welland ran to the burning house,
which seemed to be made of tinder, it blazed up so
quickly.

Giles was making desperate efforts to enter by a
window which vomited fire and smoke that defied
him.   An upper window was thrown open, and
Samuel Twitter appeared in his night-dress, shouting
frantically.

Stephen Welland saw that entrance or egress by
lower window or staircase was impossible.   He had
been a noted athlete at school.   There was an iron
spout which ran from the street to the roof.   He
rushed to that, and sprang up more like a monkey
than a man.

" Pitch   over   blankets ! "   roared   Giles,   as   the

youth gained a, window of the first floor, and dashed it in.

"The donkey cart!" shouted Welland, in reply, and disappeared.

Giles was quick to understand. He dragged— almost lifted—the donkey and cart on to the pavement under the window where Mr. Twitter stood waving his hands and yelling. The poor man had evidently lost his reason for the time, and was fit for nothing. A hand was seen to grasp his neck behind, and he disappeared. At the same moment a blanket came fluttering down, and Welland stood on the window-sill with Mrs. Twitter in his arms, and a sheet of flame following. The height was about thirty feet. The youth steadied himself for one moment, as if to take aim, and dropped Mrs. Twitter, as he might have dropped a bundle. She not only went into the vegetable cart, with a bursting shriek, but right through it, and reached the pavement unhurt—though terribly shaken!

Four minutes had not yet elapsed. The crowd had thickened, and a dull rumbling which had been audible for half a minute increased into a mighty roar as the fiery-red engine with its brass-helmeted heroes dashed round the corner, and pulled up with a crash, seeming to shoot the men off. These swarmed, for a few seconds, about the hose, water plug, and nozzles. At the same instant the great fire-escape came rushing on the scene, like some antediluvian monster, but by that time Giles had swept away the débris of the donkey cart, with Mrs. Twitter imbedded therein, and had stretched the blanket with five powerful volunteers to hold it. "Jump, sir, jump!" he cried. Samuel Twitter jumped—unavoidably, for Welland pushed him— just as the hiss and crackle of the water-spouts began.

He came down in a heap, rebounded like india-rubber, and was hurled to one side in time to make way for one of his young flock.

"The children! the children!" screamed Mrs. Twitter, disengaging herself from the vegetables.

"Where are they?" asked a brass-helmeted man, quietly, as the head of the Escape went crashing through an upper window.

"The top floor! all of 'em there!—top flo-o-o-r!"

"No—no-o-o! some on the second fl-o-o-or!" yelled Mr. Twitter.

"I say *top*—floo-o-o-r," repeated the wife.

"You forget—baby—ba-i-by!" roared the husband.

A wild shriek was Mrs. Twitter's reply.

The quiet man with the brass helmet had run up the Escape quite regardless of these explanations. At the same time top windows were thrown up, and little night-dressed figures appeared at them all, apparently making faces, for their cries were drowned in the shouts below.

From these upper windows smoke was issuing, but not yet in dense, suffocating volumes. The quiet man of the Escape entered a second floor window through smoke and flames as though he were a salamander.

The crowd below gave him a lusty cheer, for it was a great surging crowd by that time; nevertheless it surged within bounds, for a powerful body of police kept it back, leaving free space for the firemen to work.

A moment or two after the quiet fireman had entered, the night-dressed little ones disappeared from the other windows and congregated, as if by magic, at the window just above the head of the Escape. Almost simultaneously the fly-ladder of the Escape—used for upper windows—was swung out, and when the quiet fireman had got out on the window-sill with little Lucy in his arms and little Alice held by her dress in his teeth, its upper rounds, touched his knees, as if with a kiss of recognition!

He descended the fly-ladder, and shoved the two terrified little ones somewhat promptly into the canvas shoot, where a brother fireman was ready to pilot them safely to the ground. Molly being big had to be taken by herself, but Willie and Fred. went together.

During all this time poor Mrs. Frog had given

herself over to the one idea of screaming "baby! bai-e-by!" and struggling to get free from the two policemen, who had come to the relief of Sir Richard, and who tenderly restrained her.

In like manner Mr. and Mrs. Twitter, although not absolutely in need of restraint, went about wringing their hands and making such confused and contradictory statements that no one could understand what they meant, and the firemen quietly went on with their work quite regardless of their existence.

"Policeman!" said Sam Twitter, looking up in the face of No. 666, with a piteous expression, and almost weeping with vexation, "*nobody* will listen to me. I would go up myself, but the firemen won't let me, and my dear wife has such an idea of sticking to truth that when they ask her, 'Is your baby up there?' she yells 'No, not *our* baby;' and before she can explain she gasps, and then I try to explain, and that so bamboozles—"

"*Is* your baby there?" demanded No. 666 vehemently.

"Yes, it *is!*" cried Twitter, without the slightest twinge of conscience.

"What room?"

"That one," pointing to the left side of the house on the first floor.

Just then part of the roof gave way and fell into

the furnace of flame below, leaving visible the door of the very room to which Twitter had pointed.

A despairing groan escaped him as he saw it, for now all communication seemed cut off, and the men were about to pull the Escape away to prevent its being burned, while, more engines having arrived, something like a mountain torrent of water was descending on the devoted house.

" Stop, lads, a moment," said Giles, springing upon the Escape. He might have explained to the firemen what he had learned, but that would have taken time, and every second just then was of the utmost value. He was up on the window-sill before they well understood what he meant to do.

The heat was intolerable. A very lake of fire rolled beneath him. The door of the room pointed out by Twitter was opposite—fortunately on the side furthest from the centre of fire, but the floor was gone. Only two great beams remained, and the one Giles had to cross was more than half burned through. It was a fragile bridge on which to pass over an abyss so terrible. But heroes do not pause to calculate. Giles walked straight across it with the steadiness of a rope-dancer, and burst in the charred and splitting door.

The smoke here was not too dense to prevent his seeing. One glance revealed baby Frog lying calmly in her crib as if asleep. To seize her, wrap her in

GILES RESCUING MATTY.—PAGE 247.

the blankets, and carry her to the door of the room, was the work of a moment, but the awful abyss now lay before him, and it seemed to have been heated seven times. The beam, too, was by that time re-kindling with the increased heat, and the burden he carried prevented Giles from seeing, and balancing himself so well. He did not hesitate, but he advanced slowly and with caution.

A dead silence fell on the awe-stricken crowd, whose gaze was concentrated now on the one figure. The throbbing of the engines was heard distinctly when the roar of excitement was thus temporarily checked.

As Giles moved along, the beam cracked under his great weight. The heat became almost insupportable. His boots seemed to shrivel up and tighten round his feet.

"He's gone! No, he's not!" gasped some of the crowd, as the tall smoke and flame encompassed him, and he was seen for a moment to waver.

It was a touch of giddiness, but by a violent impulse of the will he threw it off, and at the same time bounded to the window, sending the beam, which was broken off by the shock, hissing down into the lake of fire.

The danger was past, and a loud, continuous, enthusiastic cheer greeted gallant No. 666 as he descended the shoot with the baby in his arms, and delivered it alive and well, and more solemn than ever, to its mother—its *own* mother!

When Sir Richard Brandon returned home that night, he found it uncommonly difficult to sleep. When, after many unsuccessful efforts, he did manage to slumber, his dreams re-produced the visions of his waking hours, with many surprising distortions and mixings—one of which distortions was, that all the paupers in the common lodging-houses had suddenly become rich, while he, Sir Richard, had as suddenly become poor, and a beggar in filthy rags, with nobody to care for him, and that these enriched beggars came round him and asked him, in quite a facetious way, " how he liked it! "

Next morning, when the worthy knight arose, he found his unrested brain still busy with the same theme. He also found that he had got food for meditation, and for discussion with little Di, not only for some time to come, but, for the remainder of his life.

CHAPTER XVIII.

THE OCEAN AND THE NEW WORLD.

DOCTORS tell us that change of air is usually beneficial, often necessary, nearly always agreeable. Relying on the wisdom of this opinion, we propose now to give the reader who has followed us thus far a change of air—by shifting the scene to the bosom of the broad Atlantic—and thus blow away the cobwebs and dust of the city.

Those who have not yet been out upon the great ocean cannot conceive—and those who have been out on it may not have seen—the splendours of a luminous fog on a glorious summer morning. The prevailing ideas in such circumstances are peace and liquidity! the only solid object visible above, below, or around, being the ship on which you stand.

Everything else is impalpable, floating, soft, and of a light, bright, silvery grey. The air is warm, the sea is glass; it is circular, too, like a disc, and the line where it meets with the sky is imperceptible. Your little bark is the centre of a great crystal ball, the limit of which is Immensity!

As we have said, peace, liquidity, luminosity, softness, and warmth prevail everywhere, and the fog, or rather, the silvery haze—for it is dry and warm as well as bright—has the peculiar effect of deadening sound, so that the quiet little noises of ship-board rather help than destroy the idea of that profound tranquillity which suggests irresistibly to the religious mind the higher and sweeter idea of " the peace of God."

But, although intensely still, there is no suggestion of death in such a scene. It is only that of slumber, for the ocean undulates even when at rest, and sails flap gently even when there is no wind. Besides this, on the particular morning to which we call attention, a species of what we may call " still life " was presented by a mighty iceberg—a peaked and towering mountain of snowy white and emerald blue—which floated on the sea not a quarter of a mile off on the starboard bow. Real life also was presented to the passengers of the noble bark which formed the centre of this scene, in the form of gulls floating like great snowflakes in the air, and flocks of active little divers rejoicing unspeakably on the water. The distant cries of these added to the harmony of nature, and tended to draw the mind from mere abstract contemplation to positive

sympathy with the joys of other animals besides
one's-self.

The only discordant sounds that met the ears of
those who voyaged in the bark *Ocean Queen* were
the cacklings of a creature in the hen-coops which
had laid an egg, or thought it had done so, or wished
to do so, or, having been sea-sick up to that time,
perhaps, endeavoured to revive its spirits by recal-
ling the fact that it once did so, and might perhaps
do so again ! By the way there was also one other
discord, in the form of a pugnacious baby, which
whimpered continuously, and, from some unaccountable cause, refused to be comforted. But that was
a discord which, as in some musical chords, seemed
rather to improve the harmony—at least in its
mother's ears.

The *Ocean Queen* was an emigrant ship. In her
capacious hull, besides other emigrants, there were
upwards of seventy diamonds from the Beehive in
Spitalfields on their way to seek their fortunes in
the lands that are watered by such grand fresh-
water seas as Lakes Superior and Huron and Michi-
gan and Ontario, and such rivers as the Ottawa and
the St. Lawrence.

Robert Frog and Tim Lumpy were among those
boys, so changed for the better in a few months
that, as the former remarked, " their own mothers
wouldn't know 'em," and not only improved in ap-

pearance, but in spirit, ay and even to some small extent in language—so great had been the influence for good brought to bear on them by Christian women working out of love to God and souls.

"Ain't it lovely?" said Tim.

"Splendacious!" replied Bob.

The reader will observe that we did, not say the language had, at that time, been *much* improved! only to some small extent.

"I've seen pictur's of 'em, Bob," said Tim, leaning his arms on the vessel's bulwarks as he gazed on the sleeping sea, "w'en a gen'l'man came to George Yard with a magic lantern, but I never thought they was so big, or that the holes in 'em was so blue."

"Nor I neither," said Bob.

They referred, of course, to the iceberg, the seams and especially the caverns in which graduated from the lightest azure to the deepest indigo.

"Why, I do believe," continued Bobby, as the haze grew a little thinner, "that there's rivers of water runnin' down its sides, just like as if it was a mountain o' loaf-sugar wi' the fire-brigade a-pumpin' on it. An' see, there's water-falls too, bigger I do b'lieve than the one I once saw at a pantomime."

"Ay, an' far prettier too," said Tim.

Bobby Frog did not quite see his way to assent to that. The waterfalls on the iceberg were bigger, he admitted, than those in the pantomime, but then, there was not so much glare and glitter around them.

"An' I 'm fond of glare an' glitter," he remarked, with a glance at his friend.

"So am I Bob, but—"

At that instant the dinner-bell rang, and the eyes of both glittered—they almost glared—as they turned and made for the companion-hatch, Bob exclaiming, " Ah, that 's the thing that *I 'm* fond of; glare an' glitter 's all wery well in its way, but it can't 'old a candle to grub !"

Timothy Lumpy seemed to have no difference of opinion with his friend on that point. Indeed the other sixty-eight boys seemed to be marvellously united in sentiment about it, for, without an exception, they responded to that dinner-bell with a promptitude quite equal to that secured by military discipline ! There was a rattling of feet on decks and ladderways for a few seconds, and then all was quiet while a blessing was asked on the meal.

For many years Miss Annie Macpherson has herself conducted parties of such boys to Canada, but the party of which we write happened to be in charge of a gentleman whom we will name the

Guardian. He was there to keep order, of course, but in truth this was not a difficult matter, for the affections of the boys had been enlisted, and they had already learned to practise self-restraint.

That same day a whale was seen. It produced a sensation among the boys that is not easily described. Considerately, and as if on purpose, it swam round the ship and displayed its gigantic proportions ; then it spouted as though to show what it could do in that line, and then, as if to make the performance complete and reduce the Westminster Aquarium to insignificance, it tossed its mighty tail on high, brought it down with a clap like thunder, and finally dived into its native ocean followed by a yell of joyful surprise from the rescued waifs and strays.

There were little boys, perhaps even big ones, in that band, who that day received a lesson of faith from the whale. It taught them that pictures, even extravagant ones, represent great realities. The whale also taught them a lesson of error, as was proved by the remark of one waif to a brother stray :—

"I say, Piggie, it ain't 'ard *now*, to b'lieve that the whale swallered Jonah."

"You're right, Konky."

Strange interlacing of error with error traversed by truth in this sublunary sphere ! Piggie was wrong in admitting that Konky was right, for, as every one knows, or ought to know, it was not a whale at all that swallowed Jonah, but a "great fish" which was "prepared" for the purpose.

But the voyage of the *Ocean Queen* was not entirely made up of calms, and luminous fogs, and bergs, and whales, and food. A volume would be required to describe it all. There was much foul weather as well as fair, during which periods a certain proportion of the little flock, being not very good sailors, sank to depths of misery which they had never before experienced—not even in their tattered days—and even those of them who had got their "sea-legs on," were not absolutely happy.

"I say, Piggie," asked the waif before mentioned of his chum (or dosser) Konky, "'ow long d'ee think little Mouse will go on at his present rate o' heavin' ?"

"I can't say," answered the stray, with a serious air ; "I ain't studied the 'uman frame wery much, but I should say, 'e 'll bust by to-morrow if 'e goes on like 'e 's bin doin'."

A tremendous sound from little Mouse, who lay in a neighbouring bunk, seemed to justify the prophecy.

But little Mouse did not "bust." He survived that storm and got his sea-legs on before the next one.

The voyage, however, was on the whole propitious, and, what with school-lessons and Bible-lessons and hymn-singing, and romping, and games of various kinds instituted and engaged in by the Guardian, the time passed profitably as well as pleasantly, so that there were, perhaps, some feelings of regret when the voyage drew to an end, and they came in sight of that Great Land which the Norsemen of old discovered; which Columbus, re-discovering, introduced to the civilised world, and which, we think, ought in justice to have been named Columbia.

And now a new era of life began for those rescued waifs and strays—those east-end diamonds from the great London fields. Canada—with its mighty lakes and splendid rivers, its great forests and rich lands, its interesting past, prosperous present, and hopeful future—opened up to view. But there was a shadow on the prospect, not very extensive, it is true, but dark enough to some of them just then, for here the hitherto united band was to be gradually disunited and dispersed, and friendships that had begun to ripen under the sunshine of Christian influence were to be broken up, perhaps for ever. The Guardian, too, had to be left behind by each member as he was severed from his fellows and sent to a new home among total strangers.

Still there were to set off against these things several points of importance. One of these was that the Guardian would not part with a single boy until the character of his would-be employer was inquired into, and his intention to deal kindly and fairly ascertained. Another point was, that each boy, when handed over to an employer, was not to be left thereafter to care for himself, but his interests were to be watched over and himself visited at intervals by an emissary from the Beehive, so that he would not feel friendless or forsaken even though he should have the misfortune to fall into bad hands. The Guardian also took care to point out, that amid all these leave-takings and partings, there was One who would " never leave nor forsake " them, and to whom they were indebted for the first helping hand, when they were in their rags and misery, and forsaken of man.

At last the great gulf of St. Lawrence was entered, and here the vessel was beset with ice, so that she could not advance at a greater rate than two or three miles an hour for a considerable distance.

Soon, however, those fields of frozen sea were passed, and the end of the voyage drew near. Then was there a marvellous outbreak of pens, ink, and paper, for the juvenile flock was smitten with a sudden desire to write home before going to the interior of the new land.

It was a sad truth that many of the poor boys
had neither parent nor relative to correspond with,
but these were none the less eager in their literary
work, for had they not Miss Macpherson and the
ladies of the Home to write to?

Soon after that, the party landed at the far-famed
city of Quebec, each boy with his bag containing
change of linen, and garments, a rug, etc.; and there,
under a shed, thanks were rendered to God for a
happy voyage, and prayer offered for future guidance.

Then the Guardian commenced business. He had
momentous work to do. The Home of Industry
and its work are well known in Canada. Dusty
diamonds sent out from the Beehive were by that
time appreciated, and therefore coveted; for the
western land is vast, and the labourers are comparatively few. People were eager to get the boys,
but the character of intending employers had to be
inquired into, and this involved care. Then the
suitability of boys to situations had to be considered. However, this was finally got over, and
a few of the reclaimed waifs were left at Quebec.
This was the beginning of the dispersion.

"I don't like it at all," said Bobby Frog to his
friend Tim Lumpy, that evening in the sleeping car
of the railway train that bore them onward to
Montreal; "they'll soon be partin' you an' me, an'

that 'll be worse than wallerin' in the mud of Vitechapel."

Bobby said this with such an expression of serious anxiety that his little friend was quite touched.

" I hope not, Bob," he replied. " What d' ee say to axin' our Guardian to put us both into the same sitivation ?"

Bobby thought that this was not a bad idea, and as they rolled along these two little waifs gravely discussed their future prospects. It was the same with many others of the band, though not a few were content to gaze out of the carriage windows, pass a running commentary on the new country, and leave their future entirely to their Guardian. Soon, however, the busy little tongues and brains ceased to work, and ere long were steeped in slumber.

At midnight the train stopped, and great was the sighing and groaning, and earnest were the requests to be let alone, for a batch of the boys had to be dropped at a town by the way. At last they were aroused, and with their bags on their shoulders prepared to set off under a guide to their various homes. Soon the sleepiness wore off, and, when the train was about to start, the reality of the parting seemed to strike home, and the final hand-shakings and good wishes were earnest and hearty.

Thus, little by little, the band grew less and less.

Montreal swallowed up a good many. While there the whole band went out for a walk on the heights above the reservoir with their Guardian, guided by a young Scotsman.

"That's a jolly-lookin' 'ouse, Tim," said Bob Frog to his friend.

The Scotsman overheard the remark.

"Yes," said he, "it is a nice house, and a good jolly man owns it. He began life as a poor boy. And do you see that other villa—the white one with the green veranda among the trees? That was built by a man who came out from England just as you have done, only without anybody to take care of him; God however cared for him, and now you see his house. He began life without a penny, but he had three qualities which will make a man of any boy, no matter what circumstances he may be placed in. He was truthful, thorough, and trust-worthy. Men knew that they might believe what he said, be sure of the quality of what he did, and could rely upon his promises. There was another thing much in his favour, he was a total abstainer. Drink in this country ruins hundreds of men and women, just as in England. Shun drink, boys, as you would a serpent."

"I wouldn't shun a drink o' water just now if I could get it," whispered Bobby to his friend, "for I'm uncommon thirsty."

At this point the whole band were permitted to disperse in the woods, where they went about climbing and skipping like wild squirrels, for these novel sights, and scents, and circumstances were overwhelmingly delightful after the dirt and smoke of London.

When pretty well breathed—our waifs were grown too hardy by that time to be easily exhausted —the Guardian got them to sit round him and sing that sweet hymn:—

"Shall we gather at the river?"

And tears bedewed many eyes, for they were reminded that there were yet many partings in store before that gathering should take place.

And now the remnant of the band—still a goodly number—proceeded in the direction of the far west. All night they travelled, and reached Belleville, where they were received joyfully in the large house presented as a free gift to Miss Macpherson by the Council of the County of Hastings. It served as a " Distributing Home" and centre in Canada for the little ones till they could be placed in suitable situations, and to it they might be returned if necessary, or a change of employer required it. This Belleville Home was afterwards burned to the ground, and rebuilt by sympathising Canadian friends.

But we may not pause long here. The far west

still lies before us.   Our gradually diminishing band
must push on.

"It's the sea!" exclaimed the boy who had been
named little Mouse, *alias* Robbie Dell.

"No, it aint," said Konky, who was a good deal
older; "it's a lake."

"Ontario," said the Guardian, "one of the noble
fresh-water seas of Canada."

Onward, ever onward, is the watchword just now
—dropping boys like seed-corn as they go!   Woods
and fields, and villas, and farms, and waste-lands,
and forests, and water, fly past in endless variety
and loveliness.

"A panoramy without no end!" exclaimed Tim
Lumpy after one of his long gazes of silent admiration.

"*Wot* a diff'rence!" murmured Bobby Frog.
"Wouldn't mother an' daddy an' Hetty like it,
just!"

The city of Toronto came in sight.   The wise
arrangements for washing in Canadian railway-cars
had been well used by the boys, and pocket-combs
also.   They looked clean and neat and wonderfully
solemn as they landed at the station.

But their fame had preceded them.   An earnest
crowd came to see the boys, among whom were
some eager to appropriate.

"I'll take that lad," said one bluff farmer, stepping

forward, and pointing to a boy whose face had taken his fancy.

"And I want six boys for our village," said another.

"I want one to learn my business," said a third, "and I'll learn him as my own son. Here are my certificates of character from my clergyman and the mayor of the place I belong to."

"I like the looks of that little fellow," said another, pointing to Bob Frog, "and should like to have him."

"Does you, my tulip?" said Bobby, whose natural tendency to insolence had not yet been subdued; "an' don't you vish you may get 'im!"

It is but justice to Bobby, however, to add, that this remark was made entirely to himself.

To all these flattering offers the Guardian turned a deaf ear, until he had passed through the crowd and marshalled his boys in an empty room of the depôt. Then inquiries were made; the boys' characters and capacities explained; suitability on both sides considered; the needs of the soul as well as the body referred to and pressed; and, finally, the party went on its way greatly reduced in numbers.

Thus they dwindled and travelled westward until only our friend Bobby, Tim, Konky, and little Mouse remained with the Guardian, whose affections seemed to intensify as fewer numbers were left on which they might concentrate.

Soon the little Mouse was caught. A huge backwoods farmer, who could have almost put him in his coat-pocket, took a fancy to him. The fancy seemed to be mutual, for, after a tearful farewell to the Guardian, the Mouse went off with the backwoodsman quite contentedly.

Then Konky was disposed of. A hearty old lady with a pretty daughter and a slim son went away with him in triumph, and the band was reduced to two.

"I do believe," whispered Bob to Tim, "that he's goin' to let us stick together after all."

"You are right, my dear boy," said the Guardian, who overheard the remark. "A family living a considerable distance off wishes to have two boys. I have reason to believe that they love the Lord Jesus, and will treat you well. So, as I knew you wished to be together, I have arranged for your going to live with them."

As the journey drew to a close, the Guardian seemed to concentrate his whole heart on the little waifs whom he had conducted so far, and he gave them many words of counsel, besides praying with and for them.

At last, towards evening, the train rushed into a grand pine wood. It soon rushed out of it again and entered a beautiful piece of country which was diversified by lakelet and rivulet, hill and vale, with rich meadow lands in the hollows, where cattle browsed or lay in the evening sunshine.

The train drew up sharply at a small road-side station. There was no one to get into the cars there, and no one to get out except our two waifs. On the road beyond stood a wagon with a couple of spanking bays in it. On the platform stood a broad-shouldered, deep-chested, short-legged farmer with a face like the sun, and a wide-awake on the back of his bald head.

"Mr. Merryboy, I presume?" said the Guardian, descending from the car.

"The same. Glad to see you. Are these my boys?"

He spoke in a quick, hearty, off-hand manner, but Bobby and Tim hated him at once, for were they not on the point of leaving their last and best friend, and was not this man the cause?

They turned to their Guardian to say farewell, and, even to their own surprise, burst into tears.

"God bless you, dear boys," he said, while the guard held open the door of the car as if to suggest haste; "good-bye. It won't be *very* long I think before I see you again. Farewell."

He sprang into the car, the train glided away, and the two waifs stood looking wistfully after it with the first feelings of desolation that had entered their hearts since landing in Canada.

"My poor lads," said Mr. Merryboy, laying a hand on the shoulder of each, "come along with me. Home is only six miles off, and I've got a pair of spanking horses that will trundle us over in no time."

The tone of voice, to say nothing of "home" and "spanking horses," improved matters greatly. Both boys thought, as they entered the wagon, that they did not hate him quite so much as at first.

The bays proved worthy of their master's praise. They went over the road through the forest in grand style, and in little more than half an hour landed Bobby and Tim at the door of their Canadian home.

It was dark by that time, and the ruddy light that shone in the windows and streamed through the door as it opened to receive them seemed to our waifs like a gleam of celestial light.

CHAPTER XIX.

AT HOME IN CANADA.

THE family of Mr. Merryboy was a small one. Besides those who assisted him on the farm—and who were in some cases temporary servants—his household consisted of his wife, his aged mother, a female servant, and a small girl. The latter was a diamond from the London diggings, who had been imported the year before. She was undergoing the process of being polished, and gave promise of soon becoming a very valuable gem. It was this that induced her employer to secure our two masculine gems from the same diggings.

Mrs. Merryboy was a vigorous, hearty, able-bodied lady, who loved work very much for the mere exercise it afforded her; who, like her husband, was constitutionally kind, and whose mind was of that serious type which takes concern with the souls of the people with whom it has to do as well as with their bodies. Hence she gave her waif a daily lesson in religious and secular knowledge;

she reduced work on the Sabbath-days to the lowest possible point in the establishment, and induced her husband, who was a little shy as well as bluff and off-hand, to institute family worship, besides hanging on her walls here and there sweet and striking texts from the Word of God.

Old Mrs. Merryboy, the mother, must have been a merry girl in her youth; for, even though at the age of eighty and partially deaf, she was extremely fond of a joke, practical or otherwise, and had her face so seamed with the lines of appreciative humour, and her nut-cracker mouth so set in a smile of amiable fun, and her coal-black eyes so lit up with the fires of unutterable wit, that a mere glance at her stirred up your sources of comicality to their depths, while a steady gaze usually resulted in a laugh, in which she was sure to join with an apparent belief that, whatever the joke might be, it was uncommonly good. She did not speak much. Her looks and smiles rendered speech almost unnecessary. Her figure was unusually diminutive.

Little Martha, the waif, was one of those mild, reticent, tiny things that one feels a desire to fondle without knowing why. Her very small face was always, and, as Bobby remarked, awfully grave, yet a ready smile must have lurked close at hand somewhere, for it could be evoked by the smallest provocation at any time, but fled the instant the provoking cause ceased. She seldom laughed, but when she did the burst was a hearty one, and over immediately. Her brown hair was smooth, her brown eyes were gentle, her red mouth was small and round. Obedience was ingrained in her nature. Original action seemed never to have entered her imagination. She appeared to have been born with the idea that her sphere in life was to do as she was directed. To resist and fight were to her impossibilities. To be defended and kissed seemed to be her natural perquisites. Yet her early life had been calculated to foster other and far different qualities, as we shall learn ere long.

Tim Lumpy took to this little creature amazingly. She was *so* little that by contrast he became quite big, and felt so! When in Martha's presence he absolutely felt big and like a lion, a roaring lion capable of defending her against all comers! Bobby was also attracted by her, but in a comparatively mild degree.

On the morning after their arrival the two boys awoke to find that the windows of their separate little rooms opened upon a magnificent prospect of wood and water, and that, the partition of their apartment consisting of a single plank-wall, with sundry knots knocked out, they were not only able to converse freely, but to peep at each other awkwardly

—facts which they had not observed the night before, owing to sleepiness.

"I say, Tim," said Bob, "you seem to have a jolly place in there."

"First-rate," replied Tim, "an' much the same as your own. I had a good squint at you before you awoke. Isn't the place splendacious?"

"Yes, Tim, it is. I've been lookin' about all the mornin' for Adam an' Eve, but can't see 'em nowhere."

"What d'ee mean?"

"Why, that we've got into the garden of Eden, to be sure."

"Oh! stoopid," returned Tim, "don't you know that they was both banished from Eden?"

"So they was. I forgot that. Well, it don't much matter, for there's a prettier girl than Eve here. Don't you see her? Martha, I think they called her—down there by the summer-'ouse, feedin' the hanimals, or givin' 'em their names."

"There you go again, you ignorant booby," said Tim; "it wasn't Eve as gave the beasts their names. It was Adam."

"An' wot's the difference, I should like to know? wasn't they both made *one* flesh? However, I think little Martha would have named 'em better if she'd bin there. What a funny little thing she is!"

"Funny!" returned Tim, contemptuously; "she's a trump!"

During the conversation both boys had washed and rubbed their faces till they absolutely shone like rosy apples. They also combed and brushed their hair to such an extent that each mass lay quite flat on its little head, and bade fair to become solid, for the Guardian's loving counsels had not been forgotten, and they had a sensation of wishing to please him even although absent.

Presently the house, which had hitherto been very quiet, began suddenly to resound with the barking of a little dog and the noisy voice of a huge man. The former rushed about, saying " Good-morning " as well as it could with tail and tongue to every one, including the household cat, which resented the familiarity with arched back and demoniacal glare. The latter stamped about on the wooden floors, and addressed similar salutations right and left in tones that would have suited the commander of an army. There was a sudden stoppage of the hurricane, and a pleasant female voice was heard.

" I say, Bob, that's the missus," whispered Tim through a knot-hole.

Then there came another squall, which seemed to drive madly about all the echoes in the corridors above and in the cellars below. Again the noise ceased, and there came up a sound like a wheezy squeak.

" I say, Tim, that's the old 'un," whispered Bob through the knot-hole.

Bob was right, for immediately on the wheezy squeak ceasing, the hurricane burst forth in reply :—

"Yes, mother, that's just what I shall do. You're always right. I never knew such an old thing for wise suggestions! I'll set both boys to milk the cows after breakfast. The sooner they learn the better, for our new girl has too much to do in the house to attend to that; besides, she's either clumsy or nervous, for she has twice overturned the milk-pail. But after all, I don't wonder, for that red cow has several times showed a desire to fling a hind-leg into the girl's face, and stick a horn in her gizzard. The boys won't mind that, you know. Pity that Martha's too small for the work; but she'll grow—she'll grow."

"Yes, she'll grow, Franky," replied the old lady, with as knowing a look as if the richest of jokes had been cracked. The look was, of course, lost on the boys above, and so was the reply, because it reached them in the form of a wheezy squeak.

"Oh! I say! Did you ever! Milk the keows! On'y think!" whispered Bob.

"Ay, an' won't I do it with my mouth open too, an' learn 'ow to send the stream up'ards!" said Tim.

Their comments were cut short by the breakfast bell; at the same time the hurricane again burst forth :—

"Hallo! lads—boys! Youngsters! Are you up?

—ah! here you are. Good-morning, and as tidy as two pins. That's the way to get along in life. Come now, sit down. Where's Martha? Oh! here we are. Sit beside me, little one."

The hurricane suddenly fell to a gentle breeze, while part of a chapter of the Bible and a short prayer were read. Then it burst forth again with redoubled fury, checked only now and then by the unavoidable stuffing of the vent-hole.

"You've slept well, dears, I hope?" said Mrs. Merryboy, helping each of our waifs to a splendid fried fish.

Sitting there, partially awe-stricken by the novelty of their surroundings, they admitted that they had slept well.

"Get ready for work then," said Mr. Merryboy, through a rather large mouthful. "No time to lose. Eat—eat well—for there's lots to do. No idlers on Brankly Farm, I can tell you. And we don't let young folk lie abed till breakfast-time every day. We let you rest this morning, Bob and Tim, just by way of an extra refresher before beginning. Here, tuck into the bread and butter, little man, it'll make you grow. More tea, Susy (to his wife). Why, mother, you're eating nothing—nothing at all. I declare you'll come to live on air at last."

The old lady smiled benignly, as though rather tickled with that joke, and was understood by the boys to protest that she had eaten more than

S

enough, though her squeak had not yet become intelligible to them.

"If you do take to living on air, mother," said her daughter-in-law, "we shall have to boil it up with a bit of beef and butter to make it strong."

Mrs. Merryboy, senior, smiled again at this, though she had not heard a word of it. Obviously she made no pretence of hearing, but took it as good on credit, for she immediately turned to her son, put her hand to her right ear, and asked what Susy said.

In thunderous tones the joke was repeated, and the old lady almost went into fits over it, insomuch that Bob and Tim regarded her with a spice of anxiety mingled with their amusement, while little Martha looked at her in solemn wonder.

Twelve months' experience had done much to increase Martha's love for the old lady, but it had done nothing to reduce her surprise; for Martha, as yet, did not understand a joke. This, of itself, formed a subject of intense amusement to old Mrs. Merryboy, who certainly made the most of circumstances, if ever woman did.

"Have some more fish, Bob," said Mrs. Merryboy, junior.

Bob accepted more, gratefully. So did Tim, with alacrity.

"What sort of a home had you in London, Tim?" asked Mrs. Merryboy.

" Well, ma'am, I hadn't no home at all."

" No home at all, boy ; what do you mean ? You *must* have lived somewhere."

" Oh yes, ma'am, I always lived somewheres, but it wasn't nowheres in partikler. You see I'd neither father nor mother, an' though a good old 'ooman did take me in, she couldu't purvide a bed or blankets, an' her 'ome was stuffy, so I preferred to live in the streets, an' sleep of a night w'en I couldn't pay for a lodgin', in empty casks and under wegitable carts in Covent Garden Market, or in empty sugar 'ogsheads. I liked the 'ogsheads best w'en I was 'ungry, an' that was most always, 'cause I could sometimes pick a little sugar that was left in the cracks an' 'oles, w'en they 'adn't bin cleaned out a'ready. Also I slep' under railway arches, and on door-steps. But sometimes I 'ad raither disturbed nights, 'cause the coppers wouldu't let a feller sleep in sitch places if they could 'elp it."

" Who are the ' coppers ?' " asked the good lady of the house, who listened in wonder to Tim's narration.

" The slopps, ma'am, the—the—pl'eece."

" Oh ! the police ? "

" Yes, ma'am."

"Where in the world did they expect you to sleep?" asked Mrs. Merryboy with some indignation.

" That's best known to themselves, ma'um," returned Tim;" "p'raps we might 'ave bin allowed to sleep on the Thames, if we'd 'ad a mind to, or on the hatmosphere, but never 'avin' tried it on, I can't say."

"Did you lead the same sort of life, Bob?" asked the farmer, who had by that time appeased his appetite.

"Pretty much so, sir," replied Bobby, "though I wasn't quite so 'ard up as Tim, havin' both a father and mother as well as a 'ome. But they was costly possessions, so I was forced to give 'em up."

"What! you don't mean that you forsook them?" said Mr. Merryboy with a touch of severity.

"No, sir, but father forsook me and the rest of us, by gettin' into the Stone Jug—wery much agin' my earnest advice,—an' mother an' sister both thought it was best for me to come out here."

The two waifs, being thus encouraged, came out with their experiences pretty freely, and made such a number of surprising revelations, that the worthy backwoodsman and his wife were lost in astonishment, to the obvious advantage of old Mrs. Merryboy, who, regarding the varying expressions of face around her as the result of a series of excellent jokes, went into a state of chronic laughter of a mild type.

"Have some more bread and butter, and tea, Bob and some more sausage," said Mrs. Merryboy, under a sudden impulse.

Bob declined. Yes, that London street-arab absolutely declined food! So did Tim Lumpy!

"Now, my lads, are you quite sure," said Mr. Merryboy, "that you've had enough to eat?"

They both protested, with some regret, that they had.

"You couldn't eat another bite if you was to try, could you?"

"Vell, sir," said Bob, with a spice of the 'old country' insolence strong upon him, "there's no sayin' what might be accomplished with a heffort, but the consikences, you know, might be serious."

The farmer received this with a thunderous guffaw, and, bidding the boys follow him, went out.

He took them round the farm buildings, commenting on and explaining everything, showed them cattle and horses, pigs and poultry, barns and stables, and then asked them how they thought they'd like to work there.

"Uncommon!" was Bobby Frog's prompt reply, delivered with emphasis.

"Fust rate!" was Tim Lumpy's sympathetic sentiment.

"Well, then, the sooner we begin the better. D'you see that lot of cord-wood lying tumbled about in the yard, Bob?"

"Yes, sir."

"You go to work on it, then, and pile it up against

that fence, same as you see this one done. An' let's
see how neatly you'll do it. Don't hurry. What
we want in Canada is not so much to see work done
quickly as done well."

Taking Tim to another part of the farm, he set
him to remove a huge heap of stones with a barrow
and shovel, and, leaving them, returned to the house.

Both boys set to work with a will. It was to
them the beginning of life; they felt that, and were
the more anxious to do well in consequence. Remembering the farmer's caution, they did not hurry,
but Tim built a cone of stones with the care and
artistic exactitude of an architect, while Bobby
piled his billets of wood with as much regard to sym-
metrical proportion as was possible in the circumstances.

About noon they became hungry, but hunger was
an old foe whom they had been well trained to defy,
so they worked on utterly regardless of him.

Thereafter a welcome sound was heard—the
dinner-bell!

Having been told to come in on hearing it, they
left work at once, ran to the pump, washed themselves, and appeared in the dining-room looking hot,
but bright and jovial, for nothing brightens the
human countenance so much (by gladdening the
heart) as the consciousness of having performed
duty well.

From the first this worthy couple, who were
childless, received the boys into their home as sons,
and on all occasions treated them as such. Martha
Mild (her surname was derived from her character)
had been similarly received and treated.

"Well, lads," said the farmer as they commenced
the meal—which was a second edition of breakfast,
tea included, but with more meat and vegetables—
"how did you find the work ? pretty hard—eh ?"

"Oh! no, sir, nothink of the kind," said Bobby,
who was resolved to show a disposition to work like
a man and think nothing of it.

"Ah, good. I'll find you some harder work
after dinner."

Bobby blamed himself for having been so prompt
in reply.

"The end of this month, too, I'll have you both
sent to school," continued the farmer with a look
of hearty good-will, that Tim thought would have
harmonised better with a promise to give them jam-
tart and cream. "It's vacation time just now, and
the schoolmaster's away for a holiday. When he
comes back you'll have to cultivate mind as well as
soil, my boys, for I've come under an obligation to
look after your education, and even if I hadn't, I'd
do it to satisfy my own conscience."

The *couleur-de-rose* with which Bob and Tim had
begun to invest their future faded perceptibly on

hearing this. The viands, however, were so good that it did not disturb them very much. They ate away heartily, and in silence. Little Martha was not less diligent, for she had been busy all the morning in the dairy and kitchen, playing, rather than working, at domestic concerns, yet in her play doing much real work, and acquiring useful knowledge, as well as an appetite.

After dinner the farmer rose at once. He was one of those who find it unnecessary either to drink or smoke after meals. Indeed, strong drink and tobacco were unknown in his house, and, curiously enough, nobody seemed to be a whit the worse for their absence. There were some people, indeed, who even went the length of asserting that they were all the better for their absence!

"Now for the hard work I promised you, boys; come along."

CHAPTER XX.

OCCUPATIONS AT BRANKLY FARM.

THE farmer led our two boys through a deliciously
scented pine-wood at the rear of his house, to a
valley which seemed to extend and widen out into a
multitude of lesser valleys and clumps of woodland,
where lakelets and rivulets and waterfalls glittered
in the afternoon sun like shields and bands of bur-
nished silver.

Taking a ball of twine from one of his capacious
pockets, he gave it to Bobby along with a small
pocket-book.

"Have you got clasp-knives?" he asked.

"Yes, sir," said both boys, at once producing in-
struments which were very much the worse for
wear.

"Very well, now, here is the work I want you to
do for me this afternoon. D'you see the creek
down in the hollow yonder—about half a mile off?"

"Yes, yes, sir."

"Well, go down there and cut two sticks about
ten feet long each; tie strings to the small ends of

them; fix hooks that you'll find in that pocket-book to the lines. The creek below the fall is swarming with fish; you'll find grasshoppers and worms enough for bait if you choose to look for 'em. Go, and see what you can do."

A reminiscence of ancient times induced Bobby Frog to say "Walke-e-r!" to himself, but he had too much wisdom to say it aloud. He did, however, venture modestly to remark—

"I knows nothink about fishin', sir. Never cotched so much as a eel in—"

"When I give you orders, *obey* them!" inter-rupted the farmer, in a tone and with a look that sent Bobby and Tim to the right-about double-quick. They did not even venture to look back until they reached the pool pointed out, and when they did look back Mr. Merryboy had disappeared.

"Vell, I say," began Bobby, but Tim interrupted him with, "Now Bob you *must* git off that 'abit you've got o' puttin' v's for double-u's. Wasn't we told by the genl'm'n that gave us a partin' had-dress that we'd never git on in the noo world if we didn't mind our p's and q's? An' here you are as regardless of your v's as if they'd no connection wi' the alphabet."

"Pretty cove *you* are, to find fault wi' *me*," re-torted Bob, "w'en you're far wuss wi' your haitches —a-droppin' of 'em w'en you shouldn't ought to, an'

stickin' of 'em in where you oughtn't should to. Go
along an' cut your stick, as master told you."

The sticks were cut, pieces of string were measured off, and hooks attached thereto. Then grasshoppers were caught, impaled, and dropped into a
pool. The immediate result was almost electrify-
ing to lads who had never caught even a minnow
before. Bobby's hook had barely sunk when it was
seized and run away with so forcibly as to draw a
tremendous "Hi! hallo!! ho!!! I've got 'im!!!"
from the fisher.

"Hoy! hurroo!!" responded Tim, "so 'v I!!!"

Both boys, blazing with excitement, held on.

The fish, bursting, apparently, with even greater
excitement, rushed off.

"He'll smash my stick!" cried Bob.

"The twine's sure to go!" cried Tim.   "Hold
o-o-on!"

This command was addressed to his fish, which
leaped high out of the pool and went wriggling
back with a heavy splash. It did not obey the
order, but the hook did, which came to the same
thing.

"A ten-pounder if he's a' ounce," said Tim.

"You tell that to the horse—hi ho! stop that,
will you?"

But Bobby's fish was what himself used to be,
troublesome to deal with. It would not "stop that."

It kept darting from side to side and leaping out of
the water until, in one of its bursts, it got entangled
with Tim's fish, and the boys were obliged to haul
them both ashore together.

" Splendid ! " exclaimed Bobby, as they unhooked
two fine trout and laid them on a place of safety;
" At 'em again ! "

At them they went, and soon had two more fish,
but the disturbance created by these had the effect
of frightening the others. At all events, at their
third effort their patience was severely tried, for
nothing came to their hooks to reward the intense
gaze and the nervous readiness to act which marked
each boy during the next half hour or so.

At the end of that time there came a change in
their favour, for little Martha Mild appeared on the
scene. She had been sent, she said, to work with
them.

" To play with us, you mean," suggested Tim.

" No, father said work," the child returned simply.

" It's jolly work, then! But I say, old 'ooman,
d' you call Mr. Merryboy father ? " asked Bob in
surprise.

" Yes, I 've called him father ever since I came."

" An' who 's your real father ? "

" I have none.   Never had one."

" An' your mother ? "

" Never had a mother either."

" Well, you air a curiosity."

" Hallo ! Bob, don't forget your purliteness," said Tim. " Come, Mumpy; father calls you Mumpy, doesn't he ? "

" Yes."

"Then so will I. Well, Mumpy, as I was goin' to say, you may come an' *work* with my rod if you like, an' we 'll make a game of it. We 'll play at work. Let me see where shall we be ? "

" In the garden of Eden," suggested Bob.

" The very thing," said Tim; " I 'll be Adam an' you 'll be Eve, Mumpy."

" Very well," said Martha with ready assent.

She would have assented quite as readily to have personated Jezebel or the Witch of Endor.

" And I 'll be Cain," said Bobby, moving his line in a manner that was meant to be persuasive.

" Oh !" said Martha, with much diffidence, " Cain was wicked, wasn't he ? "

" Well, my dear Eve," said Tim, " Bobby Frog is wicked enough for half-a-dozen Cains. In fact, you can't cane him enough to pay him off for all his wickedness."

" Bah ! go to bed," said Cain, still intent on his line, which seemed to quiver as if with a nibble.

As for Eve, being as innocent of pun-appreciation as her great original probably was, she looked at the two boys in pleased gravity.

"Hi! Cain's got another bite," cried Adam, while Eve went into a state of gentle excitement, and fluttered near with an evidently strong desire to help in some way.

"Hallo! got 'im again!" shouted Tim, as his rod bent to the water with jerky violence; "out o' the way, Eve, else you'll get shoved into Gihon."

"Euphrates, you stoopid!" said Cain, turning his Beehive training to account. Having lost his fish, you see, he could afford to be critical while he fixed on another bait.

But Tim cared not for rivers or names just then, having hooked a "real wopper," which gave him some trouble to land. When landed, it proved to be the finest fish of the lot, much to Eve's satisfaction, who sat down to watch the process when Adam renewed the bait.

Now, Bobby Frog, not having as yet been quite reformed, and, perhaps, having imbibed some of the spirit of his celebrated prototype with his name, felt a strong impulse to give Tim a gentle push behind. For Tim sat in an irresistibly tempting position on the bank, with his little boots overhanging the dark pool from which the fish had been dragged.

"Tim," said Bob.

"Adam, if you please—or call me father, if you prefer it!"

"Well, then, father, since I haven't got an

Abel to kill, I'm only too 'appy to have a Adam to souse."

Saying which, he gave him a sufficient impulse to send him off!

Eve gave vent to a treble shriek, on beholding her husband struggling in the water, and Cain himself felt somewhat alarmed at what he had done. He quickly extended the butt of his rod to his father, and dragged him safe to land, to poor Eve's inexpressible relief.

"What d'ee mean by that, Bob?" demanded Tim fiercely, as he sprang towards his companion.

"Cain, if you please—or call me son, if you prefers it," cried Bob, as he ran out of his friend's way; "but don't be waxy, father Adam, with your own darlin' boy. I couldn't 'elp it. You'd ha' done just the same to me if you'd had the chance. Come, shake 'ands on it."

Tim Lumpy was not the boy to cherish bad feeling. He grinned in a ghastly manner, and shook the extended hand.

"I forgive you, Cain, but please go an' look for Abel an' pitch into *him* w'en next you git into that state o' mind, for it's agin common sense, as well as history, to pitch into your old father so." Saying which, Tim went off to wring out his dripping garments, after which the fishing was resumed.

"Wot a re-markable difference," said Bobby,

breaking a rather long silence of expectancy, as he glanced round on the splendid landscape which was all aglow with the descending sun, "'tween these 'ere diggin's an' Commercial Road, or George Yard, or Ratcliffe 'Ighway. Ain't it, Tim?"

Before Tim could reply, Mr. Merryboy came forward.

"Capital!" he exclaimed, on catching sight of the fish; "well done, lads, well done. We shall have a glorious supper to-night. Now, Mumpy, you run home and tell mother to have the big frying-pan ready. She'll want your help. Ha!" he added, turning to the boys, as Martha ran off with her wonted alacrity, "I thought you'd soon teach yourselves how to catch fish. It's not difficult here. And what do you think of Martha, my boys?"

"She's a trump!" said Bobby, with decision.

"Fust rate!" said Tim, bestowing his highest conception of praise.

"Quite true, lads; though why you should say "fust" instead of *first*-rate, Tim, is more than I can understand. However, you'll get cured of suchlike queer pronunciations in course of time. Now, I want you to look on little Mumpy as your sister, and she's a good deal of your sister too in reality, for she came out of that same great nest of good and bad, rich and poor—London. Has she told you anything about herself yet?"

"Nothin', sir," answered Bob, "'cept that when we axed—asked, I mean—I ax—ask, your parding—she said she'd neither father nor mother."

"Ah! poor thing; that's too true. Come, pick up your fish, and I'll tell you about her as we go along."

The boys strung their fish on a couple of branches, and followed their new master home.

"Martha came to us only last year," said the farmer. "She's a little older than she looks, having been somewhat stunted in her growth, by bad treatment, I suppose, and starvation and cold in her infancy. No one knows who was her father or mother. She was "found" in the streets one day, when about three years of age, by a man who took her home, and made use of her by sending her to sell matches in public-houses. Being small, very intelligent for her years, and attractively modest, she succeeded, I suppose, in her sales, and I doubt not the man would have continued to keep her, if he had not been taken ill and carried to hospital, where he died. Of course the man's lodging was given up the day he left it. As the man had been a misanthrope—that's a hater of everybody, lads—nobody cared anything about him, or made inquiry after him. The consequence was, that poor Martha was forgotten, strayed away into the streets, and got lost a second time. She was picked up this time by a widow lady in very reduced circumstances, who questioned her closely; but all that the poor little creature knew was that she didn't know where her home was, that she had no father or mother, and that her name was Martha

"The widow took her home, made inquiries about her parentage in vain, and then adopted and began to train her, which accounts for her having so little of that slang and knowledge of London low life that you have so much of, you rascals! The lady gave the child the pet surname of Mild, for it was so descriptive of her character. But poor Martha was not destined to have this mother very long. After a few years she died, leaving not a sixpence or a rag behind her worth having. Thus little Mumpy was thrown a third time on the world, but God found a protector for her in a friend of the widow, who sent her to the Refuge—the Beehive as you call it—which has been such a blessing to you, my lads, and to so many like you, and along with her the £10 required to pay her passage and outfit to Canada. They kept her for some time and trained her, and then, knowing that I wanted a little lass here, they sent her to me, for which I thank God, for she's a dear little child."

The tone in which the last sentence was uttered told more than any words could have conveyed the feelings of the bluff farmer towards the little gem that had been dug out of the London mines and thus given to him.

Reader, they are prolific mines, those East-end mines of London! If you doubt it, go, hear and see for yourself. Perhaps it were better advice to say, go and dig, or help the miners!

Need it be said that our waifs and strays grew and flourished in that rich Canadian soil? It need not! One of the most curious consequences of the new connection was the powerful affection that sprang up between Bobby Frog and Mrs. Merryboy, senior. It seemed as if that jovial old lady and our London waif had fallen in love with each other at first sight. Perhaps the fact that the lady was intensely appreciative of fun, and the young gentleman wonderfully full of the same, had something to do with it. Whatever the cause, these two were constantly flirting with each other, and Bob often took the old lady out for little rambles in the wood behind the farm.

There was a particular spot in the woods, near a waterfall, of which this curious couple were particularly fond, and to which they frequently resorted, and there, under the pleasant shade, with the roar of the fall for a symphony, Bob poured out his hopes and fears, reminiscences and prospects into the willing ears of the little old lady, who was so very small that Bob seemed quite a big man by contrast. He had to roar almost as loud as the cataract to make her hear, but he was well rewarded. The old lady, it is true, did not speak much, perhaps because she understood little, but she expressed enough of sympathy, by means of nods, and winks with her brilliant black eyes, and smiles with her toothless mouth, to satisfy any boy of moderate expectations.

And Bobby *was* satisfied. So, also, were the other waifs and strays, not only with old granny, but with everything in and around their home in the New World.

CHAPTER XXI.

TREATS OF ALTERED CIRCUMSTANCES AND BLUE RIBBONISM.

ONCE again we return to the great city, and to
Mrs. Frog's poor lodging.

But it is not poor now, for the woman has
at last got riches and joy—such riches as the
ungodly care not for, and a joy that they cannot
understand.

It is not all riches and joy, however. The Master
has told us that we shall have " much tribulation."
What then ? Are we worse off than the unbelievers ?
Do *they* escape the tribulation ? It is easy to
prove that the Christian has the advantage of the
worldling, for, while both have worries and tribulation without fail, the one has a little joy along
with these—nay, much joy if you choose—which,
however, will end with life, if not before ; while
the other has joy unspeakable and full of glory,
which will increase with years, and end in absolute
felicity !

Let us look at Mrs. Frog's room now, and listen
to her as she sits on one side of a cheerful fire, sew-

ing, while Hetty sits on the other side, similarly occupied, and Matty, *alias* Mita, lies in her crib sound asleep.

It is the same room, the same London atmosphere, which no moral influence will ever purify, and pretty much the same surroundings, for Mrs. Frog's outward circumstances have not altered much in a worldly point of view. The neighbours in the court are not less filthy and violent. One drunken nuisance has left the next room, but another almost as bad has taken his place. Nevertheless, although not altered much, things are decidedly improved in the poor pitiful dwelling. Whereas, in time past, it used to be dirty, now it is clean. The table is the same table, obviously, for you can see the crack across the top caused by Ned's great fist on that occasion when, failing rather in force of argument while laying down the law, he sought to emphasise his remarks with an effective blow; but a craftsman has been at work on the table, and it is no longer rickety. The chair, too, on which Mrs. Frog sits, is the same identical chair which missed the head of Bobby Frog that time he and his father differed in opinion on some trifling matter, and smashed a panel of the door; but the chair has been to see the doctor, and its constitution is stronger now. The other chair, on which Hetty sits, is a distinct innovation. So is baby's crib. It has replaced the heap of straw which formerly sufficed, and there are two low bedsteads in corners which once were empty.

Besides all this there are numerous articles of varied shape and size glittering on the walls, such as sauce-pans and pot-lids, etc., which are made to do ornamental as well as useful duty, being polished to the highest possible degree of brilliancy. Everywhere there is evidence of order and care, showing that the inmates of the room are somehow in better circumstances.

Let it not be supposed that this has been accomplished by charity. Mrs. Samuel Twitter is very charitable undoubtedly. There can be no question as to that; but if she were a hundred times more charitable than she is, and were to give away a hundred thousand times more money than she does give, she could not greatly diminish the vast poverty of London. Mrs. Twitter had done what she could in this case, but that was little, in a money point of view, for there were others who had stronger claims upon her than Mrs. Frog. But Mrs. Twitter had put her little finger under Mrs. Frog's chin when her lips were about to go under water, and so, figuratively, she kept her from drowning. Mrs. Twitter had put out a hand when Mrs. Frog tripped and was about to tumble, and thus kept her from falling. When Mrs. Frog, weary of life, was on the point of rushing once again to London Bridge, with a purpose, Mrs. Twitter caught the skirt of her ragged robe with a firm but kindly grasp and held her back, thus saving her from destruction; but, best of all, when the poor woman, under the influence of the Spirit of God, ceased to strive with her Maker and cried out earnestly, "What must I do to be saved?" Mrs. Twitter grasped her with both hands and dragged her with tender violence towards the Fold, but not quite into it.

For Mrs. Twitter was a wise, unselfish woman, as well as good. At a certain point she ceased to act, and said, "Mrs. Frog, go to your own Hetty, and she will tell you what to do."

And Mrs. Frog went, and Hetty, with joyful surprise in her heart, and warm tears of gratitude in her eyes, pointed her to Jesus the Saviour of mankind. It was nothing new to the poor woman to be thus directed. It is nothing new to almost any one in a Christian land to be pointed to Christ; but it *is* something new to many a one to have the eyes opened to see, and the will influenced to accept. It was so now with this poor, self-willed, and long-tried—or, rather, long-resisting—woman. The Spirit's time had come, and she was made willing. But now she had to face the difficulties of the new life. Conscience—never killed, and now revived—began to act.

"I must work," she said, internally, and conscience nodded approval. "I must drink less," she said, but conscience shook her head. "It will be very hard, you see," she continued, apologetically, "for a poor woman like me to get through a hard day without just *one* glass of beer to strengthen me."

Conscience did all her work by looks alone. She was naturally dumb, but she had a grand majestic countenance with great expressive eyes, and at the mention of *one* glass of beer she frowned so that poor Mrs. Frog almost trembled.

At this point Hetty stepped into the conversation. All unaware of what had been going on in her mother's mind, she said, suddenly, "Mother, I'm going to a meeting to-night; will you come?"

Mrs. Frog was quite willing. In fact she had fairly given in and become biddable like a little child,—though, after all, that interesting creature does not always, or necessarily, convey the most perfect idea of obedience!

It was a rough meeting, composed of rude elements, in a large but ungilded hall in Whitechapel. The people were listening intently to a powerful speaker.

The theme was strong drink. There were opponents and sympathisers there. "It is the greatest curse, I think, in London," said the speaker, as Hetty and her mother entered. "Bah!" exclaimed a powerful man beside whom they chanced to sit down. "I've drank a lot on't an' don't find it no curse, at all." "Silence," cried some in the audience. "I tell 'ee it's all bam wot 'e's talkin'," said the powerful man. "Put 'im out," cried some of the audience. But the powerful man had a powerful look, and a great bristly jaw, and a fierce pair of eyes which had often been blackened, and still bore the hues of the last fight; no one, therefore, attempted to put him out, so he snapped his fingers at the entire meeting, said, "Bah!" again, with a look of contempt, and relapsed into silence, while the speaker, heedless of the slight interruption, went on.

"Why, it's a Blue Ribbon meeting, Hetty," whispered Mrs. Frog.

"Yes, mother," whispered Hetty in reply, "that's one of its names, but its real title, I heard one gentleman say, is the Gospel-Temperance Association, for, you see, they're very anxious to put the gospel first and temperance second; temperance bein' only one of the fruits of the gospel of Jesus."

The speaker went on in eloquent strains pleading the great cause—now drawing out the sympathies of his hearers, then appealing to their reason; sometimes relating incidents of deepest pathos, at other times convulsing the audience with touches of the broadest humour, insomuch that the man who said "bah!" modified his objections to "pooh!" and ere long came to that turning-point where silence is consent. In this condition he remained until reference was made by the speaker to a man—not such a bad fellow too, when sober—who, under the influence of drink, had thrown his big shoe at his wife's head and cut it so badly that she was even then—while he was addressing them—lying in hospital hovering between life and death.

"That's me!" cried the powerful man, jumping up in a state of great excitement mingled with indignation, while he towered head and shoulders above the audience, "though how *you* come for to 'ear on 't beats me holler. An' it shows 'ow lies git about, for she's *not* gone to the hospital, an' it wasn't shoes at all, but boots I flung at 'er, an' they only just grazed 'er, thank goodness, an' sent the cat flyin' through the winder. So—"

A burst of laughter with mingled applause and cheers cut off the end of the sentence and caused the powerful man to sit down in much confusion, quite puzzled what to think of it all.

"My friend," said the speaker, when order had been restored, "you are mistaken. I did not refer to you at all, never having seen or heard of you before, but there are too many men like you—men who would be good men and true if they would only come to the Saviour, who would soon convince them that it is wise to give up the drink and put on the blue ribbon. Let it not be supposed, my friends,

that I say it is the *duty* of every one to put on the
blue ribbon and become a total abstainer. There
are circumstances in which a ' little wine ' may be
advisable. Why, the apostle Paul himself, when
Timothy's stomach got into a chronic state of disease
which subjected him, apparently, to ' frequent
infirmities,' advised him to take a ' little wine,' but
he didn't advise him to take many quarts of beer, or
numerous glasses of brandy and water, or oceans of
Old Tom, or to get daily fuddled on the poisons
which are sold by many publicans under these
names. Still less did Paul advise poor dyspeptic
Timothy to become his own medical man and prescribe all these medicines to himself, whenever he
felt inclined for them. Yes, there are the old and
the feeble and the diseased, who may (observe I
don't say who *do*, for I am not a doctor, but who
may) require stimulants under medical advice. To
these we do not speak, and to these we would not
grudge the small alleviation to their sad case which
may be found in stimulants ; but to the young and
strong and healthy we are surely entitled to say,
to plead, and to entreat—put on the blue ribbon if
you see your way to it. And by the young we
mean not only all boys and girls, but all men and
women in the prime of life, ay, and beyond the
prime, if in good health. Surely you will all admit
that the young require no stimulants. Are they not

superabounding in energy? Do they not require the very opposite—sedatives, and do they not find these in constant and violent muscular exercise?"

With many similar and other arguments did the speaker seek to influence the mass of human beings before him, taking advantage of every idea that cropped up and every incident in the meeting that occurred to enforce his advice—namely, total abstinence for the young and the healthy—until he had stirred them up to a state of considerable enthusiasm. Then he said:—

"I am glad to see you enthusiastic. Nothing great can be done without enthusiasm. You may potter along the even tenor of your way without it, but you'll never come to much good, and you'll never accomplish great things, without it. What is enthusiasm? Is it not seeing the length, breadth, height, depth, and bearing of a good thing, and being zealously affected in helping to bring it about? There are many kinds of enthusiasts, though but one quality of enthusiasm. Weak people show their enthusiasm too much on the surface. Powerful folk keep it too deep in their hearts to be seen at all. What then, are we to scout it in the impulsive because too obvious; to undervalue it in the reticent because almost invisible? Nay, let us be thankful for it in any form, for the *thing* is good, though the individual's manner of displaying it may be faulty. Let us hope that the too gushing may learn to clap on the breaks a little—a very little; but far more let us pray that the reticent and the self-possessed, and the oh!-dear-no-you'll-never-catch-me-doing-*that*-sort-of-thing people, may be enabled to get up more steam. Better far in my estimation the wild enthusiast than the self-possessed and self-sufficient cynic. Just look at your gentlemanly cynic; good-natured very likely, for he's mightily pleased with himself and excessively wise in regard to all things sublunary. Why, even *he* has enthusiasm, though not always in a good cause. Follow him to the races. Watch him while he sees the sleek and beautiful creatures straining every muscle, and his own favourite drawing ahead, inch by inch, until it bids fair to win. Is *that* our cynic, bending forward on his steed, with gleaming eyes and glowing cheek, and partly open mouth and quick-coming breath, and so forgetful of himself that he swings off his hat and gives vent to a lusty cheer as the favourite passes the winning-post?

" But follow him still further. Don't let him go. Hold on to his horse's tail till we see him safe into his club, and wait there till he has dined and gone to the opera. There he sits, immaculate in dress and bearing, in the stalls. It is a huge audience. A great star is to appear. The star comes on—music such as might cause the very angels to bend and listen.

The sweet singer exerts herself; her rich voice swells in volume and sweeps round the hall, filling every ear and thrilling every heart, until, unable to restrain themselves, the vast concourse rises *en masse*, and, with waving scarf and kerchief, thunders forth applause ! And what of our cynic? There he is, the wildest of the wild—for he happens to love music—shouting like a maniac and waving his hat, regardless of the fact that he has broken the brim, and that the old gentleman whose corns he has trodden on frowns at him with savage indignation.

"Yes," continued the speaker, "the whole world is enthusiastic when the key-note of each individual, or class of individuals, is struck; and shall *we* be ashamed of our enthusiasm for this little bit of heavenly blue, which symbolises the great fact that those who wear it are racing with the demon Drink to save men and women (ourselves included, perhaps) from his clutches; racing with Despair to place Hope before the eyes of those who are blindly rushing to destruction; racing with Time to snatch the young out of the way of the Destroyer before he lays hand on them; and singing—ay shouting—songs of triumph and glory to God because of the tens of thousands of souls and bodies already saved; because of the bright prospect of the tens of thousands more to follow ; because of the innumerable voices added to

the celestial choir, and the glad assurance that the
hymns of praise thus begun shall not die out with
our feeble frames, but will grow stronger in sweetness as they diminish in volume, until, the river
crossed, they shall burst forth again with indescrib-
able intensity in the New Song.

"Some people tell us that these things are not
true. Others say they won't last. My friends, I
know, and many of you know, that they *are* true,
and even if they were *not* to last, have we not even
now ground for praise ? Shall we not rejoice that
the lifeboat has saved some, because others have
refused to embark and perished ? But we don't
admit that these things won't last. Very likely, in
the apostolic days, some of the unbelievers said of
them and their creed, " How long will it last ?" If
these objectors be now able to take note of the
world's doings, they have their answer from Father
Time himself ; for does he not say, ' Christianity has
lasted nearly nineteen hundred years, and is the
strongest moral motive-power in the world to-day' ?
The Blue Ribbon, my friends, or what it represents,
is founded on Christianity ; therefore the principles
which it represents are sure to stand. Who will
come now and put it on ?"

" I will !" shouted a strong voice from among the
audience, and up rose the powerful man who began
the evening with " bah !" and " pooh !" He soon

made his way to the platform amid uproarious cheering, and donned the blue.

"Hetty," whispered Mrs. Frog in a low, timid voice, "I think I would like to put it on too."

If the voice had been much lower and more timid, Hetty would have heard it, for she sat there watching for her mother as one might watch for a parent in the crisis of a dread disease. She knew that no power on earth can change the will, and she had waited and prayed till the arrow was sent home by the hand of God.

"Come along, mother," she said—but said no more, for her heart was too full.

Mrs. Frog was led to the platform, to which multitudes of men, women, and children were pressing, and the little badge was pinned to her breast.

Thus did that poor woman begin her Christian course with the fruit of self-denial.

She then set about the work of putting her house in order. It was up-hill work at first, and very hard, but the promise did not fail her, "Lo! I am with you alway." In all her walk she found Hetty a guardian angel.

"I must work, Hetty, dear," she said, "for it will never do to make you support us all; but what am I to do with baby? There is no one to take charge of her when I go out."

"I am quite able to keep the whole of us, mother,

U

now that I get such good pay from the lady I work for, but as you want to work, I can easily manage for baby. You know I've often wished to speak of the Infant Nursery in George Yard. Before you sent Matty away I wanted you to send her there, but—" Hetty paused.

"Go on, dear. I was mad agin' you an' your religious ways; wasn't that it?" said Mrs. Frog.

"Well, mother, it don't matter now, thank God. The Infant Nursery, you know, is a part of the Institution there. The hearts of the people who manage it were touched by the death of so many thousands of little ones every year in London through want and neglect, so they set up this nursery to enable poor widowed mothers and others to send their babies to be cared for—nursed, fed, and amused in nice airy rooms—while the mothers are at work. They charge only fourpence a day for this, and each baby has its own bag of clothing, brush and comb, towel and cot. They will keep Matty from half-past seven in the morning till eight at night for you, so that will give you plenty of time to work, won't it, mother?"

"It will indeed, Hetty, and all for fourpence a day, say you?"

"Yes, the ordinary charge is fourpence, but widows get it for twopence for each child, and, perhaps, they may regard a deserted wife as a widow! There is a fine of twopence per hour for any child not taken away after eight, so you'll have to be up to time, mother."

Mrs. Frog acted on this advice, and thus was enabled to earn a sufficiency to enable her to pay her daily rent, to clothe and feed herself and child, to give a little to the various missions undertaken by the Institutions near her, to put a little now and then into the farthing bank, and even to give a little in charity to the poor!

Now, reader, you may have forgotten it, but if you turn back to near the beginning of this chapter, you will perceive that all we have been writing about is a huge digression, for which we refuse to make the usual apology.

We return again to Mrs. Frog where we left her, sitting beside her cheerful fire, sewing and conversing with Hetty.

"I can't bear to think of 'im, Hetty," said Mrs. Frog. "You an' me sittin' here so comfortable, with as much to eat as we want, an' to spare, while your poor father is in a cold cell. He's bin pretty bad to me of late, it's true, wi' that drink, but he wasn't always like that, Hetty; even you can remember him before he took to the drink."

"Yes, mother, I can, and, bless the Lord, he may yet be better than he ever was. When is his time up?"

"'This day three weeks. The twelve months will be out then. We must pray for 'im, Hetty."

"Yes, mother. I am always prayin' for him. You know that."

There was a touch of anxiety in the tones and faces of both mother and daughter as they talked of the father, for his home-coming might, perhaps, nay probably would, be attended with serious consequences to the renovated household. They soon changed the subject to one more agreeable.

"Isn't Bobby's letter a nice one, mother?" said Hetty, "and so well written, though the spellin' might have been better; but then he's had so little schoolin'."

"It just makes my heart sing," returned Mrs. Frog. "Read it again to me, Hetty. I'll never tire o' hearin' it. I only wish it was longer."

The poor mother's wish was not unnatural, for the letter which Bobby had written was not calculated to tax the reader's patience, and, as Hetty hinted, there was room for improvement, not only in the spelling but in the writing. Nevertheless, it had carried great joy to the mother's heart. We shall therefore give it *verbatim et literatim* :—

BRANKLY FARM—KANADA.

"DEER MUTHER. wen i left you i promisd to rite so heer gos. this Plase is eaven upon arth. so pritty an grand. O you never did see the likes. ide park is nuffin to it, an as for Kensintn gardings—wy to kompair thems rediklis. theres sitch a nice litle gal here. shes wun of deer mis mukfersons gals— wot the vestenders calls a wafe and sometimes a strai. were all very fond of er spesially tim lumpy. i shuvd im in the river wun dai. my—ow e spluterd. but e was non the wus—all the better. mister an mistress meryboi aint that a joly naim are as good as gold to us. we as prairs nite and mornin an no end o witls an as appy as kings and kueens asitin on there throns. give all our luv to deer father, an etty an baiby an mis mukferson an mister olland an all our deer teechers. sai we ll never forgit wot they told us. your deer sun BOBBY."

" Isn't it beautiful?" said Mrs. Frog, wiping away a tear with the sock she was darning in preparation for her husband's return.

" Yes, mother. Bless the people that sent 'im out to Canada," said Hetty, " for he would never have got on here."

There came a tap to the door as she spoke, and Mrs. Twitter, entering, was received with a hearty welcome.

" I came, Mrs. Frog," she said, accepting the chair —for there was even a third chair—which Hetty placed for her, " to ask when your husband will be home again."

Good Mrs. Twitter carefully avoided the risk of

hurting the poor woman's feelings by needless reference to jail.

"I expect him this day three weeks, ma'am," replied Mrs. Frog.

"That will do nicely," returned Mrs. Twitter. "You see, my husband knows a gentleman who takes great pleasure in getting con—in getting men like Ned, you know, into places, and giving them a chance of—of getting on in life, you understand?"

"Yes, ma'am, we must all try to git on in life if we would keep in life," said Mrs. Frog, sadly.

"Well, there is a situation open just now, which the gentleman—the same gentleman who was so kind in helping us after the fire; you see we all need help of one another, Mrs. Frog—which the gentleman said he could keep open for a month, but not longer, so, as I happened to be passing your house to-night on my way to the Yard, to the mothers' meeting, I thought I'd just look in and tell you, and ask you to be sure and send Ned to me the moment he comes home."

"I will, ma'am, and God bless you for thinkin' of us so much."

"Remember, now," said Mrs. Twitter, impressively, "*before* he has time to meet any of his old comrades. Tell him if he comes straight to me he will hear something that will please him very much. I won't tell you what. That is my message to him. And now, how is my Mita? Oh! I need not ask. There she lies like a little angel! (Mrs. Twitter rose and went to the crib, but did not disturb the little sleeper.) I wish I saw roses on her little cheeks and more fat, Mrs. Frog."

Mrs. Frog admitted that there was possible improvement in the direction of roses and fat, but feared that the air (it would have been more correct to have said the smoke and smells) of the court went against roses and fat, somehow. She was thankful, however, to the good Lord for the health they all enjoyed in spite of local disadvantages.

"Ah!" sighed Mrs. Twitter, "if we could only transport you all to Canada—"

"Oh! ma'am," exclaimed Mrs. Frog, brightening up suddenly, "we've had *such* a nice letter from our Bobby. Let her see it, Hetty."

"Yes, and so nicely written, too," remarked Hetty, with a beaming face, as she handed Bobby's production to the visitor, "though he doesn't quite understand yet the need for capital letters."

"Never mind, Hetty, so long as he sends you capital letters," returned Mrs. Twitter, perpetrating the first pun she had been guilty of since she was a baby; "and, truly, this is a charming letter, though short."

"Yes, it's rather short, but it might have been shorter," said Mrs. Frog, indulging in a truism.

Mrs. Twitter was already late for the mothers'

meeting, but she felt at once that it would be better to be still later than to disappoint Mrs. Frog of a little sympathy in a matter which touched her feelings so deeply. She sat down, therefore, and read the letter over, slowly, commenting on it as she went along in a pleasant sort of way, which impressed the anxious mother with, not quite the belief, but the sensation that Bobby was the most hopeful immigrant which Canada had received since it was discovered.

"Now, mind, send Ned up *at once*," said the amiable lady when about to quit the little room.

"Yes, Mrs. Twitter, I will; good-night."

CHAPTER XXII.

NED FROG'S EXPERIENCES AND SAMMY TWITTER'S WOES.

BUT Ned Frog, with strong drink combined, rendered fruitless all the efforts that were put forth in his behalf at that time.

When discharged with a lot of other jail-birds, none of whom, however, he knew, he sauntered leisurely homeward, wondering whether his wife was alive, and, if so, in what condition he should find her.

It may have been that better thoughts were struggling in his breast for ascendency, because he sighed deeply once or twice, which was not a usual mode with Ned of expressing his feelings. A growl was more common and more natural, considering his character.

Drawing nearer and nearer to his old haunts, yet taking a roundabout road, as the moth is drawn to the candle, or as water descends to its level, he went slowly on, having little hope of comfort in his home, and not knowing very well what to do.

As he passed down one of the less frequented

streets leading into Whitechapel, he was arrested
by the sight of a purse lying on the pavement. To
become suddenly alive, pick it up, glance stealthily
round, and thrust it into his pocket, was the work of
an instant. The saunter was changed into a steady
business-like walk. As he turned into Commercial
Street, Ned met No. 666 full in the face. He knew
that constable intimately, but refrained from taking
notice of him, and passed on with an air and
expression which were meant to convey the idea of
infantine innocence. Guilty men usually over-reach
themselves. Giles noted the air, and suspected
guilt, but, not being in a position to prove it,
walked gravely on, with his stern eyes straight to
the front.

In a retired spot Ned examined his " find." It
contained six sovereigns, four shillings, threepence,
a metropolitan railway return ticket, several cut-
tings from newspapers, and a recipe for the concoc-
tion of a cheap and wholesome pudding, along with
a card bearing the name of Mrs. Samuel Twitter,
written in ink and without any address.

" You 're in luck, Ned," he remarked to himself,
as he examined these treasures. " Now, old boy,
you 'aven't stole this 'ere purse, so you ain't a thief;
you don't know w'ere Mrs. S. T. lives, so you can't
find 'er to return it to 'er. Besides, it 's more than
likely she won't feel the want of it—w'ereas I feels

in want of it wery much indeed. Of course it's my dooty to 'and it over to the p'lice, but, in the fust place, I refuse to 'ave any communication wi' the p'lice, friendly or otherwise; in the second place, I 'ad no 'and in makin' the laws, so I don't feel bound to obey 'em; thirdly, I'm both 'ungry an' thirsty, an' 'ere you 'ave the remedy for them afflictions, so, fourthly—'ere goes !"

Having thus cleared his conscience, Ned committed the cash to his vest pocket, and presented the purse with its remaining contents to the rats in a neighbouring sewer.

Almost immediately afterwards he met an Irishman, an old friend.

"Terence, my boy, well met!" he said, offering his hand.

"Hooroo! Ned Frog, sure I thought ye was in limbo !"

"You thought right, Terry; only half-an-hour out. Come along, I'll stand you somethin' for the sake of old times. By the way, have you done that job yet?"

"What job ?"

"Why, the dynamite job, of course."

"No, I've gi'n that up," returned the Irishman with a look of contempt. "To tell you the honest truth, I don't believe that the way to right Ireland is to blow up England. But there's an Englishman you'll find at the Swan an' Anchor—a sneakin' blackguard, as would sell his own mother for dhrink—he'll help you if you wants to have a hand in the job.   I'm off it."

Notwithstanding this want of sympathy on that point, the two friends found that they held enough in common to induce a prolonged stay at the public-house, from which Ned finally issued rather late at night, and staggered homewards. He met no acquaintance on the way, and was about to knock at his own door when the sound of a voice within arrested him.

It was Hetty, praying. The poor wife and daughter had given up hope of his returning at so late an hour that night, and had betaken themselves to their usual refuge in distress. Ned knew the sound well, and it seemed to rouse a demon in his breast, for he raised his foot with the intention of driving in the door, when he was again arrested by another sound.

It was the voice of little Matty, who, awaking suddenly out of a terrifying dream, set up a shrieking which at once drowned all other sounds.

Ned lowered his foot, thrust his hands into his pockets, and stood gazing in a state of indecision at the broken pavement for a few minutes.

"No peace there," he said, sternly. "Prayin' an' squallin' don't suit me, so good-night to 'ee all."

With that he turned sharp round, and staggered away, resolving never more to return!

"Is that you, Ned Frog?" inquired a squalid, dirty-looking woman, thrusting her head out of a window as he passed.

"No, 'tain't," said Ned, fiercely, as he left the court.

He went straight to a low lodging-house, but before entering tied his money in a bit of rag, and thrust it into an inner pocket of his vest, which he buttoned tight, and fastened his coat over it. Paying the requisite fourpence for the night's lodging, he entered, and was immediately hailed by several men who knew him, but being in no humour for good fellowship, he merely nodded and went straight up to his lowly bed. It was one of seventy beds that occupied the entire floor of an immense room. Police supervision had secured that this room should be well ventilated, and that the bedding should be reasonably clean, though far from clean-looking, and Ned slept soundly in spite of drink, for, as we have said before, he was unusually strong.

Next day, having thought over his plans in bed, and, being a man of strong determination, he went forth to carry them into immediate execution. He went to a lofty tenement in the neighbourhood of Dean and Flower Street, one of the poorest parts of the city, and hired a garret, which was so high up that even the staircase ended before you reached it, and the remainder of the upward flight had to be performed on a ladder, at the top of which was a trap-door, the only entrance to Ned's new home.

Having paid a week's rent in advance he took possession, furnished the apartment with one old chair, one older table, one bundle of straw in a sack, one extremely old blanket, and one brand-new pipe with a corresponding ounce or two of tobacco. Then he locked the trap door, put the key in his pocket, and descended to the street, where at Bird-Fair he provided himself with sundry little cages and a few birds. Having conveyed these with some food for himself and the little birds to his lodging he again descended to the street, and treated himself to a pint of beer.

While thus engaged he was saluted by an old friend, the owner of a low music-hall, who begged for a few minutes' conversation with him outside.

"Ned," he said, "I'm glad I fell in with you, for I'm uncommon 'ard up just now."

"I never lends money," said Ned, brusquely turning away.

"'Old on, Ned, I don't want yer money, bless yer! I wants to *give* you money."

'Oh! that's quite another story; fire away, old man."

"Well, you see, I'm 'ard up, as I said, for a man to keep order in my place. The last man I 'ad was a good un, 'e was. Six futt one in 'is socks, an' as strong as a 'orse, but by ill luck one night, a sailor-chap that was bigger than 'im come in to the 'all, an' they 'ad a row, an' my man got sitch a lickin' that he 'ad to go to hospital, an' 'e's been there for a week, an' won't be out they say for a month or more. Now, Ned, will you take the job? The pay's good an' the fun's considerable. So's the fightin', sometimes, but you 'd put a stop to that you know. An', then, you 'll 'ave all the day to yourself to do as you like."

" I 'm your man," said Ned, promptly.

Thus it came to pass that the pugilist obtained suitable employment as a peacemaker and keeper of order, for a time at least, in one of those disreputable places of amusement where the unfortunate poor of London are taught lessons of vice and vanity which end often in vexation of spirit, not only to themselves, but to the strata of society which rest above them.

One night Ned betook himself to this temple of vice, and on the way was struck by the appearance of a man with a barrow—a sort of book-stall on wheels—who was pushing his way through the crowded street. It was the man who at the temperance meeting had begun with " bah !" and " pooh !" and had ended by putting on the Blue Ribbon. He had once been a comrade of Ned Frog, but had become so very respectable that his old chum scarcely recognised him.

"Hallo! Reggie North, can that be you?"

North let down his barrow, wheeled round, and held out his hand with a hearty, "how are 'ee, old man? W'y you're lookin' well, close cropped an' comfortable, eh! Livin' at Her Majesty's expense lately? Where d'ee live now, Ned? I'd like to come and see you."

Ned told his old comrade the locality of his new abode.

"But I say, North, how respectable you are! What's come over you? not become a travellin' bookseller, have you?"

"That's just what I am, Ned."

"Well, there's no accountin' for taste. I hope it pays."

"Ay, pays splendidly—pays the seller of the books and pays the buyers better."

"How's that?" asked Ned, in some surprise, going up to the barrow; "oh! I see, Bibles."

"Yes, Ned, Bibles, the Word of God. Will you buy one?"

"No, thank 'ee," said Ned, drily.

"Here, I'll make you a present o' one, then," returned North, thrusting a Bible into the other's hand; "you can't refuse it of an old comrade. Good-night. I'll look in on you soon."

"You needn't trouble yourself," Ned called out as his friend went off, and he felt half inclined to fling the Bible after him, but checked himself. It was worth money! so he put it in his pocket and went his way.

The hall was very full that night, a new comic singer of great promise having been announced, and oh! it was sad to see the youths of both sexes, little more than big boys and girls, who went there to smoke, and drink, and enjoy ribald songs and indecent jests!

We do not mean to describe the proceedings. Let it suffice to say that, after one or two songs and a dance had been got through, Ned, part of whose duty it was to announce the performances, rose and in a loud voice said—

"Seignor Twittorini will now sing."

The Signor stepped forward at once, and was received with a roar of enthusiastic laughter, for anything more lugubrious and wobegone than the expression of his face had never been seen on these boards before. There was a slight look of shyness about him, too, which increased the absurdity of the thing, and it was all *so natural*, as one half-tipsy woman remarked.

So it was—intensely natural—for Seignor Twittor-ini was no other than poor Sammy Twitter in the extremest depths of his despair. Half-starved, half-

X

mad, yet ashamed to return to his father's house, the miserable boy had wandered in bye streets, and slept in low lodging-houses as long as his funds lasted. Then he tried to get employment with only partial success, until at last, recollecting that he had been noted among his companions for a sweet voice and a certain power of singing serio-comic songs, he thought of a low music-hall into which he had staggered one evening when drunk—as much with misery as with beer. The manager, on hearing a song or two, at once engaged him and brought him out. As poor Sammy knew nothing about acting, it was decided that he should appear in his own garments, which, being shabby genteel, were pretty well suited for a great Italian singer in low society.

But Sammy had overrated his own powers. After the first burst of applause was over, he stood gazing at the audience with his mouth half open, vainly attempting to recollect the song he meant to sing, and making such involuntary contortions with his thin visage, that a renewed burst of laughter broke forth. When it had partially subsided, Sammy once more opened his mouth, gave vent to a gasp, burst into tears, and rushed from the stage.

This was the climax! It brought down the house! Never before had they seen such an actor. He was inimitable, and the people made the usual demand for an *encore* with tremendous fervour, expecting that Signor Twittorini would repeat the scene, probably with variations, and finish off with the promised song. But poor Sammy did not respond.

" I see,—you can improvise," said the manager, quite pleased, " and I've no objection when it's well done like that; but you'd better go on now, and stick to the programme."

" I *can't* sing," said Sammy, in passionate despair.

" Come, come, young feller, I don't like actin' *off* the stage, an' the audience is gittin' impatient."

" But I tell you I can't sing a note," repeated Sam.

" What! D'ye mean to tell me you're not actin'?"

" I wish I was!" cried poor Sam, glancing upward with tearful eyes and clasping his hands.

" Come now. You've joked enough. Go on and do your part," said the puzzled manager.

" But I tell you I'm *not* joking. I couldn't sing just now if you was to give me ten thousand pounds!"

It might have been the amount of the sum stated, or the tone in which it was stated—we know not— but the truth of what Sam said was borne so forcibly in upon the manager, that he went into a violent passion; sprang at Sam's throat; hustled him towards a back door, and kicked him out into a back lane, where he sat down on an empty packing case, covered his face with his hands, bowed his head on his knees, and wept.

The manager returned on the stage, and, with a calm voice and manner, which proved himself to be a very fair actor, stated that Signor Twittorini had met with a sudden disaster—not a very serious one —which, however, rendered it impossible for him to re-appear just then, but that, if sufficiently recovered, he would appear towards the close of the evening.

This, with a very significant look and gesture from Ned Frog, quieted the audience to the extent at least of inducing them to do nothing worse than howl continuously for ten minutes, after which they allowed the performances to go on, and saved the keeper of order the trouble of knocking down a few of the most unruly.

Ned was the first to quit the hall when all was over. He did so by the back door, and found Sam still sitting on the door-step.

"What's the matter with ye, youngster?" he said, going up to him. "You've made a pretty mess of it to-night."

"I couldn't help it—indeed I couldn't. Perhaps I'll do better next time."

"Better! ha! ha! You couldn't ha' done better —if you'd on'y gone on. But why do ye sit there?"

"Because I've nowhere to go to."

"There's plenty o' common lodgin' 'ouses, ain't there?"

" Yes, but I haven't got a single rap."

" Well, then, ain't there the casual ward? W'y don't you go there? You'll git bed and board for nothin' there."

Having put this question, and received no answer, Ned turned away without further remark.

Hardened though Ned was to suffering, there was something in the fallen boy's face that had touched this fallen man. He turned back with a sort of remonstrative growl, and re-entered the back lane, but Signor Twittorini was gone. He had heard the manager's voice, and fled.

A policeman directed him to the nearest casual ward, where the lowest stratum of abject poverty finds its nightly level.

Here he knocked with trembling hand. He was received; he was put in a lukewarm bath and washed; he was fed on gruel and a bit of bread—quite sufficient to allay the cravings of hunger; he was shown to a room in which appeared to be a row of corpses—so dead was the silence—each rolled in a covering of some dark brown substance, and stretched out stiff on a tressel with a canvas bottom. One of the tressels was empty. He was told he might appropriate it.

" Are they dead?" he asked, looking round with a shudder.

" Not quite," replied his jailer, with a short laugh,

"but dead-beat most of 'em—tired out, I should say, and disinclined to move."

Sam Twitter fell on the couch, drew the coverlet over him, and became a brown corpse like the rest, while the guardian retired and locked the door to prevent the egress of any who might chance to come to life again.

In the morning Sam had a breakfast similar to the supper; was made to pick oakum for a few hours by way of payment for hospitality, and left with a feeling that he had at last reached the lowest possible depth of degradation.

So he had in that direction, but there are other and varied depths in London—depths of crime and of sickness, as well as of suffering and sorrow!

Aimlessly he wandered about for another day, almost fainting with hunger, but still so ashamed to face his father and mother that he would rather have died than done so.

Some touch of pathos, or gruff tenderness mayhap, in Ned Frog's voice, induced him to return at night to the scene of his discreditable failure, and await the pugilist's coming out. He followed him a short way, and then running forward, said—

"Oh, sir! I'm very low!"

"Hallo! Signor Twittorini again!" said Ned, wheeling round, sternly. "What have I to do with your being low? I've been low enough myself at times, an' nobody helped—"

Ned checked himself, for he knew that what he said was false.

"I think I'm dying," said Sam, leaning against a house for support.

"Well, if you do die, you'll be well out of it all," replied Ned, bitterly. "What's your name?"

"Twitter," replied Sam, forgetting in his woe that he had not intended to reveal his real name.

"Twitter—Twitter. I've heard that name before. Why, yes. Father's name Samuel—eh? Mother alive—got cards with Mrs. Samuel Twitter on 'em, an' no address?"

"Yes—yes. How do you come to know?" asked Sam in surprise.

"Never you mind that, youngster, but you come along wi' me. I've got a sort o' right to feed you. Ha! ha! come along."

Sam became frightened at this sudden burst of hilarity, and shrank away, but Ned grasped him by the arm, and led him along with such decision, that resistance he felt would be useless.

In a few minutes he was in Ned's garret eating bread and cheese with ravenous satisfaction.

"Have some beer?" said Ned, filling a pewter pot.

"No—no—no—*no!*" said Sam, shuddering as he turned his head away.

"Well, youngster," returned Ned, with a slight look of surprise, "please yourself, and here's your health."

He drained the pot to the bottom, after which, dividing his straw into two heaps, and throwing them into two corners, he bade Sam lie down and rest.

The miserable boy was only too glad to do so. He flung himself on the little heap pointed out, and the last thing he remembered seeing before the "sweet restorer" embraced him was the huge form of Ned Frog sitting in his own corner with his back to the wall, the pewter pot at his elbow, and a long clay pipe in his mouth.

CHAPTER XXIII.

HOPES REVIVE.

MR. THOMAS BALLS, butler to Sir Richard Brandon, standing with his legs wide apart and his hands under his coat tails in the servants' hall, delivered himself of the opinion that "things was comin' to a wonderful pass when Sir Richard Brandon would condescend to go visitin' of a low family in Whitechapel."

"But the family is no more low than you are, Mr. Balls," objected Jessie Summers, who, being not very high herself, felt that the remark was slightly personal.

"Of course not, my dear," replied Balls, with a paternal smile. " I did not for a moment mean that Mr. Samuel Twitter was low in an offensive sense, but in a social sense. Sir Richard, you know, belongs to the hupper ten, an' he 'as not been used to associate with people so much further down in the scale. Whether he 's right or whether he 's wrong ain't for me to say. I merely remark that, things being as they are, the master 'as come to a wonderful pass."

"It's all along of Miss Diana," said Mrs. Screw-bury. "That dear child 'as taken the firm belief into her pretty 'ead that all people are equal in the sight of their Maker, and that we should look on each other as brothers and sisters, and you know she can twist Sir Richard round her little finger, and she's taken a great fancy to that Twitter family ever since she's been introduced to them at that 'Ome of Industry by Mr. Welland, who used to be a great friend of their poor boy that ran away. And Mrs. Twitter goes about the 'Ome, and among the poor so much, and can tell her so many stories about poor people, that she's grown quite fond of her."

"But we *ain't* all equal, Mrs. Screwbury," said the cook, recurring, with some asperity, to a former remark, "an' nothink you or anybody else can ever say will bring me to believe it."

"Quite right, cook," said Balls. "For instance, no one would ever admit that I was as good a cook as you are, or that you was equal to Mrs. Screwbury as a nurse, or that any of us could compare with Jessie Summers as a 'ouse-maid, or that I was equal to Sir Richard in the matters of edication, or station, or wealth. No, it is in the more serious matters that concern our souls that we are equal, and I fear that when Death comes, he's not very particular as to who it is he's cuttin' down when he's got the order."

A ring at the bell cut short this learned discourse. "That's for the cab," remarked Mr. Balls as he went out.

Now, while these things were taking place at the "West End," in the "East End" the Twitters were assembled round the social board enjoying themselves—that is to say, enjoying themselves as much as in the circumstances was possible. For the cloud that Sammy's disappearance had thrown over them was not to be easily or soon removed.

Since the terrible day on which he was lost, a settled expression of melancholy had descended on the once cheery couple, which extended in varying degree down to their youngest. Allusion was never made to the erring one; yet it must not be supposed he was forgotten. On the contrary, Sammy was never out of his parents' thoughts. They prayed for him night and morning aloud, and at all times silently. They also took every possible step to discover their boy's retreat, by means of the ordinary police, as well as detectives whom they employed for the purpose of hunting Sammy up; but all in vain.

It must not be supposed, however, that this private sorrow induced Mrs. Twitter selfishly to forget the poor, or intermit her labours among them. She did not for an hour relax her efforts in their behalf at George Yard and at Commercial Street.

At the Twitter social board—which, by the way, was spread in another house not far from that which had been burned—sat not only Mr. and Mrs. Twitter and all the little Twitters, but also Mrs. Loper, who had dropped in just to make inquiries, and Mrs. Larrabel, who was anxious to hear what news they had to tell, and Mr. Crackaby, who was very sympathetic, and Mr. Stickler, who was oracular. Thus the small table was full.

"Mariar, my dear," said Mr. Twitter, referring to some remarkable truism which his wife had just uttered, "we must just take things as we find 'em. The world is not goin' to change its course on purpose to please *us*. Things might be worse, you know, and when the spoke in your wheel is at its lowest there must of necessity be a rise unless it stands still altogether."

"You're right, Mr. Twitter. I always said so," remarked Mrs. Loper, adopting all these sentiments with a sigh of resignation. "If we did not submit to fortune when it is adverse, why then we'd have to—have to—"

"Succumb to it," suggested Mrs. Larrabel, with one of her sweetest smiles.

"No, Mrs. Larrabel, I never succumb—from principle I never do so. The last thing that any woman of good feeling ought to do is to succumb. I would bow to it."

"Quite right, ma'am, quite right," said Stickler, who now found time to speak, having finished his first cup of tea and second muffin; "to bow is, to say the least of it, polite and simple, and is always safe, for it commits one to nothing; but then, suppose that Fortune is impolite and refuses to return the bow, what, I ask you, would be the result?"

As Mrs. Loper could not form the slightest conception what the result would be, she replied with a weak smile and a request for more sausage.

These remarks, although calculated to enlist the sympathies of Crackaby and excite the mental energies of Twitter, had no effect whatever on those gentlemen, for the latter was deeply depressed, and his friend Crackaby felt for him sincerely. Thus the black sheep remained victorious in argument— which was not always the case.

Poor Twitter! He was indeed at that time utterly crestfallen, for not only had he lost considerably by the fire—his house having been uninsured—but business in the city had gone wrong somehow. A few heavy failures had occurred among speculators, and as these had always a row of minor speculators at their backs, like a row of child's bricks, which only needs the fall of one to insure the downcome of all behind it, there had been a general tumble of speculative bricks, tailing off with a number of unspeculative ones, such as tailors, grocers, butchers, and shopkeepers generally. Mr. Twitter was one of the unspeculative unfortunates, but he had not come quite down. He had only been twisted uncomfortably to one side, just as a toy brick is sometimes seen standing up here and there in the midst of surrounding wreck. Mr. Twitter was not absolutely ruined. He had only "got into difficulties."

But this was a small matter in his and his good wife's eyes compared with the terrible fall and disappearance of their beloved Sammy. He had always been such a good, obedient boy; and, as his mother said, "*so* sensitive." It never occurred to Mrs. Twitter that this sensitiveness was very much the cause of his fall and disappearance, for the same weakness, or cowardice, that rendered him unable to resist the playful banter of his drinking comrades, prevented him from returning to his family in disgrace.

"You have not yet advertised, I think?" said Crackaby.

"No, not yet," answered Twitter; "we cannot bear to publish it. But we have set several detectives on his track. In fact we expect one of them this very evening; and I shouldn't wonder if that was him," he added, as a loud knock was heard at the door.

"Please, ma'am," said the domestic, "Mr. Welland's at the door with another gentleman. 'E says 'e won't come in—'e merely wishes to speak to you for a moment."

" Oh ! bid 'em come in, bid 'em come in," said Mrs. Twitter in the exuberance of a hospitality which never turned any one away, and utterly regardless of the fact that her parlour was extremely small.

Another moment, and Stephen Welland entered, apologising for the intrusion, and saying that he merely called with Sir Richard Brandon, on their way to the Beehive meeting, to ask if anything had been heard of Sam.

" Come in, and welcome, *do*," said Mrs. Twitter to Sir Richard, whose face had become a not unfamiliar one at the Beehive meetings by that time. " And Miss Diana, too ! I 'm *so* glad you 've brought her. Sit down, dear. Not so near the door. To be sure there ain't much room anywhere else, but—get out of the way, Stickler."

The black sheep hopped to one side instantly, and Di was accommodated with his chair. Stickler was one of those toadies who worship rank for its own sake. If a lamp-post had been knighted Stickler would have bowed down to it. If an ass had been what he styled " barrow-knighted," he would have lain down and let it walk over him—perhaps would even have solicited a passing kick—certainly would not have resented one.

"Allow me, Sir Richard," he said, with some reference to the knight's hat.

"Hush, Stickler!" said Mrs. Twitter.

The black sheep hushed, while the bustling lady took the hat and placed it on the sideboard.

"Your stick, Sir Richard," said Stickler, "permit—"

"Hold your tongue, Stickler," said Mrs. Twitter.

The black sheep held his tongue—between his teeth,—and wished that some day he might have the opportunity of punching Mrs. Twitter's head, without, if possible, her knowing who did it. Though thus reduced to silence, he cleared his throat in a demonstratively subservient manner and awaited his opportunity.

Sir Richard was about to apologise for the intrusion when another knock was heard at the outer door, and immediately after, the City Missionary, John Seaward, came in. He evidently did not expect to see company, but, after a cordial salutation to every one, said that he had called on his way to the meeting.

"You are heartily welcome. Come in," said Mrs. Twitter, looking about for a chair, "come, sit beside me, Mr. Seaward, on the stool. You'll not object to a humble seat, I know."

"I am afraid," said Sir Richard, "that the meeting

has much to answer for in the way of flooding you
with unexpected guests."

"Oh! dear, no, sir, I love unexpected guests—the
more unexpected the more I—Molly, dear" (to her
eldest girl), "take all the children up-stairs."

Mrs. Twitter was beginning to get confused in
her excitement, but the last stroke of generalship
relieved the threatened block and her anxieties at
the same time.

"But what of Sam?" asked young Welland in a
low tone; "any news yet?"

"None," said the poor mother, suddenly losing
all her vivacity, and looking so pitifully miserable
that the sympathetic Di incontinently jumped off
her chair, ran up to her, and threw her arms round
her neck.

"Dear, darling child," said Mrs. Twitter, returning the embrace with interest.

"But I have brought you news," said the missionary, in a quiet voice which produced a general hush.

"News!" echoed Twitter with sudden vehemence.

"Oh! Mr. Seaward," exclaimed the poor mother,
clasping her hands and turning pale.

"Yes," continued Seaward; "as all here seem
to be friends, I may tell you that Sam has been
heard of at last. He has not, indeed, yet been
found, but he has been seen in the company of
a man well known as a rough disorderly character,

but who it seems has lately put on the blue ribbon, so we may hope that his influence over Sam will be for good instead of evil."

An expression of intense thankfulness escaped from the poor mother on hearing this, but the father became suddenly much excited, and plied the missionary with innumerable questions, which, however, resulted in nothing, for the good reason that nothing more was known.

At this point the company were startled by another knock, and so persuaded was Mrs. Twitter that it must be Sammy himself, that she rushed out of the room, opened the door, and almost flung herself into the arms of No. 666.

"I—I—beg your pardon, Mr. Scott, I thought that—"

"No harm done, ma'am," said Giles. "May I come in?"

"Certainly, and most welcome."

When the tall constable bowed his head to pass under the ridiculously small doorway, and stood erect in the still more ridiculously small parlour, it seemed as though the last point of capacity had been touched, and the walls of the room must infallibly burst out. But they did not! Probably the house had been built before domiciles warranted to last twenty years had come into fashion.

"You have found him!" exclaimed Mrs. Twitter,

clasping her hands and looking up in Giles's calm countenance with tearful eyes.

"Yes, ma'am, I am happy to tell you that we have at last traced him. I have just left him."

"And does he know you have come here? Is he expecting us?" asked the poor woman breathlessly.

"Oh! dear, no, ma'am, I rather think that if he knew I had come here, he would not await my return, for the young gentleman does not seem quite willing to come home. Indeed he is not quite fit; excuse me."

"How d' you know he's not willing?" demanded Mr. Twitter, who felt a rising disposition to stand up for Sammy.

"Because I heard him say so, sir. I went into the place where he was, to look for some people who are wanted, and saw your son sitting with a well-known rough of the name of North, who has become a changed man, however, and has put on the blue ribbon. I knew North well, and recognised your son at once. North seemed to have been trying to persuade your boy to return ['bless him! bless him!' from Mrs. Twitter], for I heard him say as I passed—'Oh! no, no, no, I can *never* return home!'"

"Where is he? Take me to him at once. My bonnet and shawl, Molly!"

"Pardon me, ma'am," said Giles. "It is not a

very fit place for a lady—though there are *some*
ladies who go to low lodging-houses regularly to
preach; but unless you go for that purpose it—"

"Yes, my dear, it would be quite out of place,"
interposed Twitter. "Come, it is *my* duty to go to
this place. Can you lead me to it, Mr. Scott?"

"Oh! and I should like to go too—*so* much, so
very much!"

It was little Di who spoke, but her father said
that the idea was preposterous.

"Pardon me, Sir Richard," said Mr. Seaward;
"this happens to be my night for preaching in the
common lodging-house where Mr. Scott says poor
Sam is staying. If you choose to accompany me,
there is nothing to prevent your little daughter
going. Of course it would be as well that no one
whom the boy might recognise should accompany
us, but his father might go and stand at the door
outside, while the owner of the lodging might be
directed to tell Sam that some one wishes to see
him."

"Your plan is pretty good, but I will arrange
my plans myself," said Mr. Twitter, who suddenly
roused himself to action with a degree of vigour
that carried all before it. "Go and do your own
part, Mr. Seaward. Give no directions to the pro-
prietor of the lodging, and leave Sammy to me. I
will have a cab ready for him, and his mother in

the cab waiting, with a suit of his own clothes. Are you ready ?"

"Quite ready," said the missionary, amused as well as interested by the good man's sudden display of resolution. Mrs. Twitter, also, was reduced to silence by surprise, as well as by submission. Sir Richard agreed to go and take Di with him, if Giles promised to hold himself in readiness within call.

"You see," he said, "I have been in similar places before now, but—not with my little child!"

As for Loper, Larrabel, Crackaby, Stickler, and Co.—feeling that it would be improper to remain after the host and hostess were gone; that it would be equally wrong to offer to go with them, and quite inappropriate to witness the home-coming,—they took themselves off, but each resolved to flutter unseen in the neighbourhood until he, or she, could make quite sure that the prodigal had returned.

It was to one of the lowest of the common lodging-houses that Sam Twitter the younger had resorted on the night he had been discovered by No. 666. That day he had earned sixpence by carrying a carpet bag to a railway station. One penny he laid out in bread, one penny in cheese. With the remaining fourpence he could purchase the right to sit in the lodging-house kitchen, and to

sleep in a bed in a room with thirty or forty homeless ones like himself.

On his way to this abode of the destitute, he was
overtaken by a huge man with a little bit of blue
ribbon in his button-hole.

"Hallo! young feller," exclaimed the man,
"you're the chap that was livin' wi' Ned Frog the
night I called to see 'im—eh? Sam Twitter, ain't
you?"

"Yes," said young Sam, blushing scarlet with
alarm at the abruptness of the question. "Yes, I
am. T—Twitter *is* my name. You're the man
that gave him the Bible, are you not, whom he
turned out of his house for tryin' to speak to him
about his soul?"

"The same, young feller. That's me, an' Reggie
North is my name. He'd 'ave 'ad some trouble
to turn me out *once*, though, but I've given up
quarrellin' and fightin' now, havin' enlisted under
the banner of the Prince of Peace," replied the man,
who was none other than our Bible-salesman, the
man who contributed the memorable speech—
"Bah!" and "Pooh!" at the Gospel temperance
meeting. "Where are you going?"

Sam, who never could withhold information or
retain a secret if asked suddenly, gave the name of
the common lodging-house to which he was bound.

"Well, I'm going there too, so, come along."

Sam could not choose but go with the man. He would rather have been alone, but could not shake him off.

Entering, they sat down at a table together near the kitchen fire, and North, pulling out of his pocket a small loaf, cut it in two and offered Sam half.

Several men were disputing in the box or compartment next to them, and as they made a great noise, attracting the attention of all around, North and his friend Sam were enabled the more easily to hold confidential talk unnoticed, by putting their heads together and chatting low as they ate their frugal meal.

" What made you leave Ned ? " asked North.

" How did you know I 'd left him ? "

" Why, because if you was still with him you wouldn't be here ! "

This was so obvious that Sam smiled; but it was a sad apology for a smile.

" I left him, because he constantly offered me beer, and I 've got such an awful desire for beer now, somehow, that I can't resist it, so I came away. And there 's no chance of any one offering me beer in this place."

" Not much," said North, with a grin. " But, young feller (and there was something earnestly kind in the man's manner here), if you feel an *awful* desire for drink, you 'd better put on this."

He touched his bit of blue ribbon.

"No use," returned Sam, sorrowfully, "I once put it on, and—and—I've broke the pledge."

"That's bad, no doubt; but what then?" returned North; "are we never to tell the truth any more 'cause once we told a lie? Are we never to give up swearin' 'cause once we uttered a curse? The Lord is able to save us, no matter how much we may have sinned. Why, sin is the very thing He saves us from—if we'll only come to Him."

Sam shook his head, but the manner of the man had attracted him, and eventually he told all his story to him. Reggie North listened earnestly, but the noise of the disputants in the next box was so great that they rose, intending to go to a quieter part of the large room. The words they heard at the moment, however, arrested them. The speaker was, for such a place, a comparatively well-dressed man, and wore a top-coat. He was discoursing on poverty and its causes.

"It is nothing more nor less," he said, with emphasis, "than the absence of equality that produces so much poverty."

"Hear! hear!" cried several voices, mingled with which, however, were the scoffing laughs of several men who knew too well and bitterly that the cause of their poverty was not the absence of equality, but, drink with improvidence.

"What right," asked the man, somewhat indig-nantly, "what right has Sir Crossly Cowel, for instance, the great capitalist, to his millions that 'e don't know what to do with, when we 're starvin'? (Hear!) He didn't earn these millions; they was left to 'im by his father, an' *he* didn't earn 'em, nor did his grandfather, or his great-grandfather, and so, back an' back to the time of the robber who came over with William—the greatest robber of all—an' stole the money, or cattle, from our forefathers. (Hear! hear!) An' what right has Lord Lorrumdoddy to the thousands of acres of land he's got? ('Ha! you may say that!' from an outrageously miserable-looking man, who seemed too wretched to think, and only spoke for a species of pastime.) What right has he, I say, to his lands? The ministers of religion, too, are to be blamed, for they toady the rich and uphold the unjust system. My friends, it is these rich capitalists and landowners who oppress the people. What right have they, I ask again, to their wealth, when the inmates of this house, and thousands of others, are ill-fed and in rags? If I had my way (*Hear!* hear! and a laugh), I would dis-tribute the wealth of the country, and have no poor people at all such as I see before me—such as this poor fellow (laying his hand on the shoulder of the outrageously miserable man, who said 'Just so' feebly, but seemed to shrink from his touch). Do

I- not speak the truth?" he added, looking round with the air of a man who feels that he carries his audience with him.

"Well, mister, I ain't just quite clear about that," said Reggie North, rising up and looking over the heads of those in front of him. There was an immediate and complete silence, for North had both a voice and a face fitted to command attention. "I'm not a learned man, you see, an' hain't studied the subjec', but isn't there a line in the Bible which says, 'Blessed are they that consider the poor'? Now it do seem to me that if we was all equally rich, there would be no poor to consider, an' no rich to consider 'em!"

There was a considerable guffaw at this, and the argumentative man was about to reply, but North checked him with—

"'Old on, sir, I ain't done yet. You said that Sir Cowley Cross—"

"Crossly Cowel," cried his opponent, correcting.

"I ax your pardon; Sir Crossly Cowel—that 'e 'ad no right to 'is millions, 'cause 'e didn't earn 'em, and because 'is father left 'em to 'im. Now, I 'ad a grandmother with one eye, poor thing—but of coorse that's nothin' to do wi' the argiment—an' she was left a fi' pun note by 'er father as 'ad a game leg—though that's nothin' to do wi' the argiment neither. Now, what puzzles me is, that if Sir Cow—Cross—"

A great shout of laughter interrupted North here, for he looked so innocently stupid, that most of the audience saw he was making game of the social reformer.

" What puzzles me is," continued North, " that if Sir Crossly Cowel 'as no right to 'is millions, my old grandmother 'ad no right to 'er fi' pun note! (Hear, hear, and applause.) I don't know nothin' about that there big thief Willum you mentioned, nor yet Lord Lorrumdoddy, not bein' 'ighly connected, you see, mates, but no doubt this gentleman believes in 'is principles—"

" Of course I do," said the social reformer indignantly.

" Well, then," resumed North, suddenly throwing off his sheepish look and sternly gazing at the reformer while he pointed to the outrageously miserable man, who had neither coat, vest, shoes, nor socks, " do you see that man ?   If you are in earnest, take off your coat and give it to him.   What right have you to two coats when he has none ?"

The reformer looked surprised, and the proposal was received with loud laughter; all the more that he seemed so little to relish the idea of parting with one of his coats in order to prove the justice of his principles and his own sincerity.

To give his argument more force, Reggie North took a sixpence from his pocket and held it up.

"See here, mates, when I came to this house I said to myself, 'The Lord 'as given me success to-day in sellin' His word'—you know, some of you, that I'm a seller of Bibles and Testaments?"

"Ay, ay, old boy. *We* know you," said several voices.

"And I wasn't always that," added North.

"*That's* true, anyhow," said a voice with a laugh.

"Well. For what I was, I might thank drink and a sinful heart. For what I am I thank the Lord. But, as I was goin' to say, I came here intendin' to give this sixpence—it ain't much, but it's all I can spare—to some poor feller in distress, for I practise what I preach, and I meant to do it in a quiet way. But it seems to me that, seein' what's turned up, I'll do more good by givin' it in a public way—so, there it is, old man," and he put the sixpence on the table in front of the outrageously miserable man, who could hardly believe his eyes.

The change to an outrageously jovial man, with the marks of misery still strong upon him, was worthy of a pantomime, and spoke volumes; for, small though the sum might seem to Sir Crossly Cowel, or Lord Lorrumdoddy, it represented a full instead of an empty stomach and a peaceful instead of a miserable night to one wreck of humanity.

The poor man swept the little coin into his pocket and rose in haste with a "thank 'ee," to go out and invest it at once, but was checked by North.

"Stop, stop, my fine fellow! Not quite so fast. If you'll wait till I've finished my little business here, I'll take you to where you'll get some warm grub for nothin', and maybe an old coat too." Encouraged by such brilliant prospects, the now jovially-miserable man sat down and waited while North and Sam went to a more retired spot near the door, where they resumed the confidential talk that had been interrupted.

"The first thing you must do, my boy," said North, kindly, "is to return to your father's 'ouse; an' that advice cuts two ways—'eaven-ward an' earth-ward."

"Oh! no, no, *no*, I can never return home," replied Sam, hurriedly, and thinking only of the shame of returning in his wretched condition to his earthly father.

It was at this point that the couple had come under the sharp stern eye of No. 666, who, as we have seen, went quietly out and conveyed the information direct to the Twitter family.

CHAPTER XXIV.

THE RETURNING PRODIGAL.

FOR a considerable time the Bible-seller plied Sam with every argument he could think of in order to induce him to return home, and he was still in the middle of his effort when the door opened, and two young men of gentlemanly appearance walked in, bearing a portable harmonium between them.

They were followed by one of the ladies of the Beehive, who devote all their time—and, may we not add, all their hearts—to the rescue of the perishing. Along with her came a tall, sweet-faced girl. She was our friend Hetty Frog, who, after spending her days at steady work, spent some of her night hours in labours of love. Hetty was passionately fond of music, and had taught herself to play the harmonium sufficiently to accompany simple hymns.

After her came the missionary, whose kind face was familiar to most of the homeless ones there. They greeted him with good-natured familiarity, but some of their faces assumed a somewhat vinegar aspect when the tall form of Sir Richard Brandon followed Seaward.

"A bloated haristocrat!" growled one of the men.

"Got a smart little darter, anyhow," remarked another, as Di, holding tight to her father's hand, glanced from side to side with looks of mingled pity and alarm.

For poor little Di had a not uncommon habit of investing everything in *couleur de rose*, and the stern reality which met her had not the slightest tinge of that colour. Di had pictured to herself clean rags and picturesque poverty. The reality was dirty rags and disgusting poverty. She had imagined sorrowful faces. Had she noted them when the missionary passed, she might indeed have seen kindly looks; but when her father passed there were only scowling faces, nearly all of which were unshaven and dirty. Di had not thought at all of stubbly beards or dirt! Neither had she thought of smells, or of stifling heat that it was not easy to bear. Altogether poor little Di was taken down from a height on that occasion to which she never again attained, because it was a false height. In after years she reached one of the true heights—which was out of sight higher than the false one!

There was something very business-like in these missionaries, for there was nothing of the simply amateur in their work—like the visit of Di and her

father. They were familiar with the East-end mines ;
knew where splendid gems and rich gold were to be
found, and went about digging with the steady per-
sistence of the labourer, coupled, however, with the
fire of the enthusiast.

They carried the harmonium promptly to the most
conspicuous part of the room, planted it there,
opened it, placed a stool in front of it, and one of the
brightest diamonds from that mine—in the person
of Hetty Frog—sat down before it. Simply, and in
sweet silvery tones, she sang—

"Come to the Saviour—"

The others joined—even Sir Richard Brandon
made an attempt to sing—as he had done on a
previous occasion, but without much success, musi-
cally speaking. Meanwhile, John Seaward turned
up the passage from which he had prepared to speak
that evening. And so eloquent with nature's simplicity was the missionary, that the party soon forgot
all about the Twitters while the comforting Gospel
was being urged upon the unhappy creatures around.

But *we* must not forget the Twitters. They are
our text and sermon just now !

Young Sam Twitter had risen with the intention
of going out when the missionary entered, for words
of truth only cut him to the heart. But his companion whispered him to wait a bit. Soon his
attention was riveted.

While he sat there spell-bound, a shabby-genteel man entered and sat down beside him. He wore a broad wide-awake, very much slouched over his face, and a coat which had once been fine, but now bore marks of having been severely handled—as if recently rubbed by a drunken wearer on white-washed and dirty places. The man's hands were not so dirty, however, as one might have expected from his general appearance, and they trembled much. On one of his fingers was a gold ring. This incongruity was lost on Sam, who was too much absorbed to care for the new comer, and did not even notice that he pushed somewhat needlessly close to him.

These things were not, however, lost on Reggie North, who regarded the man with some surprise, not unmixed with suspicion.

When, after a short time, however, this man laid his hand gently on that of Sam and held it, the boy could no longer neglect his eccentricities. He naturally made an effort to pull the hand away, but the stranger held it fast. Having his mind by that time entirely detached from the discourse of the missionary, Sam looked at the stranger in surprise, but could not see his face because of the dis-reputable wide-awake which he wore. But great was his astonishment, not to say alarm, when he felt two or three warm tears drop on his hand.

z

Again he tried to pull it away, but the strange man held it tighter.   Still further, he bent his head over it and kissed it.

A strange unaccountable thrill ran through the boy's frame.   He stooped, looked under the brim of the hat, and beheld his father !

"Sammy—dear, dear Sammy," whispered the man, in a husky voice.

But Sammy could not reply.   He was thunder-struck.   Neither could his father speak, for he was choking.

But Reggie North had heard enough.   He was quick-witted, and at once guessed the situation.

"Now then, old gen'lm'n," he whispered, "don't you go an' make a fuss, if you're wise.   Go out as quiet as you came in, an' leave this young 'un to me.   It's all right.   I'm on *your* side."

Samuel Twitter senior was impressed with the honesty of the man's manner, and the wisdom of his advice.   Letting go the hand, after a parting squeeze, he rose up and left the room.   Two minutes later, North and Sammy followed

They found the old father outside, who again grasped his son's hand with the words, "Sammy, my boy—dear Sammy;" but he never got further than that.

No. 666 was there too.

"You'll find the cab at the end of the street, sir," he

said, and next moment Sammy found himself borne along—not unwillingly—by North and his father.

A cab door was opened. A female form was seen with outstretched arms.

"Mother!"

"Sammy—darling—"

The returning prodigal disappeared into the cab. Mr. Twitter turned round.

"Thank you. God bless you, whoever you are," he said, fumbling in his vest pocket; having forgotten that he represented an abject beggar, and had no money there.

"No thanks to me, sir. Look higher," said the Bible-seller, thrusting the old gentleman almost forcibly into the vehicle. "Now then, cabby, drive on."

The cabby obeyed. Having already received his instructions he did not drive home. Where he drove to is a matter of small consequence. It was to an unknown house, and a perfect stranger to Sammy opened the door. Mrs. Twitter remained in the cab while Sammy and his father entered the house, the latter carrying a bundle in his hand. They were shown into what the boy must have considered—if he considered anything at all just then—a preposterously small room.

The lady of the house evidently expected them, for she said, "The bath is quite ready, sir."

"Now, Sammy,—dear boy," said Mr. Twitter, "off with your rags—and g—git into that b—bath."

Obviously Mr. Twitter did not speak with ease. In truth it was all he could do to contain himself, and he felt that his only chance of bearing up was to say nothing more than was absolutely necessary in short ejaculatory phrases. Sammy was deeply touched, and began to wash his dirty face with a few quiet tears before taking his bath.

"Now then, Sammy—look sharp! You didn't use—to—be—so—slow! eh?"

"No, father. I suppose it—it—is want of habit. I haven't undressed much of late."

This very nearly upset poor Mr. Twitter. He made no reply, but assisted his son to disrobe with a degree of awkwardness that tended to delay progress.

"It—it's not too hot—eh?"

"Oh! no, father. It's—it's—v—very nice."

"Go at it with a will, Sammy. Head and all, my boy—down with it. And don't spare the soap. Lots of soap here, Sammy—no end of soap!"

The truth of which Mr. Twitter proceeded to illustrate by covering his son with a lather that caused him quickly to resemble whipt cream.

"Oh! hold on, father, it's getting into my eyes."

"My boy—dear Sammy—forgive me. I didn't quite know what I was doing. Never mind. Down you go again, Sammy—head and all. That's it. Now, that's enough; out you come."

" Oh! father," said the poor boy, while invisible tears trickled over his wet face, as he stepped out of the bath, " it's so good of you to forgive me so freely."

"Forgive you, my son! forgive! why, I'd—I'd—"

He could say no more, but suddenly clasped Sammy to his heart, thereby rendering his face and person soap-suddy and wet to a ridiculous extént.

Unclasping his arms and stepping back, he looked down at himself.

" You dirty boy! what d' you mean by it?"

" It's your own fault, daddy," replied Sam, with a hysterical laugh, as he enveloped himself in a towel.

A knock at the bath-room door here produced dead silence.

" Please, sir," said a female voice, " the lady in the cab sends to say that she's gettin' impatient."

" Tell the lady in the cab to drive about and take an airing for ten minutes," replied Mr. Twitter with reckless hilarity.

" Yes, sir."

" Now, my boy, here's your toggery," said the irrepressible father, hovering round his recovered son like a moth round a candle—" your best suit, Sammy; the one you used to wear only on Sundays, you extravagant fellow."

Sammy put it on with some difficulty from want
of practice, and, after combing out and brushing his
hair, he presented such a changed appearance that
none of his late companions could have recognised
him.   His father, after fastening up his coat with
every button in its wrong hole, and causing as
much delay as possible by assisting him to dress,
finally hustled him down-stairs and into the cab,
where he was immediately re-enveloped by Mrs.
Twitter.

He was not permitted to see any one that night,
but was taken straight to his room, where his mother
comforted, prayed with, fed and fondled him, and
then allowed him to go to bed.

Next morning early—before breakfast—Mrs.
Twitter assembled all the little Twitters, and put
them on chairs in a row—according to order, for
Mrs. Twitter's mind was orderly in a remarkable
degree.   They ranged from right to left thus:—
Molly, Willie, Fred, Lucy, and Alice—with Alice's
doll on a doll's chair at the left flank of the line.

"Now children," said Mrs. Twitter, sitting down
in front of the row with an aspect so solemn that
they all immediately made their mouths very small
and their eyes very large—in which respect they
brought themselves into wonderful correspondence
with Alice's doll.   "Now children, your dear
brother Sammy has come home."

SAMUEL TWITTER AND SON.—Page 358

"Oh! how nice! Where has he been? What has he seen? Why has he been away so long? How jolly!" were the various expressions with which the news was received.

"Silence."

The stillness that followed was almost oppressive, for the little Twitters had been trained to prompt obedience. To say truth they had not been difficult to train, for they were all essentially mild.

"Now, remember, when he comes down to breakfast you are to take no notice whatever of his having been away—no notice at all."

"Are we not even to say good-morning or kiss him, mamma?" asked little Alice with a look of wonder.

"Dear child, you do not understand me. We are all charmed to see Sammy back, and so thankful—so glad—that he has come, and we will kiss him and say whatever we please to him *except*" (here she cast an awful eye along the line and dropt her voice) *except* ask him *where—he—has—been.*

"Mayn't we ask him how he liked it, mamma?" said Alice.

"Liked what, child?"

"Where he has been, mamma."

"No, not a word about where he has been; only that we are so glad, so very glad, to see him back."

Fred, who had an argumentative turn of mind, thought that this would be a rather demonstrative though indirect recognition of the fact that Sammy had been *somewhere* that was wrong, but, having been trained to unquestioning obedience, Fred said nothing.

"Now, dolly," whispered little Alice, bending down, " 'member dat—you 're so glad Sammy's come back; mustn't say more—not a word more."

"It is enough for you to know, my darlings," continued Mrs. Twitter, "that Sammy has been wandering and has come back."

"Listen, Dolly, you hear? Sammy's been wondering an' come back. Dat 's 'nuff for *you*."

"You see, dears," continued Mrs. Twitter, with a slightly perplexed look, caused by her desire to save poor Sammy's feelings, and her anxiety to steer clear of the slightest approach to deception, "you see, Sammy has been long away, and has been very tired, and won't like to be troubled with too many questions at breakfast, you know, so I want you all to talk a good deal about anything you like—your lessons,—for instance, when he comes down."

"Before we say good-morning, mamma, or after?" asked Alice, who was extremely conscientious.

"Darling child," exclaimed the perplexed mother, "you 'll never take it in. What I want to impress on you is—"

She stopped, suddenly, and what it was she meant to impress we shall never more clearly know, for at that moment the foot of Sammy himself was heard on the stair.

"Now, mind, children, not a word—not—a—word!"

The almost preternatural solemnity induced by this injunction was at once put to flight by Sammy, at whom the whole family flew with one accord and a united shriek—pulling him down on a chair and embracing him almost to extinction.

Fortunately for Sammy, and his anxious mother, that which the most earnest desire to obey orders would have failed to accomplish was brought about by the native selfishness of poor humanity, for, the first burst of welcome over, Alice began an elaborate account of her Dolly's recent proceedings, which seemed to consist of knocking her head against articles of furniture, punching out her own eyes and flattening her own nose; while Fred talked of his latest efforts in shipbuilding; Willie of his hopes in regard to soldiering, and Lucy of her attempts to draw and paint.

Mr. and Mrs. Twitter contented themselves with gazing on Sammy's somewhat worn face, and lying in watch, so that, when Alice or any of the young members of the flock seemed about to stray on the forbidden ground, they should be ready to descend, like two wolves on the fold, remorselessly change the subject of conversation, and carry all before them.

Thus tenderly was that prodigal son received back to his father's house.

CHAPTER XXV.

CANADA AGAIN—AND SURPRISING NEWS.

IT is most refreshing to those who have been long cooped up in a city to fly on the wings of steam to the country and take refuge among the scents of flowers and fields and trees. We have said this, or something like it, before, and remorselessly repeat it—for it is a grand truism.

Let us then indulge ourselves a little with a glance at the farm of Brankly in Canada.

Lake Ontario, with its expanse of boundless blue, rolls like an ocean in the far distance. We can see it from the hill-top where the sweet-smelling red-pines grow. At the bottom of the hill lies Brankly itself, with its orchards and homestead and fields of golden grain, and its little river, with the little sawmill going as pertinaciously as if it, like the river, had resolved to go on for ever. Cattle are there, sheep are there, horses and wagons are there, wealth and prosperity are there, above all happiness is there, because there also dwells the love of God.

It is a good many years, reader, since you and I
were last here. Then, the farm buildings and
fences were brand-new. Now, although of course
not old, they bear decided traces of exposure to the
weather. But these marks only give compactness
of look and unity of tone to everything, improving
the appearance of the place vastly.

The fences, which at first looked blank and
staring, as if wondering how they had got there, are
now more in harmony with the fields they enclose.
The plants which at first struggled as if unwillingly
on the dwelling-house, now cling to it and climb
about it with the affectionate embrace of old friends.
Everything is improved—

Well, no, not everything. Mr. Merryboy's legs
have not improved. They will not move as actively
as they were wont to do. They will not go so far,
and they demand the assistance of a stick. But Mr.
Merryboy's spirit has improved—though it was pretty
good before, and his tendency to universal philanthropy has increased to such an extent that the
people of the district have got into a way of
sending their bad men and boys to work on his
farm in order that they may become good!

Mrs. Merryboy, however, has improved in every
way, and is more blooming than ever, as well as a
trifle stouter, but Mrs. Merryboy senior, although
advanced spiritually, has degenerated a little physi-

cally. The few teeth that kept her nose and chin
apart having disappeared, her mouth has also vanished,
though there is a decided mark which tells where it
was—especially when she speaks or smiles. The
hair on her forehead has become as pure white as
the winter snows of Canada. Wrinkles on her
visage have become the rule, not the exception, but
as they all run into comical twists, and play in the
forms of humour, they may, perhaps, be regarded as
a physical improvement. She is stone deaf now,
but this also may be put to the credit side of her
account, for it has rendered needless those awkward
efforts to speak loud and painful attempts to hear
which used to trouble the family in days gone by.
It is quite clear, however, when you look into
granny's coal-black eyes, that if she were to live to
the age of Methuselah she will never be blind, nor
ill-natured, nor less pleased with herself, her surroundings, and the whole order of things created!

But who are these that sit so gravely and busily
engaged with breakfast as though they had not the
prospect of another meal that year? Two young
men and a young girl. One young man is broad
and powerful though short, with an incipient
moustache and a fluff of whisker. The other is
rather tall, slim, and gentlemanly, and still beardless.
The girl is little, neat, well-made, at the budding
period of life, brown-haired, brown-eyed, round, soft

—just such a creature as one feels disposed to pat on the head and say, "My little pet!"

Why, these are two "waifs" and a "stray!" Don't you know them? Look again. Is not the stout fellow our friend Bobby Frog, the slim one Tim Lumpy, and the girl Martha Mild? But who, in all London, would believe that these were children who had been picked out of the gutter? Nobody— except those good Samaritans who had helped to pick them up, and who could show you the photographs of what they once were and what they now are.

Mr. Merryboy, although changed a little as regards legs, was not in the least deteriorated as to lungs. As Granny, Mrs. Merryboy, and the young people sat at breakfast he was heard at an immense distance off, gradually making his way towards the house.

"Something seems to be wrong with father this morning, I think," said Mrs. Merryboy, junior, listening.

Granny, observing the action, pretended to listen, and smiled.

"He's either unusually jolly or unusually savage —a little more tea, mother," said Tim Lumpy, pushing in his cup.

Tim, being father-and-motherless, called Mr. Merryboy father and the wife mother. So did Martha, but Bobby Frog, remembering those whom

he had left at home, loyally declined, though he did
not object to call the elder Mrs. Merryboy granny.

" Something for good or evil must have happened,"
said Bobby, laying down his knife and fork as the
growling sound drew nearer.

At last the door flew open and the storm burst in.

And we may remark that Mr. Merryboy's stormy
nature was, if possible, a little more obtrusive than
it used to be, for whereas in former days his toes
and heels did most of the rattling-thunder-business,
the stick now came into play as a prominent creator
of din—not only when flourished by hand, but often
on its own account and unexpectedly, when propped
clumsily in awkward places.

" Hallo! good people all, how are 'ee? morning—
morning. Boys, d'ee know that the saw-mill's come
to grief?"

"No, are you in earnest, father?" cried Tim,
jumping up.

" In earnest! Of course I am. Pretty engineers
you are. Sawed its own bed in two, or burst itself.
Don't know which, and what's more I don't care.
Come, Martha, my bantam chicken, let's have a cup
of tea. Bother that stick, it can't keep its legs much
better than myself. How are you, mother? Glorious
weather, isn't it?"

Mr. Merryboy ignored deafness. He continued to
speak to his mother just as though she heard him.

And she continued to nod and smile, and make-believe to hear with more demonstration of face and cap than ever. After all, her total loss of hearing made little difference, her sentiments being what Bobby Frog in his early days would have described in the words, "Wot's the hodds so long as you're 'appy?"

But Bobby had now ceased to drop or misapply his h's—though he still had some trouble with his r's.

As he was chief engineer of the saw-mill, having turned out quite a mechanical genius, he ran down to the scene of disaster with much concern on hearing the old gentleman's report.

And, truly, when he and Tim reached the picturesque spot where, at the water's edge among fine trees and shrubs, the mill stood clearly reflected in its own dam, they found that the mischief done was considerable. The machinery, by which the frame with its log to be sawn was moved along quarter-inch by quarter-inch at each stroke, was indeed all right, but it had not been made self-regulating. The result was that, on one of the attendant workmen omitting to do his duty, the saw not only ripped off a beautiful plank from a log, but continued to cross-cut the end of the heavy framework, and then proceeded to cut the iron which held the log in its place. The result, of course, was that the iron refused to be cut, and savagely revenged itself by

DUSTY DIAMONDS. 369

scraping off, flattening down, turning up, and otherwise damaging, the teeth of the saw!

"H'm! that comes of haste," muttered Bob, as he
surveyed the wreck. "If I had taken time to make
the whole affair complete before setting the mill to
work, this would not have happened."

"Never mind, Bob, we must learn by experience,
you know," said Tim, examining the damage done
with a critical eye. "Luckily, we have a spare saw
in the store."

"Run and fetch it," said Bob to the man in charge
of the mill, whose carelessness had caused the damage, and who stared silently at his work with a look
of horrified resignation.

When he was gone Bob and Tim threw off their
coats, rolled up their sleeves to the shoulder, and set
to work with a degree of promptitude and skill which
proved them to be both earnest and capable workmen.

The first thing to be done was to detach the
damaged saw from its frame.

"There," said Bob, as he flung it down, "you
won't use your teeth again on the wrong subject for
some time to come. Have we dry timber heavy
enough to mend the frame, Tim?"

"Plenty—more than we want."

"Well, you go to work on it while I fix up the
new saw."

To work the two went accordingly—adjusting,

2 A

screwing, squaring, sawing, planing, mortising, until the dinner-bell called them to the house.

"So soon!" exclaimed Bob; "dinner is a great bother when a man is very busy."

"D' ye think so, Bob? Well, now, I look on it as a great comfort—specially when you 're hungry."

"Ah! but that 's because you are greedy, Tim. You always were too fond o' your grub."

"Come, Bob, no slang. You know that mother doesn't like it. By the way, talkin' of mothers, is it on Wednesday or Thursday that you expect *your* mother?"

"Thursday, my boy," replied Bob, with a bright look. "Ha! that *will* be a day for me!"

"So it will, Bob, I 'm glad for your sake," returned Tim with a sigh, which was a very unusual expression of feeling for him. His friend at once understood its significance.

"Tim, my boy, I 'm sorry for you. I wish I could split my mother in two and give you half of her."

"Yes," said Tim, somewhat absently, "it *is* sad to have not one soul in the world related to you."

"But there are many who care for you as much as if they were relations," said Bob, taking his friend's arm as they approached the house.

"Come along, come along, youngsters," shouted Mr. Merryboy from the window, "the dinner 's gettin' cold, and granny 's gettin' in a passion. Look sharp.

If you knew what news I have for you you'd look sharper."

"What news, sir?" asked Bob, as they sat down to a table which did not exactly "groan" with viands —it was too strong for that—but which was heavily weighted therewith.

"I won't tell you till after dinner—just to punish you for being late; besides, it might spoil your appetite."

"But suspense is apt to spoil appetite, father, isn't it?" said Tim, who, well accustomed to the old farmer's eccentricities, did not believe much in the news he professed to have in keeping.

"Well, then, you must just lose your appetites, for I won't tell you," said Mr. Merryboy firmly. "It will do you good—eh! mother, won't a touch of starvation improve them, bring back the memory of old times—eh?"

The old lady, observing that her son was addressing her, shot forth such a beam of intelligence and goodwill that it was as though a gleam of sunshine had burst into the room.

"I knew you'd agree with me—ha! ha! you always do, mother," cried the farmer, flinging his handkerchief at a small kitten which was sporting on the floor and went into fits of delight at the attention.

After dinner the young men were about to return

to their saw-mill when Mr. Merryboy called them back.

"What would you say, boys, to hear that Sir Richard Brandon, with a troop of emigrants, is going to settle somewhere in Canada?'

"I would think he'd gone mad, sir, or changed his nature," responded Bob.

."Well, as to whether he's gone mad or not I can't tell—he may have changed his nature, who knows? That's not beyond the bounds of possibility. Anyway, he is coming. I've got a letter from a friend of mine in London who says he read it in the papers. But perhaps you may learn more about it in *that*."

He tossed a letter to Bob, who eagerly seized it. "From sister Hetty," he cried, and tore it open.

The complete unity and unanimity of this family was well illustrated by the fact, that Bob began to read the letter aloud without asking leave and without apology.

"Dearest Bob," it ran, "you will get this letter only a mail before our arrival. I had not meant to write again, but cannot resist doing so, to give you the earliest news about it. Sir Richard has changed his mind! You know, in my last, I told you he had helped to assist several poor families from this quarter—as well as mother and me, and Matty. He is a real friend to the poor, for he doesn't merely fling coppers and old clothes at them, but takes trouble to find out about them, and helps them in the way that seems best for each. It's all owing to that sweet Miss Di, who comes so much about here that she's almost as well known as Giles Scot the policeman, or our missionary. By the way, Giles has been made an Inspector lately, and has got no end of medals and a silver watch, and other testimonials, for bravery in saving people from fires, and canals, and cart wheels, and—he's a wonderful man is Giles, and they say his son is to be taken into the force as soon as he's old enough. He's big enough and sensible enough already, and looks twice his age. After all, if he can knock people down, and take people up, and keep order, what does it matter how young he is?

"But I'm wandering, I always do wander, Bob, when I write to you! Well, as I was saying, Sir Richard has changed his mind and has resolved to emigrate himself, with Miss Di and a whole lot of friends and work-people. He wants, as he says, to establish a colony of likeminded people, and so you may be sure that all who have fixed to go with him are followers of the Lord Jesus—and not ashamed to say so. As I had already taken our passages in the *Amazon* steamer—"

"The *Amazon*!" interrupted Mr. Merryboy, with a shout, "why, that steamer has arrived already!"

"So it has," said Bob, becoming excited; "their letter must have been delayed, and they must have come by the same steamer that brought it; why, they'll be here immediately!"

"Perhaps to-night!" exclaimed Mrs. Merryboy.

"Oh! *how* nice!" murmured Martha, her great brown eyes glittering with joy at the near prospect of seeing that Hetty about whom she had heard so much.

"Impossible!" said Tim Lumpy, coming down on them all with his wet-blanket of common-sense. "They would never come on without dropping us a line from Quebec, or Montreal, to announce their arrival."

"That's true, Tim," said Mr. Merryboy, "but you've not finished the letter, Bob—go on. Mother, mother, what a variety of faces you *are* making!"

This also was true, for old Mrs. Merryboy, seeing that something unusual was occurring, had all this time been watching the various speakers with her coal-black eyes, changing aspect with their varied expressions, and wrinkling her visage up into such inexpressible contortions of sympathetic good-will, that she really could not have been more sociable if she had been in full possession and use of her five senses.

"As I had already," continued Bob, reading,

"taken our passages in the *Amazon* steamer, Sir Richard thought it best that we should come on before, along with his agent, who goes to see after the land, so that we might have a good long stay with you, and dear Mr. and Mrs. Merryboy, who have been so kind to you, before going on to Brandon—which, I believe, is the name of the place in the backwoods where Sir Richard means us all to go to. I don't know exactly where it is—and I don't know anybody who does, but that's no matter. Enough for mother, and Matty, and me to know that it's within a few hundred miles of you, which is very different from three thousand miles of an ocean!

" You'll also be glad to hear that Mr. Twitter with all his family is to join this band. It quite puts me in mind of the story of the Pilgrim Fathers, that I once heard in dear Mr. Holland's meeting hall, long ago. I wish he could come too, and all his people with him, and all the ladies from the Beehive. Wouldn't that be charming! But, then,—who would be left to look after London? No, it is better that they should remain at home.

" Poor Mr. Twitter never quite got the better of his fire, you see, so he sold his share in his business, and is getting ready to come. His boys and girls will be a great help to him in Canada, instead of a burden as they have been in London—the younger ones I mean, of course, for Molly, and Sammy, and

Willie have been helping their parents for a long time past. I don't think Mrs. Twitter quite likes it, and I'm sure she's almost breaking her heart at the thought of leaving George Yard. It is said that their friends Mrs. Loper, Mrs. Larrabel, Stickler, and Crackaby, want to join, but I rather think Sir Richard isn't very keen to have them. Mr. Stephen Welland is also coming. One of Sir Richard's friends, Mr. Brisbane I think, got him a good situation in the Mint—that's where all the money is coined, you know—but, on hearing of this expedition to Canada, he made up his mind to go there instead; so he gave up the Mint—very unwillingly, however, I believe, for he wanted very much to go into the Mint. Now, no more at present from your loving and much hurried sister (for I'm in the middle of packing), HETTY."

Now, while Bob Frog was in the act of putting Hetty's letter in his pocket, a little boy was seen on horseback, galloping up to the door.

He brought a telegram addressed to "Mr. Robert Frog." It was from Montreal, and ran thus : "We have arrived, and leave this on Tuesday forenoon."

"Why, they're almost here *now*," cried Bob.

"Harness up, my boy, and off you go—not a moment to lose!" cried Mr. Merryboy, as Bob dashed out of the room. "Take the bays, Bob," he added in a stentorian voice, thrusting his head out of the window, "and the biggest wagon. Don't forget the rugs!"

Ten minutes later, and Bob Frog, with Tim Lumpy beside him, was driving the spanking pair of bays to the railway station.

CHAPTER XXVI.

HAPPY MEETINGS.

IT was to the same railway station as that at which they had parted from their guardian and been handed over to Mr. Merryboy years before that Bobby Frog now drove. The train was not due for half an hour.

"Tim," said Bob after they had walked up and down the platform for about five minutes, "how slowly time seems to fly when one's in a hurry!"

"Doesn't it?" assented Tim, "crawls like a snail."

"Tim," said Bob, after ten minutes had elapsed, "what a difficult thing it is to wait patiently when one's anxious!"

"Isn't it?" assented Tim, "so hard to keep from fretting and stamping."

"Tim," said Bob, after twenty minutes had passed, "I wonder if the two or three dozen people on this platform are all as uncomfortably impatient as I am."

"Perhaps they are," said Tim, "but certainly possessed of more power to restrain themselves."

"Tim," said Bob, after the lapse of five-and-twenty minutes, "did you ever hear of such a long half-hour since you were born?"

"Never," replied the sympathetic Tim, "except once long ago when I was starving, and stood for about that length of time in front of a confectioner's window till I nearly collapsed and had to run away at last for fear I should smash in the glass and feed."

"Tim, I'll take a look round and see that the bays are all right."

"You've done that four times already, Bob."

"Well, I'll do it five times, Tim. There's luck, you know, in odd numbers."

There was a sharpish curve on the line close to the station. While Bob Frog was away the train, being five minutes before its time, came thundering round the curve and rushed alongside the platform.

Bob ran back of course and stood vainly trying to see the people in each carriage as it went past.

"Oh! *what* a sweet eager face!" exclaimed Tim, gazing after a young girl who had thrust her head out of a first-class carriage.

"Let alone sweet faces, Tim—this way. The third classes are all behind."

By this time the train had stopped, and great was the commotion as friends and relatives met or said good-bye hurriedly, and bustled into and out of the carriages—commotion which was increased by the

cheering of a fresh band of rescued waifs going to new
homes in the west, and the hissing of the safety
valve which took it into its head at that inconvenient moment to let off superfluous steam. Some of
the people rushing about on that platform and jost-
ling each other would have been the better for safety
valves! Poor Bobby Frog was one of these.

"Not there!" he exclaimed despairingly, as he
looked into the last carriage of the train.

"Impossible," said Tim, " we 've only missed them ;
come back."

They went back, looking eagerly into carriage
after carriage—Bob even glancing under the seats in
a sort of wild hope that his mother might be hiding
there, but no one resembling Mrs. Frog was to be
seen.

A commotion at the front part of the train, more
pronounced than the general hubbub, attracted their
attention.

" Oh ! where is he—where is he ?" cried a female
voice, which was followed up by the female herself,
a respectable elderly woman, who went about the
platform scattering people right and left in a fit of
temporary insanity, "where is my Bobby, where *is*
he, I say ? Oh ! *why* won't people git out o' my
way ? *Git* out o' the way (shoving a sluggish man
forcibly), where are you, Bobby ? Bo-o-o-o-o-by !"

It was Mrs. Frog! Bob saw her, but did not

move. His heart was in his throat ! He *could* not
move. As he afterwards said, he was struck all of
a heap, and could only stand and gaze with his hands
clasped.

"Out o' the *way*, young man !" cried Mrs. Frog,
brushing indignantly past him, in one of her erratic
bursts. "Oh ! Bobby—where *has* that boy gone
to ?"

"Mother !" gasped Bob.

"Who said that ?" cried Mrs. Frog, turning round
with a sharp look, as if prepared to retort "you 're
another" on the shortest notice.

"Mother !" again said Bob, unclasping his hands
and holding them out.

Mrs. Frog had hitherto, regardless of the well-
known effect of time, kept staring at heads on
the level which Bobby's had reached when he
left home. She now looked up with a startled
expression.

"Can it—is it—oh ! Bo—" she got no further, but
sprang forward and was caught and fervently clasped
in the arms of her son.

Tim fluttered round them, blowing his nose
violently though quite free from cold in the head
—which complaint, indeed, is not common in those
regions.

Hetty, who had lost her mother in the crowd, now
ran forward with Matty. Bob saw them, let go his

mother, and received one in each arm—squeezing
them both at once to his capacious bosom.

Mrs. Frog might have fallen, though that was not
probable, but Tim made sure of her by holding out
a hand which the good woman grasped, and laid her
head on his breast, quite willing to make use of
him as a convenient post to lean against, while she
observed the meeting of the young people with a
contented smile.

Tim observed that meeting too, but with very
different feelings, for the "sweet eager face" that
he had seen in the first-class carriage belonged to
Hetty! Long-continued love to human souls had
given to her face a sweetness—and sympathy with
human spirits and bodies in the depths of poverty,
sorrow, and deep despair had invested it with a
pitiful tenderness and refinement—which one looks
for more naturally among the innocent in the
higher ranks of life.

Poor Tim gazed unutterably, and his heart went
on in such a way that even Mrs. Frog's attention was
arrested. Looking up, she asked if he was took
bad.

"Oh! dear no. By no means," said Tim, quickly.

"You 're tremblin' so," she returned, "an' it ain't
cold—but your colour 's all right. I suppose it 's the
natur' o' you Canadians. But only to think that my
Bobby," she added, quitting her leaning-post, and again

seizing her son, " that my Bobby should 'ave grow'd up, an' his poor mother knowed nothink about it! I can't believe my eyes—it ain't like Bobby a bit, yet some'ow I *know* it's 'im! Why, you've grow'd into a gentleman, you 'ave."

" And you have grown into a flatterer," said Bob, with a laugh. " But come, mother, this way; I've brought the wagon for you. Look after the luggage, Tim—Oh! I forgot. This is Tim, Hetty Tim Lumpy. You remember, you used to see us playing together when we were city Arabs."

Hetty looked at Tim, and, remembering Bobby's strong love for jesting, did not believe him. She smiled, however, and bowed to the tall good-looking youth, who seemed unaccountably shy and confused as he went off to look after the luggage.

" Here is the wagon; come along," said Bob, leading his mother out of the station.

" The waggin, boy; I don't see no waggin."

" Why, there, with the pair of bay horses."

" You don't mean the carridge by the fence, do you ?"

" Well, yes, only we call them wagons here."

" An' you calls the 'osses *bay* 'osses, do you ?"

" Yes."

" Well now, *I* would call 'em beautiful 'osses, but I suppose bay means the same thing here. You've got strange ways in Canada."

"Yes, mother, and pleasant ways too, as I hope you shall find out ere long. Get in, now. Take care! Now then, Hetty—come, Matty. How difficult to believe that such a strapping young thing can be the squalling Matty I left in London!"

Matty laughed as she got in, by way of reply, for she did not yet quite believe in her big brother.

"Do you drive, Tim; I'll stay inside," said Bob.

In another moment the spanking bays were whirling the wagon over the road to Brankly Farm at the rate of ten miles an hour.

Need it be said that the amiable Merryboys did not fail of their duty on that occasion? That Hetty and Matty took violently to brown-eyed Martha at first sight, having heard all about her from Bob long ago—as she of them; that Mrs. Merryboy was, we may say, one glowing beam of hospitality; that Mrs. Frog was, so to speak, one blazing personification of amazement, which threatened to become chronic—there was so much that was contrary to previous experience and she was so slow to take it in; that Mr. Merryboy became noisier than ever, and that, what between his stick and his legs, to say nothing of his voice, he managed to create in one day hubbub enough to last ten families for a fortnight; that the domestics and the dogs were sympathetically joyful; that even the kitten gave unmistakeable evidences of unusual hilarity—though some attributed the

BOBBY FROG AND HIS MOTHER.—PAGE 385.

effect to surreptitiously-obtained cream ; and, finally, that old granny became something like a Chinese image in the matter of nodding and gazing and smirking and wrinkling, so that there seemed some danger of her terminating her career in a gush of universal philanthropy—need all this be said, we ask ? We think not ; therefore we won't say it.

But it was not till Bob Frog got his mother all to himself, under the trees, near the waterfall, down by the river that drove the still unmended saw-mill, that they had real and satisfactory communion. It would have been interesting to have listened to these two— with memories and sympathies and feelings towards the Saviour of sinners so closely intertwined, yet with knowledge and intellectual powers in many respects so far apart. But we may not intrude too closely.

Towards the end of their walk, Bob touched on a subject which had been uppermost in the minds of both all the time, but from which they had shrunk equally, the one being afraid to ask, the other disinclined to tell.

"Mother," said Bob, at last, "what about father ?"

"Ah ! Bobby," replied Mrs. Frog, beginning to weep, gently, "I know'd ye would come to that— you was always so fond of 'im, an' he was so fond o' you too, indeed—"

"I know it, mother," interrupted Bob, "but have you never heard of him ? "

"Never. I might 'ave, p'r'aps, if he'd bin took an' tried under his own name, but you know he had so many aliases, an' the old 'ouse we used to live in we was obliged to quit, so p'r'aps he tried to find us and couldn't."

"May God help him—dear father!" said the son in a low sad voice.

"I'd never 've left 'im, Bobby, if he 'adn't left me. You know that. An' if I thought he was alive and know'd w'ere he was, I'd go back to 'im yet, but—"

The subject was dropped here, for the new mill came suddenly into view, and Bob was glad to draw his mother's attention to it.

"See, we were mending that just before we got the news you were so near us. Come, I'll show it to you. Tim Lumpy and I made it all by ourselves, and I think you'll call it a first-class article. By the way, how came you to travel first-class?"

"Oh! that's all along of Sir Richard Brandon. He's sitch a liberal gentleman, an' said that as it was by his advice we were goin' to Canada, he would pay our expenses; and he's so grand that he never remembered there was any other class but first, when he took the tickets, an' when he was show'd what he'd done he laughed an' said he wouldn't alter it, an' we must go all the way first-class. He's a strange man, but a good 'un!"

By this time they had reached the platform of

the damaged saw-mill, and Bob pointed out, with elaborate care, the details of the mill in all its minute particulars, commenting specially on the fact that most of the telling improvements on it were due to the fertile brain and inventive genius of Tim Lumpy. He also explained the different kinds of saws—the ripping saw, and the cross-cut saw, and the circular saw, and the eccentric saw— just as if his mother were an embryo mill-wright, for he *felt* that she took a deep interest in it all, and Mrs. Frog listened with the profound attention of a civil engineer, and remarked on everything with such comments as—oh! indeed! ah! well now! ain't it wonderful? amazin'! an' you made it all too! Oh! Bobby!—and other more or less appropriate phrases.

On quitting the mill to return to the house they saw a couple of figures walking down another avenue, so absorbed in conversation that they did not at first observe Bob and his mother, or take note of the fact that Matty, being a bouncing girl, had gone after butterflies or some such child-alluring insects.

It was Tim Lumpy and Hetty Frog.

And no wonder that they were absorbed, for was not their conversation on subjects of the profoundest interest to both?—George Yard, White-chapel, Commercial Street, Spitalfields, and the

Sailor's Home, and the Rests, and all the other
agencies for rescuing poor souls in monstrous
London, and the teachers and school companions
whom they had known there and never could forget!
No wonder, we say, that these two were absorbed
while comparing notes, and still less wonder that
they were even more deeply absorbed when they
got upon the theme of Bobby Frog—so much loved,
nay, almost worshipped, by both.

At last they observed Mrs. Frog's scarlet shawl—
which was very conspicuous—and her son, and
tried to look unconscious, and wondered with quite
needless surprise where Matty could have gone to.

Bobby Frog, being a sharp youth, noted these
things, but made no comment to any one, for the air
of Canada had, somehow, invested this waif with
wonderful delicacy of feeling.

Although Bob and his mother left off talking of
Ned Frog somewhat abruptly, as well as sorrowfully, it does not follow that we are bound to do the
same.   On the contrary, we now ask the reader to
leave Brankly Farm rather abruptly, and return to
London for the purpose of paying Ned a visit.

CHAPTER XXVII.

A STRANGE VISIT AND ITS RESULTS.

EDWARD FROG, bird-fancier, pugilist, etc. (and the etc. represents an unknown quantity) has changed somewhat like the rest, for a few years have thinned the short-cropped though once curly locks above his knotted forehead, besides sprinkling them with grey. But in other respects he has not fallen off—nay he has rather improved, owing to the peculiar system of diet and discipline and regularity of life to which, during these years, he has been subjected.

When Ned returned from what we may style his outing, he went straight to the old court with something like a feeling of anxiety in his heart, but found the old home deserted and the old door, which still bore deep marks of his knuckles on the upper panels and his boots on the lower, was padlocked. He inquired for Mrs. Frog, but was told she had left the place long ago,—and no one knew where she had gone.

With a heavy heart Ned turned from the door and sauntered away, friendless and homeless. He thought of making further inquiries about his family, but at the corner of the street smelt the old shop that had swallowed up so much of his earnings.

"If I'd on'y put it all in the savin's bank," he said bitterly, stopping in front of the gin-palace, "I'd 'ave bin well off to-day."

An old comrade turned the corner at that moment.

"What! Ned Frog!" he cried, seizing his hand and shaking it with genuine goodwill. "Well, this *is* good luck. Come along, old boy!"

It was pleasant to the desolate man to be thus recognised. He went along like an ox to the slaughter, though, unlike the ox, he knew well what he was going to.

He was "treated." He drank beer. Other old friends came in. He drank gin. If good resolves had been coming up in his mind earlier in the day he forgot them now. If better feelings had been struggling for the mastery, he crushed them now. He got drunk. He became disorderly. He went into High Street, Whitechapel, with a view to do damage to somebody. He succeeded. He tumbled over a barrow, and damaged his own shins. He encountered No. 666 soon after, and, through his influence, passed the night in a police cell.

After this Ned gave up all thought of searching for his wife and family.

" Better let 'em alone," he growled to himself on being discharged from the police office with a caution.

But, as we have said or hinted elsewhere, Ned was a man of iron will. He resolved to avoid the public-house, to drink in moderation, and to do his drinking at home. Being as powerful and active as ever he had been, he soon managed, in the capacity of a common labourer, to scrape enough money together to enable him to retake his old garret, which chanced to be vacant. Indeed its situation was so airy, and it was so undesirable, that it was almost always vacant. He bought a few cages and birds; found that the old manager of the low music-hall was still at work and ready to employ him, and thus fell very much into his old line of life.

One night, as he was passing into his place of business—the music-hall—a man saw him and recognised him. This was a city missionary of the John Seaward type, who chanced to be fishing for souls that night in these troubled waters. There are many such fishermen about, thank God, doing their grand work unostentatiously, and not only rescuing souls for eternity, but helping, more perhaps than even the best informed are aware of, to save London from tremendous evil.

What it was in Ned Frog that attracted this man of God we know not, but, after casting his lines for some hours in other places, he returned to the music-hall and loitered about the door.

At a late hour its audience came pouring out with discordant cries and ribald laughter. Soon Ned appeared and took his way homeward. The missionary followed at a safe distance till he saw Ned disappear through the doorway that led to his garret. Then, running forward, he entered the dark passage and heard Ned's heavy foot clanking on the stone steps as he mounted upwards.

The sound became fainter, and the missionary, fearing lest he should fail to find the room in which his man dwelt—for there were many rooms in the old tenement—ran hastily up-stairs and paused to listen. The footsteps were still sounding above him, but louder now, because Ned was mounting a wooden stair. A few seconds later a heavy door was banged, and all was quiet.

The city missionary now groped his way upwards until he came to the highest landing, where in the thick darkness he saw a light under a door. With a feeling of uncertainty and a silent prayer for help he knocked gently. The door was opened at once by a middle-aged woman, whose outline only could be seen, her back being to the light.

"Is it here that the man lives who came up just now?" asked the missionary.

"What man?" she replied, fiercely, "I know

nothink about men, an' 'ave nothink to do with 'em.
Ned Frog's the on'y man as ever comes 'ere, an' *he*
lives up there."

She made a motion, as if pointing upwards somewhere, and banged the door in her visitor's face.

"Up there!" The missionary had reached the
highest landing, and saw no other gleam of light anywhere. Groping about, however, his hand struck
against a ladder. All doubt as to the use of this
was immediately banished, for a man's heavy tread
was heard in the room above as he crossed it.

Mounting the ladder, the missionary, instead of
coming to a higher landing as he had expected,
thrust his hat against a trap-door in the roof. Immediately he heard a savage human growl. Evidently
the man was in a bad humour, but the missionary
knocked.

"Who's there?" demanded the man, fiercely, for
his visitors were few, and these generally connected
with the police force.

"May I come in?" asked the missionary in a
mild voice—not that he put the mildness on for
the occasion. He was naturally mild—additionally
so by grace.

"Oh! yes—you may come in," cried the man,
lifting the trap-door.

The visitor stepped into the room and was startled
by Ned letting fall the trap-door with a crash that

shook the whole tenement. Planting himself upon it, he rendered retreat impossible.

It was a trying situation, for the man was in a savage humour, and evidently the worse for drink. But missionaries are bold men.

"Now," demanded Ned, "what may *you* want?"

"I want your soul," replied his visitor, quietly.

"You needn't trouble yourself, then, for the devil's got it already."

"No—he has not got it *yet*, Ned."

"Oh! you know me then?"

"No. I never saw you till to-night, but I learned your name accidentally, and I'm anxious about your soul."

"You don't know me," Ned repeated, slowly, "you never saw me till to-night, yet you're anxious about my soul! What stuff are you talkin'! 'Ow can that be?"

"Now, you have puzzled *me*," said the missionary. "I cannot tell how that can be, but it is no 'stuff,' I assure you. I think it probable, however, that your own experience may help you. Didn't you once see a young girl whom you had never seen before, whom you didn't know, whom you had never even heard of, yet you became desperately anxious to win her?"

Ned instantly thought of a certain woman whom he had often abused and beaten, and whose heart he had probably broken.

"Yes," he said, "I did; but then I had falled in love wi' her at first sight, and you can't have falled in love wi' *me*, you know."

Ned grinned at this idea in spite of himself.

"Well, no," replied the missionary, "not exactly. You're not a very lovable object to look at just now. Nevertheless, I *am* anxious about your soul *at first sight*. I can't tell how it is, but so it is."

"Come, now," said Ned, becoming suddenly stern. "I don't believe in your religion, or your Bible, or your prayin' and psalm-singin'. I tell you plainly, I'm a infidel. But if you can say anything in favour o' your views, fire away; I'll listen, only don't let me have any o' your sing-songin' or whinin', else I'll kick you down the trap-door and down the stair an' up the court and out into the street—speak out, like a man."

"I will speak as God the Holy Spirit shall enable me," returned the missionary, without the slightest change in tone or manner.

"Well, then, sit down," said Ned, pointing to the only chair in the room, while he seated himself on the rickety table, which threatened to give way altogether, while the reckless man swung his right leg to and fro quite regardless of its complainings.

"Have you ever studied the Bible?" asked the missionary, somewhat abruptly.

"Well, no, of course not. I'm not a parson, but

I have read a bit here and there, an' it's all rubbish. I don't believe a word of it."

"There's a part of it," returned the visitor, "which says that God maketh his rain to fall on the just and on the unjust. Do you not believe that?"

"Of course I do. A man can't help believin' that, for he sees it—it falls on houses, fields, birds and beasts as well."

"Then you *do* believe a word of it?"

"Oh! come, you're a deal too sharp. You know what I mean."

"No," said his visitor, quickly, "I don't quite know what you mean. One who professes to be an infidel professes more or less intelligent disbelief in the Bible, yet you admit that you have never studied the book which you profess to disbelieve—much less, I suppose, have you studied the books which give us the evidences of its truth."

"Don't suppose, Mr. parson, or missioner, or whatever you are," said Ned, "that you're goin' to floor me wi' your larnin'. I'm too old a bird for that. Do you suppose that I'm bound to study everything on the face o' the earth like a lawyer before I'm entitled to say I don't believe it. If I see that a thing don't work well, that's enough for me to condemn it."

"You're quite right there. I quite go with that line of reasoning. By their fruits shall ye know them. A man don't usually go to a thistle to find grapes. But let me ask you, Ned, do you usually find that murderers, drunkards, burglars, thieves, and blackguards in general are students of the Bible and given to prayer and psalm-singing?"

"Ha! ha! I should rather think not," said Ned, much tickled by the supposition.

"Then," continued the other, "tell me, honestly, Ned, do you find that people who read God's Word and sing His praise and ask His blessing on all they do, are generally bad fathers, and mothers, and masters, and servants, and children, and that from their ranks come the worst people in society?"

"Now, look here, Mr. missioner," cried Ned, leaping suddenly from the table, which overturned with a crash, "I'm one o' them fellers that's not to be floored by a puff o' wind. I can hold my own agin most men wi' fist or tongue. But I like fair-play in the ring or in argiment. I have *not* studied this matter, as you say, an' so I won't speak on it. But I'll look into it, an' if you come back here this day three weeks I'll let you know what I think. You may trust me, for when I say a thing I mean it."

"Will you accept a Testament, then," said the missionary, rising and pulling one out of his pocket.

"No, I won't," said Ned, "I've got one."

The missionary looked surprised, and hesitated.

"Don't you believe me?" asked Ned, angrily.

"At first I did not," was the reply, "but now that I stand before your face and look in your eyes I *do* believe you."

Ned gave a cynical laugh. "You're easy to gull," he said; "why, when it serves my purpose I can lie like a trooper."

"I know that," returned the visitor, quietly, "but it serves your purpose to-night to speak the truth. I can see that. May I pray that God should guide you?"

"Yes, you may, but not here. I'll have no hypo-critical goin' down on my knees till I see my way to it. If I don't see my way to it, I'll let you know when you come back this day three weeks."

"Well, I'll pray for you in my own room, Ned Frog."

"You may do what you like in your own room. Good-night."

He lifted the trap-door as he spoke, and pointed downward. The missionary at once descended after a brief "good-night," and a pleasant nod. Ned just gave him time to get his head out of the way when he let the trap fall with a clap like thunder, and then began to pace up and down his little room with his hands in his pockets and his chin on his breast.

After a short time he went to a corner of the room where stood a small wooden box that contained the few articles of clothing which he possessed. From the bottom of this he fished up the New Testament that had been given to him long ago by Reggie North. Drawing his chair to the table and the candle to his elbow, the returned convict opened the Book, and there in his garret began for the first time to read in earnest the wonderful Word of Life!

CHAPTER XXVIII.

THE GREAT CHANGE.

PUNCTUAL to the day and the hour, the missionary returned to Ned's garret.

Much and earnestly had he prayed, in the meantime, that the man might be guided in his search after truth, and that to himself might be given words of wisdom which might have weight with him.

But the missionary's words were not now required. God had spoken to the rough man by his own Word. The Holy Spirit had carried conviction home. He had also revealed the Saviour, and the man was converted before the missionary again saw him.

Reader, we present no fancy portrait to you. Our fiction had its counterpart in actual life. Ned Frog, in essential points at least, represents a real man—though we have, doubtless, saddled on his broad shoulders a few unimportant matters, which perhaps did not belong to him.

"I believe that this is God's Word, my friend," he said, extending his hand, the moment the missionary entered, " and in proof of that I will now ask you to kneel with me and pray."

You may be sure that the man of God complied gladly and with a full heart

We may not, however, trace here the after-course of this man in detail. For our purpose it will suffice to say that this was no mere flash in the pan. Ned Frog's character did not change. It only received a new direction and a new impulse. The vigorous energy and fearless determination with which he had in former days pursued sin and self-gratification had now been turned into channels of righteousness.

Very soon after finding Jesus for himself, he began earnestly to desire the salvation of others, and, in a quiet humble way, began with the poor people in his own stair.

But this could not satisfy him. He was too strong both in body and mind to be restrained, and soon took to open-air preaching.

" I 'm going to begin a mission," he said, one day, to the missionary who had brought him to the Saviour. " There are many stout able fellows here who used to accept me as a leader in wickedness, and who will, perhaps, agree to follow me in a new walk. Some of them have come to the Lord already. I 'm goin', sir, to get these to form a band of workers, and we 'll take up a district."

"Good," said the missionary, "there's nothing like united action. What part of the district will you take up yourself, Ned?"

"The place where I stand, sir," he replied. "Where I have sinned there will I preach to men the Saviour of sinners."

And he did preach, not with eloquence, perhaps, but with such fervour that many of his old comrades were touched deeply, and some were brought to Christ and joined his "Daniel Band." Moreover, Ned kept to his own district and class. He did not assume that all rich church-goers are hypocrites, and that it was his duty to stand in conspicuous places and howl to them the message of salvation, in tones of rasping discord. No, it was noted by his mates, as particularly curious, that the voice of the man who could, when he chose, roar like a bull of Bashan, had become soft and what we may style entreative in its tone. Moreover, he did not try to imitate clerical errors. He did not get upon a deadly monotone while preaching, as so many do. He simply *spoke* when he preached—spoke loud, no doubt, but in a tone precisely similar to that in which, in former days, he would have seriously advised a brother burglar to adopt a certain course, or to carefully steer clear of another course, in order to gain his ends or to avoid falling into the hands of the police. Thus men, when listening to him, came to believe that he was really speaking to them in earnest, and not " preaching "!

Oh! that young men who aim at the high privilege of proclaiming the " good news " would reflect on this latter point, and try to steer clear of that fatal rock on which the Church—not the Episcopal, Presbyterian, or any other Church, but the whole Church militant—has been bumping so long to her own tremendous damage!

One point which told powerfully with those whom Ned sought to win was, that he went about endeavouring, as far as in him lay, to undo the evil that he had done. Some of it could never be undone— he felt that bitterly. Some could be remedied—he rejoiced in that and went about it with vigour.

For instance, he owed several debts. Being a handy fellow and strong, he worked like a horse, and soon paid off his debts to the last farthing. Again, many a time had he, in days gone by, insulted and defamed comrades and friends. These he sought out with care and begged their pardon. The bull-dog courage in him was so strong that in former days he would have struck or insulted any man who provoked him, without reference to his, it might be, superior size or strength. He now went as boldly forward to confess his sin and to apologise. Sometimes his apologies were kindly received, at other times he was rudely repelled and called a hypocrite in language that we may not repeat, but he took it well; he resented nothing now, and used to say he had been made invulnerable since he had enlisted under the banner of the Prince of Peace.

Yet, strange to say, the man's pugilistic powers were not rendered useless by his pacific life and profession.

One day he was passing down one of those streets where even the police prefer to go in couples. Suddenly a door burst open and a poor drunken woman was kicked out into the street by a big ruffian with whom Ned was not acquainted. Not satisfied with what he had done, the rough proceeded to kick the woman, who began to scream "murder!"

A crowd at once collected, for, although such incidents were common enough in such places, they always possessed sufficient interest to draw a crowd; but no one interfered, first, because no one cared, and, second, because the man was so big and powerful that every one was afraid of him.

Of course Ned interfered, not with an indignant statement that the man ought to be ashamed of himself, but, with the quiet remark—

"She's only a woman, you know, an' can't return it."

"An' wot 'ave *you* got to do with it?" cried the man with a savage curse, as he aimed a tremendous blow at Ned with his right hand.

Our pugilist expected that. He did not start or raise his hands to defend himself. He merely put his head to one side, and the huge fist went harmlessly past his ear. Savagely the rough struck out with the other fist, but Ned quietly, yet quickly put his head to the other side, and again the fist went innocently by. A loud laugh and cheer from the crowd greeted this, for, apart altogether from the occasion of the disagreement, this turning of the head aside was very pretty play on the part of Ned —being a remarkably easy-looking but exceedingly difficult action, as all boxers know. It enabled Ned to smile in the face of his foe without doing him any harm. But it enraged the rough to such an extent, that he struck out fast as well as hard, obliging Ned to put himself in the old familiar attitude, and skip about smartly.

"I don't want to hurt you, friend," said Ned at last, "but I *can*, you see!" and he gave the man a slight pat on his right cheek with one hand and a tap on the forehead with the other.

This might have convinced the rough, but he would not be convinced. Ned therefore gave him suddenly an open-handed slap on the side of the head which sent him through his own door-way; through his own kitchen—if we may so name it— and into his own coal-cellar, where he measured his length among cinders and domestic *débris*.

"I didn't want to do it, friends," said Ned in a mild voice, as soon as the laughter had subsided, " but, you see, in the Bible—a book I'm uncommon fond of—we're told, as far as we can, to live peaceably with all men. Now, you see, I couldn't live peaceably wi' this man to-day. He wouldn't let me, but I think I'll manage to do it some day, for I'll come back here to-morrow, and say I'm sorry I had to do it. Meanwhile I have a word to say to you about this matter."

Here Ned got upon the door-step of his adversary, and finished off by what is sometimes styled "improving the occasion."

Of course, one of the first things that Ned Frog did, on coming to his " right mind," was to make earnest and frequent inquiries as to the fate of his wife and family. Unfortunately the man who might have guided him to the right sources of information—the City missionary who had brought him to a knowledge of the truth—was seized with a severe illness, which not only confined him to a sick-bed for many weeks, but afterwards rendered it necessary that he should absent himself for a long time from the sphere of his labours. Thus, being left to himself, Ned's search was misdirected, and at last he came to the heart-breaking conclusion that they must have gone, as he expressed it, "to the bad;" that perhaps his wife had carried out her oft-repeated threat, and drowned herself, and that Bobby, having been only too successful a pupil in the ways of wickedness, had got himself transported.

To prosecute his inquiries among his old foes, the police, was so repugnant to Ned that he shrank from it, after the failure of one or two attempts, and the only other source which might have been successful he failed to appeal to through his own ignorance. He only knew of George Yard and the Home of Industry by name, as being places which he had hated, because his daughter Hetty was so taken up with them. Of course he was now aware that the people of George Yard did good work for his new Master, but he was so ignorant of the special phase of their work at the beginning of his Christian career that he never thought of applying to them for information. Afterwards he became so busy with his own special work, that he forgot all about these institutions.

When the missionary recovered and returned to his work, he at once—on hearing for the first time from Ned his family history—put him on the scent, and the discovery was then made that they had gone to Canada. He wrote immediately, and soon received a joyful reply from Hetty and a postscript from Bobby, which set his heart singing and his soul ablaze with gratitude to a sparing and preserving God.

About that time, however, the robust frame gave

way under the amount of labour it was called on to perform. Ned was obliged to go into hospital. When there he received pressing invitations to go out to Canada, and offers of passage-money to any extent. Mrs. Frog also offered to return home without delay and nurse him, and only waited to know whether he would allow her.

Ned declined, on the ground that he meant to accept their invitation and go to Canada as soon as he was able to undertake the voyage.

A relapse, however, interfered with his plans, and thus the visit, like many other desirable events in human affairs, was, for a time, delayed.

CHAPTER XXIX.

HOME AGAIN.

TIME passed away, and Bobby Frog said to his mother one morning, "Mother, I'm going to England."

It was a fine summer morning when he said this. His mother was sitting in a bower which had been constructed specially for her use by her son and his friend Tim Lumpy. It stood at the foot of the garden, from which could be had a magnificent view of the neighbouring lake. Rich foliage permitted the slanting sunbeams to quiver through the bower, and little birds, of a pert conceited nature, twittered among the same. Martha Mild—the very embodiment of meek, earnest simplicity, and still a mere child in face though almost a woman in years—sat on a wooden stool at Mrs. Frog's feet reading the Bible to her.

Martha loved the Bible and Mrs. Frog; they were both fond of the bower; there was a spare half hour before breakfast-time;—hence the situation, as broken in upon by Bobby.

"To England, Bobby?"

"To England, mother."

Martha said nothing, but she gave a slight—an almost imperceptible—start, and glanced at the sturdy youth with a mingled expression of anxiety and surprise.

The surprise Bob had expected; the anxiety he had hoped for; the start he had not foreseen, but now perceived and received as a glorious fact! Oh! Bobby Frog was a deep young rascal! His wild, hilarious, reckless spirit, which he found it so difficult to curb, even with all surroundings in his favour, experienced a great joy and sensation of restfulness in gazing at the pretty, soft, meek face of the little waif. He loved Martha, but, with all his recklessness, he had not the courage to tell her so, or to ask the condition of her feelings with regard to himself.

Being ingenious, however, and with much of the knowing nature of the "stray" still about him, he hit on this plan of killing two birds with one stone, as it were, by briefly announcing his intentions to his mother; and the result was more than he had hoped for.

"Yes, mother, to England—to London. You see, father's last letter was not at all satisfactory. Although he said he was convalescent and hoped to be able to travel soon, it seemed rather dull in tone, and now several posts have passed without bringing us a letter of any kind from him. I am beginning to feel anxious, and so as I have saved a good bit of money I mean to have a trip to old England and bring Daddy out with me."

"That will be grand indeed, my son. But will Mr. Merryboy let ye go, Bobby?"

"Of course he will. He lets me do whatever I please, for he's as fond o' me as if he were my father."

"Na; he ain't that," returned Mrs. Frog, with a shake of the head; "your father was rough, Bobby, specially w'en in liquor, but he 'ad a kind 'art at bottom, and he was very fond o' you, Bobby— almost as fond as he once was o' me. Mr. Merryboy could never come up to 'im in *that*."

"Did I say he came up to him, mother? I didn't say he was as fond o' me *as* my own father, but *as if he was* my father. However, it's all arranged, and I go off at once."

"Not before breakfast, Bobby?"

"No, not quite. I never do anything important on an empty stomach, but by this time to-morrow I hope to be far on my way to the sea-coast, and I expect Martha to take good care of you till I come back."

"I'll be *sure* to do that," said Martha, looking up in Mrs. Frog's face affectionately.

Bob Frog noted the look, and was satisfied.

"But, my boy, I shan't be here when you come

back. You know my visit is over in a week, and then we go to Sir Richard's estate."

"I know that, mother, but Martha goes with you there, to help you and Hetty and Matty to keep house while Tim Lumpy looks after the farm."

"Farm, my boy, what nonsense are you talking ?'

"No nonsense, mother, it has all been arranged this morning, early though it is. Mr. Merryboy has received a letter from Sir Richard, saying that he wants to gather as many people as possible round him, and offering him one of his farms on good terms, so Mr. Merryboy is to sell this place as soon as he can, and Tim and I have been offered a smaller farm on still easier terms close to his, and not far from the big farm that Sir Richard has given to his son-in-law Mr. Welland—"

"Son-in-law !" exclaimed Mrs. Frog. "Do you mean to say that Mr. Welland, who used to come down an' preach in the lodgin'-'ouses in Spitalfields 'as married that sweet hangel Miss Di ?"

"I do mean that, mother. I could easily show him a superior angel, of course, said Bob with a steady look at Martha, but he has done pretty well, on the whole."

"Pretty well !" echoed Mrs. Frog indignantly ; " he couldn't 'ave done better if 'e'd searched the wide world over."

"There I don't agree with you," returned her son ;

however, it don't matter—Hallo! there goes granny down the wrong path!"

Bob dashed off at full speed after Mrs. Merryboy, senior, who had an inveterate tendency, when attempting to reach Mrs. Frog's bower, to take a wrong turn, and pursue a path which led from the garden to a pretty extensive piece of forest-land behind. The blithe old lady was posting along this track in a tremulo-tottering way when captured by Bob. At the same moment the breakfast-bell rang; Mr. Merryboy's stentorian voice was immediately heard in concert; silvery shouts from the forest-land alluded to told where Hetty and Matty had been wandering, and a rush of pattering feet announced that the dogs of the farm were bent on being first to bid the old gentleman good-morning.

As Bob Frog had said, the following day found him far on his way to the sea-coast. A few days later found him *on* the sea,—wishing, earnestly, that he were on the land! Little more than a week after that found him in London walking down the old familiar Strand towards the city.

As he walked slowly along the crowded thoroughfare, where every brick seemed familiar and every human being strange, he could not help saying to himself mentally, "Can it be possible! was it here that I used to wander in rags? Thank God for the rescue and for the rescuers!"

" Shine yer boots, sir ?" said a facsimile of his former self.

" Certainly, my boy," said Bob, at once submitting himself to the operator, although, his boots having already been well "shined," the operation was an obvious absurdity.

The boy must have felt something of this, for, when finished, he looked up at his employer with a comical expression. Bob looked at him sternly.

" They were about as bright before you began on 'em," he said.

" They was, sir," admitted the boy, candidly.

" How much ?" demanded the old street boy.

" On'y one ha'penny, sir," replied the young street boy, " but ven the day's fine, an' the boots don't want much shinin', we gin'rally expecs a penny. Gen'l'min 'ave bin known to go the length of tuppence."

Bob pulled out half-a-crown and offered it.

The boy grinned, but did not attempt to take it.

" Why don't you take it, my boy ?"

" You *don't* mean it, do you ?" asked the boy, as the grin faded and the eyes opened.

" Yes, I do. Here, catch. I was once like you. Christ and Canada have made me what you see. Here is a little book that will tell you more about that."

He chanced to have one of Miss Macpherson's *Canadian Homes for London Wanderers* in his pocket, and gave it to the little shoe-black,—who was one of the fluttering free-lances of the metropolis, not one of the " Brigade."

Bob could not have said another word to have saved his life. He turned quickly on his heel and walked away, followed by a fixed gaze and a prolonged whistle of astonishment.

" How hungry I used to be here," he muttered as he walked along, " so uncommon hungry! The smell of roasts and pies had something to do with it, I think. Why, there's the shop—yes, the very shop, where I stood once gazing at the victuals for a full hour before I could tear myself away. I do think that, for the sake of starving boys, to say nothing of men, women, and girls, these grub-shops should be compelled to keep the victuals out o' the windows and send their enticing smells up their chimneys!"

Presently he came to a dead stop in front of a shop where a large mirror presented him with a full-length portrait of himself, and again he said mentally " Can it be possible!" for, since quitting London he had never seen himself as others saw him, having been too hurried, on both occasions of passing through Canadian cities, to note the mirrors there. In the backwoods, of course, there was nothing large enough in the way of mirror to show more than his good-looking face.

The portrait now presented to him was that of a

broad-chested, well-made, gentlemanly young man of middle height, in a grey Tweed suit.

"Not *exactly* tip-top, A1, superfine, you know, Bobby," he muttered to himself with the memory of former days strong upon him, "but—but—perhaps not altogether unworthy of—of—a thought or two from little Martha Mild."

Bob Frog increased in stature, it is said, by full half an inch on that occasion, and thereafter he walked more rapidly in the direction of White-chapel.

With sad and strangely mingled memories he went to the court where his early years had been spent. It was much the same in disreputableness of aspect as when he left it. Time had been gnawing at it so long that a few years more or less made little difference on it, and its inhabitants had not improved much.

Passing rapidly on he went straight to the Bee-hive, which he had for long regarded as his real home, and there, once again, received a hearty welcome from its ever busy superintendent and her earnest workers; but how different his circumstances now from those attending his first reception! His chief object, however, was to inquire the way to the hospital in which his father lay, and he was glad to learn that the case of Ned Frog was well known, and that he was convalescent.

It chanced that a tea-meeting was "on" when he arrived, so he had little more at the time than a warm shake of the hand from his friends in the Home, but he had the ineffable satisfaction of leaving behind him a sum sufficient to give a sixpence to each of the miserable beings who were that night receiving a plentiful meal for their bodies as well as food for their souls—those of them, at least, who chose to take the latter. None refused the former!

On his way to the hospital he saw a remarkably tall policeman approaching.

"Well, you *are* a long-legged copper," he muttered to himself, with an irrepressible laugh as he thought of old times. The old spirit seemed to revive with the old associations, for he felt a strong temptation to make a face at the policeman, execute the old double-shuffle, stick his thumb to the end of his nose, and bolt! As the man drew nearer he did actually make a face in spite of himself—a face of surprise—which caused the man to stop.

"Excuse me," said Bob, with much of his old bluntness, "are not you No. 666?"

"That is not my number now, sir, though I confess it was once," answered the policeman, with a humorous twinkle of the eye.

Bobby noticed the word "sir," and felt elated. It was almost more than waif-and-stray human nature could stand to be respectfully "sirred" by a

London policeman—his old foe, whom, in days gone
by and on occasions innumerable, he had scorned,
scouted, and insulted, with all the ingenuity of his
fertile brain.

"Your name is Giles Scott, is it not?" he asked.

"It is, sir."

"Do you remember a little ragged boy who once
had his leg broken by a runaway pony at the West
End—long ago?"

"Yes, as well as if I'd seen him yesterday. His
name was Bobby Frog, and a sad scamp he was,
though it is said he's doing well in Canada."

"He must 'ave changed considerable," returned
Bob, reverting to his old language with wonderful
facility, "w'en No. 666 don't know 'im. Yes, in
me, Robert Frog, Esquire, of Chikopow Farm,
Canada Vest, you be'old your ancient henemy, who
is on'y too 'appy to 'ave the chance of axin your
parding for all the trouble he gave you, an' all the
'ard names he called you in days gone by."

Bobby held out his hand as he spoke, and you
may be sure our huge policeman was not slow to
grasp it, and congratulate the stray on his improved
circumstances.

We have not time or space to devote to the conversation which ensued. It was brief, but rapid
and to the point, and in the course of it Bob learned
that Molly was as well, and as bright and cheery

as ever—also somewhat stouter; that Monty was in a fair way to become a real policeman, having just received encouragement to expect admission to the force when old enough, and that he was in a fair way to become as sedate, wise, zealous, and big as his father; also, that little Jo aimed at the same honourable and responsible position, and was no longer little.

Being anxious, however, to see his father, Bob cut the conversation short, and, having promised to visit his old enemy, hastened away.

The ward of the hospital in which Bob soon found himself was a sad place. Clean and fresh, no doubt, but very still, save when a weary sigh or a groan told of suffering. Among the beds, which stood in a row, each with its head against the wall, one was pointed out on which a living skeleton lay. The face was very very pale, and it seemed as if the angel of death were already brooding over it. Yet, though so changed, there was no mistaking the aspect and the once powerful frame of Ned Frog.

"I'd rather not see any one," whispered Ned, as the nurse went forward and spoke to him in a low voice, " I'll soon be home—I think."

"Father, *dear* father," said Bob, in a trembling, almost choking voice, as he knelt by the bedside and took one of his father's hands.

The prostrate man sprang up as if he had received an electric shock, and gazed eagerly into the face of his son. Then, turning his gaze on the nurse, he said—

"I'm not dreaming, am I? It's true, is it? Is this Bobby?"

"Whether he's Bobby or not I can't say," replied the nurse, in the tone with which people sometimes address children, "but you're not dreaming—it *is* a gentleman."

"Ah! then I *am* dreaming," replied the sick man, with inexpressible sadness, "for Bobby is no gentleman."

"But it *is* me, daddy," cried the poor youth, almost sobbing aloud as he kissed the hand he held, "why, you old curmudgeon, I thought you'd 'ave know'd the voice o' yer own son! I've grow'd a bit, no doubt, but it's me for all that. Look at me!"

Ned did look, with all the intensity of which he was capable, and then fell back on his pillow with a great sigh, while a death-like pallor overspread his face, almost inducing the belief that he was really dead.

"No, Bobby, I ain't dead yet," he said in a low whisper, as his terrified son bent over him. "Thank God for sendin' you back to me."

He stopped, but, gradually, strength returned, and he again looked earnestly at his son.

"Bobby," he said, in stronger tones, "I thought the end was drawin' near—or, rather, the beginnin'

—the beginnin' o' the New Life. But I don't feel like that now. I feel, some'ow, as I used to feel in the ring when they sponged my face arter a leveller. I did think I was done for this mornin'. The nurse thought so too, for I 'eerd her say so; an' the doctor said as much. Indeed I'm not sure that my own 'art didn't say so—but I'll cheat 'em all yet, Bobby, my boy. You've put new life into my old carcase, an' I'll come up to the scratch yet—see if I don't."

But Ned Frog did not "come up to the scratch." His work for the Master on earth was finished—the battle fought out and the victory gained.

"Gi' them all my love in Canada, Bobby, an' say to your dear mother that I *know* she forgives me—but I'll tell her all about that when we meet—in the better land."

Thus he died with his rugged head resting on the bosom of his loved and loving son.

CHAPTER XXX.

THE NEW HOME.

ONCE again, and for the last time, we shift our scene to Canada—to the real backwoods now—the Brandon Settlement.

Sir Richard, you see, had been a noted sportsman in his youth. He had chased the kangaroo in Australia, the springbok in Africa, and the tiger in India, and had fished salmon in Norway, so that his objections to the civilised parts of Canada were as strong as those of the Red Indians themselves. He therefore resolved, when making arrangements to found a colony, to push as far into the backwoods as was compatible with comfort and safety. Hence we now find him in the *very* far West.

We decline to indicate the exact spot, because idlers, on hearing of its fertility and beauty and the felicity of its inhabitants, might be tempted to crowd to it in rather inconvenient numbers. Let it suffice to say, in the language of the aborigines, that it lies towards the setting sun.

Around Brandon Settlement there are rolling

prairies, illimitable pasture-lands, ocean-like lakes, grand forests, and numerous rivers and rivulets, with flat-lands, low-lands, high-lands, undulating-lands, wood-lands, and, in the far-away distance, glimpses of the back-bone of America—peaked, and blue, and snow-topped.

The population of this happy region consists largely of waifs with a considerable sprinkling of strays. There are also several families of "haristo-crats," who, however, are not "bloated"—very much the reverse.

The occupation of the people is, as might be expected, agricultural; but, as the colony is very active and thriving and growing fast, many other branches of industry have sprung up, so that the hiss of the saw and the ring of the anvil, the clatter of the water-mill, and the clack of the loom, may be heard in all parts of it.

There is a rumour that a branch of the Great Pacific Railway is to be run within a mile of the Brandon Settlement; but that is not yet certain. The rumour, however, has caused much joyful hope to some, and rather sorrowful anxiety to others. Mercantile men rejoice at the prospect. Those who are fond of sport tremble, for it is generally sup-posed, though on insufficient grounds, that the railway-whistle frightens away game. Any one who has travelled in the Scottish Highlands and

seen grouse close to the line regarding your clanking train with supreme indifference, must doubt the
evil influence of railways on game. Meanwhile,
the sportsmen of Brandon Settlement pursue the
buffalo and stalk the deer, and hunt the brown and
the grizzly bear, and ply rod, net, gun, and rifle, to
their hearts' content.

There is even a bank in this thriving settlement
—a branch, if we mistake not, of the flourishing
Bank of Montreal—of which a certain Mr. Welland
is manager, and a certain Thomas Balls is hall-
porter, as well as general superintendent, when not
asleep in the hall-chair. Mrs. Welland, known
familiarly as Di, is regarded as the mother of the
settlement—or, more correctly, the guardian angel
—for she is not yet much past the prime of life.
She is looked upon as a sort of goddess by many
people; indeed she resembles one in mind, face,
figure, and capacity. We use the last word advis-
edly, for she knows and sympathises with every one,
and does so much for the good of the community,
that the bare record of her deeds would fill a large
volume. Amongst other things she trains, in the way
that they should go, a family of ten children, whose
adoration of her is said to be perilously near to
idolatry. She also finds time to visit an immense
circle of friends. There are no poor in Brandon
Settlement yet, though there are a few sick and a

good many aged, to whom she ministers. She also attends on Sir Richard, who is part of the Bank family, as well as a director.

The good knight wears well. His time is divided between the children of Di, the affairs of the settlement, and a neighbouring stream in which the trout are large and pleasantly active. Mrs. Screwbury, who spent her mature years in nursing little Di, is renewing her youth by nursing little Di's little ones, among whom there is, of course, another little Di whom her father styles Di-licious. Jessie Summers assists in the nursery, and the old cook reigns in the Canadian kitchen with as much grace as she formerly reigned in the kitchen at the " West End."

Quite close to the Bank buildings there is a charming villa, with a view of a lake in front and a peep through the woods at the mountains behind, in which dwells the cashier of the Bank with his wife and family. His name is Robert Frog, Esquire. His wife's name is Martha. His eldest son, Bobby—a boy of about nine or ten—is said to be the most larky boy in the settlement. We know not as to that, but any one with half an eye can see that he is singularly devoted to his mild little brown-eyed mother.

There is a picturesque little hut at the foot of the garden of Beehive Villa, which is inhabited by an old woman. To this hut Bobby the second is very partial, for the old woman is exceedingly fond of Bobby—quite spoils him in fact—and often entertains him with strange stories about a certain lion of her acquaintance which was turned into a lamb. Need we say that this old woman is Mrs. Frog? The Bank Cashier offered her a home in Beehive Villa, but she prefers the little hut at the foot of the garden, where she sits in state to receive visitors and is tenderly cared for by a very handsome young woman named Matty, who calls her mother. Matty is the superintendent of a neighbouring school, and it is said that one of the best of the masters of that school is anxious to make Matty and the school his own. If so, that master must be a greedy fellow —all things considered.

There is a civil engineer—often styled by Bob Frog an uncivil engineer—who has planned all the public works of the settlement, and is said to have a good prospect of being engaged in an important capacity on the projected railway. But of this we cannot speak authoritatively. His name is T. Lampay, Esquire. Ill-natured people assert that when he first came to the colony his name was Tim Lumpy, and at times his wife Hetty calls him Lumpy to his face, but, as wives do sometimes call their husbands improper names, the fact proves nothing except the perversity of woman. There is a blind old woman in his establishment, however, who has grown amiably childish in her old age, who invariably calls him Tim. Whatever may be the truth as to this, there is no question that he is a thriving man and an office-bearer in the Congregational church, whose best Sabbath-school teacher is his wife Hetty, and whose pastor is the Rev. John Seaward—a man of singular good fortune, for, besides having such men as Robert Frog, T. Lampay, and Sir Richard Brandon to back him up and sympathise with him on all occasions, he is further supported by the aid and countenance of Samuel Twitter, senior, Samuel Twitter, junior, Mrs. Twitter, and all the other Twitters, some of whom are married and have twitterers of their own.

Samuel Twitter and his sons are now farmers! Yes, reader, you may look and feel surprised to hear it, but your astonishment will never equal that of old Twitter himself at finding himself in that position. He never gets over it, and has been known, while at the tail of the plough, to stop work, clap a hand on each knee, and roar with laughter at the mere idea of his having taken to agriculture late in life! He tried to milk the cows when he first began, but, after having frightened two or three animals into fits, overturned half a dozen milk-pails, and been partially gored, he gave it up. Sammy is his right-hand man, and the hope of his declining years. True, this right hand has got the name of

being slow, but he is considered as pre-eminently
sure.

Mrs. Twitter has taken earnestly to the sick, since
there are no poor to befriend. She is also devoted
to the young—and there is no lack of them. She
is likewise strong in the tea-party line, and among
her most favoured guests are two ladies named
respectively Loper and Larrabel, and two gentlemen
named Crackaby and Stickler. It is not absolutely
certain whether these four are a blessing to the new
settlement or the reverse. Some hold that things
in general would progress more smoothly if they
were gone; others that their presence affords excellent and needful opportunity for the exercise of
forbearance and charity. At all events Mrs. Twitter
holds that she could not live without them, and
George Brisbane, Esq., who owns a lovely mansion
on the outskirts of the settlement, which he has
named Lively Hall, vows that the departure of
that quartette would be a distinct and irreparable
loss to society in Brandon Settlement.

One more old friend we have to mention, namely,
Reggie North, who has become a colporteur, and
wanders far and near over the beautiful face of
Canada, scattering the seed of Life with more
vigour and greater success than her sons scatter
the golden grain. His periodical visits to the settlement are always hailed with delight, because North

has a genial way of relating his adventures and describing his travels, which renders it necessary for him to hold forth as a public lecturer at times in the little chapel, for the benefit of the entire community. On these occasions North never fails, you may be quite sure, to advance his Master's cause.

Besides those whom we have mentioned, there are sundry persons of both sexes who go by such names as Dick Swiller, Blobby, Robin, Lilly Snow, Bobbie Dell, and Little Mouse, all of whom are grown men and women, and are said to have originally been London waifs and strays. But any one looking at them in their backwoods prosperity would pooh-pooh the idea as being utterly preposterous!

However this may be, it is quite certain that they are curiously well acquainted with the slums of London and with low life in that great city. These people sometimes mention the name of Giles Scott, and always with regret that that stalwart policeman and his not less stalwart sons are unable to see their way to emigrate, but if they did, as Bobby Frog the second asks, " what would become of London ?"

" They'd make such splendid backwoodsmen," says one.

" And the daughters would make such splendid wives for backwoodsmen," says another.

Mr. Merryboy thinks that Canada can produce

splendid men of its own without importing them from England, and Mrs. Merryboy holds that the same may be said in regard to the women of Canada, and old granny, who is still alive, with a face like a shrivelled-up potato, blinks with undimmed eyes, and nods her snow-white head, and beams her brightest smile in thorough approval of these sentiments.

Ah, reader! Brandon Settlement is a wonderful place, but we may not linger over it now. The shadows of our tale have lengthened out, and the sun is about to set. Before it goes quite down let us remind you that the Diamonds which you have seen dug out, cut, and polished, are only a few of the precious gems that lie hidden in the dust of the great cities of our land; that the harvest might be very great, and that the labourers at the present time are comparatively few.

THE END.

www.ingramcontent.com/pod-product-compliance
Lightning Source LLC
Chambersburg PA
CBHW031101110726
47900CB00003B/1008